Michael Dubis

The
Hangman

A Novel

Erica House

BALTIMORE   AMSTERDAM   SALAMANCA

Cover photo: Execution gallows at Natzweiler concentration camp, in use during World War II.

ISBN: 0-9659308-6-6

PUBLISHED BY ERICA HOUSE BOOK PUBLISHERS
www.ericahouse.com

Baltimore　　　　　Amsterdam　　　　Salamanca

Printed in the United States of America

DEDICATION

I dedicate this novel first to my wife Sandra and my children Mike and Michelle, who watched me work on it for the last four years.

I also dedicate it to my good friends Ed and Pat Huckstorf and Mick and Kathy Hane, who had the faith in me to see to it that publication became a reality.

Finally, I dedicate this book also to the millions of those unfortunates who lived in those dark years of 1938 to 1945, and died for no reason other than their nationality or heritage.
For them, this work is no fiction.

12.9.41 City of Wilna 933 Jews, 1670 Jewesses, 771 children 3,374
22.9.41 Novo-Wilejka 468 Jews, 495 Jewesses, 196 children 1,159
......
SS Einsatzkommando 3

"Today, I can confirm that our objective to solve the Jewish problem for Lithuania has been achieved by EK3. In Lithuania, there are no more Jews, apart from Jewish workers and their families."

(signed) Jager,
SS-Standartenführer

EK#3 liquidated 137,346 Jews in its campaign.

1

The Beginning

MOST would agree that weekends were meant for recreation and leisure, but that did not apply if one was employed by Weinstein Industries and its owner, Walter Weinstein. In fact, today, a Sunday no less, I was summoned to the Weinstein Estate in order to discuss what Walter called a matter of *utmost importance* to Weinstein Industries.

As I was parking my car in the circular driveway, Rachael ran out to greet me.

"Erik, Erik, I missed you so! You should have been here an hour ago. You know how Daddy gets."

I gave Rachael a peck on the cheek and entered the study with her arm in mine.

"About time you arrived, Erik!" thundered Walter.

Walter, all five-foot-four of him, was always the pompous ass. "When, and if, you marry my Rachael, things will be different."

"What did you need to see me about, Walter?"

"Erik, I want you to leave for Berlin at once. Our exports to Germany are slipping greatly and it is all because of that madman Hitler. We need to stabilize relations between Weinstein Industries and the Reich. Since Hitler wants war, war he will get, but then he will need uniforms, coats, boots, all items we can produce. Goebbels, his Minister of Propaganda, is an anti-Semitic idiot. I'm convinced he is the one who is persuading Hitler not to deal with Jewish firms. You must go and convince Goebbels, or convince anyone in power, that dealing with Weinstein Industries would be in their best interest, Jew or no Jew. You are a gentile, Erik, blond, tall, physically fit, and a former military man. Your father was a war hero. Persuade the officials in authority that it makes sense to deal with me. Tell them that I employ loyal Germans such as yourself. Tell them that I admire Hitler. Tell them anything, but get their business! I am counting on you, Erik."

Come to think of it, how did Walter know about my father?

"But Walter," I insisted, "I'm not a politician. Why would such important men even let me see them, let alone listen to me?"

Didn't Walter read the papers? It was just on the 5th of February of this year 1938 that Austrian Nazis vandalized Jewish stores in the Viennese suburbs and on the 12th of February, Austria's Von Schuschnigg, at Berchtesgaden, paved the way for a greater Nazi role in Austrian politics and public life. Anti-Jewish demonstrations were becoming more and more apparent.

"Damn it, Erik! I won't take no for an answer. If you want to marry my daughter and continue to keep this job, you will do as I say."

What an asshole! Besides insulting me, he commanded me to convince the most anti-Semitic government in the world to continue doing business with a Jew!

"Erik, please go, do it for me," Rachael whined.

I had heard enough.

"Alright. Alright, Walter. You win. When do I leave?"

2

To Berlin

THE next day was brisk and cold as the 5:00 AM train left *Süd Bahnhof* on its journey to Berlin. The trip would take about ten hours, a distance of six hundred or so kilometers. Rachael had feigned a cold the night before. It was her way of telling me that she would not be there to see me off.

I thought it would be difficult finding an empty seat, but as luck would have it, an attractive woman in dark glasses left her place just as I entered the passenger car, and I was able to take her seat on the aisle row.

The whistle blew and I was off to Berlin! Berlin, just the name filled me with excitement. I think that just knowing that I could return there had helped me decide to acquiesce to Walter's demands. To see my father and sister again would be grand. I only regretted that Mother, who died last year, would not be there as well.

Father, now in his late fifties, was doing fine, but he was still rightfully bitter over the outcome of the Great War, a war in which he had won the Iron Cross. Like many other Germans, he felt strongly that the signing of the Treaty of Versailles marked Germany's lowest moment. It was a treaty which punished Germany and took away her dignity, took away her military might and, together with the Great Depression, sunk her into economic ruin. I knew he admired Hitler's economic and military policies, but he was not sympathetic to the physical persecution many of the Jews in Germany were now undergoing.

My sister, Theresa, the smart one, taught at the local school. She was yet unmarried, but continually searching. How I missed the two of them.

Shortly after the train left the station, the man who was seated next to me, also in his thirties, began a conversation which would ultimately result in major new developments in my life, developments I couldn't even begin to imagine that brisk February morning.

"Good morning, sir. My name is Dieter Schmidt. What takes you to Berlin? Mr ..."

"Erik, Erik Byrnes."

"Glad to make your acquaintance, Erik Byrnes."

I shook his already extended hand and explained to him, in general terms, that my journey to Berlin was to promote sales of clothing, footwear, and the like. I didn't mention whom I worked for and whom I was instructed to meet.

"Sales, Erik, that's wonderful! I always wanted to be a salesman. I really think I would have been good at it, but my parents insisted I join the military and become a soldier. Oh well, there are worse things in life. I could have been born a Jew."

I couldn't help but smile at his last remark as I thought of Walter and Rachael.

"Herr Schmidt, what brought you to Vienna?"

With a smile like that of a mischievous little boy, he began. "Erik, may I call you that? I feel that I know you so well."

I nodded my approval.

"To put it quite candidly and quite bluntly, I am going to get right to the point. Small talk does little good. Erik, our meeting was not by accident. I am an Obersturmführer in the SS and my assignment is to meet with you here today."

He was smiling, yet he seemed deadly serious.

"Actually, for the last several weeks you have been under our surveillance. Do you want me to prove it?"

I thought I would play along with him. It seemed harmless enough.

"Well, just yesterday, you walked arm in arm with Rachael Weinstein into her father's beautiful mansion. I certainly wish I could live in such a home."

My God! He had been following me. "Yes, so do I. But what does all of this have to do with me and the SS?"

The *SS*. Even the very name sent shivers down my spine. I had heard stories, both in Vienna and in Berlin, about the SS, Himmler's private core of fanatic Germans, sworn to loyalty to the Führer.

"I know what is going through your mind. Erik. Please don't be alarmed. I have only positive news for you. I have your dossier here in this briefcase, and it contains your life history. You were a gifted athlete, with obvious Germanic features. We know you have a pure bloodline dating back over three hundred years, with parents who are good, sincere and loyal Germans. Your father is a decorated veteran. I will be totally honest with you. I have been instructed to watch your every move and to make a report to my superiors about your *suitability*. My report was delivered to Dr. Joseph Goebbels in Berlin just days ago. It recommended your recruitment."

"Recruitment? Suitability? For what?" I asked.

9

"Erik, I know why you were sent to Berlin by Weinstein. We have an informant in Weinstein Industries who alerted us to Walter Weinstein's mission for you, Erik, a mission, I might add, he had been planning for a considerable period of time. Didn't you think it was odd that shortly before you first were hired by Weinstein Industries you just happened to meet Rachael Weinstein on that skiing trip? She certainly wasn't shy, was she? Also, wasn't it just plain luck for you that she persuaded you to follow her to Vienna and accept that great job that Weinstein Industries just happened to have open?

Erik, wise up! You have been set up. Set up by that Jew Weinstein and your lovely Rachael who I must say is quite attractive even for a Jewess, but if you didn't already know, not very faithful."

For some strange reason, at that very moment I didn't take offense at what Dieter said about Rachael.

"How was I set up?"

"Before Weinstein sent you on your trip to Berlin, to convince that *madman* Hitler to make an exception for Weinstein Industries, and even before you were even hired at Weinstein Industries, Walter had his eyes on you. Your landlady's cousin, the Jew Saul Raeder, he was the one who schemed with his good friend Walter and with Walter's daughter, to trick you into working for them and getting close to Rachael. Raeder had known your father in Berlin and your father had told him about you. Walter hoped that, with your assistance, the Reich would agree to continue doing business with Weinstein Industries, while other Jewish manufacturers were being denied similar contracts. I'm sure Walter suspects that time is quickly running short.

When we found out about this deception, we decided to turn it against Weinstein, but to do so, we need your help. To put it quite simply, Erik, we want you to work for us. If you would, I'd like you to think about what I have just told you. You will be filled in on the details shortly. By the way, I hope you don't mind, but I took the liberty to have you booked at the Führer's old lodgings, the *Kaiserhof Hotel*, quite an improvement from the lodgings picked by Weinstein. It has already been arranged that any phone calls made to you will be immediately forwarded to the Kaiserhof. Now, Erik, I have to leave you, but we will talk again soon."

With that said, Dieter, or whatever his real name was, got up and walked away.

The train's whistle announced our arrival at Berlin's *Anhalt* railway station. As I left the train, the crowd seemed to be moving in several different directions. I fought my way through the masses and then out of the station.

I hailed a taxi and instructed the driver to proceed to the Kaiserhof where Dieter stated he had made reservations for me. I needed to find out for myself whether he actually was who he said he was, and what's more important, whether what he told me about working with the SS was true.

I was about to enter the car when a black Mercedes, with *swastikas* flying from both antennas, cut off the taxi.

"Erik, my boy, forget the taxi and get in with me."

It was Dieter, but this time he was impeccably dressed in the black uniform of the SS, with its dreaded Death's Head Insignia brilliantly exposed. A young SS officer opened the door and I sat down next to Dieter.

"Sherry, Erik?" as he held out a glass to me.

I did not refuse. In fact, I eagerly accepted his hospitality.

"To the Third Reich!"

"To the Third Reich," I answered while our glasses touched.

The ride to the hotel took us through the business district of Berlin. The large crowds reminded me of New York, when I had visited there just four years ago, the only exception being that the area seemed to be patrolled not only by the regular police but also by the SA, which to me appeared quite out of place with the peaceful surroundings.

"You noticed them too, haven't you, Erik? In the SS we call them thugs, mostly uneducated, many of them criminals and, almost to a man, drunken bullies. Hitler has reduced their presence and their importance by eliminating Röhm and many of his followers. Those of the SA who are left are of a somewhat better quality. This I assure you."

We entered the lobby and completely bypassed the check-in as if it didn't exist. It was apparent that Dieter had taken care of all arrangements.

My room was quite spacious, with a beautiful view of the surrounding area.

"I'll let you get set up, Erik, and I will contact you sometime tomorrow."

As I unpacked, I couldn't help but think of what had happened this morning. The thought of actually working against Walter bothered me somewhat, but at the same time it also filled me with great satisfaction and excitement. Speaking of Walter, I had promised him I would call upon my arrival.

"Erik, it's about time I heard from you! I hope you know how important it is that you get started right away. Remember, try to see Goebbels or Himmler, or better still, Hermann Göring. I'm told Göring is by far a more reasonable man than either of the others. If we have to, Erik, we will *pay* to get their business."

"Walter, I can hardly hear you. Is there something wrong with the phone? Your voice is fading away. I'll call you later."

"Erik, Erik!..."

I was furious with Walter. We had agreed that my assignment was to convince the Reich to deal with Weinstein but I did not care to spend the next few years in a prison on bribery charges. Obviously, putting me in jeopardy didn't bother Walter.

Since it was late and I had gotten little rest on the train, I decided to skip dinner and turn in for the evening.

After a good night's sleep, I awoke feeling very hungry, so I decided to get something to eat. Upon leaving the hotel, I couldn't help but feel that somebody was watching me, but I could see nobody suspicious.

I was so enthralled with the magic of Berlin that I actually forgot about my hunger and neglected to notice that I walked out of the main business artery and entered what could only be described as a secondary district, mostly full of merchant shops, professional offices and the like.

What I saw next made my blood run cold.

There, in the middle of the block, a crowd had gathered. As I approached, I could hear laughter and jeering. The object of their taunts was an old man, who was scrubbing the gutters on his hands and knees, toothbrush in his hand. By the behavior of his persecutors and by his appearance, I knew he was a Jew, and his persecutors were the Brown Shirts, ably assisted by local citizens.

The scene was terrible.

While the old man toiled, he was spat on and ridiculed. Finally, the crowd was broken up by the local police, and not with any vigor, I might add. I helped the man up and gave him a handkerchief to clean his face. He thanked me and then quickly walked away.

I decided I had done enough walking, and turned to go back to my hotel. On the way, remembering that I was still hungry, I found a pleasant café. There, on the table, was a local newspaper, the *Der Angriff.* The front page had a picture of Hitler. With him were Hess and Goebbels. The article spoke of a speech recently given by Hitler to the German Parliament, the *Reichstag*:

"Germany's destiny lies in the direction of Austria. We must at any cost protect the countless Germans under Austrian rule. It is our obligation to protect them and Austria itself from Bolshevism."

Even those who hate the man must admit one thing: Hitler's greatest gift was his ability to communicate, how he used the media, the radio, and the new concept of campaigning by using air travel.

The waitress brought me my food, hard boiled eggs, cheese and ham, along with fresh tomatoes. I lifted my fork, then felt a firm tap on my shoulder. It was Dieter.

"I see you found me."

"Nothing to it, Erik. You're easy. Only I would strongly advise you not to be so foolish as to assist a Jew next time. Go ahead and eat, Erik, but please hurry. We have to leave soon."

"We have to leave? Where are we going? I thought I would not see you until later."

"Well, plans have been somewhat modified. Weinstein told you that you had to approach the powers-to-be, didn't he? I fully intend to give you that very opportunity right now. Come on. You ate enough. Let's get going."

I grabbed a sweet roll, and Dieter paid the charges. We were driven away again.

I marveled at the beauty of Berlin, the architecture dating back centuries. There was the newly-built *Reichstag,* constructed after the mysterious fire of 1933. As we traveled the Autobahn, I saw what evidently was a people on the go, a people with a destiny.

The Mercedes pulled up to a governmental building. Dieter called it the Ministry of Propaganda. I had heard others call it *The Brown House.* Nearby was the British Embassy.

"Who are we going to see, Dieter?"

"Erik, you are going to have the honor of meeting Dr. Joseph Goebbels, the Minister of Public Enlightenment and Propaganda. Don't be afraid. It was his idea to recruit you. In fact, it was one of his secretaries who gave up her seat so that you could sit next to me on the train. Pretty clever, *ja.*"

We were escorted into the large interior office of Doctor Goebbels.

"Dr. Goebbels, I would like you to meet Erik Byrnes."

Goebbels held out his hand and took mine.

"Herr Byrnes, I am very glad to meet you. Please sit down. Cigarette?"

"Yes, thank you."

"Erik, I am sure Dieter has informed you of our interest in you, has he not?"

"Yes, he has, Herr Doctor."

"Good, then let me get to the specifics. As you know, we became aware of Walter Weinstein's purpose in sending you to Berlin. After some analysis, we decided that Weinstein actually was unknowingly doing us a favor. A complete background check on you told us that your heritage is pure Germanic, as far back as the records would let us search. Your parental background is excellent and your physical traits are apparent. You are the perfect man to implement our plan."

"Forgive me, Dr. Goebbels, but I don't know exactly what it is that you want me to do. Please, what is this plan you speak of?"

"Hitler's armies will soon march into Austria, Erik, either by invitation or by force. No matter how, mark my words, it *will* take place. Equally inevitable is the fact that, in the not too distant future, Jewry as Austria knows it will undergo a dramatic downfall. Germany has already passed its own economic and racial laws, such as the *Nuremberg Race Laws* of 1935. Jews are now set apart because of their race and not because of their religion. In time, Austria and eventually the entire civilized world will do the same.

As Dieter has told you, we want you to work for us in Austria. Initially, when you return to Vienna, Weinstein will be pleased at your efforts. We will see to it that your trip to Germany is not only a success for the Reich but also a tremendous success for Weinstein Industries. His firm will receive lucrative German contracts, thus enabling you to gain an even more prominent position in Weinstein Industries. After Germany takes over Austria, if you perform up to our expectations, you will run the company and perhaps, when that task is over, hold a position of importance in the new German-Austrian government. You will be able to ease into the transition from Austrian to German rule and to implement the Führer's policies. Does this sound as it would be of interest to you, Erik?"

"Herr Doctor, please forgive me. Yes, I am interested but I'd like some time before I make a final decision."

"That will be fine, Erik. Take your time. All I ask of you is your word as a German national, that if you decide not to join us, you will speak not a word of what you have learned today."

I agreed without hesitation.

With that, Goebbels bade us farewell and dismissed us from his office.

Dieter informed me that a car was there for my use so I asked the driver to drop me off at my father's home in the outskirts of Berlin.

3

I'm Home

WHAT a surprise it would be for Father and sis!

Upon entering my old neighborhood, I was filled with joy and happy memories. There had been times in my life when my only worries were how I was going to get money for the weekend and how I could talk Father into letting me use the car.

I dismissed the driver, and as I entered my home, I saw Father seated by the fire, reading the morning paper. He turned towards me.

"Erik, Erik, I can't believe it. What are you doing here and why didn't you call? I ought to..."

"I wanted to surprise you, Father." I shook his firm hand. "How are you doing, and where is Theresa?"

"She's working late, but I expect her shortly. What brings you to Berlin?"

"Oh, just sales. I am trying to solicit business for Weinstein Industries."

"What kind of business, Erik?"

"I'll tell you more later, Father, but first I'd like to freshen up a bit."

"Of course, but where is your luggage?"

"It's at my hotel."

"I'll hear nothing of a hotel, Erik..."

"Later, Father, later. We'll talk about it later."

Walking up the staircase to my old room brought back fond memories. Although I had experienced the Great Depression and general economic chaos, my father, being a decorated veteran, was able to obtain a governmental position that paid a reasonable salary. Further, my mother had inherited a tidy sum from her father when he passed away. Mind you, we were not wealthy, but I have many memories of my mother having supper for nearly all my friends because their parents were often unable to adequately feed them. As I passed my parents' room, I saw my mother's picture. Sweet Josephine, she was an angel, never a disparaging word towards anyone, kindness to all.

I entered my room and noticed that nothing had changed since I moved away. There were my soccer and gymnastic trophies, my university diploma and my Wehrmacht uniform. Why did I let Weinstein trick me into leaving home?

When I came back downstairs, Father was waiting for me.

"Erik, I won't hear anything different. You call that hotel and cancel your reservation. You're staying with us. By the way, how long will you be in Berlin?"

"At least a week, maybe longer."

"Good, now come and sit down, I want to see my son."

I would tell Father later of what had happened to me today, but for now I only wanted to savor the perfect happiness of being home.

He hardly seemed to have changed. Always a tall man, somewhat more grey, but obviously still strong as an ox and with a mind sharp as ever.

"How's retirement, Father?"

"Just fine. I get to sleep until seven and stay up until ten and I don't have to take orders from snibbling bureaucrats half my age. I get to take rides in my car and I can stop at the *Kneipen* and have a *Weissbier* any time I want to. It's great and it would be even greater if I had you back home where you belong with me and Theresa, just like before. Remember when you and Marie..."

"Alright, Father, that's enough reminiscing. How is Theresa?"

"She's fine, but I think you can see that for yourself."

"Erik, Erik!" Theresa squealed as she hugged me.

"Well, sis, you look good. Still dating my old pal Horst?"

"Yes, Erik, still with Horst for now, until somebody better comes along."

"Good, at least he has enough common sense not to marry you."

"Why, you..."

"That's enough, children. Theresa, Erik has the guts to tell me he is staying in Berlin while he is here on business. What do you think of that?"

"No way! You will stay here with us, Erik, if you know what's good for you."

"I give up. I'll stay here. Father, would you drive me into Berlin so I can check out of the hotel? But before we go, I'll have to call Rachael and let her know where I am."

Never a Rachael fan, Theresa quipped, "Of course, Erik, we wouldn't want you to *neglect* her, would we?"

"Rachael, is that you?"

"Why, yes, Erik. I left several messages today. What took you so long to get back to me?"

"I'm at my father's and sister's. I am checking out of the hotel and I will stay with them while I am here."

"But won't you be at least an hour's drive from downtown, then?"

"Well, yes. So what?"

"Really, Erik, you are supposed to be working on Father's business and if you have to drive for over an hour, that will be that much less time for you to work!"

I bit my tongue, and didn't tell Rachael what I really thought of her last comment. "Rachael, my dear, I *have* been working! In fact, Walter may soon be receiving news of a large order, and guess who obtained it."

"Why, that is lovely, Erik, Father will be so happy. Still, I will have to tell him where you'll be staying. He won't be happy about this. If I were you, I would change my mind."

"Well, you are not me, Rachael, and as far as I am concerned, I will decide where I will stay!"

With that, I hung up the phone.

Seeing the look of disgust on my face, Theresa couldn't help but tell me how she felt.

"I told you, Erik, she is not the woman for you, and to think that you left Marie for that bitch."

"Theresa, I didn't leave Marie for her. I took her father's job."

As we drove to the hotel, Father began to confide in me. "Erik, you should know that about two months ago a man came to see me. He told me that the government was doing a survey about German nationals living in Austria to determine just what the political climate would be if the Reich were to move into that country. He asked me about you and if I knew about your feelings on such a takeover. I answered his questions as best I could and didn't think much of it because I had already heard that this same man interviewed several other people I know, who also have relatives living in Austria.

The only thing that did strike me as somewhat peculiar, Erik, was his specific interest in your relationship with your employer, and with members of the Weinstein family. Since they are Jews, I would have thought that the German government would have little or no interest in them. Yet, his questions became very personal. He wanted to know about Rachael and your relationship with her. Why was he asking so many questions about you and the Weinsteins?"

"Father, something happened to me on the train ride to Berlin that I want to talk to you about, and this will probably explain why you were visited by this man. I have been watched by the SS for some time. In fact, I was approached on the train by a member of the SS who took me to see Dr. Joseph Goebbels."

"Goebbels! What in the world for, Erik? What could you have done?"

"Don't worry, Father. I have done nothing wrong. You might not believe this, but the SS want me to work for them. They want me to go back to Austria and help smooth the road for its eventual takeover. They especially want me to run Weinstein Industries. If all goes well, I might even join them permanently!"

"What did you decide, Erik?"

"I told them I need time to think about it. I have to admit that I have had second thoughts for some time now about my relationship with Rachael and her family. In fact, Goebbels informed me that my meeting Rachael and working for Weinstein was all a setup. All Walter Weinstein and Rachael ever saw in me was my German background. I realize now that all they ever wanted was to use me to further their own selfish purposes. The purpose of this very trip here was to muster as much trade as I could for Weinstein from the Reich. That bastard even went so far as to tell me to bribe whomever I could."

"Why would he need to do that, Erik? I always thought he was a very wealthy man."

"He is, but not wealthy enough for his needs. It seems that orders from Germany have slackened off quite a bit in the past few years and this has hurt his business. I need your advice, Father. What do you think I should do?"

"Erik, you know I have been a public servant most of my life. First the military and then civil service. I have always been proud of Germany, more so now than I have ever been. I admit Hitler may be eccentric or even somewhat mad, but Germany has a sense of pride now that it hasn't had since before the Great War. Our economy is on an upswing, the military is now respected worldwide, and our people have hopes for a brighter future. Just walk down a street, Erik. See for yourself."

"Well, Father, I did walk down the street, just hours ago. But what I saw could hardly be described as pride."

He gave me a puzzled look. "How can you say that?"

"While taking a walk in Berlin, I saw a mob led by the SA, picking on and taunting an old Jewish man and forcing him to clean the street with a toothbrush. Is this the sense of German pride you were referring to?"

"Of course not, Erik. Why, many fine Jews fought with me in the war. I don't share the view that all Jews are bad but I do see them now in a different light. For example, I never knew before Hitler told us just how much control the Jews have over the every-day life of Germany. Did you know that they control the courts, the theater, the sciences, but especially that they control the economy? This control must be stopped. Mind you, I don't approve of the physical abuse they are receiving, even though it is no different than what the negroes receive in America, but I am totally in favor of limiting Jewish

18

influence. So, in answer to your question, my advice would be that the offer you have received may be a tremendous opportunity for you. You should consider it carefully. As far as you and Rachael are concerned, it is about time you saw the light, Erik, and time you begin to understand that there will never be any real life for you with her. Germans and Jews might be able to be friends but nothing more."

"Maybe you're right, Father, but the rest of the world doesn't necessarily believe all this talk about a Jewish conspiracy."

"Erik, soon the Führer's policies will become dogma across Europe. All enlightened countries will come to understand that by minimizing the influence of the Jews, their economies and their very nations will soon begin to prosper, as is Germany. In any event, I am glad we had this talk, and since you are going to stay for awhile, perhaps we can discuss this again."

"I agree, Father, but for now this talk is just between you and me, alright?"

"Alright, son."

"I am sorry you are leaving so soon, Herr Byrnes. I hope we have done nothing to offend you."

"No, of course not, I'm just going to accept my father's invitation to stay with him while I'm here in Berlin."

The hotel manager seemed to breathe easier now since he obviously would not want to be accused of mistreating a guest of the SS.

While Father was helping me put my luggage in the trunk, a voice which would soon become very familiar called out to me.

"Erik, I see you are taking up lodging with your family. Good. This is as it should be."

It was Dieter. "Why, hello there. What took you so long to find me?"

"You're obviously too clever for me, Erik," he quipped. Then turning to my father and extending his hand, he said, "Good evening, Herr Byrnes. I believe we have met before. My name is Dieter Schmidt."

Father looked at Dieter carefully, and after shaking his hand he removed his glasses and smiled. "Yes, we have. In fact, just a little while ago I told Erik that I was interviewed by someone who I believe belonged with the government. Erik, this is the man who asked me about you."

"In the back of my mind I knew it was you, Dieter."

"Yes, well, now that the formalities are out of the way, let me help you with the luggage."

"Dieter, I have a great idea! Why don't you join my son and me for dinner. My daughter will have it ready when we return."

"Thank you, Herr Byrnes. A home-cooked German meal sounds great."

"Father, why don't you go with Dieter to the house in his auto and I'll meet you later. There is somebody I need to see."

I realized right then and there that I must now see Marie. I had to make things right and I knew that this was the time to do it. She must know why I left her and how I now recognized the stupidity of my actions. I knew with every instinct I had that I still loved her and that I had never had really stopped loving her. She must know how I feel.

I saw Marie's light. My heart pounded as I climbed the steps to her third-floor flat. I hesitated, wondering how she would react to seeing me again. Would she let me talk to her or would she slam the door in my face? I took a deep breath and forced myself to rap softly. When she opened the door, we both just stood there for what seemed an eternity, looking at each other before one of us spoke.

With tears in her eyes, she asked, "Erik, what are you doing here?"

"May I come in, Marie?"

She hesitated, then motioned for me to enter.

"Marie, I don't know if you will believe me, but I can't begin to tell you how sorry I am for what I did to you."

"Why, Erik? Why? Why did you leave me?" she whispered.

"Let me try to explain, Marie. We both know that I've never been good at holding any responsible position. How many jobs did I go through since I left the military? On top of it all, even though there was no doubt I was in love with you, Marie, what kind of life could I give you? So, being afraid to make a commitment or to take a chance, I decided to leave and go to Vienna. Marie, I never stopped loving you. I want you to know that, and I want you to know everything that happened to me since I left Berlin and especially what happened today. If after you have heard everything you don't want to see me, I'll leave for good."

"How do I know you won't leave me again? Without your father and sister's help, I would never have made it through my grief and shame. I don't think I could take it again."

"I promise you won't have to. Come with me now. I am having dinner at home with Father and Theresa and there you will meet the man whom I met today who has changed my life."

Upon entering the doorway, both Father and Theresa threw their arms around Marie. Dieter did the same.

"*Fraulein*, I am very pleased to meet you. My name is Dieter, Dieter Schmidt." Dieter's theatrics were so comical that we all, including Marie, broke out in laughter.

"Marie, how glad I am to see you! Sit down and join us," Father insisted.

"Thank God he has finally come to his senses!" exclaimed Theresa.

Before dinner, Dieter told Marie and the rest of us the entire story about Weinstein, Rachael, me and the SS. I then professed, in front of all of them, my true feelings for Marie and my contempt for Rachael. When I finished, I felt Marie's hand tightly grasp mine. I knew then that I was forgiven, and I silently vowed that I would never leave her again. To the applause of all present, I kissed her.

"Alright everyone, now that Erik has regained his senses, let's eat," said Theresa.

As usual, she showed off her superb talent at cooking. The meal was supreme, *Jägerschnitzel* with fresh mushrooms and red cabbage.

Theresa and Marie did the dishes while Father went upstairs to find his slippers. Dieter and I retired to the den where he quietly told me about Rachael and her lover. "Erik, forgive me, but I haven't yet told you that Rachael has been secretly sleeping with a Jewish doctor behind your back. So I am sure she has been, so to speak, *taken care of* in your absence."

Before I could respond, Father returned. Surprisingly enough, I was not bothered by the news.

When the dishes were finished, Theresa and Marie joined us in the den where we all enjoyed a crackling fire and listened to music on the radio recorded at the Kroll Opera House.

After the performance ended, Dieter broke the ice. "Marie... may I call you that?"

"Of course."

"Don't worry about Erik. As long as Weinstein gets business from the Reich, Walter could care less about what Erik is doing."

Before we called it an evening, Dieter grasped my hand. "Erik, is it too early to ask for your answer?"

He then turned towards Marie and my family, clearly looking for their approval.

"Yes, Dieter, if Marie and my family agree, I will join you."

I looked at the three of them, and could tell by the expressions on their faces that they did agree. My voice deep with emotion, I turned to them. "I want all of you to know just how happy this day has made me. It's like a great weight being taken off my shoulders. Yesterday, I was buried in a lifestyle that I know would never lead to happiness. Now, I have my family, my love, and my country back."

Father quickly went and poured five glasses of an aged *Liebfraumilch*, and as we all lifted our glasses, he said, "I want to make a toast to Erik. Welcome home, son!"

The glasses touched, and after pledging all of us to secrecy, Dieter exclaimed, "Heil Hitler!" which we all repeated in unison.

My time in Berlin passed quickly. While I pretended to be working diligently for Weinstein, the truth was that most of my efforts were directed towards learning my new position.

I called Walter daily. He congratulated me more and more each time I called. Dieter saw to it that sizable contracts, some even carrying the personal approval of Goebbels, no less, filtered onto Walter's desk.

I even forced myself to call Rachael. I sincerely hoped that someday I would meet her *doctor* and be able to show both of them that they were the fool, not me.

Dieter clandestinely took me to several indoctrination meetings. There I learned much about the background of the SS and also much about the Jews. I don't know how I could have been so blind as not to see the treachery and deceit practiced every day by these *chosen people*. Yet, how could this be? Frankly, I knew many decent and fine Jews. Could I blame an entire race for the actions of some of its members?

My work in Berlin was about to be finished, and all too soon it would be time for me to return to Vienna. I promised Marie that I would send for her quickly so that she could be with me when I would hopefully have at least a menial position with the Reich.

I said goodbye to Marie, my father and my sister, and I promised I would call often and that I would return to Berlin in the near future.

4

Back To Vienna

IT was a bright, cold day, as Dieter and I boarded the train at Anhalt Station for the return trip to Vienna. It had been pre-arranged that we would have separate seating and upon arrival we would each go our separate way until we could safely make contact.

I had been instructed that I should persuade Walter to hire Dieter on the pretext that he had influential friends in Berlin who would be grateful that Weinstein gave him employment.

The return trip back to Vienna was hardly as interesting as the trip to Berlin, but what I did notice, more so on this return trip, was the obvious presence of numerous uniformed SS personnel. It seemed quite obvious that soon Hitler would move upon Austria, whether she liked it or not. I really had no moral dilemma in accepting this since I now felt, as did countless thousands of Austrian-Germans, that Austria needed Germany's protection from Bolshevism. As the trip proceeded, I again thought about the moral dilemma that I *did* have, the Reich's philosophy towards the Jews. We all knew fine Jews, but by the same token, could I refuse to act for the good of the people because of my personal beliefs?

Outside the train terminal I noticed that Dieter had already flagged down a taxi and was on his way to his hotel. I told my driver to take me to my flat where I hopefully could get some rest.

My landlady was good enough to have placed my mail on the kitchen table and I knew that she checked on my room on a daily basis. Knowing how kind she was, it saddened me to know that she was a Jew and to realize how bleak her future in Austria would soon be. I dare say neither the Jews nor the gentile Austrians were even remotely aware of the full ramifications of the coming Nazi rule.

"Erik, I was just going to check on your room. I didn't mean to disturb you. How glad I am to see you! It gets lonely not having you around with us to play our weekly game of euchre. How was your trip to Berlin?" Not waiting for an answer, she continued. "My, it has been so long since my mother and I visited Berlin. We often stopped at the many fine cafés and shopped in the many beautiful stores on the *Unter den Linden*. While we were in Berlin, we always visited my uncle, who was then the chief Rabbi at his synagogue. Those were such great times! Did you know that my uncle had a fatal heart attack recently?"

"Why, no, I did not."

"Yes, while he was going to the market, he had a severe attack of chest pains and he collapsed on the sidewalk. As he lay dying, his good and dear German friends, friends he had known for years, friends whom he had helped so much, walked past and did nothing but watch as the noble *Hitler Youth* stood over him and taunted him with awful words like, "Die, dirty Jew, die!" And, of course, being the *good Jew* that he was, he obeyed the command of the *Master Race* and died on the spot. Tell me, Mr. Byrnes, why are the Germans so cruel to us? Why can't they all be kind like you?"

She started to cry softly at these words and closed my door behind her. I would have appreciated the opportunity to tell her why the Germans despised the Jews and I also wanted to tell her that she wasn't like those other Jews. I thought about going after her but I knew she didn't hate me and that we would talk again.

The next day, when I reported back to work at Weinstein Industries, my desk was full of mail and messages, but what really stood out was a card of congratulations from Walter, attached to a liter of champagne. During my brief stay in Berlin, four major contracts were let to Weinstein Industries. This was more business than it had received from the Reich in the prior six months.

"How are you, Erik? Things certainly have been dull around here since you left."

"Sarah, you know that you were the only person whom I missed. I've always said you'd make a great wife for any man. Why don't you marry me?"

Her face turned a crimson red.

I always kidded her that way. She was a wonderful secretary, loyal, although much older than me. She and her husband were originally from Berlin, just like me, but he had died in the Great War, and she had never remarried.

"By the way, Sarah, how is Walter doing?"

"Oh, he is quite happy. The plant is now running three shifts, and the rumor is that he owes it all to you, Erik. Come now, how did you do it?"

"Remind me to tell you about it later. I had better go and see Walter now."

As I walked toward his office, I suddenly became very nervous, going over in my mind just how Dieter instructed me to act. *Act friendly, but firm. Make sure Walter understands that changes will have to be made.*

Walter's door was open.

"Erik, Erik, come in. Come in! I see that your trip must have gone fabulously well. I want you to know that I won't forget what you have done. Is there anything that I can do now for you? Don't be shy, *son*, just let me know."

"Well, yes, Walter, there is something. In Berlin, I met a German by the name of Dieter Schmidt. You might say, Herr Schmidt assisted me. I also found out that he has important friends in high places in the German government. In fact, he helped me obtain those contracts for you. I would like you to give him a job, a good job, working under me. It would be helpful for the both of us."

"Erik, I said I was grateful, but don't push it. You know I am not hiring any more Germans. If anything, if I have an opening, I must hire Jews. I wouldn't hear the end of it if I didn't."

"Walter, if you want more contracts from Germany, you need to accommodate me. I'm sure I could leave Weinstein and find employment elsewhere in Vienna with one of your competitors. Goebbels has taken quite an interest in me. I don't think he would care what firm I worked for."

There was a long silence.

"Erik, Erik, why are we arguing? Of course, Dieter... what's his name? Dieter Schmidt! He will, of course, get a job here. Bring him in tomorrow. I would like to meet him."

As I walked out of the room, he called out, "Erik, don't forget to call Rachael! She has been very lonely without you."

The day passed by very quickly, with me catching up on the local gossip, returning phone calls, and scanning over the mail on my desk. In fact, the day went by so fast that I didn't notice until late that afternoon that I had forgotten to call Rachael.

Mustn't keep the bitch waiting!

"Erik, I missed you so much. When are you going to see me?"

"Tonight, Rachael, tonight. I'll see you tonight, at about seven."

The rest of our conversation was devoted to small talk. After I hung up, I felt nothing but contempt for her, for Rachael and her entire family. She had been sleeping with her doctor-lover while all the time she was using me to help her and the Weinsteins. But rather than dwell on her, I decided to call Dieter right away. He would be happy to know that he had just been hired to a reasonably good position at Weinstein Industries.

25

"Dieter, you're working for me now. You start tomorrow at 8:00 AM sharp and don't be late."

"Don't worry, boss. I won't embarrass you. How did the old man take it all?"

"Well, at first he wasn't too happy, but what could he do about it?"

"That's right Erik, there is *nothing* he can do about it, and unfortunately for him and his family, it will get worse, *much worse*. Erik, we probably should meet later tonight so that we can go over some information I received today from Berlin. Better that we do this outside the workplace so that we don't cause any suspicions. How about eight this evening?"

"Sounds good, Dieter, but let's make it about nine because I have to see Rachael first."

"See you at nine. My room number is 209."

With that, we ended the conversation, and since it was getting close to the end of the day, I decided to leave early for the Weinstein mansion.

It was Sophia, Rachael's mother, who answered the door.

"Erik, what a surprise! What are you doing here?"

She smelled of liquor and cheap perfume. I knew that Walter only kept her around for show. It wouldn't be socially acceptable in his group to be without a mate, even though he and most of his friends were rumored to have a mistress on the side.

I actually felt sorry for Sophia. She was, by all accounts, a kept woman.

"Good to see you, too, Sophia. Is Rachael in?"

"Why, no, Erik. Was she expecting you?"

"I thought I would surprise her and come by a little early. By the way, has Walter returned from work yet?"

Looking rather sadly, she shook her head. "No, Erik, he seldom gets home before nine anymore. He is very busy, you know."

"If you don't mind, Sophia, I will wait for her in the garden."

"Wait, Erik, ah, well... that might not be a good idea. I really don't know when she is coming..."

At that very moment, I heard a car pull up and two doors slam shut almost simultaneously.

"We're home, Mother. Is supper ready yet? You know David can't stay long. Erik will be here soon... Erik, I didn't..."

"What, Rachael? You didn't expect me so early? I thought that I would surprise you and I see that I did. Aren't you going to introduce me to your friend, Rachael?"

Her face was pale, very, very pale.

Seeing that she was not the polite hostess, I said, "Excuse me, sir. I didn't catch your name."

"Eh, David Herus. Dr. David Herus."

"Well, Herr Doctor, I hope you take good care of Rachael."

"Rachael and I are only friends, Herr Byrnes."

"Yes, I'm sure."

Turning back to Rachael, I decided there would be no better time than now to break up this farce of a relationship.

"Rachael, this is to officially inform you that you and I no longer have any commitments to each other."

"But, Erik, David is just a friend. Aren't you, David?"

"Please, Rachael, please, no more lies. I already know what Dr. Herus is to you and what you are to him."

Now, with our relationship out of the way and knowing that Walter would certainly find out about this, I suspected that he would be even more *kind* to me. To Walter, losing me as a prospective son-in-law had to equate with the potential loss of Nazi Germany's lucrative contracts, a definite blow to his pocket book!

"Rachael, I knew about you and David before I came here tonight. In fact, the real purpose of my visit was to let you know that you're free."

She sobbed. "But Erik, I don't want to be free from you."

Suddenly, Sophia began to scream. "Rachael, Rachael, see how you have ruined everything! Erik is going to leave now. Your father will be so displeased, and without the military contracts..."

I had to stop this pathetic display. "Frau Weinstein, the fact that I am leaving Rachael doesn't mean I am leaving Weinstein Industries. Actually, I intend to stay on as long as it takes to finish my job. Good luck, David. I know you'll need it."

With that, I bade goodbye and left. I had promised Dieter I would meet him at nine.

"How did your little visit with Rachael go?"

"It's all over, Dieter, all over. You don't know how happy I feel. Rachael made it easy."

"What do you mean, easy?"

"I caught her and her doctor friend together and that gave me the excuse to break up our relationship. I did, however, have to soothe her mother's fears about my leaving Weinstein Industries."

"Good, Erik, very good, but we have more important matters to discuss now. There will be more than enough time to deal with the Weinsteins at a later date. Erik, some of our agents are moving into Vienna, even as we speak. In fact, I feel that the talks between the Reich's Rosenberg and Austria's Von Schuschnigg are moving in a positive direction. I think Von Schuschnigg will see the light very, very soon. As you know, Erik, the Reich prefers to march peacefully into Austria, much as was done in '35 when Germany was awarded the Saar Basin by the League of Nations. But if Austria doesn't capitulate any time soon, there will be war earlier than we might think, and no matter what, we have to be ready for either scenario. Soon after the occupation, all Jewish manufacturing firms will be nationalized. It means that these businesses will be *voluntarily* sold by the present owners to people loyal to our cause or directly to the new government. Weinstein Industries and all similarly owned industries will no longer be in Jewish hands."

"Dieter, what will happen to Walter and his family?"

"If he were smart, he would immediately emigrate out of the country, to England, Palestine, or even to America. He should do that now because there will come a time when all doors will be closed to him. After the occupation, the Austrian Jews won't find it as easy to leave. Also, any Jew, and especially someone like Walter Weinstein, could find himself subject to *special treatment*, that is immediate arrest and deportation to a camp. But again, enough about the Jews, there are more immediate tasks to handle."

"Such as?"

"First of all, we must quickly find lodging for the new agents, jobs for some, and *sightseeing tours* for others who are posing as visitors. There must be coordination with individuals in the Austrian government sympathetic to our cause and also with individuals like yourself who are in strategic manufacturing and industrial positions throughout Austria. Erik, there are many like you, but none that I know of have so won the favor of Goebbels and, yes, of Heydrich, too. Needless to say, you have made a great impression upon both of them. In Vienna alone, Erik, there are many SS officers such as myself, each of whom is supervising and coordinating with men like you. When the time is right, you will meet these officers and your co-collaborators."

I couldn't help but feel overwhelmed. This was a monumental undertaking. Was I up to it? Time would tell.

For dinner, I ate duck and Dieter devoured a roast. It was after eleven when we finished eating, but it was obvious that neither of us were interested in calling it a night yet. The restaurant had an adjoining stand-up bar and we decided to continue our evening in that room. They had a three-piece orchestra playing and there was a crowd of people drinking, singing and having a good time.

"Beer for the house!" Dieter shouted.

Soon, I, too, bought a round, and before we knew it, the half-dozen or so patrons each did the same. It was half past twelve when Dieter began to sing *The Horst Wessel Song.*

Die Fahne Hoch! Die Reihe dicht geschlossen!
SA marchiert mit ruhig festem Schritt.
Bald flattern Hitler's Fahnen über alle Strassen!

The flags held high! The ranks stand firm together!
The SA marches with steady, resolute tread.
Soon Hitler's flags will fly over every street.

At first, upon hearing the singing, the room became silent, an uneasy silence inundated with apprehension regarding the two strangers who invaded the pub, but also apprehension about the country and the men for whom the song was created. Sensing this, Dieter jumped up and put his arm around the largest man there and soon both began singing with the orchestra playing. I then joined in as well, not knowing the precise words, and within minutes the bar room, followed by the dining area patrons, all joined in a rousing chorus. Arms high and with steins in hand, they all praised the Reich. At the end, all glasses were raised to the cry of "Heil Hitler! Austria for the Reich!" The room was full of electricity. We drank and sang until closing time and we all agreed to meet again in the near future.

I drove Dieter back to his hotel. How I managed in my condition, I don't know. As he stumbled out of my car, drink in hand, he cried out, "Erik, we'll be friends fur..ever! Oh! By the way, tell Weinstein I'll be late for my firs da..day."

It was eleven in the morning before Dieter made it in for his first day at work. Muttering something totally indiscernible, he stumbled right past Walter and into my office.

"Erik, what a time last night! We have to do that again."

Suddenly it was as if I were looking at a different person. Dieter glanced around the room, making sure we weren't being overheard, and closed the door, but not before looking down the corridor to convince himself that indeed no one was there. He walked over to his briefcase, opened it, and pulled out a file with several typewritten pages. Then, with a tone of absolute sobriety, he began to read them to me.

"I hereby direct that Obersturmführer Schmidt and ... are to coordinate with their operatives no later than 10 PM, 3.11.38. A group meeting, to include all those involved, should be undertaken as soon as possible.

... Heydrich will be present to explain Operations ...

The following is a brief agenda of topics to be covered:

1. Time table for entry of German forces into Austria.
2. Level of pre-entry infiltration and expected ground-
   work to be in place before troop movement.
3. Alternatives to be used in the event of confrontational
   entry.
4. Post-occupation approach to local government,
   and civilians.
5. The Jewish/Bolshevik problem."

Dieter looked at me. "Erik, I've read to you the main topics. You should know that I wouldn't have if I didn't totally trust you." He put the documents away, and continued. "I think I am right in my belief that you will not only be our chief operative at Weinstein Industries but also I think, Erik, that you will soon rise to levels above that.

What I want you to do, is to continually remind Weinstein of just why he is getting these contracts from the Reich. We will see to it that letters are written to him describing just how influential you are in Berlin. He must know that it is *only* because of you that this work is still coming in.

Also, you must make dossiers on all the important Jews at Weinstein Industries. Include all those in management positions. We need to know their ages, birthplaces, parental lineage, whether they have been Christianized, whether their spouses, if any, are Jewish or gentile, number of children, schools attended by the children, what assets they own, and any other information that could be essential to the Reich. Start on this now, and obtain as many details as you can."

"What is the ultimate plan for these Jews, Dieter?"

"I am not totally sure, but I have heard a term Heydrich mentioned one day in passing. It isn't yet a routine term, but I assure you that you *will* hear it again." He turned and walked to the window. With a slight catch in his voice and with some obvious distress, he told me, "Heydrich called it *The Final Solution*. I think what this means, Erik, is that ultimately there will be few or no Jews left in Germany or any of its Protectorates. Mind you, this is not official policy at this time, but I feel quite sure that in time what I say will come to pass."

I tried to find out what Dieter meant by there being *no Jews left* and I was also very concerned as to where the Jews were going, but he cut me off before I could question him further. He obviously did not want to speak about this term any more.

"Well, enough of that now, Erik. Please show me to my office and formally introduce me to Walter Weinstein."

"Jawohl, Herr executive," I chuckled as I led Dieter to Walter's office.

"Walter Weinstein, I would like you to meet your new employee, Dieter Schmidt."

"Mr. Weinstein, my pleasure, of course." Dieter held out his hand.

Not taking Dieter's hand, Walter bellowed, "Herr Schmidt, I want you to know that it is only through the intercession of Erik that you have this position. I must also state that your tardiness today will leave an imprint on your record at Weinstein Industries. You will be docked pay for the time you missed."

"I apologize, Herr Weinstein. I will see to it that this never happens again and I realize fully well that I owe this opportunity to my friend Erik. As to the docketing of pay, I totally agree with you. I also promise you, Herr Weinstein, that when my time has come to an end at Weinstein Industries, you will agree that I have helped to accomplish here what nobody else has done in the past."

Walter was caught off guard by Dieter's comments and, amazingly, he seemed pleased to hear what he said.

"Perhaps I have misjudged you, Mr. Schmidt. I hope you do accomplish your goals. If I can be of service to you and assist you, please don't hesitate to ask me or Erik, for that matter. We will do everything we can to help. By the way, as for that bit about your pay, forget it. I'm sure it will not happen again."

As Dieter and I walked out of the office, neither of us could refrain from laughing. What a fool Walter was!

I started working on my assignments that evening and after an hour or so, I decided to take a break and give Marie a call.

"Erik, it's about time you called! I was afraid that something had happened to you."

"Don't worry, Marie. I'm fine, but also very busy with my new assignments. By the way, I want you to know that Rachael's out of the way now and things couldn't be better."

"Good, if you hadn't done something soon about her, I would have."

"How's Father and Theresa?"

"Just fine, but we all miss you already."

"And I miss you too, but I just noticed the time and I'm afraid I have to go now, but I promise you I'll call you again very soon. I love you. Give my love to Father and sis."

I noticed that since my return from Berlin Walter had hardly worked me to death. Obviously, he didn't care much what I did since he knew all the contracts were a direct result of my efforts with the German authorities.

Likewise, I saw to it that Dieter had also little to do except pick up his paycheck. What Walter did not know, however, was that Dieter and I spent the greater part of our days educating ourselves for the Reich's takeover and for the part that we might play in the future government.

As I was instructed, I quickly developed personnel files on all key employees at Weinstein Industries, making great detail in the reports of the Jewish employees. Dieter busied himself not only with training me, but also with familiarizing himself with the system of government in Austria, and in Vienna in particular. He made clandestine contacts with the officials who were sympathetic to Germany and kept dossiers on those whom he felt to be opposed to German rule. These first days were quite productive, to say the least.

We often discussed the considerable progress I made in obtaining the information Dieter requested. It was surprisingly easy, mainly because the personnel files that Walter kept had all the information I needed. Walter was very good at inserting information that was not necessarily relevant to a job application, but very relevant to his desire to obtain information about everyone's wealth and assets. It was equally surprising to find out just how much wealth these Jews possessed. I learned quite a bit about their families.

There would be many surprised and shocked Jews in a very short period of time.

I admit it wasn't very romantic, but romantic or not, I proposed to Marie over the phone two days later. She accepted, and the wedding was set for June of this year, 1938. Naturally, I asked Dieter to be the best man.

It was in this same week in March when Dieter entered my office to tell me, "Erik, soon we will see the product of our work. Do you remember the meeting we are going to have? Well, it will be tomorrow evening at nine. We will use a theater that I have secretly set up for the occasion."

"Good. Is there anything you want me to do in preparation?"

"No, not yet. We will get more directives at the meeting. Incidentally, Obergruppenführer Heydrich is chairing this occasion."

I was impressed. I had heard stories about Heydrich.

Upon returning to my desk, I noticed an envelope with the Weinstein family seal firmly implanted. I opened it and found this note from Walter.

"Congratulations upon your promotion to Executive Vice President. Walter."

Executive Vice President! Obviously, things must be going very well for Walter. He was the envy of all his fellow Jew industrialists. While they were seeing their businesses slowly coming to a standstill, Weinstein Industries was working three shifts.

Just within the last few days, I noticed how Walter now relied on me, even to the exclusion of his employed relatives. He consulted me on all important corporate decisions, and even went so far as asking me for my advice on hiring, firing, promoting or demoting the very Jews whom he sought to protect. Just one month ago, he never would have dreamed of asking me that. In fact, I had heard that just one day ago when the local Rabbi complained to him that Weinstein Industries was hiring hardly any Jews anymore, Walter actually swore at him, telling him to stay out of his affairs.

I also noticed that just this last week he had begun to drink at work. I had never seen him do that before. More out of curiosity than anything else, when I had asked him if anything was bothering him, he told me about the problems he was having with Rachael, namely her total irresponsibility, her constant partying, and her infatuation with her doctor-lover. Incidentally, Dr. David Herus, because of *somebody's* suggestion, had just lost his position at the city hospital. Walter couldn't seem to find out why.

He also complained about Sophia who, according to Walter, was becoming a total drunk and a constant spendthrift. Perhaps she knew that soon she would have no more money.

Walter also lost the love of his gentile mistress who ran away with a young soldier in the Austrian Army. But what I believe concerned him the most was his fear about the very real threat of a Nazi takeover of Austria. He already knew about the Aryanization of German industries, the confiscation of German-Jewish property, and the elimination of Jewish professionals in Germany from practicing their professions except amongst Jews only. In all, Germany had passed dozens of anti-Jewish pieces of legislation and before the year would be up, Walter felt this was a real possibility in Austria. Many of his Jewish business associates in Germany had even found their way to Dachau, up to now only a "work prison."

Knowing all of this, Walter felt that for some reason I had a *magic touch* with the German government. I don't think he cared why or how I got this gift. He just knew I had it and I knew he was going to do his best to keep it alive for his benefit.

When he confided in me, I could tell he was counting on me to intercede in the event of a takeover. To calm him and also to amuse myself, I often told him words to the effect that I would see to it that I would personally take care of him and his family if indeed the German presence in Austria became a reality. Little did he know, then, how really serious I was when I made that statement.

The very first day he was employed, I saw to it that Dieter was able to hire his own personal secretary. In no time, he hired a beautiful Austrian girl, named Ursula. It was obvious to me that she was an operative. Dieter and Ursula did little work for Weinstein Industries while spending most of their time working towards the eventual occupation. There were secret phone calls to nameless destinations, many hours spent with the office door closed, the obvious way in which she showed me warmth and affection while expressing nothing but icy cold indifference to most of the other employees, especially those who were Jewish. She knew too well that Dieter would protect her and I would protect the both of them.

5

Austria And Germany Become One

THE political climate in Austria was very tense this second week of March. Some Austrians, foolishly, even promoted the use of force against Germany. Just lately, Von Schuschnigg, the Austrian politician, was at odds with Hitler and wanted no part of a German occupation. In fact, he had called for a popular vote on the issue but I'm afraid that if he'd ever gotten the chance to hold that election, it certainly would not be a fair vote.

It really didn't matter since I'm sure Hitler couldn't care less about any election and Austria was no match for his armies. If he were to be stopped, it should have been earlier, at the Saar. Now I was quite sure that Austria would fall, one way or another.

Up to now, I had only seen pictures of Heydrich, but upon entering the theater hall, and seeing him in person, I felt I was in the presence of a man, not just any man, but truly a *superman*.

He was tall and handsome. His eyes, although small and sinister looking, were deep blue. His hands were large and his fingers were long and slender. I was told he excelled in sports, especially fencing.

"Herr Obergruppenführer, it is my honor to introduce you to..."

"Enough, Dieter, I need no introduction of Erik Byrnes. I congratulate you in your decision to join us, Erik. The next few months will be history-in-the-making and you will be part of it, and if I'm indeed the good judge of character that I think I am, it will not be a small part. I have taken a personal interest in you. Your work for the Reich, in this short period of time, has been nothing less than outstanding. You have definite leadership and administrative qualities. Goebbels and I are totally pleased with our decision to seek you out. I also believe that the Austrian government will freely capitulate and our Führer will peacefully enter Vienna within days. We must all be ready for him, both physically and mentally.

Some of the duties that will be required of you would have seemed a year ago to be immoral and totally against everything you had learned. By now, however, I know that you will gladly perform these tasks if asked. What you and Dieter must both understand is that Germany is seeking its own destiny.

We are truly a super race, and as such, we must remove the slavs, bolsheviks, Jews, and gypsies who inhabit lands to which Germany lays a claim and which morally belong to the Reich. These subhumans will be dealt with in short fashion, but enough of that for now. I must begin my speech."

We all took our seats. There were guards at all entrances and at all exits.

Heydrich began by introducing himself and he then proceeded to show us a film, produced in 1934 by Leni Riefenstahl, called *Triumph of the Will.* Although I had seen it before, I didn't pay much attention to it at the time. Watching it now, however, was totally different. This film showed the greatness of Adolf Hitler, his magnetism, and his ability to work the crowd into a frenzy. At least a dozen times throughout the film, our group stood and raised our voices in the Nazi salute, *Heil Hitler! Heil Hitler*! We could not stop ourselves. At its conclusion, I noticed my clothes were wet from perspiration and my face felt flushed.

After the shouting and clapping was over, Heydrich, standing in front of a lectern, praised what he called the *accuracy* of the film. He then pointed out what he believed would be the course of development in Austria within the next few days and the coming months: (1) the entry, preferably peacefully, which he said would be within days; (2) the removal of those governmental officials, military leaders, educators, and professionals not sympathetic to the Reich; (3) the passing of numerous race purification laws intended to remove Jews, gypsies, Freemasons and Jehovah's witnesses from any positions of importance, even if their philosophy was pro-German.

"Immediately following the entry of the Führer's armies, agents of the Gestapo and SS will openly enter Austria. They will need your assistance and you will need theirs. The local police will be under our control. The police will keep some type of order, of course, but they will be instructed not to oppose any of our policies. When things have settled down, most of you will be thanked for your services and then you will be retired from further operative work. It is not because your performance was anything but excellent, but rather it is either because your particular function will be absorbed by incoming operatives or because your particular tasks were completed to their fullest and no further work in that area needs to be done. I want you to know that the Reich is eternally grateful to you and may very well call on you again. Others of you will continue in your particular endeavors for a short period thereafter and, finally, a few of you, perhaps only one or two, will be, let's say, promoted to positions in the SS and will be prominent in the future of Austria and the Reich. Those of you whose names are now called will receive instructions by your contact. And to all of you, remember that what you have heard here may never be repeated, upon penalty of death to yourself and your family. I mention this not because I believe there are traitors among us, but rather to impress upon you how serious this matter is. *Heil Hitler!*"

As I sat contemplating what Heydrich had just said, it was evident to me that only hours stood in the way of the occupation. Our sources led us to believe that Austria would never go to war but would capitulate at the last minute. She could not count on Italy as was once hoped. England and France, on the other hand, would rather negotiate for peace than to fight.

I still couldn't help but think about what would happen to the Jews, who were now a very frightened lot. Every day one could see them lining up at the various consulates to try to secure immigration papers for France, England, Palestine, or America. Unfortunately for them, departure was not easy at all because they had to pay a high economic price in order to make the move. Walter had the money and the resources to leave Austria, but his greed prevented him from seeing the total absurdity of staying here.

Speaking of Walter, he would often go off in tangents. One time, he was babbling about how Austria would fight off Germany, another time he would say that England and France would come to Austria's aid, and the most ridiculous of them all, that he would use me to speak to the authorities to guarantee the safety and continued prosperity of the Weinstein family. I guess from Walter's perspective this made sense since, because of my deceit, he still believed that somehow I could make things right. Shortly after my return from Berlin, I told him to "get out and leave, take Rachael and Sophia with you," but he would not listen. He just shook his head in despair. "Erik, if I leave, I will lose so much." The fool didn't understand that soon he would lose everything!

It was March 12, 1938, a day that would go down in history as the *Anschluss*, the day that Austria capitulated to Hitler and the two countries were made one.

The news spread fast and the entire Jewish workforce at Weinstein Industries was in shock. I had to be careful not to show my glee as I walked through the plant. Husbands hurried home to be with their families and the women cried at the thought that they or their loved ones would soon face the same persecution that Jews in Germany had suffered for the last five years.

As I passed Walter's office, he motioned for me to come in. He had been drinking heavily and his face was pale. He asked me to close the door and to sit down. "Erik, the end has come. Soon all Austrian Jews will be doomed. Just now, I received a call from Karl Burmeister, one of my oldest Austrian competitors, and one of the few gentiles whom I considered a friend. He asked me if he could buy me out. I thought for awhile and then I gave him a price. The amount I asked was more than reasonable. Do you know what he told me, Erik?"

He took another drink from his glass, and continued. "He told me, 'Why should I pay so much, Walter? In a month, you will sell me your plant for one-tenth of what you are asking me now.' One-tenth, Erik, one-tenth." At this point, he drank what was left in his cup, spilling much of it on his wrinkled shirt. He walked over to a file cabinet, pulled out another bottle, filled up the cup, and turned to me, pleading as he spoke.

"Erik, I know that Rachael has treated you badly. But can you find it in your heart to help her, Sophia, and even myself? I'm told if a Jew marries a gentile, the Jew will be saved. If you marry her before any laws are passed prohibiting this type of marriage, she would be safe. Perhaps this would even help Sophia and myself. Please Erik, I'm begging you."

I looked at him, clasped my hands behind my back, and strolled around the room.

"Walter, I can't marry Rachael. She is in love with her Doctor Herus. It would be improper for me to interfere."

"To hell with her doctor, Erik! If she stays with that Jew, all of us will be doomed."

I shrugged my shoulders, turned around, and left the room.

Before I closed the door, I turned back and saw Walter hunched over the desk, sobbing quietly to himself. I simply went about my duties in this practically deserted plant.

After a few more hours, I decided to call it a day. It made no sense to remain any longer as there was no activity going on.

The streets were filled with people, many going home from work as if nothing had happened. Others were joyful, ready to welcome the Führer. Then there were those who seemed to be in a daze, befuddled and bewildered, with fear in their faces and tears in their eyes.

Those were the Jews.

As I turned the corner, down the Prinz Eugenstrasse, I saw that the line at the Palais Rothschildt, the governmental building that housed the *Auswanderungsabteilung*, at Kohlmessergasse #4, was at least three blocks long. People were shoving and pushing in order to enter so they could expedite their tax clearances, which were required in order to leave the country. They all wanted out of Austria.

Why hadn't they left sooner?

My car seemed to crawl in the traffic. Fortunately, I only had two more blocks to travel. Dieter and I were to meet at *Der Ratskeller*, a favorite place for both of us.

He had already arrived by the time I got there, and was seated in the second booth from the rear.

"Erik, Erik, over here!"

I sat down across from him and shook his hand.

"Well, Erik, all the time we spent and the preparations that we made are finally going to pay off. Hitler himself will soon arrive. It will truly be a great day for Germany and perhaps even a greater day for Austria."

We both toasted this grand news, but as I put my beer to my lips, I heard a loud *pop!* coming from the exit hall, to the rear.

Dieter and I turned to see were the sound came from and noticed a crowd forming near the rear door. We decided to see what was going on. Dieter took the lead and, as the crowd saw his SS uniform, it parted and we were able to get through with no trouble. I could see a middle-aged man on the ground, a pistol by his side, his temple distinctively marked by a neat, cylindrical hole, with a crimson river of blood slowly oozing out.

A woman pushed us both to the side and took the dead man in her arms. Sobbing, she looked up at us.

"Swine, you are all swine, German pigs. My Otto wasn't a strong man. He couldn't bear the thought of living and dying like his cousins in Germany under Hitler's rule. Because of you, he killed himself and left me and our children alone."

Hearing this, the crowd that had gathered around began to laugh and jeer at her. "Move that garbage out of here before someone shoots you too."

Dieter moved towards her. I think he wanted to help her, but the Jewess spat at him. She bent over and picked up the pistol. Dieter warned her to put the gun down but she continued to raise it. Instinctively, Dieter pulled out his Luger. "Put the gun down! I won't warn you again." It was all so strange, as if she wanted him to shoot her. She continued to raise the weapon and began to point it towards *me*, when Dieter, still begging with her to stop, shot her. She fell to the ground, looking first at Dieter and then at me with eyes full of hate. Her body went limp.

Like her husband, she too was dead.

After a momentary pause of silence, most of the patrons began to applaud and cheer Dieter and his *noble* deed. Dieter put away his Luger and walked out into the street without saying a word.

As expected, the local police made little of the shootings. After all, what's two less Jews to worry about? Soon several patrons dragged the two bodies out and dumped them in the gutter.

"Erik, I hope you know that I truly did not want to shoot that woman."

I looked at Dieter and assured him that there was no need to apologize. I must confess that I couldn't understand why he was so upset.

Before we left, he instructed me to meet him at his hotel room, precisely at 7:00 AM the next day.

After leaving Dieter, I hurried to my flat, and prayed that my landlady would be home. Now that time was running out for the Jews of Austria, I suddenly realized that Frau Anstrum was in great danger.

I ascended the steps to her flat and frantically knocked on her door. After a short while, she opened it up.

"Herr Byrnes, please come in. What is wrong?"

"Frau Anstrum, I must beseech you to take whatever belongings you have and leave quickly. Leave Vienna now! I will help you."

"But where should I go? To Poland? To Hungary? Where will I be safe? Even if I could escape, what of my relatives with me here? What of these little children?" She pointed to a small boy and a little girl who were playing innocently on the floor with a small wooden truck.

"What will they do? Where can they go? I cannot leave them. We have no money. How can we get exit passes without money? It is, I'm afraid, the end for all of us."

She began to sob.

"Frau Anstrum, I want you to begin packing. Take only those items you absolutely need. I'll get you and your family out of here. I promise!"

Her face lit up as she wiped away the tears with her apron hem. She believed that I would help her and her family. She gave me a hug and locked the door behind me.

I left with a cold sweat and hurried back to Dieter's place. I needed him. Would he help me? It was asking a lot, and could I trust him? I had to take the chance. I had to try.

"Dieter, are you in there? Please, open up! I need to speak with you right away."

"Erik, is that you? You're way early."

"Never mind that, Dieter, please open the door!"

"Ja! I'll be right there."

As he opened the door, I pushed him in and closed the door behind us. "Are you alone, Dieter?"

"Well, I will be soon, Erik, thanks to you."

The half-dressed woman inside was obviously upset, but after Dieter promised he would make it up to her, she left without incident.

"Dieter, I have a big favor to ask and you are the only one I can turn to."

"How can I help you, Erik?"

"I need exit visas for my landlady and her family."

"That should pose no problem, Erik..."

"Dieter, before you agree to help, there is something I must tell you. They are all Jews."

"Jews! Erik, are you out of your mind? Why should I, no, why should *we* risk everything we both have worked so hard for to help these people, not to mention what will happen to both of us if we are caught?"

"Yes, you're right, Dieter. It was wrong for me to ask you."

I started to leave, but he grabbed my arm.

"I will help you, Erik, but I must hurry, because as we speak the authorities are beginning to round up Jews all over Vienna, even before Hitler has actually entered the city. I guarantee you that it will be much worse after he has actually arrived. I have much to do myself before his arrival, so give me her name and address and I will work on it right away. Go now, Erik, there isn't much time."

I returned to my flat and called Frau Anstrum to assure her that help would soon be coming. She seemed relieved to hear my words.

I now could get some rest, knowing that Frau Anstrum and her family would be taken care of.

I arrived at Dieter's precisely at 7:00 AM. He greeted me at the door with a big grin. He said he had a surprise for me.

"Erik, look what I have for you." He walked to his closet and opened the door. There, hanging from the coat rack, was an SS uniform, complete with boots, hat and a coat.

"You can try it on, Erik, but I'm sure it will fit."

I went into Dieter's bedroom, and immediately tried it on. It fit like a glove. I went over to the mirror. There I was, an officer in the SS!

"Just in case you don't know, Erik, you now hold the rank of an SS Untersturmführer. You should be impressed. My rank is only one level above yours and I have been in the service for some time now. You have made a great impression on Heydrich and Goebbels. With them supporting you, you need no others. It is common knowledge that Hitler himself has been grooming Heydrich to be his eventual successor. If that happens, who knows how far you can rise in rank?"

I embraced him, then stepped back and placed my hands on his shoulders, saying, "Till my dying day, Dieter, you will be my brother, the brother I never had. I promise you that I will always be there for you. I can never repay you for all you have done for me, never."

Removing my hands from his shoulders, Dieter paused, then looked me in the eyes. "Erik, in this business you should be careful about making promises, but nonetheless there is a promise I make to you as well. Until my dying day, you too will be my brother, the brother I never had. I will watch out for you the best I can. History is unfolding right before our eyes. Today Austria is ours. Tomorrow, it will be all of Europe."

"Thank you, Dieter. Thank you!"

"Hitler will arrive tomorrow, on the 14th. Now, you must command a contingent of troops to Weinstein Industries. They are waiting for you in the lobby. When you get to the plant, you will have Weinstein arrested. I suggest you place him under what we will call *house arrest*. That way, no harm should come to him or his family. He will cooperate with you since he will find out that only a word from you will mean the difference between relative freedom and deportation to Dachau or Buchenwald."

With that I left, feeling exceptionally good. In fact, I felt doubly good because I knew Dieter would help Frau Anstrum and I was elated at knowing of my new position.

I found a dozen troops waiting for me outside. For my first of many commands to come, I ordered them to accompany me to Weinstein Industries. There, I would find Walter.

As we traveled through the city, I could see that crowds were beginning to line up on the *Ringstrasse,* awaiting the Führer. There were cheering Viennese waiving miniature swastika flags. Little did they know how different their lives would soon be after this glorious day.

The plant was deserted. With several armed SS men, I ascended to the main office area. There I saw Walter slumped over his desk, a bottle of whiskey clamped between his hands. One of my men, a young SS officer in his early twenties, quickly moved around the desk, grabbed Walter by his collar, and slapped him in the face.

"*Oben, Saujude*! Up, Jewish pig."

Walter awoke from his drunken stupor. I'm sure he had never been treated like this before. He looked up at me, and appeared to be in a daze. I am quite sure he didn't recognize me, or, if he did, he couldn't believe what he was seeing.

"Walter Weinstein, in the name of the Reich, you are placed under house arrest. Take him away and confine him to his home along with his family. If he behaves, see that no harm comes to him."

Immediately, obeying my command, my men lifted Walter out of his chair and dragged him out of the room. For once in Walter's life, he said absolutely nothing.

The SS quickly moved throughout the office area, removing any and all personal belongings of Jewish executives and arresting those few Jews who still remained in their offices. They would not be as fortunate as Walter was for the time being. These people would likely be sent to a camp immediately.

Thinking that all personnel had been removed, I found it unusual that the last office in the corridor appeared to be lit and that Wagner's *Ride of the Valkyres* emanated from it. I entered and immediately recognized the individual behind the desk. It was Jonathan Bach, to me only known as an individual who had begun working at Weinstein Industries just prior to my time. I must confess that I never liked him. He was short, somewhat overweight, and his voice was loud and obnoxious. I was shocked to see that he was also dressed in the uniform of the *SS*, with the rank of *SS Sturmscharführer*.

"Herr Untersturmführer Byrnes. Heil Hitler."

I returned the salute.

As he remained at attention, he said, "Herr Untersturmführer, I was the contact at Weinstein Industries that alerted the SS to Walter Weinstein's plans for you. You might say that I got you your present position. I am here to serve you and the Reich, and I am under your command."

"Good, Bach," I said, as I tried not to show how disagreeable the concept of being indebted to him was.

"The first thing to do is that all Jewish executives who are not already in custody are to be arrested this evening without delay. If they are in hiding, their immediate families must be detained until the cowards can be apprehended. If the missing executives are not located or do not surrender within forty-eight hours, then send the family to Dachau. There will be no exceptions, except for Weinstein and his family and my secretary, Sarah."

I could tell he was not happy about my exempting Sarah but he said nothing. I was about to dismiss him when I realized that this was a perfect time to settle an old score.

"And there is one more piece of business I would like you to handle this evening."

"Anything, Herr Untersturmführer. What order do you give me?"

"I want you to arrest a doctor who has been in the constant company of Rachael Weinstein. I believe his name is David Herus. Send him immediately to Dachau."

The chime from the grandfather clock indicated that I still had time to check on Frau Anstrum. Hopefully, Dieter had gotten her moved by now.

I slipped out of the plant, making sure I was not followed. I flagged down a taxi whose driver was more than happy to take me wherever I wanted to go.

I barely got in when he began to speak. "I want you to know, Herr Untersturmführer, that the citizens of Vienna are proud to have the Führer as our leader. I will be so glad to finally see those Jewish dogs get their just deserve. How many times did I have to drive their rich, fat asses around as they barked orders to me and talked about how they were screwing the public with their inflated prices."

As I listened, I too felt pride for Vienna and for the Führer, knowing that I was a part of all of this, but would *all* the Jews "get their just deserve"? What about Sarah and Frau Anstrum?

The taxi ride seemed to take an eternity. I think the driver purposely delayed so that he could continue talking to me.

Climbing the stairs to her flat, I could hear the crying of a little child. This whimpering seemed to be coming from Frau Anstrum's apartment. I found the door wide open and the apartment in disarray. Windows and furniture were broken. Records and pictures were shattered. Hearing that noise again, I opened the closet door and found the little girl I had seen the other evening playing on the floor with a boy. She was Frau Anstrum's little niece. Upon seeing me, she began screaming and crying uncontrollably. *"Mutter! Vater! Mutter!"*

I reached into the closet and picked up the struggling child. "Child, stop! Your mother and father are not here. I won't hurt you. I'm your friend. Look at me. Do you remember me? I came the other night to help Frau Anstrum. Remember? I am her friend."

This seemed to quiet her down.

By this time, the tenants across the hall had entered the doorway. They appeared alarmed by the sight of my uniform.

"Don't be afraid. I am not here to harm you. Do you know where Frau Anstrum has been taken?"

"Oh, Herr Byrnes! It's you. We're sorry. We didn't recognize you in your uniform. Frau Anstrum and her family were taken away, barely one-half hour ago. I don't know where they went or why the Gestapo chose them. The child must have hid in the closet until they left. Herr Byrnes, what will become of them?"

"Try not to worry," I told them reassuringly, even though I was extremely concerned about their welfare. I asked the neighbors to watch the child, and left the flat.

I had to get to the Gestapo headquarters immediately.

I found Frau Anstrum. There was an SS officer present and another man, presumably a Gestapo agent. Her face was bruised and bleeding, and her left arm appeared to be out of joint. Her head was tilted back and her eyes were open. I think she saw me as I walked in, yet her eyes did not move.

"What is the meaning of this?" I shouted.

With a look of surprise at the tone of my voice, the officer in charge hesitantly answered. "Herr Untersturmführer, forgive me. What is wrong? She is a Jewess who had been reported to us as being a Bolshevik spy. I am merely interrogating the bitch."

"Herr Sturmscharführer! She is no bitch! This lady is my landlady who supplied me with a place to stay while I was planning for the Führer's arrival." I had to lie to try to save her. "She is pro-German. What have you done with the rest of her family?"

The young officer could hardly speak.

"Answer me!" I shouted.

"I am sorry to report that a Jew, one Jewess and one male child were shot for resisting arrest and trying to escape."

I couldn't believe what I was hearing. How could this have gone so very, very wrong? Again, I yelled. "Resisting arrest! How does a small child of not more than seven years resist arrest? It is you and whoever ordered this that may wind up being shot. You will stop this interrogation at once and leave now."

"As you wish." He saluted and quickly left.

I turned to Frau Anstrum. She was motionless, a small trickle of blood was now oozing from her left eye. I tried to find her pulse. There was none.

She was dead.

I didn't even knock as I stormed through the door of Dieter's suite.

"I trusted you! I trusted you and you did this to me."

"Erik, calm down. Why are you screaming at me? What did I do?"

"It's not what you did! It's what you did *not* do. The woman I asked you to protect, Frau Anstrum, she is dead. Her young nephew was shot for *resisting arrest* along with other members of the family. Her niece, who somehow was not arrested, is now all alone."

"Erik, please, listen. You must listen and you must believe me. Right after I told you I would help, I received a call from Headquarters insisting that I appear at once. I had no choice, so I called Jonathan Bach and explained to him that I had some people, Jews, who needed exit visas. I did not mention your name. He promised me all would be taken care of. Erik, I would never do anything to betray you or to hurt those people. I trusted Bach!"

My rage abated. Sadly, I knew that Dieter had only done what I myself had done. Instead of seeing to it myself, I had handed the matter over to Dieter, a man I could trust. He only did the same by trusting Bach.

"Bach!" I said, as if he were a bad taste in my mouth.

"Some day, Dieter, he will pay dearly for what he did to Frau Anstrum and her family."

I put my arm on Dieter's shoulders. I told him to say nothing to Bach and, by my gaze, he knew that I had forgiven him.

Germany's entry into Austria was known as the *Anschluss*. Dieter and I had VIP seats at the *Heldenplatz*. The Vienna residents greeted Hitler by the thousands. They cheered his every word.

If the crowds were any indication of Hitler's popularity in Austria, the takeover was a success and, obviously, the correct move.

"Dieter, have you ever personally met our Führer?"

He was happy that I asked the question.

"Yes, I did. It was in 1936 at a reception held by Himmler, shortly before the opening of the Olympics in Berlin. Heydrich introduced me. Hitler shook my hand and thanked me! Can you imagine, Erik, *he* thanked *me* for helping him save the Reich! I hear that the Führer will be at the reception after the speeches. Perhaps you will meet him there, Erik."

After the ceremonies had ended, Dieter and I made our way to the reception that followed.

I had never seen in person as many Nazi dignitaries as I did that evening at the *Hotel Metropole*. Among those present was Adolf Eichmann, said to be a rising star in the Nazi ranks, and a man who would be concentrating much of his efforts towards *cleansing* Austria of its Jews. Dieter saw to it that I was introduced to practically all of those present. He went out of his way to compliment me in front of most of them. He told them and thereby he educated me as to what my new position here in Vienna would entail. I learned much that night.

Predictably, Hitler arrived one hour after schedule. He had earlier signed the law on the reunification of Austria and Germany at the *Weinzinger Hotel* in Linz. When he entered the room in the company of General Wilhelm Keitel, the OKW Chief, the crowd raised its hands in the Nazi salute and shouted *'Heil Hitler!'* To this ovation, Hitler raised his right arm in the same fashion. He mingled with the crowd, the perfect statesman, not staying with any one group too long but still providing the necessary amount of attention to everyone there. Soon he reached our little group which consisted of Dieter, myself and, to our silent disdain, Jonathan Bach.

"Herr Führer, Dieter Schmidt at your service."

Hitler patted Dieter on the shoulder, much as a father would show affection towards a favorite son, and said words to the effect that it was men like Dieter who exemplified the SS. As he turned his attention my way, Dieter introduced me. "My Führer, Erik Byrnes." I immediately stood at attention as Hitler reached out to me and took my hand, all the time gazing appreciatively into me eyes. He put me entirely at ease. "Erik, I understand from my friend Dr. Goebbels that you are to play an important part in the annexed Austria. Tell me, is that true?"

"Yes, my Führer, I am here to obey you and to follow your every directive. I am very proud of my country."

"You should be proud of yourself as well, Erik. If I don't send for you before then, you must stop to see me the next time you are in Berlin. I want to spend some time with you. Heydrich and I have been discussing for some time now an important project that will be implemented shortly. If you continue to perform as you have, you will play an important part in this plan."

He then spoke a few quick words to Bach, and left.

The reception continued into the early morning hours, being interrupted only momentarily for a few short side meetings in the various hotel conference rooms. It was at these meetings that I learned that I would temporarily continue being in charge of Weinstein Industries.

Walter would, of course, be available to counsel me on any points where I needed his help. It was for this reason that he and his family were being allowed to live, albeit certainly not in the lifestyle they were use to. Sophia would lose her gentile housekeepers, because Jews would be prohibited from employing them in such circumstances. Rachael would, for the first time in her life, be forced to find some type of employment. Her problem would be to find a job she would be qualified for. She never held any type of position in the past. Now she couldn't even become a decent prostitute since her only Johns would, by law, now be limited to Jews who soon would have no money to spend on such luxuries. It gave me a sense of pleasure to know that when I was done with Walter and his family, they would be paid back for the deceit they imposed on me.

I would soon be turning over to the Gestapo my final dossiers on the management-level Jews employed at Weinstein Industries. I'm proud to say that over this very short period of time I had compiled a rather detailed listing of their bloodline and their asset structure. I also knew who met the definition of a *full Jew* as opposed to those who were merely *half Jews,* and those among the ever growing crowd who practiced the Christian faith.

As had happened in Germany, the plan called for the taking of the assets of the wealthy Jews. We would call it a tax, for appearance sake. In order to pay these taxes the Jews would, as expected, be forced to sell their property for one-tenth of its value. The same requirements would apply if they tried to leave the country. If they refused to cooperate, ultimately their property would be taken from them and they would receive nothing.

Soon, laws effectuating these policies and others would be passed in Austria, similar to *The Nuremberg Laws* in Germany. Jewish doctors would only be allowed to practice on Jews, Jewish lawyers and judges would be removed from practice in the Austrian courts, interracial marriage would be prohibited.

As for the Jews at Weinstein Industries, those who worked in the labor section of the plant would be retained for the time being. They were essential for the company's continued service to the Reich. Finally, Weinstein Industries would be Germanically re-named.

I think Walter would be pleased when told just how many more contracts his former firm would now receive from the Reich, even more than when I first returned from Berlin.

Too bad. He would never benefit from them.

Heydrich had informed me that after my role at Weinstein Industries was finished, I would be involved in what was to be called *deportation* or *re-*

settlement of the Jews and other undesirables. As far as I could tell, they would be put in camps such as Dachau, or concentrations of Jews would be temporarily placed in *ghettos*, near urban areas. In fact, I was told that such a ghetto would be created not far from Vienna. For the present time, however, we would still encourage voluntary departures, at a great financial cost to them. I knew, though, that if they did not leave very quickly and *en masse*, free movement from Austria would soon no longer be the norm.

6

My Soul Falls To Hell

I FOUND out that there was more to running Weinstein Industries than I thought. What was worse, I was forced to seek Walter's assistance more often than I wanted.

The plant was operating at full capacity, being Vienna's premier manufacturer of German military uniforms and boots. Our work force was still primarily Jewish, but if a skilled non-Jewish laborer appeared, I terminated the Jew who held that post and replaced him with the gentile worker. What eventually happened to him or her was not my concern. I was following the procedure which I was ordered to adhere to.

I did make, however, one exception to that rule, my secretary Sarah. The feelings I had for her were similar to what I had felt for my landlady, Frau Anstrum. When I moved up to the Presidency of the company, Sarah replaced Walter's secretary who was, by the way, a gentile. She was a loyal friend to me and, despite outside disapproval, I would be loyal to her. By coincidence, and what made me feel even closer to her, I knew that she had known and been friends with Marie's mother when they all had lived in Berlin.

Against constant opposition, primarily from Bach, I made an endless number of excuses in order to keep her: she was the only one who was thoroughly familiar with all aspects of the plant's operation, she would be a spy for the Reich amongst the Jews, and I even went so far as to state that I felt she was not a Jew at all.

I was concerned about Bach, though. To him, it was not enough that Jews were being removed from their positions. He reveled in physically intimidating them, slapping them in the face, and allowing German-Austrians to beat them. He was an animal and not a soldier like me. Besides, I heard he had some disagreements with Sarah in the past, and that made him especially dangerous to her.

I would never let him do to Sarah what he did to Frau Anstrum and her family. I had to find a way to get her to safety and away from Bach. I would rely on Dieter again. I knew he would not fail me this time.

As to the Jews in general, often Bach would say to me, "Soon, Vienna will be *Judenfrei*." He would ask me to accompany him to various pogroms that he knew would be taking place on certain evenings. I declined, as I was always able to make a reasonable excuse, lying that I was busy that evening working on some Jewish *Action*. This always seemed to satisfy him. In fact, he asked on more than one occasion if he could accompany me.

In Germany, the demise of the Jews had been a slow process, taking several years. In Austria it happened almost overnight. Although the Jews only comprised about fifteen percent of Vienna's population, government policies against them became a number one priority rather quickly. In some areas of Austria, Jews were required to register and list their assets, and in other places Jewish men were forced to change their name to *Israel* and Jewish women theirs to *Sarah*. I was told that soon their passports would have the capital J stamped on its face.

More and more pogroms followed. They initially began as small demonstrations in which violence was not necessarily the norm. For example, Jews were forced to paint *Juden* on their store fronts or to scrub the streets and gutters amongst jeers and laughter. As time progressed, however, the pogroms became larger in scope and more violent in nature. Synagogues were set on fire. Shootings and even hangings were occurring. Deportations to Dachau and Buchenwald were now routine and caused little concern.

I abhorred the violence.

My time at Weinstein Industries had come to an end. I had been replaced by a civilian, loyal to the Reich and quite familiar with the clothing industry. I could not challenge the wisdom of this decision, nor did I want to. I was never meant to be in charge of such an industrial enterprise.

I was excited about my new position. I would be working under Eichmann's supervision. To add to my pleasure, Dieter would be joining me, and although he still outranked me, in this position I would be his superior. Unfortunately for both of us, Bach was also assigned to the same department.

Our office was located at *199 Am Wall*, the same as the Gestapo headquarters. Our initial duties would be to screen exit requests by Jews, gypsies, Jehovah's witnesses and the like. Although I held absolute authority

51

to grant these visas, I permitted exits for Jews only if there was a substantial benefit to the Reich. For example, if a Jew and his family wanted to leave, he or she would now be required to deposit a significant amount of money and only then did I decide whether or not they would be allowed to depart. Rather than going to France, Belgium, or even England, it would be in both their best interest and the best interest of the Reich to make their destination Palestine or America, since it would be better for the Reich not to have to deal with them again once these European countries came under German control.

Sitting across my desk were some of the wealthiest Jews in Austria, now humbled beyond recognition. Just a short time ago, these people wouldn't have given me the time of day. Now, when they passed me in the streets, the men had to tip their hats or suffer a severe beating without recourse. I heard pleas. I heard attempts at bribery and I also heard, from Jews who still possessed some dignity, cursing at my very existence and that of Germany in general. For the latter, their time remaining in Austria would be limited. I took great care to pass onto the Gestapo their names and where they could be found for immediate deportation to a concentration camp.

I grew callous in my dealings with these people. Except for Sarah, no longer did I hold the belief that there were Jews who should be exempt from the nightmare that surrounded them. My decision-making process was entirely pragmatic, I was only obeying orders. I held no personal animosity towards the people whose fate I decided.

To add to their misfortune, England was beginning to close the borders to Palestine, and the United States took a similar position by limiting access to its shores. It was ironic to see how hypocritical America and England were. They berated Germany for its treatment of the Jews, while at the same time they refused them entry.

Suicide was common, especially among those turned down for immigration. I always read the obituaries. Many of the names were familiar to me. Some were former Weinstein Industries workers, others were people whom I had turned down for visas only days before. Why they chose the *coward's* way out, I never could understand. They appeared to be in good health only days before.

Upon my arrival at work on April 30, 1938, I found a telegram on my desk. It came from Heydrich.

Berlin
30.4.38

Dear Erik:

I am pleased to inform you that the Führer himself has instructed me to promote you to the rank of Hauptsturmführer in the SS.

Keep up the fine work and good luck in your new assignment.

Heil Hitler!

Heydrich

I rushed out of my office looking for Dieter. After what seemed to be an eternity, I found him in the lounge, just staring into space.

"Dieter, you won't believe this! I have been promoted to Hauptsturmführer. Isn't that great?"

"Congratulations, Erik. I truly hope, for your sake, that you will be happy."

We shook hands, but I noticed that his smile seemed to be forced. He didn't seem as pleased with my promotion as I thought he would be. What could be troubling him?

As Dieter had promised, he arranged for Sarah's departure out of Vienna to a not too distant small village, called Elevas. She would leave within the week. I would miss her dearly, but she was much better off out of this city. I only needed to keep her departure secret from Bach. This wouldn't be easy, and Bach would not quickly forget her. Fortunately, Dieter would have her well hidden. She would be safe.

I believe it was approximately two weeks after starting my new assignment that Rachael Weinstein made an appointment to see me one afternoon. I remember it being a Wednesday and I spent the entire day in bated anticipation of her arrival. I wasn't sure if I should present myself as sympathetic, indifferent, or callous.

It didn't take me long to decide.

53

When she entered the room, I could see that she had lost weight. Her clothes were a size too large for her thin body and they were showing signs of wear. Her facial makeup was overdone in an attempt, I'm sure, to try to cover the dark circles under her eyes and her protruding cheek bones, all of which aged her considerably. Her once lovely dark hair was pinned up in a raggedy ball. Her painted nails had numerous chips in them.

She cleary made an effort to impress me.

"Good morning, Rachael. What can I do for you?"

"Hello, er...Herr..."

"*Erik* will be fine, Rachael. Again, what can I do for you?"

"Well, Erik," hesitating slightly, then looking directly at me, with a bit more confidence in her voice, "I know that my father has talked to you several times about our family. I also know that you warned him to leave but he wouldn't do it. Well, I think I have finally convinced him, and I am here to ask you to approve exit visas for him, my mother and myself."

I couldn't believe what I was hearing. Had Walter finally come to his senses?

"You understand, Rachael, that the standard policy is for your family to surrender at least 90% of all its wealth. Will your father agree to this?"

Her face lit up and a small smile crossed her lips.

"Yes, yes, Erik. I'm sure he will agree."

I didn't respond immediately. Here was my chance. I was not going to waste it now.

"Rachael, I believe that Walter is too important to the Reich to allow him to emigrate. He is needed to give advice to the new head of what you used to call Weinstein Industries. Unfortunately for your mother and yourself, I know that Walter would be lost without his wife and daughter at his side and therefore, for the sake of the common good, you all must remain here."

She began to sob.

"Erik, have you no mercy? Have you no compassion? Do you not have at least *some* feelings left for me? Help me, Erik. Help me! Look at me. I have lost weight. I have little food. I have no money. Most of my friends have been taken away. I sit at home, which is falling apart. I see my mother drinking herself to death and my father growing insane. I was told that it was you who had my lover arrested and sent to Dachau. I will never see him again. Erik, for the love of God, haven't you punished me and my family enough? Please, help me. I'll do anything you want, *anything* at all!"

I had to make the most of this opportunity.

"Rachael, if I could perhaps get you one exit visa instead of three, would that be satisfactory to you?"

It didn't take her more than a couple of seconds to answer my question.

"Oh, oh... yes... my parents... They will understand. They are old and have lived a good life. They would want what is the best for me. I am still young. Please..."

I had to turn away from her. I didn't want her to see the smile on my face. Should I give the bitch what she deserved or should I show compassion? Here was a woman who just months ago was vibrant, wealthy, and free of any material wants. Never would she have suspected, and, in fact, nor would I have suspected, that she would fall to these depths. She now begged me for her life.

To think, I might have married her!

I turned back towards her. Now was the time to pay her back for betraying me.

"Rachael, you said you would do anything I ask. Is this true?"

"Yes, Erik, anything, anything you ask!"

"Fine, I want you to take off all your clothes right now."

She looked at me, her mouth slightly opened, surprised by the request. Then she smiled.

"Do it now, Rachael!"

Slowly, she removed all her clothing until she stood there before me, naked, just skin and bones. I buzzed Dieter and Bach and told them to come into my office at once. Within seconds, there was a knock on the door.

"Hereinkommen!"

At first, they just watched in stark amazement, saying nothing. But then the grin on Bach's face became especially noticeable. At the same time, the smile on Rachael's face quickly disappeared.

"Now Rachael, I want you to stand on top of my desk and bark like a dog."

She hesitated.

"Do it now or forget the visa."

With tears in her eyes, she climbed onto my desk and began to make feeble barking-type sounds.

"Louder! Louder!" Bach shouted.

After a minute or so of this, I told her to climb off the table and I instructed Dieter and Bach to leave. Bach was laughing uncontrollably as he left the room. Dieter, on the other hand, just shook his head and quickly left.

When they were gone, I instructed Rachael to dress and told her to sit down.

"Rachael, I must admit that your performance was excellent and quite well done."

Unbelievably, she actually thanked me for saying so.

"But after giving it more thought, I have decided that you must stay."

She opened her mouth wide, as if to speak, but before she could, I continued. "You and your father had it all thought out, didn't you. My chance meeting with you, my move to Vienna, the sudden and unexpected job offer, my rise to prominence at Weinstein Industries. You did all this so you could use me with the German authorities. It would have worked, Rachael, were it not for Dieter and Dr. Goebbels."

"It was my father, Erik. He made me do it. You promised!" She shouted even louder. "You promised! *You promised*!!"

"Sit down! Now!"

Rachael did as she was told, her voice now barely above a whisper. "Just save me, Erik, just me."

"Rachael, I would rather save a rabid dog than to save you. But I will do what you asked. I am going to secure your departure from Austria, and besides that, I am also going to re-unite you with your doctor-lover. Just before you arrived, I checked with the commandant at Dachau, and I was told that David is still alive, but I'm afraid he is not doing so well. Typhus, I believe. I think it would be good for both of you if you could spend some time with him. So you see, Rachael, I am going to help you leave Vienna, just as you asked. In fact, you will leave tonight."

With that and the push of a button, two SS agents entered the room and took a screaming Rachael away.

I couldn't contain my anxiety as I waited for Marie at the *Süd Bahnhof* railway station. She was joining me at last!

The wait for the train, although only minutes, seemed like an eternity. Then, there she was. She was so lovely, her long blonde hair contrasted so beautifully with her dark, piercing eyes. I always chided her about her strange eyes.

Before we even embraced, Marie complained. "Erik, when did you start wearing this new uniform? I'm not sure I like it on you."

"I'm required to wear it, Marie. I am an officer in the SS. This uniform symbolizes the strength of Germany and it is the SS who will lead Germany to glory, as the Führer states, 'for the next thousand years.'"

"Well, I still don't think I like it."

The driver dropped us off at my hotel. After the incident with Frau Anstrum, I felt that I could no longer remain in that apartment building. This would only be our temporary residence, though. Once Marie and I were married, we would be wanting a home of our own where we would raise our family.

"Marie, there is one matter that must be taken care of before we can get married. It is just routine, you understand, but you must undergo a background check, just like I had to."

"Background check? What do you mean?"

"Don't worry, Marie. They only check your genealogy to see if you have any Jewish blood. You see, it is forbidden for an SS officer to marry anybody with Jewish blood."

Marie gave a sigh of relief.

"Like I said, Marie, don't worry."

We made love that night just as we did years ago. I truly loved her and I knew she loved me. Hopefully, we would have many children.

The next day we set the wedding for four weeks later. It would be in the tradition of the SS, a pagan wedding ceremony to begin with, and a Christian proceeding to follow. I knew that Father and Marie would not approve of the SS ceremony, but hopefully the Christian proceeding would make them happy. I would impress upon Father that I had no choice. Himmler himself had made it quite clear that he wanted this type of ceremony for Germany's *elite*.

The daily inquiries for exit visas had multiplied tenfold just in the last few weeks. If the Jews had money and young children, I could look the other way since I felt especially sorry for the very young. I knew that living in Austria could only mean eventual internment and even death for them and their parents.

It was at about this time that I began to notice that Dieter granted more exit visas than myself and Bach combined. His attitude towards the Jews was certainly different from mine and totally opposite from Bach's. I noticed that this conciliatory attitude began to surface right after he shot the woman in the restaurant, or was it when Frau Anstrum was murdered? I know that Bach had noticed this as well, and more than once he had complained to me about it. After the wedding, Dieter and I must talk.

The wedding was only a week away when he burst into my office, shouting that he needed to see me right away. His face was pale, and his voice cracked as he spoke. "Erik, close the door and sit down!"

"What is it, Dieter? You look like you've seen a ghost."

"Sit down, I said. We have big trouble."

I sat down and waited for him to tell me what was bothering him so much.

"Erik, Marie's genealogy check established beyond doubt that she has Jewish blood."

"That's impossible!" I shouted as I stood up and leaned over the desk. "Her parents are as German as mine."

"Unfortunately, that's not true. There is Jewish blood on her mother's side. Her maternal grandmother was definitely a Jew."

I couldn't believe what I was hearing.

"Are you sure? There must be some mistake."

"No! No mistake. I checked it myself."

I was in shock. How could this be? What could I do? What *could* I do?

"Who else knows about this, Dieter?"

"At this point, only you and I and the officer who did the search. He is a good friend and I already have his promise of silence. Erik, I am willing to falsify the report."

"Dieter, do you know what you are saying? If you are discovered, it would mean imprisonment or worse."

"I think I can do it, Erik. Nobody will suspect, not even Bach. Just don't tell Marie or even your father or sister. Nobody must find out. No one. You understand? I'm afraid that if any of your family found out, they might reveal the information to someone they mistakingly think they can trust."

Once again, Dieter proved his loyalty and friendship to me. "You have my word, Dieter, and my friendship for life. I will never breathe a word of this to anyone."

7

My Love, My Life

THE day was beautiful. A warm breeze and the sweet scent of flowers permeated the air. It was my wedding day! My father and sister had arrived from Berlin and I had arranged for accommodations at my hotel. Marie's parents would also stay there.

Various Nazi dignitaries were also present, including Eichmann. Goebbels, Himmler, and Heydrich had all sent telegrams and gifts. Even the Führer sent a note of his congratulations. Dieter had secured the permission of Himmler himself for the ceremony with, no less, a certification that both bride and groom were of true Aryan bloodlines. Heaven help us all if anybody actually discovered the truth. What would happen to my Jewish wife and to any children we might have?

The SS ceremony went off perfectly, as did the church ceremony that followed.

All in attendance at the reception seemed to have a wonderful time. I did feel badly, however, that Sarah could not attend, but it was better for her that she was out of harm's way.

At one point during the evening, my father drew me aside. "Erik, my son, I hope you will be very happy. Marie is a wonderful girl. I hope you will not wait long before giving me grandchildren."

"*Nein*, Father. It will not be long. I am looking forward to raising a family."

"*Das ist gut,* Erik, that is good."

But I could tell there was something else on his mind. "Something is bothering you, Father. What is it?"

"Erik, I am very proud of the position you hold. I cannot deny it, and I realize that this is certainly not the proper place to bring this up, but since I talk to you so rarely, I must say what I am feeling."

"Tell me what is bothering you, Father."

"What troubles me, Erik, are the rumors I hear back in Berlin about certain directives that you are said to have ordered. Is it true, Erik, that you had Rachael sent to Dachau? Is it also true that you ordered the deportation of hundreds of Jews within the last few weeks? Are these rumors true?"

"Father, the climate we now live in requires all Germans to accept the fact that our duty to our country and to our Führer sometimes requires the performance of *unpleasant* tasks. Yes, I did do exactly what you have heard, and more, Father, much more. I did it for Germany and I did it for us. Father, I am following orders. Who am I to question the Reich's policy that these Jews are traitors and communists? Of all people, I thought you would understand."

A tear came to my father's eyes. He looked straight at me, tried to say something, but was unable to utter a word. Then he just walked away.

Theresa, always to my rescue and sensing something was wrong, approached me and asked what the problem was. I told her what Father and I had discussed. She said she was proud of what I was doing and that she would talk to Father.

"*Danke,*" I said.

Before she left, she put her arm around me. "Erik, it takes Father a long time to get used to something new. You have to remember that he fought together with many Jews in the Great War. Although he does not agree with their economic domination, many of them were friends of his. He has seen that they are now suffering badly, but deservedly so, if you ask me. He has much difficulty with the new philosophy of the Third Reich because it deals with physically abusing those Jews. He will change. I promise you. I will see to that. In the meantime, go have some fun with Marie, and thank God that you didn't marry a Jewish girl like Rachael."

It was very difficult to laugh at Theresa's last statement.

I spent most of the night at the bar drinking with my old friends who had traveled here from Berlin and with my new friends, members of the SS, the Gestapo, and party leaders. Stories and jokes were tossed about in every direction. I must give credit to a quite drunk Bach, who even went so far as to call the Commandant at Dachau to see if he could have Rachael flown in as entertainment for the reception. It took a pair of scissors to cut the phone line before he would give up. He told us that Rachael would have come but that she couldn't find anything proper to wear on such short notice.

Marie and I received dozens of telegrams and gifts, but what impressed me the most is what took place precisely at eight that evening. It was something that I would never forget. An impeccably dressed SS officer entered the reception hall, holding a package about sixteen by eleven inches, wrapped in blue. He walked straight towards Marie and me.

"Herr Hauptsturmführer! It is my pleasure to bring you and your wife this wedding gift from our Führer, Adolf Hitler."

He handed the package to Marie, and raised his hand in the traditional Nazi salute. All present raised their hands accordingly.

Marie struggled to open the package, carefully, trying not to destroy the wrapping in the process. She read the enclosed card out loud.

"Marie and Erik Byrnes. May this day be only the beginning of your happiness. Erik, continue working as you have for your Fatherland. Marie, bear him and the Reich many children. Adolf Hitler."

The gift was a painting, autographed by the Führer himself, depicting a scene from Vienna's recent past when he had lived here. To Marie and me, the gift was breathtaking.

8

The World Will Be Ours

IT was March of 1940. Czechoslovakia had fallen without a shot being fired, while Poland had capitulated within a month's time.

England and France had declared war on the Reich, but with the treaties in place with Italy, Japan, and Russia, there was little worry as to what France and England would, or could, do. America, thank God, was still neutral.

I was the father of twin girls, Susanne and Louisa. We lived in a cute cottage-style home on the outskirts of Vienna. The house had been once owned by a Jewish industrialist for whom, by coincidence, I had previously approved an exit visa. Just a few months ago, I had made him what I thought was a fair offer for the home. With the money he received, he was able to leave Austria for Palestine.

My position with the SS had been again elevated, this time to the rank of SS Sturmbannführer, the British equivalent of a major.

It is interesting to note that by August of 1938, well over ten thousand Jews had already left Vienna. By September 1, 1939, at the beginning of the war, another two hundred sixty thousand had left, prompted by the events following the *Kristallnacht*, the Night of the Broken Glass, November 9, 1938, in which Jews were beaten, killed, or imprisoned and their property confiscated. There is no doubt in my mind that those events were ignited by Goebbels and Himmler and not by the assassination of Ernst vom Rath in Paris by a Jewish nobody.

Although he was, in my opinion, far too sympathetic towards the Jews, Dieter still was my best friend. Bach, on the other hand, seemed more in tune with the philosophy of the Reich, but in him I noticed a total lack of compassion for the Jewish race. He seemed to revel in his cruelty. However, I could not find fault in how he carried out his duties.

Often, Bach would say words to the effect, "Erik, how is your lovely wife and your two charming daughters?"

I cringed every time he asked that question. I suspected that he might know the truth about Marie and the children. I wish I knew for sure. How could I find out?

It was the Fall of 1940 when I was summoned, by Goebbels no less, to come to Berlin to discuss propaganda dissemination in Vienna. It would give me a chance to see Father and sister and hopefully to solidify my position with Himmler and Heydrich. I also remembered very well that Hitler insisted I see him the next time I was in Berlin. I would not pass up that opportunity, especially since we were able to get a sitter for the girls. It would be the first time Marie and I were alone in many, many months.

While on the train, one could hear nothing but discussions about the war. News on the Western front had been encouraging. France, Belgium, and Holland had fallen more quickly than anyone could have imagined, and if England would not agree to Hitler's peace, it would be only a matter of time before she would fall as well.

I felt that Hitler would continue the quest for peace with Britain since he held a deep admiration for the British people, but the consensus was that Churchill would never surrender, and never would England forgive us for the bombings of her cities. Germany would have no choice but to crush England into the ground. It was unfortunate, because the British and German people had so much in common!

On the train, I did make one observation. For the first time that I could recall in my frequent train rides, I saw wounded German soldiers being transported back home, obviously from the West. This was in stark contrast to my past travels when I had observed military personnel with clean, pressed uniforms and polished boots, and with beautiful women hanging on their arms. How different were the campaigns of true war compared to the bloodless coups in Austria and Czechoslovakia.

At the depot, we were greeted by the customary chauffeured Mercedes. I instructed the driver to take us first to see my father and sister. Later, we would see Marie's parents. And tomorrow I was to see Dr. Goebbels, and then Marie and I were invited to see the Führer at Berchtesgaden!

As usual, the dinner cooked by Theresa was fabulous. We had *Wiener schitzel*, made with veal rather than pork. It was sliced thin and covered ever so lightly with egg and bread crumbs, then fried to perfection. And, of course, Theresa did not forget my favorite, red cabbage. For dessert, *apfelstrudel*. What a treat!

After dinner, Father and I retired to the living room while Theresa and Marie did the dishes.

"Your sister prepared a superb meal, Erik."

"Yes, and with all my favorites!"

Father lit his pipe.

"Erik, I know you don't want to talk about this, but again, I feel that I have to say it."

There was nothing I could do to stop him from continuing.

"Your name is becoming a household word here in Berlin. You have rapidly risen in rank, and there are those who say you are a protégé of Heydrich. You have a reputation as one who does not let his conscience interfere with his duties. Some are even calling you *The Hangman*."

"Father, as I have told you time and again before, I am just following orders. I am a soldier. My position dictates that I do whatever I can to make Austria *Judenfrei*. I have personally allowed many Jews to leave the Reich, but it is true that I have also sent our enemies to work camps. Father, you must understand that I only send those who have betrayed our country and our Führer. They are our enemies and *must* be punished."

I noticed myself becoming agitated. I could not believe that he would doubt me. Why was it so difficult for him to realize that I was just doing my duty as he did when he served in the Wehrmacht?

"Father, I find it hard to believe that you, a decorated member of the Wehrmacht, would consider my duties so distressful. Don't you understand that I have been *ordered* to remove the Jews from Vienna, and from all of Austria for that matter? Did you disobey the orders to kill that you received in the Great War?"

"Erik, my orders, as you put it, had nothing to do with murder! How could my son, a son who was always a good boy, a boy who cried when he saw a dead animal or bird, a boy who would go out of his way to help a stranger, no matter what their nationality was, how could such a boy now feel such hate?"

Raising my voice in anger, I fought back. "That is where you are wrong, Father. I feel no hate. I tell you again that I am merely following orders!"

Just in the nick of time, Theresa entered the room. "Erik, stop shouting at Father. What is wrong here?"

Sitting down again, I looked at Theresa, and in a calmer voice I told her, "Oh, the usual. Father cannot accept what I do."

Theresa began to scold Father. "Erik came here to be with his family and to see the Führer. How can you criticize him for what he does? He has a very important job. Come now, both of you, let's change the subject."

Father stood up and sighed sadly. "Yes, I'm sorry, Erik, if I spoiled your evening. I'm tired. Perhaps a little rest would help."

He drifted off into his room.

Theresa sat down next to me and put her arm around me.

"Erik, give Father time. I know he will eventually see how important your work is and that what you are doing is for the good of Germany. Every day I try as much as I can to convince him. When I see your name in the paper or hear it on the radio, I feel so proud of you. I've even started a scrap book for you. Don't ever let criticisms stop you, even if they come from your own family or friends."

"My dear Theresa, how is it that you have always been there for your big brother? Why, even when we were in school, if anybody criticized me, you would stand up for me. I truly love you, but it hurts when I see the pain I am causing Father."

After saying goodbye to Father and Theresa, we went to visit with Marie's parents, Johan and Brunhilda, only a short distance away. They had a spacious, modestly furnished home. After much small talk, mostly centered on how quickly the children were growing and how they wished we would have brought them along, we all retired to the living room. I noticed that Brunhilda would, as usual, do her best to avoid eye contact with me. She would bow her head and say as little as possible. It wasn't that she exhibited any hostility or dislike. It was more like she was afraid of me. A few months ago, I wouldn't have thought anything of it, but now that I knew she had Jewish blood, I could see that she was truly scared.

But why? She must wonder if I knew and, if I did, what I would do about it. She probably feared that her daughter, and now her grandchildren too, would be in danger if they were discovered. I hoped she understood that I would do nothing to harm Marie or the children. I needed to talk to her alone to ease her fears, to tell her that I would do nothing to hurt any one of them, to tell her that they would be protected. I wondered if her husband knew. If he did, he was very good at hiding his true feelings.

I arrived early the next morning at the office of Dr. Joseph Goebbels.

"Why, good morning, Herr Byrnes."

"Good morning, Dr. Goebbels. It's a great honor to see you again."

After flipping through what appeared to be a date book, he began. "Erik, do you know that it seems only like yesterday that Dieter Schmidt and yourself were first present in this office? Am I correct in assuming that you are comfortable with your position?"

"Yes, Herr Doctor, very comfortable. I feel that my work has had some positive results."

"It certainly has, Erik. Your performance has been nothing less than excellent. But, Erik, I didn't send for you only to tell you how splendid your performance has been. I assume you know that."

"Yes, Herr Doctor, I guessed there was something important you wanted to discuss with me."

"Well, Erik, I normally don't get involved in this type of work, but since I was the one who initially recruited you, Heydrich asked that I have this chat with you. What I am going to say next is something that will never be put in writing, but I can assure you it comes from the Führer himself. I have heard it from his own lips."

Goebbels' eyes seemed on fire.

"Is there something that you want me to do, Herr Doctor?"

"Erik, even as we speak new camps are being built, exclusively in Poland. You have sent Jews to Dachau and Buchenwald, have you not?"

"Yes, I have, but I still don't understand the significance of what you mean by *new camps*, sir."

"Well, Dachau, for example, is not what one would refer to as a death camp. At Dachau, there is still the possibility of release. The prisoner can rehabilitate himself through work. Work can, in effect, guide the prisoner so that he can set himself free, so to speak. At these new camps, true death camps named Treblinka, Sobibor, Chelmno and Belzec, the only arrivals who will not be immediately exterminated will be those who we will put to work there, at the gas chambers, gas vans, ovens, and burial squads. Workers will also be responsible for making sure that all usable parts of the deceased be gathered to serve the Reich. Selections will be made. Over eighty percent of those who arrive will be selected for extermination. The other twenty percent will be selected to work either at the camp itself or at neighboring industrial compounds. As opposed to Dachau, no prisoner will ever be set free except through his or her death."

Eichmann had told me before about the concept of the mobile gas vans. I understood that the van's exhaust would be connected by a hose to a vent in the floor. After picking up the Jews, the exhaust switch would be turned on and after a short drive the van would arrive at a burial pit, its inhabitants dead of carbon monoxide poisoning. Chelmno would be the first camp to use this type of procedure.

"I have heard of the gas vans, Herr Doctor. Will this procedure be used in all of these new camps?"

"I see someone has been talking to you already, Erik. Well, you would have found out in any event. No, Erik, only at Chelmno will these gas vans be utilized. At Sobibor, Belzec, and Treblinka the exhaust from a tank engine, or the like, will be pumped into a sealed room which will have hundreds of Jews packed into it. After twenty minutes or so, they will all be dead. We will trick them into believing they are entering a *shower* in order to delouse them."

A smile crossed Goebbels' face.

"Erik, can you believe this? The Jews will to told to breathe deeply because the fumes are very good for cleaning out the lungs. Can you imagine that? But I have saved the best for last, Erik. The *premier* camp will be Auschwitz-Birkenau, which will eventually be able to exterminate up to fifteen thousand Jews a day! It will use a refined system of gassing, probably not carbon monoxide but rather some other chemical. It has not been decided yet, but there is talk that zyklon B gas will be used. Zyklon B is now only used for rodents and insects. It is far more dependable than diesel motors, which often fail. After as many as 3,000 Jews are packed into the shower room, pellets would be dropped from above. Upon contact with the air, a gas cloud would develop, starting at the bottom of the room and working its way up. For the fortunate ones, death would be instantaneous, but the stronger ones will find that death could take up to twenty minutes. These folks will climb on top of the old and very young, fighting their way to the top of the pile of human unfortunates, hoping to get that last breath of air."

I couldn't believe what I was hearing. He was actually serious, dead serious.

"Think of it, soon Europe will be truly *Judenfrei*. This is where you fit in, Erik. Eichmann, you, and Bach, as your assistant, will be in charge of deportations from Vienna and its surrounding communities. You will no longer use Dachau or other similar camps, except for the real political prisoners. The destination of your cargo will be to the new camps. As such, you must go and see the operation in action when Auschwitz is functional. I insist."

"If I understand you correctly, Herr Doctor, I assume the Führer himself wants the pace of the deportations in Austria stepped up."

"That is true, Erik. Just as Greater Germany is proceeding ahead of schedule to be free of Jews, Vienna, which the Führer considers his adoptive birthplace, and all of Austria must quickly be free of them as well. They had their chance to leave voluntarily. Those that still remain must now be exterminated!"

This must be what Dieter referred to some years ago when Heydrich had mentioned *The Final Solution*. Surprisingly, I was not shocked by what Goebbels just said. I could see that something like this was the next logical step.

"Herr Doctor, forgive me for questioning your choice of Bach as my assistant, but Dieter Schmidt and I have worked closely over the past few years. Would it be too much to ask for us to continue working together?"

"Erik, I know that you and Dieter have worked together and that you are good friends. Dieter has in the past served the Reich admirably. But there is one problem. I am told that he has become too soft on undesirables such as the Jews, gypsies, and even the Jehovah's witnesses, and although I have seen no hard evidence to prove it, I have also been told that he has even falsified official documents in order to facilitate visas and the like. You're not aware of any falsifications, are you, Erik?"

His last question caught me completely off guard. I hoped my hesitation did not give myself away.

"Of course not, Herr Doctor! If anything of this nature would be brought to my attention, I would certainly take immediate action, friend or not."

"I'm glad to hear that, Erik. If I do allow Dieter to work with you, you must take full responsibility for his actions. He shall report to Bach. That way, your friendship will not influence you."

"Herr Doctor, please, let Dieter report directly to me, rather than to Bach. Jonathan Bach, although in a different manner than Dieter, also has his deficiencies."

"Erik, Bach is a loyal SS member. I acknowledge that he reminds me of that snake Bormann, although I will deny that I have ever said so. Bormann, like Bach, would kiss the Führer's ass if it would benefit him, and he would turn on anyone to further his position. Be careful of him, Erik. Never trust him. I like you. It would be a shame if Bach were allowed to use his treachery to get the best of you. There might come a time where neither myself or Heydrich would be able to protect you."

Goebbels was silent for the next minute.

"I will do what you ask, Erik. I will see to it that Dieter reports directly to you, but he will be closely scrutinized as to his performance. I also expect that your friendship with him will not cause you to lose your objectivity."

"It will not, Herr Doctor. This I swear."

"Erik, your word will not be sufficient if Dieter fails. I grant you your wish, but in return I will hold you personally responsible for his actions. Do you understand?"

I hesitated briefly, realizing the enormous responsibility I would be undertaking. Not only would I have to watch Bach but I would also have to watch Dieter. Could I protect Dieter from Bach? Could I protect myself and my family from Bach as well?

"I do understand. I do understand, Herr Doctor."

My heart raced as the time for our scheduled appointment with the Führer drew near. We were to see him at Berchtesgaden, his mountain retreat. I was informed, some time later, that it was at the request of Eva Braun that Hitler invited Marie to join us.

The drive through the mountain countryside was beautiful. Our SS driver obviously had performed this task before. Much like a travel guide, he pointed out each and every interesting site.

Upon arrival, we both underwent a thorough search, Marie by a female guard, and I by a male counterpart. It was said that the Führer was obsessed with ensuring that his personal security was not compromised, ever since the failed assassination attempt at *Bürgerbraukeller* in November of 1939.

We were escorted to an elevator which took us up a couple of stories. An attendant then opened the door, and we were greeted by Bormann, Hitler's adjutant.

"Welcome, Herr Byrnes and Frau Byrnes. I hope you had a pleasant trip. This way. Our Führer awaits you!"

Using both hands, he opened the doors.

There stood Adolf Hitler!

"Welcome Erik, welcome Marie. Thank you for coming."

Hitler extended his hand, first to Marie, then to me.

"Thank you, my Führer," Marie humbly uttered.

As he turned toward me, I said, "Heil Hitler," and raised my arm in the traditional Nazi salute.

Hitler did the same.

"Come, come with me, I want you to meet my other guests."

As we followed him, he introduced me first to Albert Speer, his architect, whom I found then and later to be a man separate and distinct from the others who surrounded the Führer. He had a superior intellect, and he possessed something most of Hitler's inner circle did not have, a sense of morality. Next, we were introduced to SS Obergruppenführer Karl Wolff, Himmler's adjutant, who would hold a rank higher than Heydrich. Although more of a politician than a military man, he also seemed to possess a certain *class* lacking in the others, much like Speer.

While I conducted small talk with the entourage, Marie managed to find Eva Braun, or rather Eva Braun found Marie. Braun, the Führer's mistress, was truly beautiful. She was blonde, athletic, and very shapely. She also impressed me as a down-to-earth person, and Marie certainly took a liking to her. They hadn't been together more than a few minutes before Eva made an excuse for them to leave us. I found out later that they went to the upper balcony and played with Blondie, Hitler's dog.

Hitler took me gently by the arm. "Erik, while the women are away, come sit here with Speer and me. There is something I want to discuss with you."

I took a seat next to the architect.

"Erik, I know that Goebbels has already spoken to you. What he told you has to be disturbing to any good German, even more so to a family man such as yourself. It disturbs me to consider, Erik, that if the Jews had not started this war, I would be working full-time with Albert in designing the greatest buildings the world has ever seen! And you would be performing tasks certainly more pleasant than what you have undertaken. Isn't that true, Albert?"

Speer merely nodded.

"Erik, I force no one to do what you are doing. Just like Albert, you are free to stop, and no one, I promise you, no one, will take any actions against you. I would allow you to move onto a less stressful post in the SS, or even outside of the SS altogether, if that is what you want. Do you understand, Erik?"

His compassion and understanding overwhelmed me. In him, I saw my own father. How I loved this man!

"My Führer, I serve because of my devotion to you and to the Fatherland. You force no one. I serve of my own free will."

"Good, Erik, good. That is what I hoped you would say. Didn't I tell you, Speer, that he would say that? You are much like Speer, Erik, much, much like him."

Smiling, Speer again just nodded.

Hitler then stood up, gave a short, quick bow, and proceeded to the far end of the room, directly to the chocolate sweets located there.

After the Führer left, Speer turned to me and offered me this advice. "Erik, I share your obvious affection towards the Führer. He has the ability to make those close to him give up their own identity. I'm afraid that you, as I, would do anything he would ask, without raising any questions. We would sell our souls to the devil for him. Wouldn't we? I only hope that God will forgive us."

I looked at Speer, puzzled. Why would he speak so openly with me? And what was it we were doing that would require us to ask for God's forgiveness?

"Oh, by the way, Erik, I don't really believe that either you or I could quit as easily as the Führer implies. I have no doubt that he, personally, would take no action against us, but the others, well... they just can't be trusted."

As I continued to stare at him, he again gave me that same smile, then he walked away too, to be with his Führer.

9

I Sink Deeper Into Hell

NINETEEN forty-one began much as 1940 ended. No matter how hard the Luftwaffe tried, it could not break the RAF, nor, it seemed, the will of the British people. Göring continually made excuses to Hitler, but eventually even the Führer turned his attention away from the tenacious British, who now were even engaging in bombing Germany itself.

There would be time for the British later.

Also in 1941, *T4,* the Euthanasia Program, was operating with great vigor. It involved the killing of those who were mentally feeble or physically beyond cure, although quite often its victims didn't meet either of these definitions. Contrary to the elimination of the Jews, the T4 Program had the official written sanction of the Führer himself, beginning back in 1939. Also contrary to what would take place soon, T4's primary victims were German-Austrian gentiles.

Austria had its own T4 killing centers. The primary one was Hartheim, a castle located in the village of Alkoven, not far from the Mauthausen concentration camp. If my memory serves me correctly, it was in May of 1940 that Hartheim received its first *patients.* The center had its own gas chamber and two crematoriums. The gas chamber could handle between one and two hundred victims, and was disguised as a shower room.

I visited Hartheim on several occasions in 1941. The extermination process began with the patients arriving in large black busses. They were then taken into a reception area. Here, they were forced to undress and then taken into an examining room where a physician performed an examination. They were assigned a number and were thereafter photographed. After all this had taken place, the naked patients were led into the gas chambers, thinking that they were going to take a shower. Sedatives were used for those patients who resisted, and physical force was applied if the medication did not work. It was said that Christian Wirth, who supervised Hartheim and would later rule the death camp at Belzec, actually shot four female patients who resisted gassing.

After the patients had died, the bodies were looted for gold and other valuables and then taken to the crematorium.

Besides Hartheim, there was a killing center especially designed for children, called *Am Seinhof*. It was located in Vienna itself. I refused to go there to watch the children be exterminated.

My only contact with the T4 project was as an observer, but one hundred years from now, as history looks back, it will see that T4 was the forerunner of the greatest mass genocide the world had ever witnessed, and that those who manned the T4 centers would ultimately run the death camps.

Perhaps the most important event of 1941 was Operation Barbarossa, the Russian campaign, which began on June 22. One only had to have read Hitler's *Mein Kampf* to understand that the conquest of Russia and the extermination of the Jews was, after all, Hitler's ultimate aim. The Anti-Aggression Pact between Germany and Russia, signed in August 1939, was merely a ploy to guarantee that Russia would stand by quietly as Germany tore apart Poland. Just like Chamberlain and Daladier before him, I was amazed how foolish Stalin was to trust Hitler.

The initial thrusts into Belorussia were tremendously successful. Within just the first days, hundreds of miles of territory were taken, almost at will. Hundreds of thousands of prisoners were captured. It appeared as though Moscow itself would soon fall.

But with success comes responsibility. This increased territory, which Hitler liked to call *Lebensraum* or 'living space', created what could be referred to as either a new problem or a wonderful challenge for Himmler, Heydrich, Eichmann, and others such as myself. Russia had at least two million Jews!

How would the Reich deal with such increased numbers? Within a few short weeks after the invasion, I found out the answer.

At my desk, on a daily basis, I received reports from the *Einsatzgruppen*, our Action Units. I was told there were four such units: Einsatzgruppe A,B,C and D. They followed the advancing army into Russia, and their only purpose was extermination of the Jews and Russian sympathizers. One such report, which I read some time later, was from the commanding officer of Einsatzgruppe A, Franz W. Stahlecker. It was typical of the reports of all four units.

Total eliminated: 135,567.

80,311 in Lithuania;
30,025 in Latvia;
474 in Estonia;
7,620 in White Russia...

The report went on to indicate how many of the victims were male, female, or mere children.

The numbers were indeed impressive, but as Heydrich had said before, and what had been shown to be the fact in Poland, the difficulty with this type of solution to the Jewish problem was twofold. First, the executions by these units were extremely brutal and thus had an adverse effect on many of the personnel involved in carrying them out, even if they were well-trained SS, Reserve Order Police, or even Wehrmacht members. Many could handle only one *action* and then had to be relieved. There was one exception: just the opposite was true when the job was done by Ukrainian and Latvian volunteers. They seemed to have a particular hatred for the Jews, and they actually enjoyed the killing.

The second difficulty was the lack of efficiency. The typical action involved rounding up the Jews and marching them out of town into a nearby forest and then shooting them, which made this type of procedure rather time consuming and costly. Germany needed to use a more efficient process if her goal in eliminating the Jews was to be successful.

Finally, there was a third event in 1941 that would have a profound effect on Germany. Sunday, December 7, 1941, began as a day when I finally would have time for myself and my family. St. Nikolaus had recently arrived, to the delight of the children, and Christmas was not far away.

As Marie and I were sitting in the living room listening to a radio presentation of Mozart, the phone rang. It was Dieter.

"Erik, you had better sit down before you hear this."

Although I thought it to be somewhat foolish, for some reason I complied.

"Japan has just bombed Pearl Harbor. Thousands of Americans were killed and much of their Pacific Fleet has been destroyed."

I grabbed for the phone after it fell from my hands, and my heart seemed to sink into my stomach.

"Are you sure, Dieter? Could this be a mistake?"

"No mistake, Erik."

Just then, there was an interruption on the radio station confirming what Dieter had just said.

Up to now, Germany seemed able to hold its own with a two-front campaign. Hitler had gone out of his way so as not to give the Americans an excuse to enter the war, while president Roosevelt went out of *his* way to insult and belittle the Führer. Hitler, to his credit, had wisely shown his ability to control his temper and to ignore the crippled American leader.

"Erik, are you there?... What will Roosevelt do? What will Hitler do?"

"Dieter, I fear that Hitler will honor his commitment to Japan."

"But, but... that would be suicide for the German people! How can we fight Britain, Russia *and* America along with all its allies? How can we?"

"Dieter, I am just as worried as you, but especially we of the SS cannot at this time doubt Hitler or his genius. He will, as he has done in the past, lead Germany to victory! Dieter, you are a friend, a dear friend, but never, and I mean never, do I want to hear doubt from you again."

"Erik, how I wish I had never gotten you into this wretched business. I feel responsible for all of this. I feel responsible for the Jews you have murdered. I feel especially responsible for the real danger Marie and your children may one day face."

Before I could say anything else, he had hung up.

I poured myself a brandy and sat by the fire, as if in a trance, gazing into the crackling flames. Could Dieter be right? Would Hitler go too far this time?

"Who was that on the phone, Papa?"

"Oh, it was Uncle Dieter, Susanne."

"Goody! Goody! Will he be coming here for Christmas, Papa?"

"I'm not sure darling... Susanne, it isn't good that you and Louisa are so attached to Uncle Dieter. He may be going away soon, for a long time."

She was too young to understand what I just said. I was relieved that I wasn't forced to lie.

One day later, Germany declared war on the United States.

Christmas in 1941 could best be described as a season of reserved celebration. In the East, our troops were stalled by the severe Russian winter, a winter that Hitler had not banked on. If only the invasion had started earlier than it did. Instead, the Wehrmacht had to *save* the Italians from the Greeks. As history will undoubtedly prove someday, having *El Duce* Benito Mussolini for an ally was more of a detriment than any help, and Italy's poorly trained armies couldn't make up for that fact.

On the Western front, America's recent entry into the war had not yet produced any adverse effects. She would be too busy in the Pacific for some time to come.

The holidays brought with them the usual family gatherings. The children and Marie spent several days with her parents while I was called to Berlin for meetings with Heydrich and Eichmann. I joined my family in the evenings. Christmas Eve was spent with Father and Theresa and her new beau, a Wehrmacht captain by the name of Hugo Streicher. He was pleasant enough, but too much of an idealist for me. Why he did not belong to the SS, I'll never know. He made several toasts that evening to Germany's destiny as the *savior of the whole world*. He would quote verbatim from the speeches of Hitler and Goebbels. I was glad that Father, who found his rambling just as distasteful as I did, finally shut him up by suggesting we all join in a game of pinochle.

Shortly before midnight, Dieter appeared, drunk and in civilian clothes. He had come to Berlin for the holidays, too.

The children, who were up long past their bedtime waiting for him, greeted him at the door.

"Here, my girls," he slurred. "I have something for you."

They jumped with joy, dancing around him while he handed each of them what appeared to be expensive and identical dolls made in Switzerland. "One for Susanne and one for Louisa. Now, girls, what do I get for giving you these presents?"

They both climbed on his lap and gave him a big hug. "Nothing but the best for my girls," he smiled, at the same time accepting a stein of beer from Father. The girls were not the only ones who showed obvious affection, Father also openly exhibited his fondness. I think one of the reasons Father liked him so much was because he could sense that Dieter, like himself, bore a clear disgust for the extermination policies of the Reich. It was for this reason that I often felt very uneasy at these family get-togethers when Dieter was present. It saddened me to think that Dieter was beginning to occupy a place in my father's heart that was once exclusively reserved for me. If it were not for Theresa, I would have no ally, no ally at all, in this family.

It was after one in the morning when the children finally let Marie put them to bed. It didn't take long for Dieter and Theresa's captain to get into a heated discussion. This young man was obviously shocked to hear an SS officer speaking against racial policies, like Dieter did.

I privately assured Hugo that Dieter was just joking and that the Schnapps and beer had gotten the best of him. I hoped that he believed me. I also hoped, because of his affection towards Theresa, that he would not denounce Dieter to the Gestapo, as was the mandate for all good Germans hearing such talk. It would especially not go very well for me if he did, especially after Goebbels had warned me.

Most Germans believed that 1942 would bring the Russian Campaign to a successful end. The consensus was that the winter of '41 was a mere temporary setback and that, as soon as the weather warmed, victory would be swift.

It was in early January of 1942, I can't remember the exact date, that I received a call from Eichmann. He told me to make preparations to attend a conference where I and others in authority would be informed of the horrible specifics and objectives of the Final Solution.

The conference would be held at Wannsee, a resort outside of Berlin. The key speaker would be Heydrich, although I heard that Eichmann actually prepared all the documents. All those invited to attend were viewed by Himmler and Heydrich as key personnel in carrying out the plan. Unfortunately, Bach would accompany me.

I was looking forward to this gathering.

As I mentioned before, visa exists were by now virtually impossible to obtain. Even so, it never ceased to amaze me that there wasn't a day when I wasn't called by either a top-ranking SS official, or by a senior military officer, or even by a well-heeled Austrian asking that I arrange for this or that Jew to obtain safe passage from Austria. Some time later, in 1943 at Posen, Himmler gave a speech which touched upon these types of requests:

"I also want to refer before you here, in complete frankness, to a really grave matter. Among ourselves, this one, it shall be uttered quite frankly, but in public we will never speak of it...

I am referring to the evacuation of the Jews, the annihilation of the Jewish people. This is one of those things that are easily said. 'The Jewish people is going to be annihilated,' says every party member. 'Sure, it's in our program, elimination of the Jews, annihilation - we'll take care of it.' And then they all come trudging, eighty million worthy Germans, and each one has his one decent Jew. Sure, the others are swine, but this one is an A-1 Jew.

Of all those who talk this way, not one has seen it happen, not one has been through it. Most of you must know what it means to see a hundred corpses lie side by side, or five hundred, or a thousand. To have stuck this out and - excepting cases of human weakness - to have kept our integrity, this is what has made us hard. In our history, this is an unwritten and never-to-be-written page of glory..."

As I stated, at times I still interviewed some Jews, but for the most part my primary function now was to effectuate the deportations of Jews from Austria, and from Vienna in particular. I tried hard not to consider the personal effects of the stroke of my pen. For example, after signing an order for the removal of a family of four to a transit ghetto or directly to a camp, I typically placed it in an *Out* basket and took up the next file, and so on and so on. I decided then that it was important for me to see the *non-administrative* side of dealing with the Jews of Vienna with my own eyes.

It was arranged that Bach and I were to be present at SS headquarters at precisely 5:00 AM the following morning. We would accompany two Gestapo officers who were going to take into custody a family of Jews suspected of being hidden by a well-to-do Viennese Christian family.

It was dawn, with a cold sleet falling, when we drove into a highly respectable neighborhood to visit the Jews and their protectors. Ironically, these Christians had been betrayed by their own daughter, a staunch party member. The punishment for harboring Jews was, at best, deportation to a concentration camp, but summary execution was a definite reality.

The four of us left the car without as much as a sound. I accompanied one officer to the front door while Bach went to the rear with the other. Pounding on the door, my Gestapo officer shouted for the occupants to open up.

It was all very still inside.

"Machen Sie die Tür auf. Open now or we'll break down the door!"

At that precise time, from the rear of the house I could hear a sound, like an automobile backfiring. Seconds later, I heard a second pop, then the terrifying scream of a young child. We ran to the rear and, lying on the ground with Bach standing over her, was a young Jewess in her early twenties. She lay there, twitching and moaning, in much pain, with two gaping holes, one in her stomach and one in her shoulder. Hugging her was a small child, a young girl, about five years old.

"Mommy, Mommy, get up! Please!"

The child turned to me, and pleaded with me to help her. I started to reach out for her, but before I could touch her or even say a word, the Gestapo agent who accompanied me struck the child a severe blow to the face which sent her flying against the door. The other agent, who had accompanied Bach, then raised his Luger and put a third bullet into the young, helpless woman. The shot blew off half her skull.

She was in pain no more.

By this time, the other agent and Bach had grabbed the young, screaming child and marched her back into the house. I followed closely behind. Inside, gathered in the corner of the kitchen, were the remainder of the Jewish family, consisting of an old couple and a young man, who apparently was the husband of the murdered woman and presumably the father of this frightened and crying child. I assumed that the mother had tried to escape with her daughter when we knocked on the door but she was felled by the Gestapo's bullet. Also present was a well-dressed woman in her late fifties, probably one of the Austrians who had hidden the Jews.

"Shut up that Jewish swine or, by God, I will shoot her," yelled the same Gestapo agent who had so calmly murdered her mother. Quickly, the Austrian woman put her arm around the young girl and whispered something to her that seemed to put her at ease. Turning to this woman, I said, "Where is your husband?"

Looking me straight in the eyes, and with a proud look of indignation and defiance, she replied, "He is a professor at the University. He has already left for work."

"Don't worry," Bach replied. "We soon will have the traitor in custody."

After a quick search of the home which resulted in no one else being found, the suspects were herded out the back door and marched past the still body of the dead woman, into a waiting police van. Their destination would be the Gestapo headquarters to find out if other Jews, similar to this family, were being hidden by other sympathetic Austrians.

My hands were trembling and I could not speak. All I could think about was the young girl, hovering over the body of her dying mother. It was awful.

The four Jews, including the young girl, were placed in separate cells. The Viennese woman had been taken to another location. The interrogation then began with the husband of the dead woman. The interrogator, by the name of Karl, was a very young SS Untersturmführer of barely twenty-two. He had deep blue eyes and very blond hair, and an almost boyish look about him, with striking Nordic features.

Bach and I, along with Karl and the two Gestapo officers, sat around a long table with the young man seated at the head position. Karl began his interrogation in a calm and endearing manner. "I want to offer my deepest apologies for the death of your wife. I promise a full investigation into this case." He then swore at the two Gestapo officers for their *unacceptable* behavior, and ordered them out of the room.

After they left, he proceeded to emphasize that what the young man should now be thinking of was the well-being of his daughter and the two older Jews, his mother and father. He was told that it was important to find out if other Jews were being hidden by Christian families so that they and their Christian protectors could be spared from this outrageous conduct practiced by the Gestapo.

This conciliatory tone continued for several minutes but it became apparent that this type of treatment would not work. The Jew sat in silence, obviously petrified and, it seemed, in a state of shock. Karl then motioned to the guard to bring the man's mother into the room. He returned in seconds, pulling the old woman by her hair. Karl stood up, still smiling at her son, then pulled out his Luger and forced it into the woman's mouth. Screaming at the top of his lungs, he yelled, "Jewish pig! Are you now ready to answer my questions, or do I shoot the whore that bore you?"

The room was silent. In the corner of my eye, I could see a smile on Bach's lips. All eyes were glued on the young man, waiting for his response. I felt genuine fear for him.

Karl briefly looked once more at the son, but seeing and hearing no concession from him, he shrugged his shoulders, removed the gun from the woman's mouth, and then shot her in the stomach. She collapsed on the floor in full view of all of us, blood staining the wooden floor. I am sure Karl was well aware that a stomach wound kills slowly and with much pain. The old Jewess, as much as she tried, could not hold back her cries while she grasped at her bleeding wound as if she were trying to stop the life from slowly oozing from within her.

Karl taunted her son. "Save your mother! Have you no respect, no compassion for her? Would you let her die when you have the power to save her? If you tell us what we want to know, I promise I will summon the physician who waits not more than ten meters away. If you say nothing and she dies, her death will be on your conscience and not mine!"

This was too much for the son. He got on his knees and crawled to Karl, begging him to help his mother.

Patting him on the head, Karl chastised the man. "Yes, of course I will help her. Your stubbornness forced me to do what I did. Will you now help me save other Jews such as yourself from this type of unnecessary treatment?"

The man nodded his head and sobbed. Karl then motioned to the guard to take the woman away, and to "make sure that she is immediately taken to see the physician."

"Now I have kept my word and your mother will soon be free of her pain. Now you, young man, keep yours."

With that, the Jew betrayed his Austrian protectors and named not only them, but also other Austrians who he said were involved in the sheltering of Jews, providing names and addresses of both Jews and gentiles. When he finished, Karl gave him a cigarette and poured him a brandy, and even got this fool to exhibit a weak smile. As cruel as it might sound, I was truly fascinated and impressed with Karl. He had a refined technique and he used it well. In the incredible hope that it would help his mother, this trusting Jew had sealed the death warrant of all those dear to him and had betrayed others in the same position.

"Splendid, young man, splendid, now I think we should all go and see how your mother is doing. I'm sure her condition has changed by now. Wouldn't you like that?"

The man thanked Karl as we all walked out of the interrogation room into the hall. We proceeded down a long corridor flanked by small prison cells on each side. Stopping the procession halfway down the corridor, Karl told the young man, "Before we see your mother, I think we should first look in on your father to make sure he is feeling good."

A short walk more and we stopped by a small eight-by-four-foot cell. I was the first to look inside. To my amazement, I saw the elderly Jew hanging by a thin strand of piano wire with a rag stuffed in his mouth, obviously to prevent his cries from being heard. There was a pool of blood mixed with urine on the ground below his feet.

When he saw his lifeless father, the Jew screamed and turned in anger to Karl. Quickly and without hesitation, Karl struck him with his Luger, grabbed him by his hair and dragged him to the next cell. I was wrong when I thought that horror such as I had just seen could never be surpassed, for in this room, in a large fish tank, we saw the heads of the mother and his child floating in crimson water, their headless, bloody torsos lying at the feet of the tank.

Seconds later, Karl slit the Jew's throat. He fell to the ground, with only a death rattle emanating from his bloody lips.

He was dead.

I knew that if I stayed longer I would throw up, so I quickly made an excuse to leave the room. As I stepped out, I heard Bach congratulate Karl for his *splendid performance.*

10

Wannsee

THE Wannsee Conference was held on January 20, 1942. I must admit that, in light of all the party elite and dignitaries present, I certainly felt both humble and at the same time also honored to have been invited to this occasion. Heydrich of course chaired the meeting. The rest of us numbered fifteen, representing a cross section of the German government.

Heydrich began by outlining the agenda for this meeting. He then listed the approximate Jewish population in various European locations, totaling them at ten million! There were other countries mentioned but I forgot the names and the numbers.

He let us know that the Führer wanted each and every one of these Jews *dealt with*, and indicated that our task was to make the elimination of these numbers a reality.

There were discussions between various SS officers as to their specific problems and concerns, such as Hans Frank's complaint that Poland had become a dumping place for Jews from Western Europe and from greater Germany. Although Heydrich listened attentively, it was apparent that he had little sympathy for such concerns.

"You are all commissioned for one greater goal. We all must strive and sacrifice in order to achieve the ultimate victory both militarily and racially. Unfortunately, you will have to temporarily bear certain inconveniences."

With a frown, he turned to Frank. "You must not consider it a cross having to assume control over millions of Jews for now. Certainly, I and all of us are aware that you would prefer to rid yourself permanently of these vermin. What you must understand, however, is that Poland is geographically located to be the central port, a momentary stopping point for all deportations to the East. Be patient. In time, we will have completed the re-settlements from the West and Poland too will be *Judenfrei*. As to those who feel that they do not have *enough* Jews and would want some more, perhaps Frank will loan you some."

Even Hans managed a smile at that comment.

The Obergruppenführer continued. "On a more serious note, I want you all to know that I truly do sympathize with your positions. You are torn between two opposing edicts. Our Economic Minister Todt demands that the areas which you control remain economically self-sufficient, while Himmler demands that you rid yourselves of Jews, even if they are skilled workers and crucial to the economy. You must, gentlemen, somehow obey *both* commands. To be quite frank, no pun intended, Hans, I leave it up to you individually to handle this dilemma because I honestly don't know the answer."

After a brief question and answer period, the meeting took on a more sinister tone.

"Gentlemen, you all know that the present methods which are being used for handling the Jews have significant drawbacks. Beatings, clubbings, hangings, and even shootings are not only dilatory but, even worse, have left significant psychological scars on many of our brave men who had to carry out these unpleasant tasks. Do you think I take pleasure in the shooting of civilian men, women and children, even if they are Jews? Do you think that any good German actually finds this agreeable? Whoever enjoys killing just for the sake of killing must be mentally unstable, I suppose.

Let me give you an example. Eichmann and Byrnes, standing here, are dedicated party members. They are responsible for re-settlement from Austria. I know them personally and very well, and believe me, they take no pleasure in the sufferings they cause. Their only satisfaction, and the only pleasure any of us can realize from our endeavors, is knowing that we are following the explicit will of our Führer, Adolf Hitler."

Heydrich waited until the room was silent.

"What I am now going to tell you is something that some of you have already heard in confidence. I assure you that none of you will ever see in writing what I am about to say. But I can assure you that what I direct you to do today comes directly from the Führer himself."

Heydrich then told all present what Goebbels had recently told me about the new camps and the methods which would now be used for exterminating the Jews.

"Quotas for deportation will be established for each of the areas that you control. You, in turn, will see to it that these quotas are met. You will find that creating ghettos in or near the major cities is a wonderful way to confine the Jews and, thereby, have the bodies necessary to meet your requirements.

Reichsführer Himmler has come up with a brilliant idea. It is advisable to set up a council of Jews in the ghettos, a *Judenrat*. The council members will be responsible for meeting the quotas that you will demand. They should be given some privileges the other Jews do not have. And if they fail to deliver what you demand, you should not hesitate in having them publicly and severely punished.

You will also give them their own police force. If you need to enter the ghetto to forcibly obtain Jews in order to meet a quota, use the Jewish police. As with the *Judenrat*, promise the police that they and their families will be spared any deportations and also receive special privileges such as extra food rations. When the ghetto is nearly *Judenfrei*, to everyone's surprise but yours, then these council members and police officers will also be deported after all.

Gentlemen, as you can see, we now are leaving the old methods and beginning the new. Mind you, I know that occasional shootings or hangings are sometimes necessary. In fact, I must confess that they are absolutely necessary in many situations for their deterrent effect on the locals.

Eichmann will now meet with you separately to inform you of your future duties and your chain of command. Any questions? None! Very well then, I would invite you all into the lounge area for drinks and food. If you think of anything later, feel free to contact either myself or Eichmann."

Bach joined me as I followed the others into the reception area. At first, only he and I stood together. There were two sides to this man. He reminded me of a mixture of Bormann and Eichmann, both a Judas but yet a terrific worker, a loyal, dedicated party member.

"Herr Byrnes, it seems to me that our offices will handle even more deportations and re-settlements," he said. "Austria still has a long way to go before it is *Judenfrei*. The new policies certainly bode well for our job security for a long time to come."

Then he drew closer and said in a lower voice, "Erik, I know that in the past you have had second thoughts about me and that you may in fact still harbor such misconceptions. You perhaps consider me cruel and I know that you feel that you cannot trust me. But you are wrong."

I said nothing, thinking it better to let him continue.

"I know you blame me for the death of the Anstrum woman. I want you to know, Erik, that if I had known she was your landlady, I would not have had her apprehended. You can blame that idiot Schmidt for this mistake. He never told me about your involvement with her. I only found out later from an officer you reprimanded at Gestapo Headquarters."

Could he be telling the truth?

"I can be trusted and I am loyal to you. In fact, I have been more trustworthy and loyal than you even know."

This last comment puzzled and bothered me. "What do you mean by that, Bach?"

An evil smile crossed his face.

"You really should be more careful when you decide to, let us say, *change* certain reports. I discovered your cover-up when I was routinely reviewing genealogy reports about married SS officers. You might say that I am a very curious individual. I noticed that certain entries concerning your lovely wife had been quite carefully altered. I suspect that Dieter did it, knowing how loyal he is to you. Seeing the alterations, I did my own study on your wife. I know that Marie has Jewish blood, Erik."

I could not hold myself silent any longer. "Bach, I could have you shot for this!"

"Please, Herr Byrnes. Keep your voice down. We wouldn't want anybody to hear us, would we?"

I let him continue.

"Don't worry. I am not so foolish as to risk repercussions. I know only too well how much you are favored by Heydrich and Goebbels, and even the Führer himself. I want you to know that whatever you are hiding is safe with me. I only ask one favor of you."

"And what is that, Bach?"

"I would be very grateful if you have Dieter Schmidt removed from our department. The man has turned into a benevolent fool and also quite a drunk. He repeatedly ignores your directives regarding the Jews. In fact, I am convinced he often helps them escape arrest. He openly tells me to 'go to hell' when I criticize his behavior. I want him removed. No... I want him arrested or at least sent to the Russian Front. This small concession I would like you to do for me."

Before I could even answer, Heydrich joined us.

"Gentlemen, I have great hopes for the success of our program in Austria."

He then took me aside and looked me straight in the eyes. "Tell me, Erik, how are you holding up?"

"Quite well, Herr Obergruppenführer, quite well."

"Come now, Erik, you must have had some reservations from time to time. Moments of conscience? You can be honest with me. I will take no offense."

"Yes, sir. I must admit that I did have bouts of momentary confusion. There have been times that I questioned the morality of the deportations and of the killings. It was harder at first, but as time passed I have convinced myself that I am justified in all my actions. I realize that I am only following orders."

"Are you only following orders, Erik, or do you truly believe in what you are doing?"

"Both, Herr Obergruppenführer, I do believe that by following the Führer's directives I am assisting the Reich in the elimination of the plague of Jewish bolshevism."

"Well put, Erik, very well put."

Bach, who I could tell was straining to overhear what Heydrich was saying, walked over.

"Forgive me, Herr Obergruppenführer. I could not help but hear what you have said. There is no need to worry about Erik Byrnes or, for that matter, myself. Our department has functioned with absolute precision. We have even gone with the Gestapo as they made official arrests and interrogations. I can assure you that we take great satisfaction in our work."

"Yes, I truly believe *you* do, Bach, perhaps even more zealously than you should."

Having said that, Heydrich left our company. Bach knew that he had been slighted, and hastily made his exit.

After speaking to Eichmann and obtaining the needed information, I retired to my hotel room, poured myself a brandy, and laid awake for another three hours before I finally managed to fall asleep, just before dawn.

I had the morning to spare before I took the return train to Vienna, just enough time to see Father.

Upon entering our home and seeing him look up at me from the kitchen chair, I knew he was going to start in on me with the same old lecture.

"Erik, the war is lost, I'm afraid. Your Goebbels is nothing but a liar. I've spoken to friends of mine who have grandsons and sons in the military. The letters they receive from the Russian Front indicate that the Soviets are far stronger than we have given them credit for. We are being driven back and when America enters the war in earnest, the Western Front will fall."

"But, Father, Hitler has not failed us before. Why should this be any different?"

"Erik, France, Poland, Norway, Holland and Denmark can't be used for a comparison. I must admit that I was impressed by the speed of those campaigns, but all that has changed. We don't have the manpower or the resources to carry on this two-front war, a war that we are basically fighting alone. Italy is useless, and Japan is having their own anti-aggression pact with Russia, so they concern themselves only with the Pacific. Why, we can't even beat England, let alone defeat England with Russia and America on her side. Erik, I want you to know that I do not so much fear losing a war. I have gone through that before. Although such a loss would be great, what I fear most of all is losing my son."

"What do you mean, Father? How are you going to lose your son... lose me?"

"I know what you do, Erik. I read about you in the newspapers. I hear about you from the few Jewish friends I have left in hiding. Did you know, Erik, that there is already talk amongst the British, Americans and Russians, that they will try as war criminals all those found responsible for the liquidation of Jews? Erik, if you are caught you will be tried, and if you are tried you will be convicted and likely be put to death! This I could not bear."

I stopped and for a moment realized that what Father said was true. I looked into his eyes and I could see the tears he was holding back. All my life, whenever I got into trouble, he had been there to help me. I knew that I could always rely on him. When I needed money, he gave it to me, but always with a lecture, mind you. He was always there. What made me cringe this time, was that I knew that there would be little he or anybody could do for me if I was captured by the Allies. Deep down in my heart I knew that he was right about what would happen to me if Germany lost the war.

The *Hangman of Vienna* would himself be hanged.

"Father, what can I do now? It is too late for me..."

"Erik, it's never too late. You have to quit this business. Resign. Why don't you just resign?"

"Father, some time ago the Führer himself told me that I actually could resign, without any repercussions."

"Well then, why don't you do so right now?"

"That was then and this is now, Father. Too much has happened since then. The war is not going as well as it did and I am sure that my superiors would not want to open the floodgate by allowing me to set a precedent which might well be taken up by many others. If I could walk away, at best I would be sent to the Russian Front. No, Father, I will take my chances with the Allies rather than face a Russian bullet."

I looked at him one last time when I left. His eyes were fixed on me as I got into the car. I called out, "I will be back, Father. I'll see you soon."

11

A Model Of Efficiency

FORTUNATELY, once I had returned to Austria, Father's pessimism found no place in my busy schedule. If the thought occurred at all, I rationalized it away by convincing myself that somehow Hitler *would* guide us through this difficult period as he had always done in the past. After all, there had been at least some positive news, this Spring of '42, from the Russian Front. A new offensive had taken place and it appeared that the Wehrmacht was gaining ground. In Africa, we still had *Desert Fox* Rommel, guiding his *Afrika Korps* to victories over the British. Perhaps we would gain enough ground that even Hitler would be satisfied and a peace could be declared before America entered the war in earnest?

As Heydrich suggested, I began working with various *Judenrats* in my area of command. It became my standard practice to create such a council in every ghetto. I found myself often traveling to such settlements and conferring with these men.

Either Bach or I would order the formation of such a group. The council leaders, in turn, would be informed that by getting involved with the SS and by working within this council they would be able to ensure the orderly function of their community, and through their efforts they would be able to prove to me that the economic benefit to the Reich justified their continued existence. As Heydrich also had suggested, I made sure that the members of the *Judenrat* and their families received extra rations of food and clothing, thereby lulling them into a false sense of security. I also promised them that, as long as they cooperated with me, they and their families would not suffer any persecution or harassment. In fact, I told them that the opposite would happen and that they would actually be *better off* cooperating with us than they were before.

After some time, when the members of the Judenrat felt comfortable in their jobs, we informed them that they must now procure for us, on a regular basis, a number of deportees for re-settlement to the East. They cooperated because we lied to them, telling them that the deportees were going to *family farms* where the work was hard but bearable and where food and lodging was definitely better than in the ghetto. In order to make it easier to secure voluntary deportation, we even provided extra rations of food to those who volunteered. We told them that families would be kept together at deportation *and* upon arrival, which also helped. Actually, it was one promise that I always kept. The Jews who were transported were always placed together with their families in the same cattle cars, and upon arrival they were gassed together.

The Jewish police maintained order in the ghettos and enforced the deportation orders. They lived a life of luxury as well, at least compared to that of their more unfortunate countrymen.

It was warm, that October day in 1942, when Dieter, Bach, and myself made our initial trip to a newly created ghetto near Vienna, by the name of *Kovnas*. It was then that I met for the first time a Jew named Abraham, a member of the Judenrat. There was something truly different about this man. I didn't know at that time just how important he would be in my life.

There were seven members in the Judenrat and Abraham had recently been elected their *elder*, a title that did not necessarily mean the oldest member, but rather the leader or the *wisest* of the council. The meeting took place at their community hall. It was common to let the Judenrat wait a considerable period of time before we arrived. This made them more apprehensive and therefore easier to deal with.

Upon our arrival, Abraham was seated at the head of the group of seven. They all rose when we entered the room.

"Good morning, council members."

"Good morning, Herr Sturmbannführer."

"The purpose of this meeting is to familiarize you with what the Reich and I expect of you as the leaders of your community. As you know, the Führer needs workers to labor in the war effort. This work will be performed here, in your ghetto. What you may not know is that the Führer also needs laborers for family farms that are being created in the East. The conditions there are much better than most of your countrymen are experiencing here. Unfortunately, we are at war and under these circumstances sacrifices must be made by all of us. Therefore, you will be in charge of seeing to it that the Führer obtains the workers he needs. You have my word that when the war is over, all those re-settled in the East will be free to return to their homes if that is what they choose to do. Don't be surprised, however, if they decide to remain at the farms because of the fine conditions there. At these re-settlements, each family would have its own private living quarters, and the food and clothing rations are twice what is being allocated here."

I could see the council members nodding their approval of what I was saying.

"There is one problem, however, and I hope, no, I know that you will help me with it. In other ghettos throughout the Reich, we have noticed that not enough Jews are volunteering for re-settlement. It seems that there is an unwarranted fear about moving. Gentlemen, nothing could be farther from the truth! Yet, this ridiculous attitude forces me to require from you a *guaranteed* number. Your initial quota will be 1,500 Jews weekly."

There was a look of shock and disbelief on all the faces, except for Abraham's.

I continued my speech.

"I am not a violent man and I dislike saying this to you, but I feel that I must speak now because it would not be fair if I didn't give you advance warning. If you fail to meet this quota, I will choose one of you and one of your family to be shot every day that the quota is not met."

The room became very silent. Again, only Abraham didn't seem surprised.

One of the seven had the courage to speak to me. "But sir, how can we accomplish this? Right now, only two to three hundred Jews volunteer for any given deportation at most. How will we be able to increase this number so dramatically?"

I turned to him in a conciliatory tone. "You need not worry about this. You just designate who of your brethren will be re-settled, and if they don't appear voluntarily, the Jewish police, along with the assistance of the SS if necessary, will apprehend them."

"But, sir, if they are in hiding, then what?"

"If that happens and if the quota cannot be met, anybody walking the street will fill the place."

I could tell that the council members were visibly agitated.

"Gentlemen, gentlemen, don't be afraid. All you need do is to draw up the list and leave the rest to the Jewish police and the SS. Isn't it better that you be able to choose who should go rather than have me or Haupsturmführer Bach make that decision for you? After all, if you make the selection, you can choose transients, anti-socials, the elderly, and if you want you can actually choose those whom you might want to, let us say, even a score with. Don't worry, just pick them out and the Reich will put them to work. As long as you do what we ask, all will be fine in the ghetto. Your daily lives and that of your family will continue to be acceptable. If you fail, however, my retribution will be swift."

I left it to Bach to handle the details. He seemed to relish in the desperate situation these Jews now found themselves in. Dieter, on the other hand, stood in the corner staring out the window throughout my entire speech. He was obviously uneasy about what was happening.

When all the particulars had been gone over, and Bach and Dieter were elsewhere, Abraham approached me and asked for permission to speak. "Herr Sturmbannführer, I appreciate the opportunity you have given us to set our own destiny. I want you to know that I don't share the feelings of many of my brethren. I know these are difficult times and we must all work together so that the Reich achieves final victory. With your permission, I would also appreciate the opportunity to report directly to you, because some council members have beliefs that are downright counter-productive to your goals."

I listened carefully as he continued. "I would like to be thought of as *your eyes* in the ghetto. I am sure I can serve you well. In fact, I am so sure of it that if I should ever seriously disappoint you, I agree that you would have every reason to have me shot."

I had heard false platitudes before, especially from the Jews. I recalled the once wealthy Jewish whore Rachael pleading for her life and offering me anything before I had her deported. But this Abraham was different. For some reason, I truly believed that he was sincere. On the other hand, could it actually be true that this Jew was really interested in helping those who were sworn to his people's destruction?

"Tell me more, Abraham, exactly what will you be able to *see* for me?"

"Herr Sturmbannführer, in the ghetto much goes on which is not known by the Germans, or even by many of the inhabitants. There are underground newspapers. There are individuals who routinely enter and leave without restraint. I will show you exactly where and how you can come and go unseen. I see a look of disbelief on your face. You wonder how it is possible for Jews to function outside the ghetto. It is possible, Herr Sturmbannführer, in part because some have false identification papers which are printed right here in the ghetto. Some of us also *look* Aryan. Even you, as skilled as you are, would not recognize them as Jews. Really, there is much I can do to help you."

"What do you want in return, Abraham? I know that there must be something in it for you. Do you want money? A home of your own? Servants? What do you want from me?"

As if he were expecting this question, "I want none of that. I have always been a very good judge of character and I have been able to make accurate observations of people, which is one reason why I have been able to survive as long as I have. It is my humble opinion that you, Herr Sturmbannführer, care

91

little for Hauptsturmführer Bach. I believe that you tolerate him only because you have to. I come to this conclusion after only a brief observation, but nonetheless this *is* my belief."

Was my contempt for Bach that obvious?

"Just for the sake of argument, Abraham, let's assume that what you say is true. What does it have to do with what you want from me in return for helping me?"

"Herr Sturmbannführer, I want only one promise from you. I want you to assure me that before you either have me shot or ship me away to a death camp, or to what you call the *family farm*, you will give me one hour alone with Bach."

"Why such a strange request?" I asked.

He hesitated, but then seemed to gather some inner strength.

"I will tell you why, even though you may have me immediately shot for what I am about to say. This may be the first time you have come to this ghetto, Herr Sturmbannführer, but it is *not* the first time for Bach. This animal was here approximately two weeks ago, apparently without your knowledge."

I now became very interested in what Abraham was telling me.

"When he was last here, in this very building, my wife was here, working on some paperwork for me. My young daughter was also present. I have been told that my wife did not notice him entering the room so she failed to rise to attention. She tried to apologize, but it was not enough for him."

Tears were forming in Abraham's eyes and his voice cracked.

"No, Herr Sturmbannführer, he had to punish my wife and of course my daughter as well. He had both of them beaten in that corner right behind you. Well, I might have been able to accept the beating. To me, that would have been merely doing one's duty after a minor infraction of the rules. But no, it was not enough for Bach. He shot my wife in front of my ten-year-old daughter, and when my daughter cried out, he shot her as well. Their bodies were then thrown onto the ghetto streets for all to see. When I arrived minutes later, Bach was gone and my wife and daughter were still lying in the gutter. My friends were afraid to move them."

There was intense rage in his eyes. Looking around to make sure that Bach could not hear us, I told him, "Abraham, I want you to know that I knew nothing of this. It was written in no reports. Had I known, I would have disciplined Bach severely. I can still do that."

"No, please, that would not be enough for me. Let me do it my way, I beg you."

I thought about it some more. Then it hit me. What a beautiful way to eliminate the one man who might turn in Marie and my children!

"Abraham, if you help me as you say you can, I give you my word that you will have your one hour with Bach. I also warn you that once it is all over and you have survived it, I will likely have you shot on the spot."

"I don't care, Herr Sturmbannführer. All I want is Bach!"

"Abraham, I will let you know when the time is right and, understand this, I will deny that I ever had this conversation with you. Do you understand?"

He nodded and left the room.

I found Dieter in the next room. I motioned to him to accompany me.

"Dieter, dear friend, let's get a drink."

He smiled, and together we left the ghetto for the nearest tavern we could find. We both ordered a large stein of dark beer, our favorite, as we leaned upon the stand-up bar.

"Dieter, I must ask what is bothering you."

With his glass in hand, he raised his head.

"Erik, do you know that I now go to church every day? Yes, every morning. When in Vienna, I sneak like a thief into the church. I go to Mass to pray for my soul and the souls of my friends, such as yourself. I also pray for the thousands of poor wretches that the Reich murders every day.

When I look at you, Erik, I feel certain that my soul will be damned for being instrumental in recruiting you. It was I who helped convince you about the *morality* of our cause. What an efficient monster I created! I keep hoping that I will see a change in you. Even though you might not notice it, I watch you every day. I see you sinking deeper and deeper into that snake pit, filled with men like Heydrich, Himmler and the devil himself, our Führer, Adolf Hitler. I dug the first hole in that pit for you, Erik, but it was you who made it deep. Perhaps it's in vain, but I still hope that I will see some semblance of humanity return, a return to the good man that I met on the train several years ago."

I responded with indignation. "Dieter, Dieter, how can you say that about me? I only perform my duty. I only obey orders!"

With a tone of outrage, he raised his voice. "Orders, duty! Is it your *duty* to carry out the murder of innocent men, women, and children? Did you know, Erik, that at Treblinka, when the gas chambers are full and can hold no more, the guards skip the gassing altogether and throw the Jews onto the fires while they are still alive? Did you also know that some SS personnel at the camps don't even bother wasting a bullet or gas on babies? They pick them up by their tiny legs, and in front of their mothers bash their heads against walls or trees before throwing them, sometimes still alive, into the pits to be burned!"

"Dieter, Dieter, we don't condone such brutality, neither me, or Eichmann, Heydrich, Himmler, and especially the Führer. I have spent time with our Führer and I can assure you he is a caring, compassionate man. What you complain about is merely a casualty of war, nothing more."

Dieter laughed, so I tried a different approach.

"Dieter, you seem to be more concerned with the welfare of the Jews and the communists than of your own people. We both know that if it wasn't for the Jews, this war would never have taken place. As disturbing as it may be to you, even you must recognize this."

Deep down, I suspected that Dieter knew that I really didn't believe what I was telling him, but how else could I justify the Reich's philosophy? So I continued, "Don't you remember how things were before 1933? Don't you remember the poverty, the unemployment, the weak military, and an economy run by Jews at the expense of true Germans?"

He shook his head in utter disbelief as to what he was hearing, and quietly asked me, "Erik, then must we eliminate *all* Jews?"

The question was so easy that I didn't hesitate. "Of course. Of course. The Führer has made no exceptions."

"*No* exceptions, Erik, are you sure?"

"You heard me, Dieter, no exceptions."

Feigning a weak smile, Dieter looked me squarely in the eyes.

"If that is true, what about your wife and your children, Erik? Should they be gassed as well? What makes them special?"

I just stood there and couldn't say a word. Had I actually forgotten about Marie and the girls? Or did I really mean what I said, that there truly would be no exceptions?

Seeing that I was speechless, Dieter finished his beer and walked back to our waiting automobile.

12

The Lion Is Dead

HITLER took great precautions when riding in the open. His fleet of Mercedes were constructed with bullet proof armor and bullet proof glass. He instructed his leaders to provide themselves with the same security. All obeyed except one, the man who was rumored to be groomed as Hitler's successor, SS Obergruppenführer Reinhard Heydrich, the head of the Protectorate of Bohemia and Czecholosvakia. It was said that when Heydrich had to be saved from behind the Russian lines after his plane was shot down, Hitler forbade him to fly anymore.

Heydrich was openly contemptuous of the Czechs. He also kept a daily departure schedule with little variation. This consistent schedule made him an easy target for Czech assassins, trained in Great Britain.

On the morning of May 27, 1942, Bach ran into my office, shouting, "Heydrich has been shot. Heydrich has been shot!"

Soon thereafter, the official report came across the teletype that Heydrich had been severely injured from shrapnel from a bomb thrown by an assassin. His condition was serious but it was believed that he would survive.

Throughout the day, the wire press carried release after release monitoring his condition. In Prague, a great manhunt was in progress to find his assassins. Only one thing appeared certain: at least the Jews could not be blamed for this crime.

Later that morning, after things had calmed down, Bach entered my office again.

"Erik, if Heydrich is hospitalized for some period of time, I would assume that Eichmann might succeed to his command which would mean that you might succeed to Eichmann's duties."

"Yes, Jonathan, but it is also quite possible that someone like Kaltenbrunner would move into control. I'm not so sure that either you or I would be especially fond of that choice."

We both looked at each other, now seriously considering all the possible alternatives if Heydrich was indeed incapacitated for some time, or worse, dead. With Eichmann, we knew where we stood. He was a man we worked with before with some success and with some pleasure. Kaltenbrunner, on the other hand, was known to be ruthless even to the SS men with whom he worked.

What bothered me the most, however, was the thought that we might lose Heydrich. I had grown to truly admire this man, and I could honestly say that I felt a deep affection for him.

On June 4, 1942, he died. People who were with him at the end said that on his deathbed he was muttering incoherently, asking the Jews for forgiveness.

Days later, the greatest funeral in Nazi history took place in Berlin. Critics compared the pomp to gangster funerals in the United States. I attended with Marie, while Bach traveled in a separate coach. Dieter made an excuse, saying that someone had to stay back to handle office affairs. I knew that his true reason for not going was his disdain for men like Heydrich and his refusal to pay them homage. I wondered if he would attend my funeral.

Seated next to the Führer were Heydrich's widow Lina and his two sons. I was sitting close enough so that I could hear Hitler whisper to them as he patted the boys on the cheek. "Heydrich, he had a heart of iron."

After the service and upon leaving the ceremonial hall, a voice called to me from behind. "Erik, may I have a word with you?"

I instantaneously came to attention. It was Himmler.

"Herr Reichsführer, may I be of service to you?"

He took me aside. "Erik, these are indeed difficult times. Germany has lost a great man, a great leader. Heydrich's death has affected the Führer greatly. I have never seen him so distressed and angry as he now is. He speaks of nothing but revenge. Although you and I know it is not true, it seems that the Führer somehow blames the Jews for Heydrich's death. Just today, he has instructed me to step up the pace of deportations. All Jews must be exterminated as quickly as possible.

Erik, there is something else. I think I owe it to you to inform you in advance that, as you might have suspected, Kaltenbrunner will assume Heydrich's position. Some hoped Eichmann would get the position, but he is far too important to The Final Solution in his present position. To be quite frank, you should be flattered to know that the choice was between you and Kaltenbrunner and that, because of Kaltenbrunner's many years of service, the Führer hesitantly picked him over you. To choose you would have caused an upheaval among the old party members. I hope you understand the Führer had no other choice, and that your time for significant advancement will come soon.

Before you say anything, Erik, I know of Kaltenbrunner's reputation and I also know that he can be unpleasant to work with. His hatred of Jews rivals that of the Führer himself. Unfortunately for all of us, and I say this to you in strict confidence, he is no Heydrich. I am fond of you, Erik. Be careful of this man."

With that, Himmler nodded and became lost in the crowd of mourners.

As Himmler had predicted, deportations increased immediately after Heydrich's death. The various Judenrats were being called on to fill their quotas on an ever more demanding scale.

I recall it was on a dreary Monday in January of 1943 that I summoned the Judenrat to meet with me. I needed to discuss what I perceived to be their unexcusable inability to meet the quotas I had set.

As Bach, Dieter, and I walked in, we were greeted by the tip of the hat, customary when a German officer entered the presence of Jews. I then addressed the group, but primarily Abraham. "You elders should be more concerned with meeting the reasonable quotas I have established. You should do so for your own well-being and that of your family members. I am tired of hearing the never-ending excuses such as sickness, your inability to serve your people with notices of deportation, or your inability to communicate with the Jewish police.

I will no longer tolerate this! I will begin to keep the promise I made some time ago. From now on, commencing with the quota set for next Monday, if there is a failure to produce the required number, I will personally see to it that one of you, and your entire family, will be the first to depart on the next available boxcar. Any questions?"

I looked around the council members but I could see no reaction. They hung their heads like schoolboys who had just been scolded for something they had done wrong.

Bach then lunged up. "Filthy Jews, answer the Sturmbannführer."

Hearing nothing, he pulled out his Luger and struck the eldest of the council members across the face, knocking him senseless to the ground. Not having enough, he then kicked the Jew in the ribs. He would have killed him on the spot were in not for the sudden blow he received to the back of his neck.

Bach turned around in amazement. What Jew would strike an officer of the SS?

To both Bach's amazement and mine, we found it was no Jew. It was Dieter.

"Schmidt, I will have you shot," Bach screamed. He started towards Dieter, but I motioned to the guard to stop him. The guard tackled Bach and drove him to the ground.

I ordered the SS to remove both Dieter and Bach. They were to wait by the automobile for me. As they were leaving, I told them that I would deal with the situation later and that no one should utter a word about this affair until I spoke to both of them.

After they had left, I again emphasized to the Jews that there could be no exceptions made to the quotas, and after taking care of some mundane business the meeting was over and the Jews were ordered to depart.

All left, but Abraham. He looked at me, and said, "Herr Sturmbannführer, don't be hard on Dieter Schmidt. He is a good man while Bach is nothing but an animal. As we discussed earlier, Herr Sturmbannführer, I am prepared to assist you. I personally guarantee that the quota will be met as you directed. I believe the only reason that it has not been met yet is because the Jews feel you are not, let's say, *sincere*."

"Sincere, I don't understand what you mean, Abraham."

"Forgive me for being so blunt. The Jews feel that you have a conscience. You are not like the others. They believe that you would not hurt them or mistreat them. Their perception must change if you want to realize your goal." Was I really hearing such talk from a Jew?

"I believe you will be successful if you put me in charge of deportations rather than leaving the matter to the entire council. With your approval, I will publicly and vehemently express my dismay with the new quotas in order to divert suspicion from me. Once I am established within a couple of days, I will have no difficulty in carrying out your demands. I will say that there is no other choice. Again, as you have agreed, in return for my service to the Reich, I only want those few moments alone with that pig Bach, when the time is right."

I nodded my head to confirm our previous and new agreements. I would now order that Abraham would be in complete charge of deportations.

"Now beat me with this. Beat me good. We must leave no doubt that I am an unwilling pawn in your game."

I took the metal ashtray from his hand, but hesitated. Was this really necessary?

"Please, Herr Sturmbannführer, do it. They must be convinced."

I reluctantly proceeded to beat this Jew as I had never beat another, or would ever beat anyone in the future.

13

Utmost Precision

TRUE to his word, Abraham met my quota of deportees. He met it at every instance, and sometimes with ruthless precision.

The Jews were told that they were being re-settled in the East to help with the war effort on the Russian Front. As an incentive, one that Abraham thought of himself, each Jew who voluntarily appeared at the railroad depot was given bread and marmalade. The people's reaction to this bribe surprised me. I had no idea that they were that hungry.

Besides Abraham's splendid work, Bach and the SS officers under his command were also to be complimented. After his constant begging, I finally allowed Bach to handle the train boardings and loadings. His officers acted with utmost courtesy to the departing Jews, obviously in an attempt to sway them into believing this journey would only be for their benefit. I never heard of any incidents of resistance. If they had resisted, I don't know what the twenty or so SS guards could have done to stop the thousands who boarded each day.

Of course, Bach's *courtesy* stopped the minute the Jews were loaded into the boxcars, with only a bucket of water for the eighty or so crammed into the car and one bucket for human waste. The cars were so crowded that the people were forced to stand because there was no room to sit. SS guards were positioned on top of various boxcars, ready to shoot any Jew who might be inclined to escape.

I remember one particular departure. The train's destination was Auschwitz/Birkenau, which meant instant death for at least eighty percent of those on board, and within three months the twenty percent selected for work would likely die from hunger or disease. On that particular day, as the train departed, I noticed a small mountain of clothes, suitcases and so forth.

"Bach, what are these items, and why are they here?"

"Please, don't be concerned. These are the belongings the Jews brought with them for their use in the East. Due to the cramped conditions, they were told to leave their luggage here and to put their names and addresses on them."

He laughed. "They were promised that these items would be shipped to them by separate train."

We all knew that there was no *separate train*, and the clothing and other belongings would never reach their owners, who would obviously have no more need for them.

After the train was out of sight and as I turned away from Bach and made my way to my vehicle, I glanced back and noticed that the pile of belongings seemed to be moving. Upon looking more carefully, I saw a little girl, probably seven or eight years old, uncovering herself from the pile, a small doll in her hand. She must have been hidden by a mother or father who were perhaps finally aware of the fate awaiting them.

Bach had also noticed her. "What do we have here? Come here, little girl. Don't be afraid."

The whimpering child hesitated, but soon a smile crossed her lips when she noticed that Bach had pulled a piece of chocolate from his pocket. She came up to him and he gave her the chocolate, which she devoured hungrily. Bach patted her head and motioned to one of the SS to take her away. As the guard grabbed her, the child started to cry, fighting to return to Bach.

"What am I to do with her?" the soldier asked.

As if quashing a bug, Bach calmly said, "Take her in the back of the station and shoot her."

The soldier was reluctant, so Bach walked up to him and put his hand on his shoulder. "Young man, you will do her a favor. You'll save her from a lonely life of starvation without any family."

In his twisted logic, he was probably correct.

The cries of the young girl, as she was being led away, will haunt me the rest of my life. After a minute or so, there was a loud *pop,* and the cries stopped.

I slid into the seat of the Mercedes and saw out of the corner of my eye, hiding under the shadows of the railway terminal, Abraham, his gaze glued on Bach.

There was still a matter I would have preferred to forget about, but Bach would not let me. What should I do with Dieter? Almost daily, Bach repeated his request to have him sent to the Russian Front. This type of transfer was indeed commonplace for *trouble makers* such as Dieter, so the problem I had was a difficult one. I knew that Bach was right in his accusations and I also knew that if it had been anyone else, I would not have hesitated to have them sent to the Front. But Dieter was my only real friend.

The drive from the railway station to headquarters was a short one. This would be as good as any other day to have my talk with him.

I could hear music coming from Dieter's office, religious music, I thought.

"Good morning, Dieter."

"Hello, Erik. Where have you been?"

"I had business outside the office." I didn't want to tell him, although I felt he knew exactly what type of business it was.

"Dieter, my dear friend, we have to talk."

I closed the outer door and gave him no chance to interrupt me.

"It is no secret that Bach would give his soul to the devil to see you removed from your position. It is also no secret, Dieter, that you spend your entire day either daydreaming or taking long walks to who knows where, or coming up with ideas on how to keep Jews from being displaced rather than just the opposite. I can't keep covering up for you! Your actions in front of the Judenrat only made things worse. *Please* tell me you'll at least give the impression that you take your work seriously. At least *pretend*. Can't you do that for me? Can't you see what is going to happen to both of us if you don't?"

Dieter smiled and shook his head.

"Can't, Erik, sorry, but I can't."

His attitude infuriated me, but I said nothing.

"Erik, do you know the Stein family?"

"The Stein family?" I snapped. "Who the hell are they?"

He raised his voice. "You ask 'Who are they?' They are a family you murdered just yesterday."

"Dieter, what in the world are you talking about? I didn't *murder* anybody yesterday."

"Just wait. Just wait! It's here somewhere." Scrambling amongst the papers on his desk, he pulled out a one-page document, similar to the order forms I signed on a weekly basis.

"He had been a school teacher. She was a mother of two, a ten-year-old boy and a fourteen-year-old girl. The day they were scheduled to leave on the train, he poisoned his wife and children. Then, because all the poison was gone and in order to kill himself, he tried hanging, but because of his *good fortune*, before he could finish the job, the SS who came to get him and his family because they were not at the train station on time, found him dangling in his kitchen. Being the *kind* men they naturally are, they cut him down and sat him down on a chair. Then they did what they do best. After beating him severely

101

they tossed him out of his third-floor window. All this because he had spared his family from the misery of the gas chambers.

To make it worse, Erik, this man will go down in history as a murderer of his family who was rightfully killed by the SS, the *protectors* of the people. But really, Erik, it was not those men who killed him and his family. It was *you* who killed them. You killed them when you signed the quota directive!"

Dieter shoved the order paper in front of my face.

"You shouldn't be asking *me* to change, Erik. Rather I am asking, no begging, *you* to change."

"Damn it, Dieter. I am what I am and it is too late for me. Haven't you read the papers? Already Roosevelt, Churchill, and Stalin have agreed to try people like me as war criminals if they win the war. I am dead if I don't follow orders and I will be dead if we lose the war. At least by following orders, I can remain alive until then."

"Erik, you still can save some lives. You still can make a difference. Join me. Renounce the SS and I will stand by your side until death strikes both of us."

For a moment my mind traveled back in time, back to my carefree youth. I remembered...

"Erik... Erik! Are you listening to me?"

I woke up from my daydream and stared across the desk at my dear friend.

"Yes, I hear you, but it is just too late."

I left Dieter and went to Bach's office. "Bach, I want you to prepare the necessary papers for SS Obersturmführer Schmidt's transfer. Please note that he is to be assigned to an administrative position. I specifically am forbidding you to assign him to any combat. Do you understand?"

"Yes, Herr Sturmbannführer. I understand."

14

Trouble At Home

THE mood in Vienna in the Summer of 1943 hardly compared to that in 1938, when it all began with Hitler's entry into Austria. It especially did not compare to those glorious moments in 1940, after France was defeated. And above all, no comparison could be made with the Autumn of 1941 when it was thought Russia would fall within weeks. Now, with the imminent loss of Stalingrad, it seemed evident to many that the last offensive thrust into the Soviet Union had faltered and the Wehrmacht was being pushed back West.

In North Africa, the Allies were giving Rommel all he could handle, and it was rumored that even he was expressing defeatism.

What was extremely distressing to me, more so than any news of German defeats, was the obvious mood swing that I now saw in Marie. She seldom inquired about my comings and goings any more. The smile she never used to be without was now rarely present, and if it was, it was reserved for the children, not for me. I believed she still cared for me and loved me, but I felt that the fear of what might happen to us if the Germans were defeated, weighed heavily on her mind.

Father's attitude toward me had also worsened. Dieter's transfer didn't help things, because Father was always very fond of Dieter. He probably suspected that I had arranged his removal.

As in the past, the only member of my family who truly seemed to approve of me and what I stood for was my dear sister Theresa. In fact, she was more of a staunch Nazi than most party members I knew. She would listen to no talk of defeat. She faithfully attended all party functions and rallies and, besides teaching full time, she managed to devote more hours than she should to volunteer war efforts.

"Erik," she would say, "it's not true what I hear that Germany will lose the war, is it?"

I would always tell her no, that these were only temporary setbacks and that soon the *super weapons* that our scientists were testing right now would be unleashed upon the Allies.

Also at this time in 1943, Abraham finally persuaded me that now was the time that I must keep my promise to him and deliver Bach.

I had devised a plan for Bach to go to the ghetto, saying that he should examine the books and records relating to the possessions of deported Jews. I explained that I suspected that some amongst the SS were stealing the treasures taken from the Jews. I told him to go alone without guards or a driver, since I could not trust anyone else. This confidence on my part seemed to please him, and he agreed. Now the trap was set. Hopefully, when it was sprung, I would be able to request Dieter's return.

I hoped my friend was well.

Although the war might not be going as smoothly as could be desired, 1943 did prove to be the most productive year of all regarding *The Final Solution*. Never before had more Jews or other undesirables been re-settled. Auschwitz was handling thousands of exterminations a day, and other camps that were still open were taking care of any excess.

My trips to the ghetto and the meetings with the Judenrat were becoming more frequent. Actually, I didn't even mind spending an evening or two there when the weather prohibited returning that night.

One such visit in particular, in late December, stands out in my mind. After the meeting, Abraham suggested that I accompany him on a walking tour of the ghetto. Bach objected immediately, citing safety reasons.

"What can this filthy Jew do to me?" I laughed. "Thank you for your concern, Jonathan, but I will amuse myself and go with Abraham."

In his sly way, Abraham smiled at Bach, indicating to him *his* approval as well.

"Herr Sturmbannführer, are you pleased with my efforts as to meeting the quotas you have imposed?"

"Why, yes, Abraham, very pleased. Why do you ask?"

"I just wanted to make sure that the *family farms* had no shortage of *laborers*, Herr Byrnes."

I looked at him, and in his eyes I could tell that he knew these places were in reality death camps where the only laborers were the *Sonderkommandos* who tended to the corpses and the belongings of the murdered.

"Abraham, don't play games with me. I can't believe that you really are interested in the welfare of the German Reich."

"But I am. I truly am! As long as I please you, I know that my survival and the survival of the fittest of our ghetto will continue."

I fought back telling him that it was quite likely that, in time, his beloved ghetto would be totally liquidated and that it was inevitable that even the *good*

Jews would be killed. To me, this was stupid because I knew from first-hand experience just how efficient and hardworking some Jews could be. Besides, I regretted the thought of losing him as a *person*. I had grown to admire and even like this man who kept every promise he made.

"What will you do after the war, Herr Sturmbannführer? Will you continue your service in the SS, or will you do other things?"

"To be very honest with you, I never gave it much thought. I mean, it seems strange but I feel that this is the only life that I ever knew."

Abraham stopped, seeming somewhat puzzled. "Forgive me, Herr Byrnes, but did you not have a life before the SS? Did you not have a past? A family?"

"Yes, Abraham. I had, and still do have, a loving father, a loyal sister, a wife, and two young daughters. Perhaps, when all of this is over, you can meet them and we can have a drink together. Perhaps, when Germany is victorious, we will all be able to do what we did before the war."

"Again, forgive me for saying this, Herr Sturmbannführer, but now you are playing games with *me!* You must know fully well that if Germany wins the war, there will be no world left for me or my kind. And if Germany is defeated, by the time that happens I will surely be dead. You may wonder why I don't exhibit the same fear or sadness that others in the ghetto feel. For me, Herr Sturmbannführer, this tragedy has already been discounted. As I have told you before, I lost my dear ones some time ago when Bach killed them. Do you know that I pleaded with the SS to kill me? But the SS, always thinking of the good of The Fatherland, *saved* me so they could use my position in the community to benefit the war effort. Unfortunately, I was too much of a coward to take my own life."

After walking a kilometer or so, we arrived at the ghetto outskirts, surrounded by run-down dwellings and deserted streets. Abraham seemed to enjoy my company as much as I did his.

"Quite frankly, I have even become callous regarding my own people as well. It no longer saddens me to enforce your re-settlement quotas every week, even though I know what fate awaits these people. I have become oblivious to the pleas of the old and the parents who beg me not to send their children away. I know that if I don't comply and fail to send the old and the very young, you or someone under your command will choose without consideration people whose presence is necessary for Kovnas to survive."

We were walking towards an area, known to me only as the *Jewish Cemetery*. As we approached, I could hear the sound of gunfire. Abraham saw my hesitation to go onward, but he continued towards the sounds. As we drew closer, I could see a group of about a hundred Jews who were surrounded by perhaps ten SS and another twenty or so *Order Police*, a Wehrmacht unit comprised of former German lawyers, mechanics, school teachers and so forth.

There, perhaps twenty meters in front of us, a large pit had been dug, about ten meters long, five meters wide, and three meters deep. I saw layers of Jews who had already been shot, lying side by side and on top of each other. The SS officer in charge then barked a command, ordering ten more men, women, and children to lie on top of those already shot, some not yet dead, squirming, bleeding and bloody. The new arrivals were then shot in the back of the neck by machine gun fire.

Of the eighty or so still standing by the edge of the pit, some were crying or pleading, but most meekly obeyed the commands of the SS. Those that did not move quickly enough were whipped into submission. After each layer of victims had been shot, the ten who were next in line were required to pick up shovels and throw lime and earth upon those lying in the pits before they were forced to join them.

It was at this time that I heard a plea coming from down in the pit, directed at one of the Jews shoveling the dirt. I will never forget what I heard until my dying day.

"Hugo, my brother, why are you burying me alive? I am not dead yet!"

His brother ignored him, and he was buried alive!

Blood oozed from below, and crimson ground moved back and forth from the struggles of not yet dead Jews who were grasping and clawing to reach the surface air. It was as if the earth had a life of its own.

I scanned over the remaining Jews. Some were old. Some were young children, holding the hands of their mothers and fathers. Many families were going to their deaths together.

For a reason I will never truly know, I ordered the shooting to halt. Those in command and those doing the shooting, most of whom were visibly drunk, looked at me with some amazement, as if to say, "By what right do you order us to stop?" But stop they did.

I asked the officer in command why these people were being shot. He looked at me, and then with disgust at Abraham.

"Herr Sturmbannführer, these Jews were conscripted for deportation to Auschwitz. But the trains were overbooked and they were left behind. We didn't want to *disappoint* them as they could not join their other countrymen, so it was decided that they be brought here and put out of their misery."

"Why was I not informed of this?" I bellowed.

The officer said that Bach had authorized the shootings and that he just assumed that I knew.

"May we continue now, Herr Sturmbannführer? The men are anxious to return to their barracks."

I looked at the remaining Jews who now cast sad eyes upon me. I recognized some of their faces. I had seen them in the ghetto. I didn't know what to do or what to say.

"Go on, Erik, let them die here rather than in the gas chambers of Auschwitz. You will be doing them a favor."

I looked at Abraham in astonishment, realizing that he had just called me Erik, and knowing that he had also just given me *permission* to kill his own people.

I again looked at the remaining Jews.

"Continue, but I don't want live Jews in that pit!"

We left that horrible scene and as we walked back towards the meeting hall, the hair on my neck bristled for a second time when I heard another and yet another volley of gunfire.

"Herr Byrnes, don't feel compassion for my wretched brethren, for unless the tide of the war changes dramatically, it may soon be you who is lying in that pit and Jews doing the shooting. I know you are a man who has some virtues, so I will offer you some advice. If I were you, I would be looking for an opportunity to leave these lands and go elsewhere before it is too late. If you don't, you will surely pay by the executioner's hand."

I remembered similar words spoken by my Father and also by Dieter.

"Even if what you predict will happen, Abraham, how would I be able to leave? Every border is shut off and the air space is closely watched."

"Erik, what do you have to lose by trying? If you stay here, someday you will surely die. If you die trying to escape, you would at least have made the effort and, who knows, maybe you will be successful. I have been thinking about you. I think I can help you. I will let you know."

I nodded to him, and with that we returned to the administration building.

15

Where Do I Go From Here?

THEY tell me that drinking while at work is a sure sign that one is an alcoholic. Apparently, that is what I had turned into as I now took to keeping a bottle of brandy in my desk and having several shots throughout the day. At noon, I would drink rather than eat, and before coming home at night I would stop and have a drink with Bach or whomever else was present. The realization that my world might soon end was getting the best of me.

At home, I had changed, too. I had become short with the girls and with Marie who complained about my behavior more than once. In rebuttal, I would tell her to keep her comments to herself. After all, how could she understand the pressure I was under? She had become so naive and, quite frankly, at times the girls were quite annoying.

It was about this time that I became convinced that the war was lost, and that, if I stayed in Austria, I would eventually be tried as a war criminal, and likely executed. At the most, I had three years left. I decided then that I would try to escape.

I would take Marie and the children with me. I considered asking Father and Theresa to come along but I knew that neither would accept, even if I explained that if I succeeded they might suffer retribution. It might be better to say nothing to them.

I needed Abraham's help, but first Bach had to be eliminated. Once he was out of the way, I would be able to bring Dieter back, and then the three of us could perhaps come up with a plan that would work. Unfortunately, I was clearly not the only one who considered such actions, since both the Gestapo and the SS had recently set up an intelligence division to investigate and guard against just these types of escapes.

"Good morning, Jonathan. Wonderful day, isn't it?"

"Why, yes, Erik. It certainly is. You have something to discuss with me?"

"Yes, I do. Do you remember that we discussed your going to Kovnas?"

"Yes, I remember it quite well."

"Jonathan, I need you to go there at once. That filthy Jew Abraham is continually complaining about his co-members in the Judenrat. He tells me that most of them are slackers and that they will attempt a marked slowdown in the deportations. I can't risk that happening, Jonathan. Until now, this ghetto has met or surpassed all our expectations, and as a consequence you and I have both received high marks from Himmler and Eichmann for our fine work. We must not let anything spoil this. He also told me that he has information about some members of the SS who are pirating the property that was taken from the deported Jews. This too must be stopped!"

Bach interrupted. "Forgive me for asking, but please tell me again what I can do that you can't."

"Jonathan, it's embarrassing but the truth of the matter is that those Jews fear you far more than me. Your presence without me will certainly scare the hell out of them, so you will get their cooperation much easier than I could. You must go there, talk to Abraham, find out who the guilty parties are and report back to me. Tell no one else about your trip."

A smile crossed Bach's face.

"Herr Sturmbannführer, now I understand. Yes, I agree, the Jews do fear me, and rightfully so. And they will fear me even more if you are not present. I will do as you ask. Will later this week be soon enough?"

I should have asked him if this week was *soon enough* for him to die. I wonder what his answer would have been, then.

"Why, yes, Jonathan. The sooner the better. Thank you."

By this time, Treblinka, Chelmno, Belzec and Sobibor deferred to the *shining star* of Operation Heydrich, Auschwitz-Birkenau. It had been some time since I had visited there, and officers of my rank were now obligated to visit the camps at periodic intervals.

Auschwitz was undoubtedly an inconsistency, much like the situation portrayed in the Emerald City, in the *Wizard of Oz*. Just as it was illogical to have a lion who was a coward, it was equally illogical to have weekly sporting events between the *Sonderkommandos,* consisting of Jewish laborers, and the SS guards who would put to death these same Jews on a regular four-month interval. Evenly shocking was the scene of the Jewish orchestra playing merry music while at the same time their brethren were being selected for either death or work, to the left or to the right, determined by SS doctors such as Josef Mengele, the infamous *Angel of Death.*

Upon arrival at Auschwitz, I left the train together with a dozen other visitors. The Camp Commandant, Rudolph Höss, was there to greet us.

109

"I am glad to see you, Sturmbannführer Byrnes. It has been some time since you have visited us."

We shook hands and proceeded to several waiting cars.

"I am told you all are under a tight schedule so I will make every effort to use the time that we have most efficiently. I would like to take you on a short tour of the camp before you view the Selection Process and its aftermath. You then will have time for a short lunch. After that, you are free to leave or spend the night, as you see fit."

We drove through the camp structure. I was amazed at the size of this place. At Himmler's direction, Auschwitz had expanded considerably since my last visit. Back then, the camp was in its early stages. Now it held up to 100,000 inmates.

We passed through sections designated as "C" Camp, "D" Camp, etc. All had their separate meanings. One might be a women's camp. Another might be a gypsy camp or a Czech camp, and so forth. There were four crematoriums, also designated by a letter of the alphabet. For each crematorium, there were approximately four to five hundred Sonderkommandos, Jews designated as workers involved in maintaining the gas chambers, the collection and sorting of clothes, the burning of the bodies, and the pulling of gold and other valuables from the corpses. Some of these Sonderkommandos were doctors who staffed the inadequate hospitals and assisted in the dissection and autopsy work. I was told that these physicians became invaluable to SS doctors such as Mengele, who used these prisoners to assist them in the various experiments that had become so famous in the inner circles of the SS.

The motor tour took about one hour, barely enough time to get even a glimpse of the magnitude of this operation. As we swung back to the point of beginning, we were very fortunate. A train load of Austrian Jews had just arrived from the Lodz ghetto.

The Selection, to be conducted under the supervision of Mengele, would soon begin.

We exited our vehicles and took a position about fifteen meters behind the *Angel of Death.*

The Jews were packed into some fifty freight cars, with about eighty to ninety Jews in each car. The occupants were men, women and children, the old and the young, the rich and the poor. Their journey, the Camp Commandant told me, had taken them about two days, whereas a normal coach ride would have taken less than a day. I shuddered at the thought of how miserable the conditions must have been throughout that trip. There were no windows to speak of, only broken boards allowing the slightest bit of air and light in. The daytime heat must have baked the cars so that the temperature inside was unbearable. Sanitary conditions were non-existent.

From every third roof top, an armed SS man was now descending. These men were posted there throughout the journey to prevent Jews from ripping out the wooden boards and escaping by jumping from the moving train. Most of those who did attempt to escape were shot, and those who managed to elude the bullets would be seriously hurt by the fall from the train and then usually turned over to the authorities by the unfriendly Polish occupants of the area. Few managed to return to their ghettos, or find safety with the partisan bands who roamed the Polish forests.

The guards opened the cars, shouting, *"Tempo, schnell!"*, "on the double, quickly!"

The Jews frantically left the boxcars. Many were thrown out, suffering broken bones and other serious injury as they hit the earth. Screaming, shouting and mass confusion permeated the area. Jews who were moving too slowly were beaten with whips or attacked by the dogs.

They all cried for water.

It took about ten minutes for all the occupants to exit the train. I excused myself and walked up to one of the cars. I had to hold my breath while I peered inside. Lying alongside the car walls were sixteen to twenty corpses of those who had not survived the journey. The bodies were covered with flies and filth from the human excrement which flowed freely on the hard wooden floor.

I had seen enough.

The Jews were divided into a line for the women and one for the men. At the front of the procession, situated between both groups, was a table. Seated at this table was Josef Mengele, along with several other SS doctors. Before the lines began to move, the Sonderkommandos moved up and down the four or five thousand souls asking if any were dentists, goldsmiths, tailors, doctors, or other skilled professionals. Those who raised their hands were taken to the side and told to wait.

Slowly the procession began to move towards the seated SS doctors. I strained to listen.

"And how are you feeling today, mama?" Mengele would sometimes ask in a seemingly conscientious tone. "Not too well? I am very sorry. Go to the left and we will take care of you."

Most of the time, however, he was silent, flipping his baton to either the left or to the right. The old, the sick, the young children and mothers with infants were processed to the left. The stronger he motioned to the right. I don't believe the Jews knew the significance of being placed in any particular line. In fact, the right line was told that those in the left were being taken to a camp where the sick and old cared for the children. More than once I saw a young man or a young woman beg Mengele to be placed in the same line as their parents. The *good Doctor* was more than happy to oblige.

"Why, of course. How inconsiderate of me to separate you from your family. Go ahead and join your parents." The poor wretches actually thanked him for his kindness. Mengele turned towards us and smiled.

The entire selection of these unfortunates took no more than an hour. When it had been completed, those to the left were ordered to move forward, surrounded on either side by armed SS along with attack dogs. The column advanced slowly. You could tell they were tired and exhausted. The little children held their mother's hands. The infants who could not walk were carried by parents, grandparents, or older brothers and sisters.

I, along with the rest of our group, followed the procession. After a short walk, we entered a courtyard. The Jews noticed the water faucets. Like a mob, they broke rank and frantically made it to the water. Some filled cups they had brought with them, others drank feverishly from the spigot. The SS guards were obviously aware that they could not control the outbreak and that it was better to let the Jews drink rather than face the chaos which would result if they did not. The guards waited patiently until all had drunk to their fill. And again, the Jews thanked the SS guards for their *kindness*.

Soon, the line twisted its way out of the courtyard like a serpent, led by a jovial SS officer.

"*Halt*, my friends, and listen carefully to me."

The Jews gathered around.

"You soon will be going to the showers and disinfection room where you will be able to clean up and also be deloused. Our camp prides itself at being free of typhus. You will then be given fresh clothes and good food and an opportunity to take care of your personal hygiene."

A thunderous applause came from the Jews.

We came upon a cinder path, which led to a ramp. At the end of the ramp we entered a huge underground room, perhaps even two hundred meters long. There were columns in the middle of the room and benches along the walls. Hooks were in place along the walls, and the SS politely told all to remember the number on their hook as they would soon return to pick up their clothes.

"Tie your shoes together. If you don't have laces, just raise your hand and we will give you some."

The German masters had learned some time ago that if the shoes were not tied together, it became very difficult to match the pairs later, after the Jews had been murdered.

There were between 2,500 and 3,000 people in this room. All were told to completely undress, and the abled were ordered to assist those who could not do so themselves. The women had to undress in the same room as the men. Many young girls were especially hesitant about this, so the Sonderkommandos were sent in to speed up the undressing.

When all were disrobed and the clothes carefully placed at the numbered hooks, an SS man opened a heavy gate at the far end of the room. The mass of people proceeded into the shower room as ordered. It was about as large as the dressing room and also well lit, but there were no benches or hooks. In the center of the room, at long intervals, were square columns of perforated iron piping.

When all had entered, a command was given for the SS and Sonderkommandos and all observers to leave the room.

The door was closed.

My heart was racing. I knew what was going to happen.

The lights were shut off and the Jews were left to themselves. I could only view what was happening from a peep hole constructed in the door. Because of the darkness, I had difficulty seeing, but for the first time since the procession began I now heard whimpering and crying coming from inside. I believe that the Jews finally began to realize that something dreadful was about to happen to them.

The Camp Commandant explained that immediately above us an SS officer was now dropping Zyklon B gas crystals into the four pipes that I had seen protruding from the lawn surface. The screaming began! I heard moans and cries of "Mother", "Father", "Help me!" permeate the air.

Within minutes, it was all over. I could see no movement within. All was silent.

Ventilators were then turned on to remove the gas, and also the lights were turned back on. The doors were opened. The Sonderkommandos entered with gas masks over their faces, because Zyklon B would still hide in the air pockets between the dead bodies and could be fatal up to until half an hour after the pellets were dropped.

The scene that I then saw rivaled any described in *Dante's Inferno*.

The bodies of the Jews were congregated in all four corners, ascending to the ceiling. The Commandant explained that this happened every time. As the gas slowly ascended up from the floor, the stronger prisoners climbed and

113

scratched and bit their way to the top in a desperate attempt to keep breathing healthy air. On the bottom of the piles, the young, the old, and the weak were trampled by their stronger brethren, seeking a few more seconds of life.

The bodies were covered with blood and excrement since people who die of gas lose control of their natural functions and defecate or bleed. The Sonderkommandos entered with large hoses and washed out the room and the bodies by forcing the filth into drain holes in the center of the room. We watched as they then dragged the bodies with ropes and chains to a room where they examined the corpses for gold fillings or other valuables hidden in private body parts, aware that Jewish women were especially adept to this deception. When this was completed, elevators lifted the bodies to the crematorium above where they were incinerated. I was told that the ashes were then shoveled into dump trucks and disposed of in the nearby Vistula River.

After an excellent lunch, some of us bade our host adieu. I decided not to stay the night. I would rather take the train and then a car to go to *my* ghetto to see Abraham and advise him of Bach's impending arrival.

When I arrived at the ghetto gates, I instructed the SS that my presence was to be mentioned to no one. As far as everyone knew, my purpose in coming was to gather information on some Judenrat members. Even if Bach found out that I had been there, he would accept that explanation.

When I arrived at the meeting room, Abraham was already there.

"Good morning, Herr Sturmbannführer. I heard you just arrived."

How did he know I had arrived?

"Good morning, Abraham. Please sit down. Abraham, I kept my promise. Bach will be here later this week."

It was unbelievable. He actually did a dance in front of me. I started to laugh.

"Erik, you don't know how happy you have made me. Ever since I buried my wife and daughter, I have thought of nothing else but this day."

"I am curious, Abraham, how will Bach die?"

"Very slowly, very slowly, and quite painfully, I might add." He laughed out loud. "The Germans, I am told, are quite fond of piano wire. They use it in certain interrogations and executions, do they not?"

I nodded affirmatively.

"After silencing Bach, I intend to hang him with piano wire. It will be a slow death. The neck does not break, so it will strangle him to death. Before he dies, I am going to tell him why I am doing what I am. I am going to show him the pictures I carry of my wife and daughter and remind him of his cruelty. He does not remember them, I'm sure. He has killed too many. But before he dies, he will remember them. I promise!"

We began discussing the fine points of his plan and I even offered some suggestions. I had to admit that I felt some guilt about what was going to happen, for Bach had in the recent past become quite friendly to me. But weighing all the positives and negatives, I knew we had to proceed as planned. I could not be sure that Bach would not reveal what he knew about Marie. And with him gone, I would be able to get Dieter back to help Abraham come up with a plan to get me and my family out of Austria.

Our conversation went on and on, and before we knew it we were both hungry. I ordered food for the two of us, much to the surprise of the young *Rottenführer* who delivered it.

Abraham ate with great reservation, hardly what I would expect from a ghetto Jew. When we finished, the conversation turned to Vienna in happier times. He asked about my family and he told me stories about his daughter and wife, how close they had been and how the three of them loved each other. Here was a man who, because of the Reich and men like me, had lost his entire family and yet he still could speak to me with civility, even with a sense of friendship. He was certainly a better man than me. Yet, wasn't I a member of the *Master Race*, and wasn't he a *Jewish Pig?*

"Herr Sturmbannführer, do you still intend to have me shot when this is all over?"

"No, Abraham, you are my friend. Call me once it is all over."

"Mommy, Mommy, Daddy's home. Daddy's home," Susanne and Louisa shouted together as if they had rehearsed it for some time.

Marie's greeting was certainly less enthusiastic than that of the girls, a weak smile and a peck on the cheek.

"Why, what are you doing here? I thought you were away on business?"

"I just got back. I really could use some sleep and, believe it or not, I thought it was important that I spend more time with you and the girls. How about if I lie down for a couple of hours and then we can all do something together?"

She just nodded.

It seemed like I had just closed my eyes when all of a sudden two little bodies were jumping on my stomach and pulling at my arm.

"Get up, Daddy. Get up. You slept long enough. Mommy has food ready."

The girls literally dragged me down the stairs into the kitchen and sat me down at the table.

"Now hurry up and eat, Daddy. We want to play."

We had a fine meal, and even though my sleep had been interrupted, I felt much better. Marie asked the girls to go play outside while she and Daddy finished some *grown-up talk*. Reluctantly, they obeyed.

"Erik, yesterday and also just this morning I received two very strange calls."

"What kind of calls? What are you talking about?"

"Now, come on, Erik. The man who called both times told me that he was working on family trees for my family and yours. He said it was at the request of the SS. He wanted the names and birthplaces of my grandparents. He was so persistent, Erik. When I first told him I did not know where they were born, or even my grandmother's maiden name, he wouldn't take no for an answer. So I told him I would check and he should call back later. He thanked me and hung up."

This did not sound good.

"Could you recognize the voice? Think hard. Who was it?"

"Erik, what's all of this about? Didn't you have this man call me?"

What could I say? What should I say?

"Marie, I want you to listen very carefully to what I am about to tell you. I don't believe that the man who called you was concerned about your family tree."

"Then what? Why did he call?"

I had been wanting to tell her this for years, but the time was never right.

"Marie, you're not going to believe this, but I believe the reason the man called was because he wanted information so he can prove that you are Jewish."

"Jewish? I'm not Jewish, Erik. You know that!"

"I'm afraid it is true, Marie. Your maternal grandmother was part Jew. That makes you and the children Jewish as well. Dieter found this out and he falsified the reports before we were married. That is how we were able to get married at all. However, Bach found out what Dieter did. Maybe it's him or somebody on his behalf who made the calls. I can't be sure."

"Erik, why didn't you tell me this before?"

"What good would that have done, Marie? I knew I could trust Dieter and it was only later that I found out that Bach knew. What good would it have done to tell you? I love you, Jewish or not, and I feel nothing less towards the girls, even if they have Jewish blood."

She started to cry.

"What will they do to me and the children, Erik? We'll be sent to a camp, won't we?"

She was correct, if the SS found out. So I did my best to lie to her.

"Of course not, Marie. First of all, they won't find out and secondly, do you really think that Eichmann and Goebbels want that kind of scandal? Even if they do find out, they won't do anything about it. *Believe me*. I'm telling you the truth."

She looked at me, with the look of a small child who needed someone to assure her that everything would be alright. I tried my best to give her the impression that I was not worried and that what had happened amounted to nothing. Deep down I knew that I had to find out exactly who was responsible for making the call. Was it Bach? If so, had he told anybody else? I had to make sure that Abraham succeeded in his plan and that any records that Bach might have would be destroyed. Tonight, I would go to Bach's office to see if I could find anything he might have on Marie.

My late night entry didn't cause the guards any concern. I had done this before.

"Heil Hitler, Herr Sturmbannführer. May we be of any assistance to you?"

"*Nein*. Please make sure I am not disturbed."

No one was on my floor except the guards. Bach's office was typically unlocked. I hoped he would be careless enough to leave my family's dossier with his other records. The file cabinet was unlocked. I paged frantically but could find no listing about me or my family. I kept searching for the next twenty minutes, but to no avail. If any file existed, it was not here. Where could he have put it? Perhaps there was no such file!

After going through the rest of his office for yet another hour, I still came up empty. Perhaps it was not Bach after all who made the calls.

But if not him, then who?

On my way home, I thought of Marie. Should I lie to her and tell her that I found the files and destroyed them? Or should I tell her that I found nothing and therefore whoever was calling her was telling the truth and indeed working on a family tree?

Deep down, I believed that Bach was too careful to leave such information in an unlocked office. If he had it at all, he probably had it safely hidden.

Just then an idea came to me.

I would ask Abraham to find out what Bach knew before he killed him. Bach would tell the truth to save his life. I realized that by making this request Abraham would also know the truth about Marie and the children, but he would not turn them in. I could trust Abraham. He was my friend.

Marie was still up, reading in bed.

"What did you find, Erik?"

"Nothing, Marie, nothing. Bach had no information in his office and it was probably true that whoever called was merely seeking information for that family tree. In any event, if he calls again, tell him that he should speak to your husband."

This seemed to please her. I always took care of everything.

First thing the next morning, I had a trustworthy private messenger deliver a note to Abraham indicating what I wanted done. I had the messenger wait until he had seen Abraham read the letter. Abraham then informed him that he would take care of the matter and, as instructed in the message, he destroyed the letter in the messenger's presence.

Thursday had finally come! I came to work early that morning to make sure that nothing stood in the way of Bach's departure.

When I arrived, Bach was already there. He was obviously in a good mood.

"Good morning, Erik. Fine day, isn't it?"

"Why, yes, Jonathan. It is a fine day. A great day, actually."

He made sure that no one was around, then said to me, "Erik, there is something I wanted to tell you. I suppose this is as good a time as any. I know that you have been uneasy because of what I know about your marriage certification. I want you to know and believe that I have destroyed all this information. At first, I had copied the files, but like I said, they have now been destroyed. No one knows anything about your wife's race. This I swear to you!"

I looked at him with a feeling of uncertainty. Was he telling me the truth or was he lying in order to lull me into a false sense of security? My God, if he was telling the truth, I was sending him today to his execution for no good reason at all!

"Jonathan, have you told anyone else about this?"

"No one!"

My mind was racing. Should I stop him from seeing Abraham or should I let him go to his death?

"Thank you, Jonathan, thank you for your loyalty. We will spend some time together when you return, but you had better be going now. Remember, you are supposed to meet Abraham at the place he designated. Don't tell anyone, because I don't know who might be a part of the conspiracy."

He agreed with everything I said. He gave me the Nazi salute, smiled, and walked out the door, not knowing that he would never walk through it again.

By the end of the day, there was still no news. I decided to stay at the office, hoping that I would receive a call or message of some sort from Abraham.

At 9:00 PM the phone rang. It was Abraham.

"It is done. The butcher is dead."

"Did he say anything?" I asked.

"Oh, he certainly did. He said quite a bit before he died, but in answer to your specific interest, Bach insisted that he was not making the calls and that he had destroyed the information about your wife. I tend to believe him, Erik. Any man in his situation would tell the truth in hopes of saving his life. But I must hang up now, I've got to be careful. I will see you the next time you come out. Then I will tell you exactly how Herr Bach died."

I had barely gotten home when the phone rang. It was the commanding officer at the ghetto.

"Herr Sturmbannführer, I have terrible news for you."

"What is it?" I asked.

"Hauptsturmführer Jonathan Bach has been murdered."

Feigning shock and outrage was truly hard to do.

"Bach, murdered? But... Start a detailed investigation immediately!"

I told him I would arrive tomorrow and that he should have a complete report for me at that time.

"Who was that, Erik?"

"Bach is dead, Marie."

"But how, Erik? How?"

"I don't know much more, sweetheart. I will go to Kovnas in the morning to find out all the details. We'll talk about it when I return."

Sleep came easy to me that night.

I arrived at the ghetto late in the morning. I entered headquarters and immediately went to see the officer in charge.

"May I see your report on Bach?"

"Yes, sir. It is lying on the desk in front of you. Please sit down and make yourself comfortable."

I took off my jacket and began reading. Usually, reports such as these were very detailed and quite well done, especially considering the short period of time. The coroner estimated that Bach had died at about seven o'clock last night. The prime cause of death was strangulation, presumably by piano wire. It was noted in the file that Bach had been tortured before he died.

"Do you have any suspects?"

"No, Herr Sturmbannführer, not yet. The body was found just outside of the ghetto. Apparently, there were no witnesses. I checked with Bach's office, but he kept this trip secret from his secretary and obviously from yourself as well. Nobody even knew he was coming here yesterday. We searched his body and found the usual identification papers, a small amount of money, and what appeared to be his calendar book."

He handed me the calendar book and I paged through it. There was nothing peculiar in it and the page date of his murder was blank, with no notations.

"I want the Judenrat convened immediately. I will return in one hour."

I arrived back within the hour, and waiting for me were the seven members, with Abraham seated at the head of the table. As was customary, they all rose and removed their caps.

"Sit down... By now, most of you must know why I have summoned you."

They nodded affirmatively.

"I will begin by asking you what any of you know about the murder of Hauptsturmführer Bach. Any information you may give me will go a long way in helping your individual position and also that of your people. But if you fail to provide this information and I find out that anyone of you is withholding it from me, I will have a hundred of your countrymen shot. This I tell you with no hesitation on my part. I have always kept my word. Your living conditions have been at least adequate and I have done my best to keep anybody else from imposing upon you. Now, in return, I want your assistance."

After a moment of silence, Abraham spoke. "Herr Sturmbannführer, none of us know how or why this terrible thing happened. We assure you it was not the work of any ghetto residents."

"That is not good enough, Abraham!"

I struck him across the head with the back of my hand. It was not a hard blow.

"You will not tell me that you know nothing! You will all go out and find me the murderer. The rest of you are dismissed. Guards, lead the filthy Jews out of here. You, Abraham, will stay with me to go over the details of what I want you and your people to do."

When the room was cleared, I asked him to sit down.

"Tell me everything, Abraham, everything!"

A smile crossed his lips.

"Bach arrived yesterday on schedule. It was obvious that nobody knew why he was coming here or even that he had come at all. I convinced him to go walking with me. The streets were dark and deserted. We left the ghetto at the place I once showed you, and entered a building where I had told him I kept my records that showed who of the Judenrat had been planning to sabotage the deportations and which SS men were dishonest.

After we entered, I closed the door behind us. He turned towards me, and I struck him hard in the face, knocking him down and rendering him semi-conscious.

I tied him up, binding his feet and his arms. I then placed a gag across his mouth. When he woke up, groggy as he was, I stood him up on a long, low table and tied piano wire around his neck that was hanging down from a ceiling fixture. Do you want me to go on?"

"Yes, Abraham, of course, I *must* hear every detail."

"I beat him in the face and body. I lit a cigarette and burned him in several places. I then jogged his memory to that day when he took such pleasure in murdering my wife and daughter. I took the gag out of his mouth, because there really was no one around to hear him cry. He begged for forgiveness."

"Did you ask him about the phone calls? Did you ask about my wife?"

"Yes, I did. Patience, Erik, I am getting to that. I played with him for half an hour or so. He was still quite conscious and in relatively good physical condition. I asked him about the calls and what he knew about your wife. He swore up and down that he did not make the calls, nor did he arrange for anyone else to do so, nor did he know who did. He also swore that he destroyed any evidence about Marie and that he had told no one about her. After he first answered, I beat him rather severely. If he was lying, he would now tell the truth. But he never changed his story, never, never, up to the time he died. I tend to believe him, Erik. I think he was telling the truth.

After he finished talking about your family, his death began in earnest. I beat and burned him some more. I then kicked the table from under his legs and the strangulation began. He was twitching, screaming and begging for his life. It took him ten minutes to die."

Once again, guilt swept over me, for I knew that I had just assisted in killing a man who had done me no harm.

"Remorse, Herr Sturmbannführer? But why? Remorse is such a worthless emotion. It does no good since the foul deed has already been done and it cannot be taken back. Remorse only weakens a man. Besides, how did you know with any certainty that it wasn't Bach, and how could you be sure he would not turn in your wife and children after all? You did what you had to do. What you should now be considering is, if not Bach, then who is making these calls? Think, Erik. Who else out there knows about your wife's lineage?"

I could not think of anyone else. "Outside of her mother and possibly her father, only you and... and Dieter!"

"Ah, yes. Dieter Schmidt, that kind SS man you had sent to a position outside of Vienna. I remember him. In fact, I was very impressed by his actions."

"But Dieter adores my children. They call him *Onkel*. I can't believe he would do anything that would even remotely harm them."

"I agree, Erik. It would seem to be out of character for him."

"In fact, Abraham, now that Bach is dead, I will try to have Dieter reassigned back to Vienna."

"That is good. With Dieter back, the three of us can work out a plan for your escape. You have kept your word by giving me justice and you have spared my life. I will now help you. I have many contacts, within and outside the ghetto. I have helped smuggle many to the Swiss border. I am working on a plan for you and your family. You must escape to a country that will not just *take* you, but rather will *welcome* you. To smuggle you into Switzerland or Spain and then just leave you there, that will do little good. The Allies will find you there after the war is over and bring you back here. No, what we want to do is to devise a plan to get you to Argentina or Peru, where fascist feelings are strong."

"It all sounds very good, Abraham, but do you believe this plan has a chance to succeed?"

"I believe so and if it does, you will be my first Nazi, and perhaps *the* first high ranking Nazi who succeeds in escaping from the Reich, with the exception of Rudolph Hess."

We walked back to the meeting room. I thanked Abraham and made my way to my waiting car for the trip back to Vienna.

16

Work As Usual

BY mid 1944 it was obvious, except to the fanatic Nazis, that the war would be lost. The long-expected invasion from the West had not yet taken place, but we all knew that it would only be a matter of time before the Allies would be on Germany's doorstep.

But although the war against the Allies was going poorly, the campaign against the Jews was in full stride, just like in '43. Not in Vienna and in Austria in general, however. Deportations had slowed up considerably. Most of the Jews who didn't manage to escape before the war began had already been deported. It was probably for that reason that I received the call from Eichmann.

"Erik, I need your services elsewhere."

"Herr Obersturmbannführer, what do you mean by elsewhere?"

"Budapest, Erik, Budapest, Hungary. There are still hundreds of thousands of Jews in Hungary and the Führer has recently ordered me to coordinate their deportations. In the past, Hungary and that idiot Horthy have been reluctant to cooperate with us, but there is now a definite change in attitude. It will be marvelous, Erik, just like the *old days*. I need you to work with me in eliminating the Jews from Hungary, much as we have done in Germany and Austria. There is a wonderful rail system which will transport them to Auschwitz and I have been promised priority in securing enough freight cars."

Eichmann's request hit me like a bombshell. He told me I could think it over for a while and he would call me back soon. This was one hell of a time to be requested to do more killing. Here, I was trying to come up with a plan to leave Austria for good and now I was offered a job which would literally take months or more to complete. By then, the war might well be over and it would be too late for me to escape. On the other hand, if I told Eichmann no, he might get suspicious and put me under some type of surveillance, or worse, have me sent to the Russian Front.

I spent the rest of the day trying to work out a solution to this dilemma, when my thoughts were interrupted by a knock on the door. My secretary was just having a break, so I called out, *"Komm herein!"*

In walked an impeccably dressed SS Hauptsturmführer. From his insignia I could tell he was an intelligence officer.

"Herr Sturmbannführer, Heil Hitler! My name is Horst Strasser."

I returned the salute.

"What brings you here, Herr Hauptsturmführer?"

"SS Headquarters in Berlin has assigned me to lead the investigation into Jonathan Bach's death."

"But isn't a murder investigation something for the local authorities to handle?"

"Yes, that would be the normal procedure, but in this case the circumstances are so puzzling that Berlin wants its own investigation."

"What circumstances are you referring to?"

"All I know at this time is that there are several unexplained events that occurred shortly before Bach's death."

"Please continue," I said.

"First of all, nobody knew of his trip to the ghetto. You didn't know about it, did you?"

"No, I did not. I was as surprised as anyone else."

"Secondly, he went with no guards, also very unusual. Third of all, his secretary told us that in the last several days he had been destroying some type of records. She didn't know what they were. All very strange, wouldn't you agree?"

I paused and walked to the window. "Vienna is very beautiful this time of year, don't you think so?"

"With all due respect, Herr Sturmbannführer, I did not travel all the way from Berlin to discuss the beauties of this city. My instructions are to find Bach's killer and I will do so. I have never failed any mission yet to which I have been assigned. Please forgive me, Herr Sturmbannführer, but I need to begin this investigation by asking you your whereabouts the day of the murder."

"Why, of course, I have nothing to hide. You can ask the night watch. I was here working late that evening. As soon as I arrived home, I received the phone call about his death."

"Thank you, Herr Sturmbannführer. Do you know anybody who would want Bach eliminated? Did he have any enemies?"

Although I knew Bach must have had a *legion* of people who hated him, I answered, "Only the Jews."

The young officer looked skeptically. "Yes, I'm sure there are many Jews who hated him, but these *meek sheep* rarely resort to such extreme measures.

124

I won't totally rule out Jewish involvement, because they do have small underground resistance groups, but the fact remains that the odds are against that theory."

If he only knew the true extent of Jewish involvement.

"Well, Herr Byrnes, I have taken enough of your time. I must arrange for quarters now. We will talk again, I'm sure. *Auf Wiedersehen*."

I must have been naive. For some reason I never suspected that the Intelligence Unit would send an officer all the way from Berlin to investigate a minor SS officer's murder. Now I had four problems to deal with. First of all, if Bach had not been the one who sought information about Marie, then that person was still at large. Secondly, would the young officer's investigation lead to Abraham and then eventually to me? Thirdly, what would I tell Eichmann when he called again? And finally, how would I under these circumstances prepare to leave Austria?

Just as I had expected, Eichmann called.

"Erik, I have some bad news for you."

I couldn't imagine anything worse than what I was already experiencing.

"I am sorry to inform you that you will not be coming to work with me in Budapest. Himmler has ordered that you should stay in Vienna, at least until a replacement for the murdered Hauptsturmführer is found. Maybe we can work together then."

What news!

"Herr Obersturmbannführer, I am very sorry to hear this but I do understand the Reichsführer's reasoning. There will be another time, I am sure."

"I knew you would understand, Erik. Talk to you later, Heil Hitler."

More good news came that very day. I found Dieter and he was alive and well. He had managed to be assigned as an adjutant to a back-line general. He would arrive in Vienna this evening, and Marie and the children would accompany me to meet him at the station.

Dieter's train arrived just as we entered the waiting area. Marie couldn't restrain the girls any longer.

"Onkel Dieter! Onkel Dieter!" they screamed as they ran up to him.

"Susanne, Louisa, how I missed both of you."

Marie and I joined them. As Dieter looked up, I strained to see the expression on his face. Would he understand that I had him sent away as much for his own good as for mine?

"Marie, it has been too long."

It did not take long to find out his true feelings. He embraced my wife and then looked me in the eyes. When he extended his hand, I knew he bore me no ill will. Our hands met and we embraced.

"Dieter, I hope you understand I did what I did to get you away from Bach. I hope you can forgive me."

"There is nothing to forgive, Erik. You had no other choice. If I had stayed, Bach would somehow have had me killed. I know that you did me a favor and besides, I never was any good at my job, was I?"

We both laughed.

I let Marie and the girls walk ahead to the automobile.

"Dieter, there is something I want to discuss with you. Do you remember when you offered to help me to end my service with the SS?"

"Like it was yesterday, Erik."

"That's good, because I have another friend who has also offered to help. Do you remember Abraham, from the ghetto?"

"Of course, he was quite a man."

"Yes, he is. Someday I will tell you just what a remarkable man he really is. You might not believe this, Dieter, but he is my only friend besides yourself. He has offered to help me, too."

Dieter looked at me in disbelief.

"A Jew? You're actually going to get help from a Jew? You are calling a Jew a friend? Perhaps you have really changed?"

"I'll tell you more about the plan when the time is right, but enough for now, let's go home."

What a grand day!

Dieter got back his old office and I intended to keep my word to him that he would perform no deportation work at all. I had him assigned to handle and process death benefits for German soldiers who had died for the Reich. He seemed quite satisfied with his new position. I appointed a young SS officer, a Herman Gonart, to actually handle Bach's duties. He was very qualified, and the more I saw of him, the more he reminded me of Bach.

The war was going quite badly for the Reich. The Russian Front came closer and closer, while from the West British bombings were becoming more frequent and more bold. It was only a matter of time before the Allied invasion would take place. The only thing we didn't know was when or where the landing would be.

Dieter was actually anxious to accompany me to the Kovnas ghetto. He wanted to see Abraham again. It would be an excellent time to discuss the plan for my escape.

As I had done many times before, I sent the guards out and gave Dieter and Abraham a chance to get reacquainted.

"Erik, I have come up with a plan that I feel might work. I don't have all the specifics finished yet but at least you and Dieter can hear the main points. You and your family will take a vacation at a resort called *The Kasdorf.* It is located not far from Lake Constance on the Swiss-Austrian border. The exact details will not be finalized until you have arrived there, but in general I can tell you that you and your family will be *kidnapped* from the resort. Once you are reported missing, you can rest assured that the SS and the Gestapo will have men combing the area for you, both in Austria and in Switzerland. We will have you and your family in hiding, hopefully for not too long. I believe the SS will eventually become convinced that you have all been murdered by partisans and they will discontinue the search. That is when you can make your move into Switzerland, and from there to South America."

"That sounds like a splendid idea, Abraham! But you will need money, Erik, a lot of money," Dieter said. "Do you have some saved or can you get it somewhere?"

"Yes, I have saved some money."

Abraham quickly picked up on this point.

"Good, Erik! The men who are going to help us do so for only one reason, and that is their personal gain, so you will need money, as Dieter said. Unfortunately, only mercenaries are willing to help you. The Allies would not help you because of what you have done, and the Germans or other Axis agents would forsake you because of your treason. Really, until you make it to South America, you will be a man without a country."

Dieter sensed my sadness. "Erik, I know this is a difficult time for you, and you are having doubts as to whether or not you are doing the right thing with a plan like this. Believe me! If you remain here or, for that matter, anywhere else in Europe, they will catch you, try you as a war criminal, and hang you, as sure as I am standing here."

"He's right, Erik. Your name is well known among the Allies."

I listened carefully to what they said. There was no doubt in my mind that they were both right. If I survived the war and if I remained anywhere on this continent, I would be caught. Any trial that I would undergo would be a sham at best, and if I were caught, the only thing I would have to look forward to was a hope that I would be shot instead of hung.

Abraham had spent considerable time on this project and I could tell that Dieter would do whatever it took to make it a success. What had I ever done to deserve two friends like them, willing to risk their own lives in an attempt to help me and my family?

We talked in generalities for the next hour or so, going over many of the plan's major points.

After a while, the conversation turned to the phone calls Marie had received. I then decided to tell Dieter everything I knew about the calls and the suspected caller. I did not tell him how Bach had died and who had killed him but I did say that Bach had found out about Marie and that Abraham and I suspected that he was the individual who made the calls.

"At least I can report one good thing to the two of you. Since Bach died, the calls have stopped."

17

More Problems

THE Jews we were now deporting were sent to either Mauthausen, Auschwitz or to the Lodz ghetto in Poland, where they would remain for a few months before going to Auschwitz. Those now being rounded up had been passed up in earlier deportations either because they were necessary for specific jobs or because they had somehow managed to evade us.

I likened what I did to *trophy fishing*. I would rather fish waters with few difficult-to-catch fish, than fishing a pond filled with many small fish. I prided myself on the time and effort I spent on these *special* cases.

I remember one family from Vienna in particular.

In late 1939, the father of this family of four had received a notice to report for deportation, but he managed to obtain a deferment based upon his occupation. He was a skilled master craftsman, and his employer was, no less, the former Weinstein Industries. I knew the man and his skill, so I approved his exemption. His deferment was renewed year after year until he was finally replaced by an equally able gentile. When his request for a deferment for 1943 came up, I did not renew it.

By the time I had prepared their Auschwitz deportation notice, he and his family had all disappeared. We devoted many hours trying to capture them. I was not displeased. Instead, their disappearance was a challenge to me. I became a detective, just like Charlie Chan in the American movies. I had to outsmart this Jew, which would not be easy.

I told my agents to be alert for families who somehow always carried more food ration coupons than normal. These Jews had to eat, and whoever was hiding them had to be getting extra rations in order to feed themselves and their guests.

I let all the local butchers know that I was looking for this family. They knew that if they would help me to capture them, they would be rewarded handsomely, but they also knew that I would not hesitate to have executed anyone of them who intentionally withheld such information.

After a month or so, a grocery store owner reported that a gentile family repeatedly came in with more ration coupons than normal.

The next time a member of this family came to do their shopping, I had her followed. She led us to a two-story residential building, not far from the store. The next day the house was surrounded and we broke down the doors. The building was searched and, cleverly hidden in a room *within* a room, we found our missing Jews. On the following day, after intense interrogation, both the family of four and the gentiles that hid them were deported to Auschwitz.

I made it a point to find out what their fate was. I learned that the Jewish father, his wife, his son of eight and daughter of seven were gassed upon arrival. Too bad. I would have thought that at least the father, due to his skills, would have passed the *Selection* process.

The gentiles who hid and fed the Jews I ordered shot.

The loud ringing of the phone disrupted my thoughts.

"Erik, I have that investigator Strasser on hold."

"Put him through, Urma."

I hadn't heard from him for some time. I wondered why he was calling.

"Good afternoon, Herr Sturmbannführer."

"Good afternoon to you as well, Herr Strasser. To what do I owe the honor of this call?"

"It has been some time since I talked to you, but I wanted to let you know that the inquiry into Bach's death is far from over. In fact, I have new information I want to share with you."

"Tell me, please. I am very interested." He didn't know how *really* interested I was.

"At first, our investigation led us nowhere. We could find neither motive nor suspect. I must admit that I almost gave up. Then, a miracle occurred. A short time ago, we intercepted a bill intended for Bach. It was a statement for rental of a locker at the Süd Bahnhof railway station. I went to the station, paid the bill and obtained a duplicate key. On opening the locker, guess what I found?"

"I really have no idea. Why don't you save us both some time and tell me?"

"That I will, Herr Byrnes. In the locker, Bach kept various papers, some inconsequential, such as pinups of American movie starlets, but also some notes about your wife. I will be honest with you. At first, I thought that Bach was having an affair with her, but when I looked more carefully, I could see he was trying to gather statistical information on Frau Byrnes. Her date of birth, birthplace, name of parents, maternal grandparents, and so forth. Do you know why he would want this information?"

I knew I had to answer him right away. Any delay, and he would be suspicious. I had to be firm. "Herr Strasser, I want to set the record straight. I have no knowledge about what he did outside this office or why he did it. Is that clear?"

"Why, of course, I never said you did. Herr Sturmbannführer, I can tell that I have upset you and, so I will be hanging up now. We will talk at a better time. I will be staying in Vienna. As you once mentioned, it is such a beautiful city. If you would be so kind, please find me a place to stay. I will be arriving within a day."

"Certainly, I will arrange suitable lodging for you. Please call on me when you arrive."

I hung up the phone. My hand was shaking. Was this all he knew or were there other notes in that locker? I had to find out and I *had* to put this investigation to an end. There was one positive note: my conscience was eased about the killing of Bach. Clearly, he had not destroyed all his notes.

I had to talk to Marie before the SS did. She would not be very good at answering their questions.

I began to dial her number, but stopped. What if my phone line was tapped? I must be careful, very careful. Should I go home now? No! It would look too suspicious if I left right after receiving that call. I decided to stay and leave at the regular hour, although it was difficult to concentrate the rest of the day.

My driver picked me up on time. I was careful not to tell him to hurry or to appear anxious or worried. He might be questioned by Strasser at a later date.

My thoughts drifted to a time in the future, to a place far away, South America. I visualized Marie there with me, and Susanne, Louisa, Father, Theresa, Dieter, and yes, Abraham. There we could start over, away from this hell. It could be Peru or Brazil or Argentina, anyone of those places would do. We would have a home next to a mountain stream. We could grow crops. We would be so happy, so very, very, happy!

"Herr Sturmbannführer... you are home. Is there something wrong?"

My driver's voice woke me.

"No, I'm fine. Thank you, Karl. That will be all."

I left the Mercedes and entered our home.

Marie could see right away that something was wrong.

"Erik, what's happened? You look pale."

"Marie, sit down. Where are the girls?"

"They're next door. What's wrong, Erik?"

131

"It appears there is going to be a further investigation into Bach's death."

"Well, is that so bad? You must have expected that this could happen?"

"It's not just the investigation into his death, Marie. I think the investigator found out that Bach was looking into you and your family. I am not sure how much he knows."

She hesitated for a moment. Then she hung her head down and sat at the kitchen table.

"Marie, what I do know for certain is that you must be very, very careful in talking to strangers, especially when talking on the phone. Trust no one but me and Dieter. Can you do this?"

"I think so..."

"No Marie! It's not, 'I think so.' You *must* do this, not only for your sake but for the sake of our daughters."

She began to cry.

Why was she so weak and so naive? Why couldn't she be strong?

"Marie, let me help you. Here is what you do. First of all, make sure that the girls don't answer the phone. Then, if anyone asks you any information, tell them nothing specific. Tell them that they must talk to me. Ask them for their phone number."

"I understand, Erik, but I am scared, very scared."

"I know, Marie. I know. Trust me. It'll all work out. I promise."

As I entered my office the next morning, I could tell by Urma's expression that something was not quite right.

"Good morning, Herr Sturmbannführer. I hope you will forgive me for waiting here for you unannounced."

Better judgment stopped me from replying.

"That is quite alright, Herr Strasser. How can I help you?"

"Thank you for your consideration. I will get right to the point. Our investigation leads us to believe that Bach was somehow involved in something affecting you, Herr Sturmbannführer. Do you know of anyone who might want to harm you or any members of your family?"

"I am sure there are many, but I can come up with no specific individual."

There was a pause in the conversation. I could tell he was getting ready to tell me something I wouldn't like to hear.

"I apologize to you in advance for what I am about to say next. I believe, Herr Sturmbannführer, that for some reason you have not been totally truthful with me. I hope that you can prove me wrong."

Now I had to feign outrage.

"How dare you accuse me of such things! To sit there and say a thing like that is unthinkable. I will certainly report you to your superiors for this."

"Sir, there is no need for such outbursts. I hope you know that I am only a detective. I say it as I see it. If it does make you feel better, you should know that I have informed both my superiors and Obersturmbannführer Eichmann about the course of my investigation and my feelings to date. I will give you time to think about what I have said before we speak again. Please consider the possible consequences of your actions."

He started to leave, but turned before he reached the door.

"Oh, by the way, please tell your wife that I will be contacting her."

"My wife... but..."

"Till we meet again, till we meet again."

I nodded tersely as he left. I had to stay strong and not break under the pressure. I only hoped that Marie would be equal to the task.

I busied myself, or at least tried to, with paperwork the rest of the day. This worked only on and off throughout the morning, but as the day wore on, I could tell that I was accomplishing little. Just as I had finished signing some administrative orders, Urma informed me that I had a call on hold from SS Headquarters in Budapest. It was Eichmann.

"Erik, how are you, my friend?"

"Quite well, Herr Obersturmbannführer, and you and your family?"

"All good, Erik. Let's get right down to business if we can."

I listened attentively.

"Erik, some time ago, we talked about a job for you in Budapest, but things turned out differently."

"Yes, I recall, Herr Obersturmbannführer."

"Well, the officer I assigned to the position happened to be killed in a car accident last evening. I must again ask you to take the job, Erik, but this time it is more than a polite request. I really do need you and I hope you won't force me to pull rank on you. Before you say anything, Erik, please let me finish.

I can arrange for magnificent accommodations for you and your family, far more luxurious than what you now have. Also, there will probably be a promotion in this for you. I am aware of your friendship with Dieter Schmidt. There will be a position for him as well, directly under you. Finally, Erik, consider this. There are still hundreds of thousand of Jews in Hungary. What a service to the Reich and to mankind in general you and I could accomplish! At this very time, we are completing a further expansion of Birkenau to accommodate all these additional *guests*. What do you say, Erik?"

What could I say? I knew I could not put him off, but I must stall for time.

"Of course, I accept, but there is one favor I need to ask, Herr Obersturmbannführer."

"Name it, Erik."

"Have you heard, sir, about the newly resurrected investigation into the death of Jonathan Bach?"

"Yes, I have, but what of it?"

"I believe that young SS Hauptsturmführer Strasser who is investigating the matter, feels that he needs time to question both me and my wife about activities Bach was involved in before his death. I really believe he is making much ado about nothing, but if I just pack up and leave for Budapest, might that not arouse suspicion? I would not want this weighing over me in my new position."

"You are right, Erik. I had heard that the investigation would be resurrected, and I even heard that Strasser suspects you have not been, shall we say, totally candid with him. But I cannot allow it to interfere with the very important work you and I have to do. I will personally put to an end this harassment."

"Thank you, Herr Obersturmbannführer."

"You're welcome, Erik. I can give you one week to get your things together. Is that enough?"

"Actually, I would appreciate it very much if I could have an additional two weeks. There is much to do, and I must train whomever you choose for my current position."

"So much time I cannot promise you, but you have my word that I will see what I can do for you, Erik."

We exchanged some small talk, then the conversation ended. I closed my office door and sat in my chair. I didn't know whether to rejoice or to cry. I might now have the SS officer out of my way, but at the same time I was being forced to move on to Budapest. Being in Budapest would make my escape almost impossible. I thought about Abraham. Without his help, the plan would be hopeless. I would have to escape before I had to leave for Budapest because I would be unable to stay in contact with Abraham anymore after I left Vienna. Finally, still buried in a corner of my mind was the ever prevailing thought that it was not Bach who had made those calls. Would that person be able to jeopardize my plans?

I went to see Dieter later that day and explained what had taken place. To put it mildly, the news bothered him. I had protected him here in Vienna and he was not forced to take part in any deportations or worse. If he had to accompany me to Hungary, he would be closer to Eichmann and less easy to watch over. It would be next to impossible to help him evade his duties.

"Erik, I don't mind saying that I don't like this at all, especially the thought of working for that pig Eichmann. Also, the plans I have made with Abraham use Vienna as a starting point. Many arrangements are already in place. We need to go see Abraham immediately and get his thoughts on this matter. The way I see it we must move up the departure date right away."

I arranged quickly that Dieter and I would go to see Abraham the following morning, and then went home to let Marie know what had happened.

She took the news, as I did initially, with mixed emotions. She was greatly relieved that the investigation which could reveal her true bloodline might finally be over. But she also knew, as did I, that a move to Budapest would place another nail in my coffin when the Allies won the war. We talked about it for at least a couple of hours until we agreed that Dieter was right and we had to make our escape before moving to Budapest. We had one week at least, and perhaps two more if we were lucky. There was much work to do.

"Erik, promise me everything will turn out alright. Promise me that nothing will happen to Louisa or Susanne?"

"I promise, Marie. We will get out of this. We'll start a new life in South America. Dieter tells me many of the details have already been worked out. In the meantime, if that SS investigator calls, try to avoid him. He should be hearing from Eichmann very soon and then he will stop bothering us. Also, don't forget we must pretend that we are indeed making preparations for a move to Budapest. Contact the school and let them know; inform the housekeeper, and tell your parents. Make it like we are truly moving. This is very important!"

"I'll start on it tomorrow, Erik."

"Good. As soon as I know more, I'll let you know."

We looked at each other with a look of longing, a desire to begin a new life. If only we could.

"Erik, I am with you all the way on this. I know you think I'm very simple and somewhat naive."

"No, Marie, that..."

"You don't have to deny it. I've seen the look in your eyes. But I promise to be better this time. I really will try. I know, Erik, that if we are caught, you will be shot or worse, and the children and I will face the same fate, or a concentration camp. I love you, Erik. I am nobody without you."

We embraced and kissed.

Early the next day, Dieter and I started out to see Abraham. We left before our escort was scheduled to arrive, telling the motor pool adjutant that we had much to do and that we had to leave early. We said there was no need for them to catch up with us.

"I told Marie about Eichmann's call, Dieter."

"How did she take it?"

"Very good, I thought. In fact, I have to tell you that I think she is finally coming to her senses."

"What do you mean by that, Erik?"

"Oh, you know, Dieter. Marie is sometimes such a fool."

"Erik, it is you who are the fool. A fool who doesn't know how lucky you are to have a wife like her."

"I didn't mean *fool* in the negative sense, Dieter. What I meant was that she just can't handle anything complicated, like this escape or the issue of the phone calls. That's all I meant to say."

"Erik, did you ever stop to think that it is because of you that these problems exist in the first place? If you had not married her, she probably would still be living in Berlin, with nobody the wiser."

Why was Dieter taking her side on this? There was silence for several minutes.

"Were you able to get through to Abraham, Dieter?"

"Yes, I did. I talked with him yesterday and I think that, between the three of us, we can come up with a good plan irrespective of Eichmann's demand."

"I hope so. I truly hope so. But whatever plan we choose, I insist that it implicates in no way you or Abraham."

"I don't think it will. Besides, who would believe that a Jew and an *unstable* SS Obersturmführer would ever team up to come up with such an ingenious plot?"

As we drove through the gate which separated the Jewish ghetto from the Aryan section, the difference between the two sides became obvious.

On the Aryan side, even though the world was in the thick of the war, there were still all the signs of life and even happiness. Children were playing while men and women walked hand in hand. The markets and shops were brimming with customers. Kovnas was in sharp contrast with that. Although the streets were full of people, it was clear that many of them were wandering aimlessly and without any particular destination. Walking was all they could do to take their minds off the hunger that pre-occupied every minute of their life. As much as I had tried, I was unable to obtain sufficient food for all of them. The war dictated that food was routed to Germany itself and to our military. The Jews were the victims of this policy. Accordingly, there were no children happily playing in the streets. The few that we did see were for the most part lying on the sidewalk, so still it was hard to tell if they were alive or dead, or they were begging with outstretched hands to anyone who would give them food or money.

Pressed close against the buildings, at every block or so, you could see bodies huddled together, with facial expressions of death.

We passed in silence as we continued towards the meeting place of the Judenrat.

Approaching the building, I wondered what Bach must have been thinking when he made a similar journey not too long ago. Was he happy? Was he sad? Did he have even the slightest idea that he would soon be tortured and murdered just blocks from here?

There was nobody present when we entered. It was as Dieter had told Abraham to make it, private, very private.

Then, the inner door swung open. "*Guten Morgen*, Erik. Good morning, Dieter. It is good to see you both."

We shook hands.

"Thank you for seeing us, Abraham. As you might guess, it was important for Erik and me to see you immediately."

We sat down at the table, and Dieter gave a summary of where we stood at the present time. When he was finished, Abraham got up and walked around with his hands clasped behind his back and his head down, obviously in deep thought. After a minute or so he came back and sat down.

"Erik, this change of circumstances troubles me. I'm not saying that it can't be done, but all the contacts we have put on hold must now be told that the time for movement is imminent."

Both Dieter and Abraham then took turns informing me about the details of the plan. I listened to them and had to smile because I could see that each tried to outdo the other in their attempt to impress me with the precise and well-thought-out details they had come up with.

Dieter seemed to lose patience with Abraham's meticulous dissertations.

"Abraham, we have less than two weeks to go. Forget the minor points and concentrate on what is important."

"Yes, yes, Dieter. I understand, but I hope *you* understand that any error in planning or execution could be fatal, no matter how small. I will stop boring you with details, but remember, Dieter, that it is up to you to make sure that in Erik's absence his office does not suffer. We can't take any chance that Eichmann would insist that he returns back home."

"That should be no problem. I really won't have to do much. Bach's successor is certainly zealous about his job and I am sure he is looking forward to showing everyone just how efficient he is in working towards the Final Solution. As to justifying the sudden vacation, Erik and his family have the perfect excuse. It is a long deserved vacation, and it makes even more sense to take a holiday now, right before such an *important* promotion, because they may not have a chance later. Since I know Erik, he has never taken time off. Even Eichmann cannot begrudge him these few days. Except for the deportations, I can handle everything else here that comes up in his absence."

The remainder of our time was spent with talk about more details and more specifics. Even Dieter, finally, agreed that this was important.

Before we left, I gave Abraham the money he needed to pay those who would assist us and to bribe those who needed bribing.

The ride back to Vienna was uneventful and quiet. I asked Dieter to drop me off at my home and once again I thanked him for all he had done.

I found the children crying by the kitchen table.

"What is wrong, little ones? Where is Mommy?"

"Daddy, Mommy is crying in her room."

I rushed upstairs.

"Marie, what's wrong? Why are you crying?"

She looked up at me, her eyes filled with tears.

"Erik, the calls, they have started again!"

I sat down next to her.

"Tell me what happened, Marie. Tell me exactly what happened!"

After wiping her eyes and blowing her nose, then catching her breath, she began telling me what had taken place.

"About eleven this morning, the phone rang. I answered and the same voice that called before was there again."

"What did he say, Marie?"

"At first, he apologized for taking so long to get back to me. He then said he had been out of the country on vacation and was just now catching up. But there was something different this time. Before, he had merely *asked* me for information about my grandparents. This time, he *insisted* on it. He said he was under a deadline and that it was all he needed to complete his study. I did what you said, Erik. I asked him to call me back later. I told him that I had a cake in the oven that I had to get to right away. Just like you told me, I also told him that you would be home later and you could help him with his questions. He seemed quite upset."

"Marie..."

"Wait, Erik, there is more."

"This time I also heard a voice in the background, a woman's voice. She kept saying, 'Find out. Find it out!', but finally he agreed with me and said he would call back. The phone rang twice this afternoon, but I didn't answer nor did I let the girls, just like you told me. I'm scared, Erik."

"Marie, could you hear anything else besides the woman's voice in the background? Anybody else talking? Any office machines? Anything at all?"

"No, Erik, nothing."

Just then, the ringing of the phone made me jump.

"Hello, who is this?"

"Who is this speaking?" the voice asked.

"This is Erik Byrnes. Again, who is this?"

The voice hesitated. In the background, I heard a second voice, the muffled sound of a woman. I could hardly hear her and I couldn't make out what she was saying.

"Herr Sturmbannführer, this is Wolfgang Strauss. I have been commissioned to do a study delineating the glorious heritage of all the top Austrian SS officers and their spouses. I am almost finished but I still lack some needed information about your lovely wife Marie. I called her today, you know."

"Yes, she told me. I am sorry you did not get to finish your conversation with her."

"If I might get directly to the point, Herr Byrnes, would you or your wife give me the names, birth dates, and places of birth of your wife's maternal grandparents?"

"I can check, but first might I ask you a question?"

I could sense hesitation, but I continued.

"Mr. Strauss, if you need information about my wife's grandparents, why don't you ask my wife's mother?"

"Uh, uh... I have tried, but for some reason she refuses to talk to me. I don't really know why."

"Nor would I know why she wouldn't talk to you either, Herr Straus, but as you know, she is an elderly woman and older people tend to be suspicious. It's the war, you know. People are afraid, afraid of talking to anyone for that matter."

"Of course, Herr Byrnes. That is precisely why I have not bothered her any more. Would you be kind enough to give me this information now? I really do need it immediately."

I could now hear the woman's voice more clearly in the background. It sounded familiar, but from where, I could not yet determine. If I heard it more, I knew that I would remember. It seemed as if this woman was listening with him on the same line.

"Herr Strauss, my wife and I would be glad to assist you. I have an idea. Why don't you visit us at our home? We have some pictures we could show you that you might be interested in."

This time there was a long silence and then that same muffled woman's voice in the background. Finally, he replied, "I thank you for your kind offer, but I cannot accept. The reason is that I am under a time pressure, Herr Byrnes. You see, I really must finish my commission immediately, or I fear that I will pay dearly for my laxity. My wife and I should never have taken the extended vacation we did."

"I sympathize with your situation, but I'm sure you can appreciate the fact that in my position I must be careful with whom I speak on the telephone. For all I know, you may not be who you say you are. You understand, don't you? Perhaps you could give me your office number and I could call you tomorrow with what you need."

The woman's voice became louder and more agitated. I listened as hard as I could. It was coming back to me. I was sure that I knew the woman behind this voice. I knew her well, but...

"Herr Strauss, my wife and I don't want to cause you any problems with your employer, certainly not. If you can't give me your phone number, won't you reconsider and agree to see us tomorrow, or maybe even tonight? Also, Herr Straus, I couldn't help but hear that there is a woman's voice in the background. She is your secretary or your wife, no doubt. Please bring her with you."

Now there was total silence, not even a whisper. I knew neither of them knew what to say.

"Thank you, Herr Byrnes. Tomorrow would be fine."

"That would be good, Herr Strauss. Come at 9:00 AM sharp. We will be happy to see both of you tomorrow. Good day."

I hung the phone up. The smile on my face was obvious. I knew they would never show up.

"Why are you smiling, Erik? This is not funny!"

"I'm sorry, Marie. Of course this is no joke, but I just can't help it. I know that the woman's voice will come back to me and I also know, Marie, that whoever it is, it is not somebody who belongs to the military or to the SS or to any other governmental organization."

Marie didn't seem to understand what I was saying.

"This is good news, Marie. Very good news! You see, whoever it is is unsure of your heritage. As long as we are careful and as long as your mother or your father, if he even knows, say nothing, we should be fine. I am sure we will not hear from this *historian* any more."

I had lied. No matter what I told Marie, I knew that these people were dangerous. I had to find out who they were and have them both eliminated!

18

The Escape

AS suspected, nobody arrived the next morning.

Marie spent the next week making all the arrangements for our so-called imminent move to Budapest. She even went so far as to call Eichmann's wife for suggestions. Dieter, under the pretext of making the ghetto more efficient, had Abraham transported to Vienna. Now they could work together without interruption.

My only contribution that first week was to supply Abraham with even more cash to make the escape possible.

It bothered me that I could not tell my father or sister anything about my plans, but to do so could only put them in danger if they were interrogated later on. I told Marie to say nothing to her parents, too.

On Wednesday of that first week I received the first challenge to my plans.

"Herr Byrnes, that young SS investigator Strasser is on the phone."

I wondered why he was calling. Eichmann had promised me that I would not be bothered anymore.

"Yes, Herr Hauptsturmführer, what can I do for you?"

"Really nothing, Herr Sturmbannführer. I just called to congratulate you on your move to Budapest. As I'm sure you know, I was told by Obersturmbannführer Eichmann, in blunt terms, that I should not bother you any further now that you will soon take on a very important mission. Of course, I will honor his request.

I also wanted to take this opportunity, Herr Sturmbannführer, to inform you that my area of jurisdiction also includes Budapest. Once you are settled, I wonder if it would be alright if I came and visited you?"

I hesitated only momentarily. Who cared if he came to see me? I wouldn't be there anyway.

"Why, of course, you're welcome to visit me any time. Just give me a couple of weeks to get settled in."

"Excellent. I will stop by in about a month. Good day and, again, congratulations."

I could tell that this young man had taken Eichmann's order to leave me alone with some indignation. I was sure he hoped that by waiting to see me until after I was settled in he would not violate Eichmann's directive and at the same time could continue to question me and Marie.

Just moments after he hung up, there was a knock at my door.

"Herr Byrnes, Dieter and the Jew Abraham are here for their appointment."

"Thank you, Urma. Please send them in and close the door behind you."

I waited until I heard Urma back at her typewriter. Although I never considered her to be disloyal to me, she still was a true Nazi, not like my Sarah.

"Dieter, before we begin, a thought just crossed my mind."

"And that is, Erik?"

"What ever did happen to Sarah? I was just thinking about her now."

"Now that you mention it, Erik, I have no idea how she is doing. As you know, I had her safely hidden with her cousin. After that, I lost touch with her. But I wouldn't worry, I'm sure she is safe. I think we would have heard otherwise."

I decided I would forget about Sarah now. Hopefully, when the war was over, I could somehow get a message to her.

Dieter continued. "Erik, next week Monday, you, Marie and the children are booked for a four-day vacation at *The Kasdorf*. As we discussed before, we don't expect that this trip will cause any suspicion because you haven't had a vacation for many years. Sometime on the second day of your stay, you and your family will be kidnapped. Abraham has made those arrangements and I will let him present the details."

"After you are abducted," Abraham said, "you and your family will be hidden at a farm about two hours away from the resort and not too terribly far from the Swiss border. There you will stay until it is safe to move you across. As Dieter said, it will appear as though you have been kidnapped. Ransom notes will be sent with postmarks far away from the place where you are being kept. We assume that the Reich will not pay the ransom. When the time seems right, we will mail a doctored picture to the Gestapo, with the dead bodies of you and your family on it. Hopefully, that will end their search."

"But Abraham, you know that murders of high-level SS officers are usually followed by a severe retaliation. Look what happened to Lidice when Heydrich was assassinated."

"I have taken that into consideration, Erik. First of all, we will make it appear that your kidnappers are renegade Italian partisans so that no retribution will be taken against any civilians. But you should also remember that when Lidice was liquidated, it still looked like Germany would win the war. It meant little, back then, what the public opinion would say. Now that the reverse is true, I doubt very much that any more Germans would want to be tried and hung as war criminals when all of this is over."

Dieter agreed with that assessment.

"He's right, Erik, and of course I will do all I can to avoid any retaliation at the local populace."

"I'm sure you will, Dieter, but I doubt you will have any influence on that front."

Dieter just smiled.

"Abraham, can you trust these individuals you have hired?"

"Without a doubt. All of them have done this before."

"Who are they?"

"Just ordinary Jews, but many with gentile features and papers that allow them to mingle freely with the local people. Above all, Erik, don't be concerned that they will betray you because of who you are. I have explained to all of them what you did for me, and for that they are thankful. Also, money is far more important to most of them than ideologies. Even though you are known as *The Hangman*, the money you have paid conveniently allows them to look the other way and forget about your background."

"You're positive about this, Abraham?" Dieter asked.

"Without a doubt, don't worry."

Fortunately, Dieter didn't ask what it was that I had done for Abraham.

The only problem I could envision would be that, somehow, whoever was making the calls would interfere with my escape plans.

It was getting late, the meeting broke up. Dieter would have to escort Abraham back to his lock-up for transport back to the ghetto tomorrow. I told Abraham I would try to meet with him at least one more time before I left. We said goodbye, and I proceeded to finish up some paperwork.

Looking around the room, I gazed at the photos on the wall. There was of course a picture of me with my parents and sister and a picture of me with Marie and the girls. There were also other photos: one of me and Dieter, one of me and Bach. There were the autographed pictures of me with Goebbels and Heydrich and me and Eichmann. The prize possession by far, however, was the photo taken with the Führer at Berchtesgaden. What would he say now if he knew what I was going to do?

All the office help had left when I prepared to go home. Then, the phone rang. I hesitated taking the call because most calls at this time of the day were more problems than they were worth, and besides, I had much to do at home. For some reason, however, I decided to answer this one.

"Byrnes speaking. Who is this please?"

It was a woman's voice. "Erik, Erik Byrnes, is this you?"

It was the same voice I had heard, muffled, in the background during that call to our home the other day!

"Yes, this is Erik Byrnes. Who is this?"

"Don't you recognize my voice, Erik? Why, I'm disappointed."

"Keep talking, please. I know it will come to me."

"Erik, my dear, sweet Erik. This is Sarah, your old secretary."

Sarah! Sarah! Of course. Now I recognized the voice!

Rage and hurt got the best of me at the same time.

"Sarah, it was you on the phone! Why have you been making these calls to my home? Why have you been so cruel to me and my family?"

"You should talk of cruelty, Erik, you who are known far and wide as The Hangman of Vienna. How many thousands have you murdered, Erik? How many Jews have you sent to their death? How many were fathers, mothers, children and babies? Do you even know the numbers, Erik? Do you even care?"

"But Sarah, I saved your life. I made sure you would be safe."

"That you did, Erik, and I must admit that I was very grateful at first. I also did not know then what you would turn out to be. When I knew you, you had not yet become the killer that you are now. Perhaps I should have seen it then, but I didn't."

"That still does not explain why you are making these calls, Sarah."

"Since you insist, I will tell you why. Do you remember that I once told you that I was on friendly terms with your wife's parents?"

I did indeed remember.

"Some time after I was re-settled here, I remembered that at one time, long ago, Marie's mother told me that she feared for her safety and her daughter's. She told me that there were some *problems* with her bloodline. I didn't think much of it then, and I put it out of my mind until about a year ago when I happened to read an underground newspaper. The paper wrote about the war criminals who would hopefully be tried, convicted and executed after the war. Your name, Erik, made the top ten on the list. I was shocked. I didn't believe it at first.

I then tried to find out more about you. I asked around and discovered that what was printed about you was true, indeed. You certainly deserve the name they call you. But this still would not have prompted me to make the calls to your wife."

"Then what did, Sarah?"

"What really did it, Erik, was that about eight months ago, my sister and her family were deported from Vienna to Auschwitz. I have heard from them no more. Do you know who authorized their re-settlement, Erik?"

There was a pause. I didn't say anything because I already knew the answer.

"It was, as I am sure you know, none other than yourself. I could not forgive you for this, Erik. You murdered my lovely sister and her little children. For this, I want and demand revenge. In the last few years, you have sent men, women and children to their death. If they did not die in the gas chambers, they died of starvation or disease. You have made the Jews the object of your hate. It made no difference to you whether they were rich or poor, young or old. If they were Jews, they were destined to die. Is this not true, Erik?"

"I cannot deny what you say I did, Sarah, but I hope you believe me when I tell you that I never *hated* any Jews. I was merely following orders."

"Orders, you say, orders! Alright, I will accept that. I will also accept the fact that you executed all Jews regardless of position or age. But if Erik Byrnes believes so strongly in the extermination of the Jewish people, and if he makes no exceptions, then I must find out if it is true that his own wife and children may have Jewish blood. If they do, I am sure Erik would want to know this, so that he could eliminate these Jewish swine from the face of the earth. And if Erik Byrnes would take no action out of sympathy towards his family, then perhaps I would see to it that his superiors would. Tell me, Erik. Is your wife a Jew?"

"Of course not, Sarah. She had a complete background check done before we were married. That is standard procedure."

"Yes, I would have expected nothing less, but if that's true, why did Marie's mother avoid me so when my cousin called her, and why did your wife and you play games with him when he called, unless you had something to hide?"

"Ridiculous, just ridiculous, Sarah. You should know that we just don't answer such questions over the phone. That is why I asked your cousin to come and see me in person."

There was no response. She apparently did not believe me.

"What made you call me today, Sarah, and what possessed you to identify yourself?"

"It became clear to me that the approach I used would never get this information from either of you. I then decided that I should call you. At least, I would make you pay for what you did by making you always think that perhaps someday someone in the Reich Hierarchy would find out about that skeleton in your closet."

I didn't know what to say to her. An apology, I'm sure, would have done no good.

"What are you going to do now, Sarah?"

"I will tell you exactly what I intend to do. As you are fully aware, a Jew such as myself could never walk into the SS offices and lodge a complaint against someone like you. I am sure that I would be arrested within seconds, and deported to my death. You did a good job, Erik, when you had me hidden. To this date, nobody knows where I am or where I live. For all practical purposes, I have disappeared from the face of the earth. No great loss. I am only a Jew."

She must have forgotten that Dieter knew where she was.

"But I can write a letter, and I plan to. By this time next week, my letter will be in the hands of the SS in Berlin. Hopefully, they will then conduct the accurate background check into your wife's past that you prevented me from doing."

"Sarah, if your suspicions about Marie's parents are correct, don't you understand what you would be doing to her and my children?"

"Yes, I have thought long and hard about that, Erik. Unfortunate as it might be, I decided that if exposing you and your family can save thousands of Jewish lives by eliminating you from your position, then what happens to your children and to Marie must be the price that has to be paid. They will suffer the same fate as millions of other Jews already have. Goodbye, Erik, or should I say, *Hangman.* I hope you rot in hell for what you have done and I hope that your children and your wife suffer in the gas chambers just like my family did..."

She then started to laugh hysterically until I could take it no more. I had to hang up the phone.

I had to stop her!

I dismissed my chauffeur and drove myself to Dieter's apartment. There was a light on in his flat. Frantically, I pounded on the door.

"Dieter, open up. Dieter, can you hear me?"

"Hang on, Erik. I'll be right there."

It seemed like an eternity until the door opened.

"Dieter, thank God you're home. I need to talk to you right away."

"What is it?"

"Dieter, it's Sarah, it's Sarah. She's the one making the calls!"

"Sarah? It can't be. You and she were very close. Impossible."

"No. It's true. She's gone mad, Dieter. She was laughing hysterically, telling me that I murdered her family. She wants revenge, Dieter, revenge. She's not going to stop now. She told me she is writing the SS and I'm afraid she is going to do so before our plans are put into effect. Dieter, you have to stop her."

"And how do you suggest I do that, Erik?"

"Go and find her. Find her and try to persuade her to stop. Tell her anything, but don't let her send the letter. You always were on good terms with her. The lives of Marie and the children are in your hands."

"I can try, Erik, but I can't guarantee success. What then?"

"Try, Dieter. Try. You must save my family!"

"Alright. I'll leave tonight. It isn't far. I will get a car tonight and call you in the morning."

"Thank you, Dieter. I won't forget this."

I left his apartment, shaking. If she wrote that letter and that investigator got a hold of it, he'd tie in Bach's murder. If Dieter couldn't persuade her to leave me alone, she might as well turn him in, too. Then not only would I and my family perish, but he would also, and Abraham as well.

The more and more I thought about it, the more and more I decided, right then and there, that I really had only one option. Even if Sarah told Dieter she would not send the letter, how could I be sure? I couldn't take that chance. Sarah and her cousin must be liquidated, immediately. I wouldn't let those *damn Jews* kill my family. I'd see them in hell before that happened. That ungrateful bitch! This was what I got for saving her life. I only wished I could be the one to put the bullet in her head!

I'd have to wait until Dieter called the next morning but, first thing, I had to arrange to have Abraham brought here. He had to know. I needed his guidance and help.

I couldn't sleep much at all that night. I tossed and turned, falling in and out of that awful semi-consciousness, when you know you're about to enter the world of nightmares, and you fight with all your might to escape by staying awake. All I could think about was how it would be if the Allies caught me after the war, how I would be interrogated, tried in a court where everyone knew verdict and punishment before the procedures were even completed. Marie and the children would, after some type of incarceration or house arrest, eventually be set free, if the Americans or British would capture them, that is, and not the Russians. I shuddered to think what would happen to Marie if she fell into the hands of thc bolsheviks, especially after what we Germans had done to the Russian women. Regardless of who captured and executed me, my family would be relegated to a life of poverty and exile, either forced or self-imposed.

It was only after hours of this painful turning and tossing that I fell asleep. I dreamt about how wonderful it would be if the escape were successful and how grand a time we would have in some small South American country lying on a warm beach, watching the children play in the sand. There Dieter and Abraham would join us.

The clock, striking five in the morning, woke me.

I was quiet because I didn't want to have to face Marie and lie to her about the events of the previous day and my plans for today.

I arrived early at the office. None of the staff had yet checked in. Fortunately, I was able to contact the officer in charge at the ghetto.

"Herr Untersturmführer, good morning. This is Sturmbannführer Byrnes."

"Heil Hitler, Herr Sturmbannführer. How can I be of service to you?"

"Heil Hitler. Do you know the Jew Abraham?"

"Yes, of course."

"I'm afraid we need him back here in Vienna. He has not told us all he knows about some irregularities in the ghetto."

"Do you want me to interrogate him, Herr Sturmbannführer? We have very effective techniques at our disposal."

"No, thank you. That stupid Jew seems to trust Schmidt and me. We can probably obtain this information quicker."

"As you wish. Besides, we have two hangings that I must supervise. I will be more than preoccupied with the *festivities*. Heil Hitler, Herr Sturmbannführer!"

I busied myself by going through old files that dealt mostly with Jews who had somehow managed to evade capture. Then it dawned on me! Quite frankly, I didn't care anymore. Now that my *career* would hopefully be coming to an end in the very near future, I saw no reason to cause more misery for some unfortunate Jew.

The seconds seemed like minutes, the minutes seemed like hours, and the hours seemed like an eternity while I waited impatiently for Dieter to call and for Abraham to arrive.

Then, the phone rang. It was Dieter.

"Dieter. How is everything going?"

"Not so good, Erik. Let me tell you. Is this line secure?"

"Yes, yes it is. Go on. What happened?"

"I got there too early so I pulled over, just outside town, and slept for a few hours. Once I got to the village, I had no trouble finding her. In fact, she hadn't moved from the place where I took her years ago. Fortunately, she held no animosity towards me and welcomed me in her home."

"Well then, what was the problem?"

"The problem started when I began to talk about you, Erik."

"What did she say?"

"It's not so much what she said. It's how she said it. There is no doubt in my mind, Erik, that she is not all there. She is clearly insane. She cannot be trusted. One minute she was telling me what a kind man you are and, seconds later, she starts screaming, calling you a hangman and a murderer."

"Did you find out what she's going to do about Marie and the children?"

"Yes, Erik, and it's not good."

"Well, what is it?"

"When I entered the kitchen, there, in full view, was a five-page letter addressed to the Reichsführer, no less."

"Are you sure it was the original and not a copy?"

"Yes, I am. Next to it was an envelope which had not yet been sealed. She told me she was going to send the letter tomorrow."

"Did you try to stop her, Dieter?"

"I tried everything. I told her you were a good family man and that what she would be doing would harm the children and Marie, not to mention her own friend, Marie's mother. At first, she agreed with me and said she would not turn them in. Then, two minutes later, she changed her mind. Even her cousin, you know, the one who made the calls to you, told her that perhaps it would be for the best that she forget about all of this. Again, at first she agreed and then it was like she forgot about everything she said before. You won't believe it, Erik. When I left, she told me to give her kisses to Marie and the children."

"Dieter, do you think she will mail the letter?"

"Yes, yes, I do, perhaps not now, but she will at *some* time mail that letter. I was tempted to take it from her but I thought it might be better to talk to you first."

"No, Dieter, you did the right thing. Taking the letter wouldn't have done any good. She just would have written another one after you left."

"What do you want me to do, Erik?"

"Let me think about it, Dieter. Call me back in a few hours, but keep her in your sight. If she goes near a mailbox, you have to stop her."

"I understand, Erik. I'll call you back."

"Erik, the Jew Abraham has arrived as you requested. He is under guard in the outer office."

"Thank you, Urma. Have him sent in and tell the guards to wait in the lobby."

Abraham entered the office and sat across from me. Urma closed the door behind him. "Good morning, Herr Sturmbannführer. How may I serve you?"

"By ceasing to exist along with the rest of the Jewish swine. But since that is not now possible, I will have to settle for explaining to you just what I need you to do for me."

It was only after I was sure nobody was listening that I told him about Sarah and what Dieter had found out.

"See what being kind to a Jew gets you, Erik?"

I was not amused.

"This is not a time for being funny, Abraham. Do you have any ideas?"

"Unfortunate as it might be, Sarah and her cousin will have to be eliminated. We have no other choice. We can't take the chance that she will carry out her threat."

"I hate to admit it, but I came to the same conclusion, Abraham. There is one problem, though."

"Don't tell me, Erik. I know what the problem is. Dieter hasn't the stomach for it."

"You're right, Abraham. You're absolutely right."

"Don't worry. I will take care of them for you, Erik."

"I hoped that you would offer, and somehow I knew that you would."

"How long of a drive is it to where she is?"

"Not far, but I'm not sure of the exact distance."

"It doesn't matter. When Dieter calls again, get exact directions and find out where he and I can meet. We will need a car and you will have to get rid of your guards."

"Do you want me to go to her house with you, Abraham?"

"No. It would be better if I dropped you off somewhere close by. I'll pick you up when it is all over. You'll need some different clothes."

"I have a set in my closet."

"And, Erik, I'll need your gun."

"Yes, I understand. When do you want to go?"

"As soon as Dieter calls. In the meantime, do you think you could get me a decent meal? Things are very bad in the ghetto and, frankly, I haven't had anything to eat for two days."

"Certainly."

151

I phoned the kitchen and ordered a meal to be brought up, ostensibly for me. It was topped off with a bottle of the wine that I kept in the credenza behind my desk. Toasting to the success of today's plan, I joined Abraham in a drink, making sure that I left only one used glass afterwards.

"It's Dieter on the line," Urma informed me.

"Put him right through. Thank you."

"Erik. It's Dieter. What's the plan?"

"Give me directions to where you are now, Dieter, and just wait for me. I'm leaving as soon as we hang up."

I decided not to tell him that Abraham would be accompanying me. He might wonder why. Within the hour, we left to meet him.

19

Goodbye, Old Friend

IT was late in the afternoon when we arrived at Elevas, the village where Dieter hid hidden Sarah so well. The weather was brisk and cool.

"Pull over in this alley, behind the tavern, Erik."

I did as he told me.

"Now it's my turn to drive. Hand me your pistol and change your clothes. It would seem out of place to have an SS Sturmbannführer drinking alone in a strange village."

I handed him my Luger and changed clothes as he directed.

"I'm sure it will be at least an hour, if not longer, before I return. I'll give Dieter some excuse why I am here instead of you. He will give me no problem I can't handle. He can show me exactly where Sarah lives. I'll come back here when it is all over."

"Thank you, Abraham. Thank you. I hope you won't have any problems with Dieter. He worries me, you know."

"He worries me too, Erik, but I'll *make* him understand."

"I know he loves my daughters dearly, but murder? I don't know what his reaction will be."

"He won't find out, Erik. After he shows me the home, I will send him somewhere else to wait for me. It will all work out. Trust me. Now, let me get to work."

As Abraham drove away, I marveled at how I put my fate into the hands of this Jew without asking any questions. It was as if we were *equals*.

The bar was typical of those found all across Greater Germany. I found a corner table and positioned myself against the wall. The bar maid brought me a large stein of beer and a bowl of pretzels.

There were only two other patrons besides myself. They were both in their sixties or seventies and, naturally, they spoke quite loud. I could hear every word they said as they stood against the stand-up bar talking about the war. They made several quick glances in my direction, a sign of the times. One did not trust one's neighbor, let alone a stranger in their local bar.

They were obviously worried about the eventual outcome of the war. One said he had a grandson in the Wehrmacht. The boy was at the Russian Front and the news was not good. The other said the Reich should free all the Jews on condition that they take up arms against the Russians. Hitler would then have the necessary manpower to match the Russian hordes. I chuckled silently. That very idea had been tossed around for the last year or so, only to be vetoed by Himmler on some ridiculous *philosophical* ground.

I ordered another stein and suddenly, for no obvious reason, I became very nervous and apprehensive. Sweat was pouring down my forehead. Were Sarah and her cousin alive this very moment? Perhaps Abraham was actually talking her out of turning Marie and my daughters in? Perhaps Abraham and Dieter had been caught by the police?

An hour and a half had passed and still no Abraham. I was on my fifth beer. A few more patrons had joined the two old men at the bar. Again, the talk was mostly of the war, and now the conversation centered on how the Jews were to blame for all that had happened.

Just then, I heard several beeps from an automobile horn. They came from the direction of the alley where Abraham had dropped me off. I waited a minute or so and then the horn sounded again.

I decided I had better go, and I left how I had entered.

It was Abraham, and he was alone.

"Hurry up, Erik. Get in. We have no time to waste!"

I got in the car and barely got the door closed when he sped away. Abraham was nervous, constantly looking over his shoulders.

"Is it over? Is she dead? What happened? Where is Dieter?"

"Wait until we get on the main highway. Then I'll tell you what happened."

Once we were several kilometers from the village and on the roadway heading back to Vienna, Abraham seemed to relax a bit.

"I've never seen you so upset before. You have to tell me."

"After I picked up Dieter, he insisted that he come with me to Sarah's home. I could not get rid of him. I think he thought he would be helpful. We met with Sarah and her cousin. We talked for about an hour. I explained to her that I was a Jew and that you had been kind to me. I told her that, SS or not, I did not want to see you or any member of your family get hurt. At first, I thought she would agree, but as Dieter had said before, she changed her mind within minutes. Nothing I or Dieter or even her cousin could do seemed to make any difference. I even picked up the letter and ripped it up in front of her. She laughed and said she would write another letter as soon as we had left. I had no choice, Erik."

When he said those words, even though I knew very well what he meant, shivers went down my spine, and my stomach felt as if I were going to throw up.

"I didn't have much time to spare. We had already been there too long and who knows who might have seen us or who might visit. I gave her one more chance, this time leaving little doubt about my purpose in being there if she didn't agree. Her cousin knew very well what would happen. He yelled at her. Dieter yelled at her. But it only made her laugh more. It was only then that I pulled out your Luger and shot her."

I felt a bit of remorse for Sarah, but better her than me and my family.

"Erik, after I shot Sarah, I turned the Luger on her cousin because I had to, but before I could pull the trigger, Dieter jumped me. We struggled. The gun flew out of my hand. I crawled to it, picked it up and shot the Jew. Dieter backed off. He just stood there, crying and asking me, 'Why, why?' I didn't know what to say, Erik. I just stood there and watched. After a few seconds, he ran past me towards the back door. I couldn't take any chances that he would tell the authorities. I shot him, Erik. I shot Dieter when he reached the door."

"You shot Dieter! My God! Is he..."

"I don't know. I think so, but I couldn't stick around and find out. The shots were loud enough, Erik. I was afraid that I would be caught. How would I explain how a Jew managed to get here and murder an SS officer and two other Jews? Besides, it was your gun and I was afraid that if I were caught, it would be traced back to you. Dieter took the shot square in the back, and although he was moaning when I left, I guess he died shortly thereafter, hopefully before anyone else arrived."

I was still in shock, thinking about Dieter.

Then I looked at Abraham. I could not be angry with him. I knew he did not intend to hurt Dieter. I gently put my arm on his shoulder.

"Dear friend, I know how bad you feel and I also know you did the best you could, not only for me, but also for my family. I mean it with all my heart."

"I know you do, Erik, but now is not the time for sentimentality. You will no doubt be questioned about Dieter's murder."

"I'm not concerned about that. I have a perfect excuse. I will tell them that Dieter himself requested permission and that I only agreed to it. I didn't know the purpose of his going there."

"That's not all of it, Erik. That investigator Strasser is going to come right back to Vienna when he hears about this. Do you realize that within a short period of time both of your second-in-commands have been murdered? Isn't that somewhat suspicious?"

My reaction was strange, to say the least. I started to laugh.

With perspiration still beating down his brow, Abraham turned towards me with a menacing glare.

"What in Jehovah's name could be so funny, Erik? This is not going to be easy to beat."

"I'm laughing, Abraham, because I know that within days I'll be gone and the young SS officer, perhaps even the Führer himself, will wonder what has happened to me, why I was the third target. First Bach, then Dieter, then poor Erik Byrnes and his fine family. I wonder who they will ultimately blame for all of this. Abraham, I want you to go with us to South America."

"I was hoping you would ask. Yes, my friend. I will go with you. Thank you. Thank you very much." For the first time since we left that village, Abraham smiled. I only prayed that the SS was not waiting to arrest us as we arrived.

It was getting towards the end of the day as we drove into the SS garage. Nothing seemed out of the ordinary.

"Luck is with us, Erik. Perhaps the bodies have not yet been discovered."

The car came to a stop, and I motioned for the guard to come forward.

"Take charge of this Jew and see to it that he is fed and taken back to the ghetto tonight."

The guard acknowledged and Abraham was taken away. I decided to go to my office and see if anything had happened.

Urma was just getting ready to leave when I entered.

"Oh, you're back, Erik. I was beginning to get worried. For the life of me, I'll never understand why you insist on traveling with that Jew and no guards. You should be more careful."

"He's harmless, Urma, and besides, I learn a lot of valuable information just from talking to him."

She shrugged her shoulders and smiled.

"Oh, Erik, Obersturmbannführer Eichmann called. You must call him back tomorrow. By the way, Erik, you don't know where Dieter is, do you? He's been gone all day! I am really beginning to get worried."

"I'm not quite sure where he is, Urma, but I guess he'll be back soon."

"Well, I certainly hope so. You know, he needs either a mother or a wife to take care of him, such a lonely man. Good night, Erik."

"Good night, Urma."

I shut the door behind her and sat down at my desk. Looking at the calendar, I could see where I had circled my vacation. Soon I would be free from this job, one way or the other.

It was almost six, and I was very tired, so I decided to go home. I called down to the motor pool and asked them to ready a car and a driver. I put the Luger in my briefcase and replaced it with the spare I kept at the office. Just as I entered the lot, a black Mercedes with the familiar SS flags screeched to a halt not more than ten feet from me.

"Herr Sturmbannführer, forgive me for this intrusion. I have terrible news to report."

Fortunately for me, the SS officer was too agitated to see my hands shaking. What if they searched my briefcase and found the gun?

"Yes, what is it?"

"It is Obersturmführer Schmidt, sir. He has been murdered."

"Dieter! No! How did this happen?" I asked, faking utter surprise and shock.

"I can only tell you what I know. In the village of Elevas, a local police officer reported that one of our vehicles had been spotted for many hours, and that it was parked near a residential area of the village. It was determined that the car had been checked out to Schmidt. We then enlisted the assistance of the local police, who did a house to house search in the neighborhood. After some time, Obersturmführer Schmidt was found, shot to death, along with two Jews."

As much as I hated it, I knew that I must ask more questions.

"Were you able to find any evidence about the killer, and why was Dieter found with two Jews? They *must* have had a part in his death."

"I don't know, sir. But there was something quite strange."

"And what would that be?"

"He was not wearing his uniform nor did he carry any identification on him. If the officer with me had not found his SS tattoo, we still might not have known who he was. Do you know, sir, why he would have behaved this way?"

"No, I don't. You must forgive me now. Dieter was a dear friend of mine and this upsets me terribly."

"I understand, Herr Sturmbannführer. Please, try not to worry. I placed a call to SS Intelligence in Berlin. They are sending Hauptsturmführer Horst Strasser here. He will arrive tomorrow by plane. I'm sure he will get to the bottom of this. Good night, sir."

Marie was in the bedroom packing some items we would need for our *vacation* when I entered the room. Her back was towards me. I called out her name. She sensed the urgency in my voice, and turned.

"Erik, what's wrong?"

"Sit down, Marie. I have some bad news to tell you."

She waited for me to speak.

"Dieter is dead."

At first she looked stunned, but when I went on to tell her what had happened, her sorrow turned into anger.

"How could you let this happen? Why Dieter? Why, Erik?"

"Abraham had no choice, Marie. He only did it to protect us and the children. What if Dieter had gone to the authorities? What would we have done?"

"I can't believe he would have done that, Erik. Shooting him was not necessary!"

"Damn it, Marie. How can you say that? You weren't there. Don't you think I feel guilty? Dieter was a good friend."

"*Ja*, some good friend! First you had him sent away. Then when you needed him to help you after Bach's death, you sent for him. This time when you thought he might interfere with another plan, you had him killed!"

"My plan! I thought this was *our* plan, yours and mine and that of Louisa and Susanne. Would you rather have had Dieter turn us in?"

"Erik, I told you before, you know damn well that he would never have done that. You sent that maniac Abraham, knowing full well that he would kill him if he thought he had to. What's the matter? Couldn't you have gone yourself? No, since you are a Sturmbannführer in the SS you have others do your killing for you."

I didn't know what to say to her. Some of what she said was true, but I also knew that she didn't really feel the hate that she now expressed to me. Deep down, she *had* to understand that nothing must interfere with my plan, or else we were all doomed.

There was no point in continuing this discussion. She would change her mind after she had a chance to think this all over. Once we were free, she would understand that Abraham and I only did what we had to do.

As I lay in bed that evening, my thoughts drifted to Dieter. I remembered that first day I met him on the train. How handsome and dashing I thought he was! I suspect it was because of him that I decided to join the SS. I admired his lifestyle, the travel, the excitement, and the intrigue.

He became a good friend, my best friend, not just to me but to my wife and especially to my children. How they would miss him, and how I would miss those old times when we hoisted a beer.

Those days were now gone.

As I entered the outer office, I heard an all too familiar voice. "Good morning, Herr Sturmbannführer. Are you surprised to see me so soon before Budapest?"

It was Strasser.

"No, Herr Hauptsturmführer, to tell you the truth, I fully expected to see you sometime today."

"Just doing my duty. Just doing my duty. There is nothing personal involved."

"I presume you are here to investigate the murder of Dieter Schmidt. Am I correct?"

"Yes, you are, Erik. May I please call you Erik?"

I nodded in agreement.

"Herr Eichmann informed me not to bother you with the investigation into Bach's death now that you were needed in Budapest. I suspected he would say the same thing about the death of Schmidt, so I decided not to bother the Obersturmbannführer. I spoke directly to Himmler himself. He authorized and directed me to investigate this matter fully, irrespective of your impending departure and your very busy schedule. Do you have any objections, Herr Sturmbannführer?"

"Of course not. I will give you whatever time I can, but I hope you know that I am scheduled for a vacation in a few days."

"Yes, I am. Somebody told me. So, if you're ready, let us get right to it."

I laughed to myself, knowing that he would never have enough time to piece together the puzzle before my departure.

"I am informed that Dieter Schmidt left Vienna the day before he was murdered, presumably to carry out an assignment authorized by you. Is that correct?"

"You are half correct. I did know Dieter was leaving but I didn't ask about the specifics. I now regret having done that."

"Please, Herr Sturmbannführer, don't be hard on yourself. I'm sure I will get to the bottom of this. The murdering of SS officers is becoming more commonplace as the war continues, and the Reichsführer is adamant about finding and punishing those responsible, whoever they might be."

What did he mean by *whoever they might be*?

"Erik, within the last year, two SS officers directly under your command have been murdered. I must say this is very unusual. In both cases, Jews figure into the picture somehow. Bach was murdered near a Jewish ghetto and we found Schmidt in a home that was occupied by Jews."

"Do you know the Jews who were found with Schmidt?" I hoped to God he didn't find out that one of the Jews was my old secretary!

"No, Erik, not yet. Their papers passed them on as Aryans, but from a physical examination we know that the male was not. We don't know yet the true identity of the female."

I felt chilled and I'm sure that all color drained from my face.

There was a momentary silence.

"Herr Sturmbannführer, you don't look too well. Are you alright?"

"I'm fine. Just continue."

"I told you before, Herr Sturmbannführer, that I believe you know more than you are telling me. This applies not only to Bach's death but now to that of Schmidt as well. Why, I don't know yet, but I am sure you were at least indirectly involved in some way in each of the assassinations. I know you didn't actually commit the murder, but my gut feeling tells me you know who did and why."

I knew I had to take the offensive.

"Herr Hauptsturmführer, your statements are highly offensive. But if I must respond, I would like to ask you why. What makes you believe that I am involved?"

"Just call it intuition. That's all I can say at this time."

I feigned indignation.

He simply ignored it. "Answer me one question, Herr Sturmbannführer. Do you know any reason why both of these men made their trips alone and without any security?"

"Obviously they must have wanted secrecy. Why else?"

Strasser smiled.

"No, I don't think so. I rather believe it was *you*, Herr Sturmbannführer, who wanted complete secrecy. These men were each on a clandestine operation involving Jews. I believe you had a major role in these missions and I also believe you have some involvement with the Jews other than your position as Sturmbannführer. I can't prove it now, but perhaps I will after I question the Jew Abraham, who I understand is frequently around here. All I need is time."

160

Time! That was what I needed too. If I could only put him off for less than a week. Perhaps it would be best if Abraham *disappeared* for awhile? I had to be very careful. If things went as planned, by this time next week it would seem that I was the next mysterious murder victim. Perhaps Herr Strasser would then investigate *my* death as well.

He began to gather his belongings.

"Before you leave, Herr Strasser, I want you to know that you are totally wrong about me. I *want* you to investigate this matter fully. Perhaps then you will believe me."

"We shall see, Herr Sturmbannführer. We shall see. But forgive me, I have taken too much of your time already. Till we meet again, hopefully sooner than later. Let me see. You are going to The Kasdorf, aren't you? Lovely place. I have been there myself. Heil Hitler."

I returned the salute and closed the door behind him. It was quite obvious that it would not be long before this bright officer found out the truth. We had only a few days to go. I hoped that neither Abraham nor myself were arrested before we left. I really should see Abraham one more time.

But, how? Would Strasser be watching?

20

Farewell, Austria

THE mood at the office was very somber. Dieter was very well liked. I left the funeral arrangements to Urma, because Dieter had no close family that we knew of and I had more important tasks to attend to regarding my departure. Urma would make sure everything was properly handled in true SS spirit.

For the past week, I had received daily memorandums from Eichmann with details about the planned deportations from Budapest. The magnitude of the project was impressive, even to me. Hundreds of thousands of Jews were scheduled to be liquidated! There would be no temporary internments in ghettos or transit camps such as the model camp Theresienstadt. With the Russians moving steadily westward, there was simply not enough time. The Hungarian Jews would be taken directly to Auschwitz/Birkenau.

Eichmann emphazised that this project must be completed as soon as possible because international pressure was now mounting to end the Jewish transports. Nations that had been neutral until now, such as Spain and Portugal, and even countries that formerly sided with Germany, such as Bulgaria, could see the handwriting on the wall, and were calling for Germany to cease this carnage. Even the formerly silent Vatican suddenly began to critize the Reich.

To indicate just how badly the war was going, the Reich was now *trading* Jews, or negotiating such trades, for supplies such as trucks, clothing, soap and so forth. Germany would never have succumbed to such depths if the war effort weren't proceeding very badly. Personally, I felt such negotiations were demeaning and not worthy of the SS, but since I would soon no longer be a party to this madness, I decided to give the topic no further thought.

Father and Theresa would arrive tomorrow morning in time for the funeral and, of course, I would be leaving Vienna for good the following day. This afternoon, I would take the chance to make my final trip to Kovnas to visit Abraham and address the Judenrat one last time.

As usual, I would give them the standard speech threatening them and their families if they did not continue to cooperate and, of course, I planned to assure them that those who would be deported would find life easier in the East.

Finally, I would inform them that this was our last meeting together because I would soon be transferred to Budapest, but they should not worry since the new officer in charge would continue my policies and work with Abraham.

For one final time, the Judenrat stood at attention when I entered the meeting room. It pleased me to see just how visibly shaken they were to learn that soon another would be in command. It made sense, though. After all, I had kept my word, and none of them, or the Jewish police, or any of their families had been deported while I was in charge.

Perhaps they were also upset because of rumors about the total liquidation of ghettos in Warsaw and Lodz, and the eventual deportations and even murders of the Judenrat and Jewish police who had served the Reich so well. I tried to assure them that they and their families were perfectly safe.

When the meeting was over, I excused my guards, saying that I needed to meet alone with the head of the Judenrat, to discuss the transition which would take place with the new SS Sturmbannführer.

Before the other Jews left, they handed me a small engravement in Dieter's memory. Obviously, they had considered him a kind man.

When Abraham and I were alone, he informed me that on the day of our abduction, we would be taken in open view of the guests. I would be struck and the four of us would be thrown into a waiting car and whisked away. Evidence would be left at the *crime* scene suggesting that Italian partisans had committed the act. If anyone got in the way, they would of course be killed.

As promised, I gave him the remaining money he had requested and he stuffed it in his shoe.

"The next time I see you will be at the farm house, dear friend. Try to convince Marie not to worry. Everything will go as planned."

"I sincerely hope so, Abraham. In the meantime, try to stay hidden if you can. Investigator Strasser has come back again and he said he was going to question you."

"Thanks for letting me know, Erik. I will make sure that I disappear. For all our sake, I can't be detained. One more thing, Erik. When your abductors try to take you, make sure you act surprised and try to resist. The kidnappers expect you to hit back so that any witness can report your struggle."

It was a cold and dreary day when Marie, Father, Theresa, the children and I entered the funeral hall.

We took places in the front row. Those who knew Dieter well, including myself, gave short eulogies. I never hated myself as much as I did then.

Marie cried uncontrollably, together with Susanne and Louisa who sensed their mother's sorrow. Father, too, had tears in his eyes. Only Theresa did not seem visibly moved.

The procession took us to a small cemetery outside Vienna. I had purchased a site for Dieter next to a grove of trees and a small stream. He would enjoy his rest there.

Farewell, old friend!

After it was over, we returned to my home in silence. Father went straight to the living room and sat in my favorite chair, just gazing at the wall. Theresa joined Marie and the children in the kitchen while I stayed with Father.

Soon, he broke the silence.

"You know, Erik, I truly did love Dieter. He so reminded me of you. I hope he rests well."

"I will miss him, too. I never had such a good friend."

Unexpectedly, a smile crossed Father's face.

"Erik, Marie has told me of your vacation plans. Heaven knows you and the family deserve it. The Kasdorf is a lovely place and although I have never been there myself, I know people who have and they tell me how grand it is. Of course, that was in a time of peace, so I hope the war has not changed it too much."

I wanted so much to tell Father what was going to happen, but if I did, and he and Theresa were interrogated by the SS, could they stand the inquiry? Before I had a chance to think about it any longer, Theresa sat down next to me.

"I wish I was an SS Sturmbannführer. Maybe then I could go on a vacation also?"

We all laughed.

"No, Theresa, you don't want to be an SS officer. It would be too boring for you."

Her tone became more serious.

"Well, that much is true. After all, you don't get to see the British and American bombers fly over Berlin and drop thousands of bombs on each raid. For God's sake, Erik, when is the Führer going to put a stop to all of this?"

I was taken aback by her question. Never before had she even hinted at doubts about Germany's handling of the war. Never before had she ever inferred that Hitler was mishandling anything.

"Theresa, these are very difficult times. Germany and the few allies that we still have are fighting on three fronts, in the East against the Russians, in the West against the British and Americans, and in the South again against the British and the Americans. I can tell you this. The Führer's scientists are very close to final development of *super weapons* which will immediately change the tide of the war. Keep your faith, Theresa. You won't be disappointed."

What good did it do for any of us if I told her the truth? I knew that these super weapons were merely the V-1 and V-2 rockets. They were very impressive, but they did little damage. What very few of us knew, but what Eichmann once told me, was that Germany was in the process of developing a new bomb, one that worked on the principle of nuclear fission. It was said that there was an underground fortress, like a small city, built into and under the mountains, where this work was going on. Unfortunately, Jews such as Einstein who had left the Reich before the war were probably helping the Americans beat the Germans in the race for the atomic bomb.

"But let's not spend the short time we have together discussing the war, Theresa. Why don't the four of us play a game of pinochle, like we used to do before? Dieter would have wanted it that way."

Father agreed.

"Yes, Erik. That's a good idea. Come on, Marie. Join us!"

The four of us spent the rest of the afternoon trying to be happy like we were before it all began.

After we finished playing, Father took me aside.

"Erik, I didn't want to say anything before, but what did you mean when you said 'the short time we have together?'"

I hesitated.

"Father, what I really meant is that I will be taking a new position in Budapest, as I told you. I doubt if I will have as much free time as I do now. That's all I meant."

"Son, ever since you were a little boy I could tell when you weren't telling the truth. You're not telling me everything now. Are you?"

I got up and walked around the room. After a minute or so, I looked at him.

"Father, I can say only this. No matter what, don't believe any rumors you might hear while we are on vacation. It may be some time before we speak again, but don't worry. Marie, the children and myself will be fine. For your own good and that of Theresa, don't ask me any more questions because I won't tell you any more. Just remember that we all love you and Theresa, and that we will be alright."

We drove Father and Theresa to the train station for their journey back to Berlin. I worried about them. Even passenger train travel was now subject to Allied bombing.

Father and Theresa hugged the children and then Marie and myself. It seemed as though Father did not want to let us go.

"Come on, Father, let's go. You'll see Erik again and I don't want to miss our train."

I shook his hand and he hugged me once more. There were tears in his eyes, and in mine as well.

"Goodbye, son. I love you."

Would I ever see them again?

The children and Marie sat in my outer office while I finished signing various orders before boarding the 10:00 AM train which would take us to a village near The Kasdorf.

"Erik, don't forget now. I don't want you to take any work with you. This is a vacation, remember!"

"Yes, Urma. I understand. Believe me. I have taken no files with me."

"Don't worry about anything. If something really important comes up, I will call you."

As I closed the door behind me, I looked around for one last time. I would have loved to take some things with me, but no, I would leave everything just the way it was. No changes whatsoever.

"What lovely children you have, Frau Byrnes. I can tell that they are very excited about their vacation."

It was Horst Strasser!

"Herr Byrnes, I see you are all ready to leave. I hope you have a good time. Before you entered the room, I told your lovely wife that I will be calling on her in Budapest."

"Oh, is that so?"

"You have no objection, do you, Herr Sturmbannführer?"

"Not at all. When we are settled down in Budapest, I promise to call you immediately."

He nodded, and that same crafty smile crossed his lips. Little did the son-of-a-bitch know that I would never be seeing his face again.

To reach the Kasdorf, one had to travel nearly three-quarters the length of Austria from Vienna. The train ride through my Austrian countryside was exquisite, to say the least. The rolling farm fields and the ancient villages were postcard-pretty. When we arrived at the village, we disembarked and waited for a pre-arranged Gestapo car to take us to our hotel. I looked around and noticed, from the corner of my eye, a group of what appeared to be students, with books in hand, seemingly doing nothing else but passing the time.

I felt they were out of place. They appeared to be too old to be in school. As I made eye contact, one of the men in the group smiled at me. I suspected, then, that they were not there for leisure but rather to check if I had arrived in time.

Just yesterday I had been told that Eichmann had, for security purposes, insisted that I have an SS escort. I had tried to persuade him that, once I had arrived, I would be safe and that we needed no further protection, but because of the present political turmoil and the deaths of Bach and Dieter he did not agree. Neither Abraham or I had seriously considered this possibility.

The drive to the hotel took less than an hour.

As a standard procedure, before allowing me or my family to enter the room, the SS guards made sure the room itself was safe and free from bombs, eavesdropping devices, or entry from the outside.

The problem I now foresaw was how to get rid of these guards. How would we get *kidnapped* with them around?

The room was lovely and smelled of sweet incense. There was a double bed for Marie and myself and one for the girls.

Louisa and Susanne were so happy. They giggled and hugged me and Marie over and over again, thanking us for this wonderful vacation. I wondered what they would have thought if they knew they were Jewish and did not *belong* in a place like this.

The SS guards had two rooms of their own, one on each side of mine. I had to come up immediately with a plan so we would be free of them.

It took us about an hour to unpack and get everything set in place. The girls had seen the indoor pool, and they insisted that Marie take them there. I had purchased some water toys for them, so off they went.

It was very strange indeed to be alone in this room, knowing that the four of us would soon be the subject of a massive manhunt. The local newspapers would speak of the SS Sturmbannführer who was brutally kidnapped along with his family. There would be stories in the papers telling how I resisted this foul act and how I was beaten into submission. Follow-up stories would appear each day reporting the progress of the investigation. Within days, I assumed, an article would appear blaming Italian partisans for the crime. Then, after a thorough SS investigation, we would hopefully all be presumed dead, the target of the partisans.

As I gazed out the window, I saw my SS guards, but only two of them. The others must have gone with Marie and the children.

I too checked the room out for eavesdropping devices, but for those the *SS* might have installed. I found none.

I went down to the pool area and sat there while Marie and the children played in the water. I looked at the other guests. They were obviously wealthy Europeans, perhaps industrialists, doctors, lawyers, and other professional folks, seemingly not touched by the war. They probably knew even better than I that it would soon be over. Since they likely belonged to no political party, they would merely re-group after the Allies had taken over and start anew.

Many of the guests stared at me and my family. It was obvious that I carried a position of some importance because SS guards were not commonplace for the average guest. I decided I would let them guard us for the rest of the day. As soon as I could, I would call Eichmann and beg him to order their removal.

We had spent about an hour by the pool when Marie suggested we stop in at the restaurant for something to eat. This sounded like a good idea and perhaps after dinner I would have an opportunity to talk to her alone. I was sure she needed to talk just as much as I did, to go over what in all likelihood would happen tomorrow.

We went to our room and changed for dinner. Both girls dressed in cute identical outfits. It was hard to tell them apart.

"I think I will have the marinated veal and, for dessert, chocolate cake."

"That sounds delicious, Erik. I will join you."

The four SS officers sat in the corner, obviously also having a good time. There was a small band playing Swiss music, much to my delight. For awhile, I almost forgot where I was and what would soon happen.

My happiness did not last long. At first, I only noticed that all four SS men quickly stood to attention. Then I noticed why.

It was Strasser! He had followed us! What was he doing here? Why had he come?

"Herr Byrnes, Frau Byrnes, how is your vacation going? This is a wonderful place. I hope you and your children enjoy your time here."

Taking me aside, he continued, "Obersturmbannführer Eichmann was very concerned about your safety, and so was I, Erik. Two deaths under mysterious circumstances worried both of us a great deal. He personally asked me to come here to supervise your escorts. I can assure you that nothing will interfere with your vacation. I will keep you and your family under close watch. I hope this does not offend you."

I replied with sarcasm.

"For your information, Herr Hauptsturmführer, I didn't ask for the four escorts who I am saddled with already and, yes, I will be candid with you. It does offend me. How do you expect me to have any time alone with my family when the five of you are constantly following us around?"

"Forgive me, Erik. As I said, it's not my doing. Eichmann needs your presence in Budapest, and he insisted on it. Don't worry, we will make every effort not to get in your way."

He made a short bow to Marie and the children and walked back to join the others at their table. Marie was visibly shaken while the children made little of his appearance. I didn't believe his suggestion that it was all Eichmann's doing.

"Don't worry, Marie. I have a plan. When we get back to the room, I will call Eichmann. He is a family man. I think I will be able to persuade him to call off the guards, at least long enough for us to make our escape." I then sent Marie off with the children to explore the resort, reminding her to stay indoors.

"Herr Obersturmbannführer, this is Erik, Erik Byrnes."

"Hello, Erik! Why in the world are you calling me at this hour of the evening and on your vacation, no less? Is it because you have found a family of Jews that we somehow missed?"

I was forced to utter a short laugh at Eichmann's joke.

"No, Herr Obersturmbannführer. No Jews. Just annoying SS guards, led by Strasser."

"Yes, yes, I know, Erik. Please forgive me. I just didn't want to take any chances that you or your family might get hurt, and Strasser convinced me that this was the right move."

"Forgive me, sir. I must ask you to reconsider. This is the only vacation I have taken in years. My wife is very upset about this intrusion on our privacy. It was difficult enough for me to convince her to accept the move to Budapest. Now this! I'm very much afraid that if this continues, I will have nothing but difficulties with her when we return. I know how much you want me to succeed in my new job and I hope you know how much I too want to succeed. But how can I perform to my fullest when my family is in disarray?"

There was silence on the other line. I knew he was considering my request.

"Erik, here is a compromise. The four SS guards will be withdrawn. Strasser will remain, but not in uniform. Does this sound alright to you and Marie?"

I paused. This would not be so bad. Strasser was only one man and I was sure my abductors could overpower him if necessary, or preferably kill him if he got in the way. Who knows?

"Thank you, Herr Obersturmbannführer. I'm sure that will be just fine with Marie. Thank you again."

"Think nothing of it, Erik. I should have given the matter more thought in the first place. I will take care of it immediately."

"Heil Hitler."

"Heil Hitler."

After Marie had returned with the children, we put them to bed and they fell asleep. Then I had a chance to tell her the good news.

"Marie, I called Eichmann. When we awake tomorrow, all the guards will be gone except for Strasser. Alone, he should not present any serious problem."

I thought that Marie would be happy to hear this news.

"Do you know, Erik, it has finally dawned on me."

"What has?"

"Do you know that we will never see our home again? We will never see Berlin again. Nor will we likely ever see our parents or any other family. You were at least able to see your father and Theresa at Dieter's funeral. I had to settle with a phone call to say goodbye."

"A phone call? When did you call your parents, Marie?" I tried not to sound worried.

"Well, I called the night before we left."

"What did you tell them?"

"I told them about our trip..."

"But you told me that you told them about our trip before. Why tell them again? Did you tell them anything about what was going to happen?"

She hesitated. I knew she had told them *something*.

"Marie, tell me. I *know* you told them something. I have to know what you said. Our lives and that of our children might depend on it."

"It was nothing, Erik. Nothing at all, honest." I was getting agitated. "Tell me!"

"Erik, all I told them was that we might not see them for a long, long time." She became distressed. "Is that why that investigator came here?"

170

"No, Marie, of course not. If he knew what we were doing, we would have all been arrested by now. He may suspect, but he doesn't know, I am sure. I promise you he will not get in our way."

"Oh, Erik, even if we succeed, we will have to start all over again with a new life and a new identity."

"I know, Marie, but it will be better. Don't you see? There will be no more killings, no more guilt, no more fear that you and the girls will be exposed by the SS."

"You're right, Erik. I know you're right. I think that I'm just scared about what is going to happen tomorrow."

"Don't be. You know it is all make-believe. Remember, the kidnappers are really *our friends*. You will see. Everything will turn out as it should."

I slept well that night and woke up to the laughter of children. They were running back and forth jumping on and off the bed that Marie and I shared.

"Come on, Papa. Come on, Mama. Let's go eat at the restaurant."

The girls started to drag us out of the bed, Susanne on my arm and Louisa on Marie's.

"Girls, you go downstairs with your father. I will be down as soon as I straighten up the room."

I got dressed in no time, and the girls raced out of the room, with me right behind.

"Don't take too long, Marie, and remember, take only what we absolutely need."

I raced down the halls with the girls in the lead. By the time we reached the lower level, I had won the chase.

"You girls have to get lots bigger before you can beat me in a race."

"It's not fair, Papa," Susanne shrieked. "You have bigger feet and legs than we do"

I smiled and took them by the hand into the restaurant. We sat by a window table and waited for Marie. It didn't take her long to arrive. She wasn't alone.

She was walking with Strasser, heading straight towards our table.

"Join us, Herr Strasser."

"Why, thank you, Herr Byrnes. I would like the company."

"Are you a married man, Herr Strasser?" Marie asked.

"No, I am not, Frau Byrnes. I have only my mother who lives in Nuremberg."

"She must be very proud of you," I said to him.

"Yes, so she has said. And what are your names, little girls?"

Giggling, they answered, "I'm Louisa," "and I'm Susanne."

"Very lovely daughters you both have. Who would you say they take after the most, Frau Byrnes?"

Marie hesitated, then, after looking at me, "Why, I think they take after Erik the most, don't you, Herr Strasser?"

"I'm not sure you are right, Frau Byrnes. They do have your husband's blond hair, but they also have your dark eyes. Your eyes, just like theirs, are *unique*, to say the least."

"Herr Strasser, I hope you are not too upset that I contacted Obersturmbannführer Eichmann."

"Well, I must admit that at first I was. But after I thought about it a little longer, I decided that his order to leave you and your family in peace was far more agreeable to me than to keep track of four SS guards while they follow you around this resort. I understand that we all need time to ourselves. You and your family must have been looking forward to this trip together for a long time and it would not be right for me or my men to upset that. We will have time to talk after you are settled in Budapest. Besides, do you know that I have not taken any time off for over three years myself? I plan to enjoy these few days here, just like you."

He hesitated, then smiled.

"In fact, Herr Byrnes, I thank you for that call! I really do."

The three of us all laughed and soon the girls joined in, not wanting to be left out. We had a very enjoyable breakfast.

As we left the table, Marie informed me that the four of us were scheduled for horseback riding within the half hour. When we returned, we would have lunch and then go fishing in the afternoon. She shocked me when she invited Strasser to accompany us riding, but he politely refused and indicated he would rather spend his time at the pool. He let it slip that he had bumped into one young lady yesterday, and he hoped she would be at the pool this morning. I wished him good luck and we went our separate ways.

My impression of this young man was beginning to change, just like it did with Bach. I was now hoping that he would not become a victim like Bach and Dieter.

Each of the girls had their own pony while Marie and I had larger horses with a definite mind of their own. We needed to do nothing. The horses knew where to go and I guess you could say we just followed along.

I was struck with awe by the beauty around Lake Constance, as we slowly followed the path along its shores. I could see farmers in the distance cultivating their fields and tending to their flocks. How simple their life was and how happy they must be. What I would give to trade places with them.

After an hour, the path started to circle back and through the trees I could see the outline of the resort. I wished the horses would turn and keep going, going, and going, so that we would never have to go back.

When we were about two hundred meters from the stable, I happened to turn my head to the left. There, standing behind a tree was a man, the same young man I had seen at the train station. Again, he didn't try to hide. Marie noticed me looking over my shoulder. I nodded to her and then turned to nod to him.

He was gone.

Our ride ended where it began. We returned our horses and walked along the path on the short walk back to the main lodge. As the girls ran ahead, I said, "It won't be long now, Marie. The man I saw at the train station was just now in these woods."

"Are you sure, Erik?"

"Yes, I'm positive. We made eye contact and I could tell that he wanted me to know he was there."

"Oh, Erik. I am getting scared. It has been so nice here the last two days and soon it will be all over."

"Marie, remember, within a year we should be in South America and away from all of this."

"Did you bring extra money, Erik?"

"Yes, I have money. Dieter was able to obtain American dollars for me. It should last us long enough until I get a job."

Marie laughed. "It sounds funny for you to say 'a job.' I haven't heard you say that word since before you left for Vienna. In fact, even then you hardly said it."

"Very funny, Marie. Very funny."

We entered the lodge without incident and proceeded to our room to change before lunch. At the pool, I noticed that Strasser was still there talking to a lovely lady who appeared to be in her late twenties, probably the woman he had mentioned before. As we passed the end of the pool area, Strasser's eyes met mine. I waved and we both smiled at each other. For his sake, I hoped he stayed out of the way.

"Papa, who sent us these pretty flowers?"

Upon entering the room, I too saw the bouquet of flowers standing on the guest table. Tucked between the flowers was a card. "Hope you are enjoying your vacation. I will see you soon." There was no signature.

Marie read the card after I did. She said nothing.

"Mama, who sent the flowers?" Susanne asked.

"It must be from Grandpa, silly," answered Louisa.

"Stop smelling the flowers and get ready for lunch, girls."

On the way to the restaurant, I noticed that Strasser and his new friend were no longer near the pool.

"I suppose Herr Strasser and his lady friend are preoccupied elsewhere."

"What a thing to say, Erik. For all we know, they might be eating lunch or walking in the garden. There are other things to do besides *that*."

Marie might be right but I knew where I would be if I were Strasser.

I scolded the children for not finishing their lunch. I suspected that they might soon be very hungry and they should take advantage of any meal they got.

Suddenly, there was a ruckus in the outer hall.

"Erik, who's shouting over there?"

"I don't know, but something is not right."

Just then, the head waiter made an announcement. "Ladies and gentlemen, would you all please follow me out of the building? It seems that we have a small fire in the kitchen area and for safety reasons we must ask all guests to leave the building until the fire is put out."

"This must be it, Marie, a diversion. Let's go."

The four of us followed the head waiter out of the dining room, through the hall, onto the parking lot. We joined thirty or forty other guests outside.

"Come with me and bring the children, Marie. Let's walk away from the building."

She took Susanne and Louisa by the hand and we walked down a dirt path.

"Erik, wait for us."

It was Strasser.

He was coming from the lodge, trying to catch up with us. His new friend was with him.

"Was it a fire inside the restaurant, Erik?"

I motioned for Marie to stop.

"Just a small fire, Horst. Everyone was asked to leave the dining room so we decided to go for a walk until the fire is put out."

"Mind if we join you?" he said.

I didn't know what to say. My heart was pounding and Marie was visibly agitated.

"Eh, eh... why, of course not." What else could I say? I had to get rid of them before it was too late.

"Horst, I just had a great idea. We were all going to go fishing this afternoon. Why don't the two of you join us there?"

I could see that this invitation pleased him. He hesitated and looked at the young lady for her approval. She smiled and nodded yes.

"Good, why don't you both go *right now* and change your clothes and meet us by the pier."

They agreed and started to turn back towards the lodge, but it was too late.

"Erik, help me!" Marie screamed. I was immediately thrown to the ground. There were four masked men. One grabbed Marie while another snatched the children. They were quickly dragged away to a parked car. Marie screamed again. I jumped to her aid and managed to strike her assailant but then I felt a sharp blow to the back of my head, which knocked me again to the ground. I couldn't move, the pain was too great. I could see that the fourth man had attacked Strasser.

At first, Strasser seemed stronger. He knocked him flat. "Get to your children, Erik. I'll try to do what I can."

He put up a heroic struggle, but then he was overcome, too. The girl who had accompanied him had managed to escape. Strasser tried to pull out his Luger but he was overpowered by the attackers. Two grabbed him while the man who had struck me pulled out a pistol. Strasser just lay there, looking helplessly at his attackers and at me.

"For God's sake, don't shoot him," I begged.

The shot blew half of Strasser's skull away. He twitched on the ground for only seconds, then he went limp.

They dragged me off to the same vehicle where Marie and the girls were being held. Bystanders were beginning to draw near. Just as we had planned it!

The car sped from the parking lot onto the public road. Pedestrians dived to avoid being hit. My head still hurt but I had all my senses back. Surprisingly, both girls were quite calm. Perhaps they were in a state of shock, I really couldn't tell. There were two kidnappers in our car, the driver and another. The other two followed in a second car.

We raced through the countryside and rolling hills, avoiding populated areas. I recognized the driver as the same young man I had seen watching us twice. The other was the man who had struck me and shot Strasser.

"Frau Byrnes, I hope you are alright," said the young man. "I apologize for the violence but I assure you, it was necessary."

Marie merely nodded. She said nothing.

We drove another fifteen minutes before the older man spoke. "Erik, we have about an hour to drive before we arrive at the safe house. You and your family will stay there until it is time to move you. Did you bring money?"

"Yes, I did. I brought money to get us through our initial period in South America."

"Give it to me," he snapped.

I was taken aback. What did he mean?

"But I have already paid Abraham all he asked for and more. He told me that all was taken care of."

The older man pulled out his pistol and slapped me with his bare hand in the back of the head.

"I will say this once and I will say it to all of you. You will do exactly as you are told or else I will not hesitate to pull this car over and shoot all of you dead, including the children. Do you understand, Herr Sturmbannführer?"

This outburst made the girls cry.

"Shut those girls up. I don't want this noise. I must keep my head clear."

Marie comforted the girls, and I handed over the money to him. I had no other choice.

21

The Hide-out

WE turned off the paved highway onto a long dirt road through a wooded area. We must have traveled at least two kilometers before we reached a large farm house, surrounded on three sides by a dense forest.

"Out now, we must get into the house," the older man ordered us. We entered the kitchen area, then walked into the living room, and I could see that the home had been neatly kept. Nothing seemed out of place.

Mere seconds later, a strikingly beautiful woman came out to greet us. "Herr Byrnes, Frau Byrnes, Louisa and Susanne, my name is Eva. Come in. My home is your home."

I couldn't take my eyes off of her. She was the most beautiful woman I had ever seen. She had blue eyes and short blonde hair, and a figure other women would kill for.

"Thank you, Frau..."

"Please, just call me Eva. Eva will do just fine. Come, Marie, let me show you where you and the children will sleep. I hope you all will like the clothing and other items I have purchased for you. Erik can stay here with Herman."

Herman was the man who had struck me in the car and who had shot Strasser. He would regret what he had done.

"Erik, you must obey every word we say. If you don't, it could mean death not only for you and your family but for us as well. The area here is full of people who would not hesitate in turning us into the Gestapo. If a lucky peasant would discover someone like you, he could be a very wealthy man. The SS would pay much to *save* you. In the same breath, I must apologize for slapping you in the car. I hope you can appreciate that it is difficult for a Jew like me to come to grips with the fact that I am saving an SS Sturmbannführer just for money."

At least the man was honest.

"I understand, Herman. If I were in your position, I would feel the same. I can't expect you to agree to what I have done and I'm sure you can't accept the *excuse* that I would give you. We will do as you say and we will cause you no problems."

I wondered if Eva and Herman were husband and wife. If so, why was such a beautiful woman living with such an ordinary man? Perhaps they were not related at all. Perhaps they were merely operatives hired by Abraham for this job. After all, why would such a beautiful woman fall for a simple Jew?

Marie and the girls returned, accompanied by Eva. For the first time since they were abducted, I saw the girls smile.

"Papa," Susanne said. "You should see the room we have. It is underneath the house and it is full of toys! You and Mommy's room is right next to ours, but you don't have any toys."

Louisa started to giggle and soon everybody smiled.

"Erik and Marie, please sit down and have the children sit as well," Eva politely asked. "I need to explain to you what is going to happen and what you must do while you are here."

We sat down and listened attentively.

"Do not wander far from this house, especially you, girls. You must do as you are told. Although we are in the countryside, we cannot assume that after the news of your disappearance is made public there will be no house-by-house search. I know the local police quite well, so I expect them not to bother me, but sometimes there are officers who drop by, so we must be on guard at all times. I don't know if you noticed, but as you drove in there was a shack about fifty meters off the road to this house. The man who drove your car is staying in that shack. He will warn us by radio if anyone approaches. There are also dogs wandering around the premises, and they will let us know, too, if strangers appear."

"How long will we be here?" Marie asked.

"It is hard to say. Abraham will arrive shortly and let us know. The next few days will be very important. By tomorrow, the Gestapo will be searching everywhere they can think of. Soon, a ransom demand will be sent to Vienna. The amount is so preposterous that the Reich will most definitely not comply. When the payment deadline has passed, photos of a *murdered* family will be sent to the SS. Hopefully, they will believe that you all are dead and we will then be able to get you safely into Switzerland."

The rest of the conversation dealt with particulars as to when we could go outside and what we could wear. We were also given a story to rehearse in case a search party arrived here and discovered us. After that, Eva treated us to a wonderful meal.

"Eva, that was delicious, and we thank you for it. Would it be alright if the girls and I went to bed? We are very tired."

"Why, of course, Marie. I will walk down with you."

I stayed upstairs with Herman who by that time had finished his sixth beer. What I feared would happen, did. He started to talk to me.

"So how do you like being *dead*, Erik?" he laughed.

The words slurred out of his mouth and beer ran down his dirty chin. I wished I was drunk like he was, then I might enjoy this conversation.

"Do you know that before the Germans invaded Latvia, I was a school teacher? Yes, it is true. I taught history, literature and the piano. I had two small children and a wonderful wife. We were not wealthy but I was able to put food on the table and clothes on our backs. We were very happy.

We lived about two hundred kilometers from the German border, in a city called Daugavpils. After the Germans arrived, within a week after the outbreak of the war, they began to beat up and shoot Jews indiscriminately, especially those highly visible Orthodox Jews, which I was not. Overnight, they came up with edicts which ordered, among other things, the Jews to appear for *work details*. I suspected they were no work details at all so I did not show up. Rather, I hid in my home, in a fruit cellar under a trap door, covered by a rug, while my wife and children stayed upstairs. I thought they would be safe. Up to then, I had not heard of mistreatment of any women and children, only of the men."

He paused to go to the kitchen and got himself another beer. When he returned to the living room, he handed me a beer as well.

"The Germans came as I hid in the cellar. There was pounding on the door and loud yelling. '*Schnell! Schnell!*. Let us in, you dirty Jews, or we'll break down the door.' My wife must have hesitated too long because the next thing I heard sounded like the door falling and my children screaming. All that time, I hid like a coward in my hole as I heard my wife pleading with the Germans. She told them the truth in perfect German, saying that we were Christians and did not practice the Jewish faith. It didn't help. The German officer asked if there were any men around and my wife told him that I had left early for work and she had not seen me since. I thought they would leave without harming my family, but I was wrong. The sound of three *pops* shattered the silence from above. I heard thuds on the floor above me and then laughter and the sound of heavy boots walking out the door. Then there was silence, cold silence. Like a coward, I waited huddled in a corner, sitting on the dirt floor, shaking."

As tears came to Herman's eyes, he continued.

"Erik, I was too afraid to go up the stairs and be with my family. I don't know exactly how long I stayed there, but finally I decided that if they were dead, life was not worth living without them and I climbed up and tried to lift the trap door, but it was stuck and it took a lot of force to open it. I felt

179

something warm running down my face and onto my lips. It was blood which had soaked through the rug, the blood of my wife who had fallen on top of the hidden trap door!"

He went to the kitchen and returned with two more beers.

"I climbed out of my hole, gently pushed aside the body of my wife, and there, lying next to her, were the bodies of my two sons. All of them had been shot. None of them said a word, Erik, not a word giving me away. They died saving me, and all I did was hide like a rat.

Before I left my home that night, I buried my family in the backyard and burned down my house. I took some food with me, and by hiding in the woods during the daytime and traveling by night, I made it to Kovnas. There I met Abraham."

I thought it better to say nothing. No matter what I might have said, I am sure he would have found fault with it, and really, what could I say? I could only imagine what he was feeling.

"Abraham has told me that you are different, Erik."

"How so, Herman?"

"He says that you never physically harmed any member of the Judenrat yourself, or any innocent people in the ghetto. According to him, you keep your word when you give it, and you have shown compassion to the Jews. How is it that you are different from so many of your colleagues?"

"Herman, I never hated any Jews. I am, or rather was, merely a soldier obeying orders."

Herman said nothing.

"When I first took office, I was told that the Jews were the scum of the earth. All those entering the SS were indoctrinated right from the beginning to think that way about your people. It wasn't until I met Abraham that my beliefs began to change."

"If that is true, why didn't you stop right there and quit your job?"

"That is easier said than done, Herman. First of all, somebody else would merely have filled my position, and also it might have jeopardized my safety and that of my wife and children. I admit that, just like you, I was afraid."

"Afraid of what, Herr Sturmbannführer? I was always told the SS feared nothing."

"It *was* fear. I was afraid what they might do to me. Would they send me to the Russian Front? Would they send me to a camp? Or worse, would they have me and my girls shot? To put it simply, I didn't want to take the chance."

"So now, Herr Sturmbannführer, now that you see that Germany will surely lose the war and that you would be hunted as a war criminal, now you are willing to take the chance?"

"Yes, Herman, now I am. My family has nothing to lose."

He nodded as if he understood, and then finished his beer.

"I think it is my turn to retire, Herman. These beers have just about put me asleep. Good night."

"Go ahead, Erik. I think I am going to turn on the radio to see if there are any reports about you. I will talk to you in the morning."

I checked up on the girls to make sure they were alright, and joined Marie in bed. She was still awake. We talked a little before we both fell asleep.

Eva had breakfast on the table by eight the next morning. I had slept well and I was very hungry. Just as we were about to eat, Herman came dashing into the kitchen.

"All of you, come in the living room, and listen to this."

"Attention! Attention! Yesterday, at The Kasdorf Resort, SS Sturmbannführer Erik Byrnes and his family were abducted at gunpoint and driven off to an unknown destination. Photos of Herr Byrnes and his family will be shown in all newspapers and posted at all police stations. Anyone who has any knowledge of their whereabouts or information leading to their safe return should inform the local police or Gestapo. A reward is being offered to those who assist in their safe return. Anyone who assists in their detention or fails to come forward with information will be shot, and so will their entire family."

"They have been playing this announcement at the top of every hour since early this morning. I wonder how much the SS is willing to pay for your safe return, Erik."

I didn't like Herman's last comment nor did I like the smile on his face.

Eva then scolded him. "You would never live to spend that reward, Herman. That I promise you."

"Yes, I suppose you are right, Eva. Why would they pay the abductor for turning in his victim? Come, let's eat. Eva makes a fine breakfast."

He was right. Eva certainly did make a fine breakfast.

She was wonderful. She had games organized for the girls and even convinced Marie to play with them.

"Come outside with me, Erik. I want you to get familiar with the surroundings."

Eva and I walked outside into the backyard.

"It is important for you, Erik, to be totally familiar with everything and *everyone* here. Don't you agree?"

She smiled as she gazed into my eyes.

"Yes, Eva, yes, you are right. Show me what I need to see."

We walked around the home and then to the outbuildings. She pointed out various hiding places such as trap doors under the hay pile and a fake wall on one side of the barn. I had to admit that this was a perfect hide-out.

"I can't believe that all this was done just for me and my family, Eva."

"No, Erik. It wasn't just for you. This has been a safe house for some time before you came."

"You mean there have been other SS whom you have helped?"

"Not, exactly, Erik. Those who have been protected here in the past were resistance fighters, communists, partisans, or governmental men not sympathetic to the Reich. You are the first SS officer who has seen these walls."

I laughed, then joked, "Am I right in saying that you are doing this for me because of your new-found devotion to the Reich?"

This time she was the one who laughed.

"Hardly, Erik, hardly. Over the past few years, I have been able to save the money given to me by those whom I have helped. When Abraham told me what you were willing to pay, I decided it would be in my best interest to open my doors to anyone. If I am successful in helping you to escape, there will be others like you who are willing to pay any price I ask. You are getting a bargain, Erik. Those who follow will pay far more."

She stopped walking, turned and looked up at me with a devilish smile. Then, after looking around to make sure nobody was watching, she placed both of her arms upon my shoulders.

"Don't think too badly of me, Erik. We both know that after the war is over, there will be little calling for an occupation such as mine. A girl has to make her money when she can."

She moved even closer to me, pressing her firm breasts against me, and then she kissed me on the lips. I couldn't help myself. I put my arms around her and returned the kiss. She was so passionate, I didn't want to let her go, but she finally pulled away.

"I'm sorry I lost control, Erik, but from the first moment I saw you, I was drawn to you."

I couldn't believe what I was hearing. Here was this woman, more beautiful than any woman I had ever seen, telling me she wanted me.

I blurted out the unthinkable.

"Eva, I felt the same way about you."

"This is not good, Erik. Neither of us can afford to take any chances. We have to be very careful or else all of us will pay with our lives."

She was right. What could I have been thinking of? I had to concentrate on one thing only, and that was saving myself and my family. As much as I might want to, I couldn't let anything else interfere.

We continued the tour of the grounds and when we were finished, we went back into the house. The girls were playing with *Onkel Herman* and Marie was busying herself with doing the dishes. Eva then showed me her rather extensive library and invited me to help myself.

I spent the rest of the day reading and playing with the children. The radio continued to broadcast information about our disappearance. In order to cause no suspicion, Eva went into the village to pick up provisions. She also said she would try to find out what she could about the Gestapo's progress in the search.

When she returned, she reported that there were several Gestapo agents in the village and that she had seen them at the café in the company of the local police chief. Apart from that, she noticed no other unusual activity. The countryside was large and there were just so many agents that could be spared. Up to now, at least, we suspected that the authorities had no real clue as to our whereabouts.

It was after supper, while we were having our coffee, that there was a knock at the door. I started to pick up our plates and move my family downstairs when Eva told us not to worry. Whoever it was had to be a friend. No stranger was able to get to the door without us being warned. Herman unlatched the door and let the visitor in.

It was Abraham!

"Erik, you made it! I am so glad to see you."

We embraced. He then went up to Marie and gave her his hand. I didn't know what she would do, considering the negative feelings she had about him, but to my surprise she behaved quite decently. She reached out to him and took his hand in hers.

"I am pleased to meet the man who has helped us so much."

"And I am pleased as well, to meet such a lovely lady."

He then approached the children and gave them a big hug. From a burlap bag he had laid on the floor, he handed each a present, a small music box.

"Now, listen to your Uncle Abraham and play with the music boxes in the living room."

They smiled and did as Abraham said.

"Herman, get me a beer. The rest of you, sit down. There is much news I have to share. It wasn't more than a few hours after your kidnapping that word spread through the ghetto about what had happened. Don't ask me how, it just did. A curfew was imposed and many were questioned about whether or not they had any information as to what had happened to you. As you know, I was in hiding from Strasser. Only later did I find out that he was at The Kasdorf with you. After the authorities were convinced we knew nothing, they left the Jews alone. As planned, Herman and his operatives *carelessly* dropped various documents at the scene, linking them to an Italian partisan unit. I am told that the Gestapo's investigation is now centered in that direction."

"Abraham, do you think they will search here?"

"I'm not sure, Eva. I don't believe that they have the slightest suspicion about this place since it has always served you well in the past. Today, a ransom note from the Italian partisans will arrive at SS Headquarters in Vïenna, demanding two million Reichmarks for your safe return. We both know that the SS will not pay that amount. It is twice as much as Hitler offered for the assassins of Heydrich. When the ransom is not paid in time, the picture will be sent showing you all dead."

Seeing the look on Marie's face, Abraham assured her that the photo was a fake and that the real people depicted on it had not been harmed. I wondered if that was really the truth.

Herman brought Abraham and me a beer. Eva and Marie then took the children outside for a walk.

"Look what I have, Erik," Abraham said. He brought out a folder containing numerous colorful pamphlets.

"What are these?"

Herman was also curious about what Abraham had brought with him.

"These, Erik, are photos of us a year from now."

I snatched the folder from a laughing Abraham. Inside were travel brochures about various places and countries in South America, especially those countries catering to the German traveler. Although the brochures pre-dated the war, I would assume that when the shooting was over these places would once again welcome the Germans and resume some normalcy.

There was information on Buenos Aires, Ecuador, Peru, San Salvador, and many more wonderful, exciting places.

We all grabbed some. We then exchanged with each other. They were beautiful.

Eva walked in.

"Where are Marie and the children?" I asked.

"Don't worry, Erik. They are safe. Marie took the children into the barn to show them the horses. They will be in soon. What are you three looking at so intensely? They wouldn't be pictures of beautiful women, would they, Erik?"

I blushed.

"No, Eva, Abraham brought travel brochures about the places we are going to. Come here and look for yourself."

She picked up the pile by my side and looked them over.

"Very nice, Erik. Very, very nice. Perhaps I will join you and Abraham there. Neither of you would mind, would you?"

She smiled that seductive smile that I had seen before. I was captivated.

"Eva, don't talk so foolishly," barked Herman. "You know very well that you and I must stay here. We can make a fortune hiding Nazis such as Herr Byrnes. There will be time for us to spend our money later."

He was definitely upset. Abraham must have noticed it as well because he attempted to quiet the storm.

"Children, children, don't get angry with each other. Eva was only kidding, Herman. There is no need for you to become so upset. Come, let's have another beer."

"*Ja*, Abraham, you're right. I'm sorry I got so upset. I thought for a moment you were serious, Eva."

Eva said nothing. She looked at Abraham and then at me, but especially at me. Was she serious about leaving with us?

When Marie and the children returned, I showed them the travel material. They were all very excited.

"Thank you for bringing these pamphlets, Abraham. They will help us pass the time and give us something to look forward to."

"You are quite welcome, Frau Byrnes. If there is anything else I can do to help you, just ask. I am at your service."

After the children went to bed, we spent the rest of the evening talking about how our plans were taking shape. We all agreed everything was proceeding well.

Our minds drifted back to days gone by. Marie took great interest in Abraham's tale of his family and how happy they were before the war. It was as if she was trying to relate to the plight of the Jews, knowing that she herself might have shared their miserable fate. She said how happy she was back in

1938 when I came back to her. Then it was my turn. Everyone, except Abraham, turned pale when I told them of one of my *brightest* times. I told my story of how proud I was when Dieter presented me with my SS uniform. Abraham was the only one in the room who acknowledged the importance of such an event. Herman's reminiscing took us back to the time of his wedding day, while Eva's topic was, strangely enough, the day of her final divorce hearing when she received a tidy settlement from her ex-husband.

After awhile, we bade each other good night. Eva walked us all to our rooms, giving Abraham the room next to mine. I slept well that night, the best sleep I had in months.

I woke early, but very refreshed. I saw no one else around, and it seemed so beautiful outside that I decided to take a walk. I wanted to see the horses again. Although I knew they weren't champion stock, they were certainly impressive.

As I opened the door to the barn, I saw Eva.

"Good morning, Herr Sturmbannführer. Did you sleep well?"

She was beautiful, her yellow hair seductively misplaced just enough to catch my attention.

"Yes, I did. In fact, I feel wonderful. Just wonderful!"

She put down the pitchfork she was using to bale the horse feed.

"Erik, you do know, don't you, that Herman was right when he suspected that I was serious about leaving with you for South America?"

"I was not surprised, Eva, not surprised at all."

"When you first arrived here, I was excited about the possibility of getting more *clients* such as yourself. The money is indeed very, very good, but it didn't take me long to change my mind. You know, it was the travel brochures that finally convinced me that life on this continent, after the war is over, even with money, will be difficult for me to bear. After all, where would I spend this money? If things continue as they are, the British or the Americans will have bombed to oblivion all the fine places in Europe where I would care to go."

"Eva, you're funny. I don't know if I really believe you're telling me the truth."

She moved closer to me, and the freshness of her scent aroused my passion. I didn't step back.

"You're partially right, Erik. I am not exactly being truthful with you. It wasn't the travel brochures that convinced me to want to go. I admit that they helped. The real reason was you, Erik. I want to be with you. I don't want to be alone anymore."

She paused and looked into my eyes.

"But, Eva, you won't be alone. You have Herman and... this is your home."

"Herman, he doesn't mean anything to me. He never did. He is only my business partner, and as for this place, yes, I like it but I would like any other place better if I knew you were there with me."

"Eva, we hardly know each other."

"I know that, Erik, but hasn't it ever happened to you, what do they call it, love at first sight? Please, try to understand."

"I'm married, Eva. I have Marie and the girls. How can I turn my back on them?"

She drew even closer.

"Eva, I can't hurt Marie. I just can't."

"I understand that, Erik, I truly do. I'm not asking you to break up your family. Marie never has to find out. I'll be happy just to be near you and maybe, later, when we are in a new country and settled in, and the past is behind us, maybe then you will be able to come to me. I'll wait, Erik. I'll be there for you whenever you are ready. I promise."

We kissed with such passion and desire...

"Eva, I can't, not here, not now."

She backed off, not out of anger but rather as if she understood.

"As I said, Erik, I'll wait for you and for the right time when you are ready."

"Eva, I've just decided that the time is right."

I pulled her towards me. She didn't resist. I put my lips to hers while she slipped her hands under my sweater and began to push it up and over my head as I unbuttoned her blouse and bra which she then removed herself.

Her round, supple breasts pressed against my bare chest. We dropped to the soft hay below and made love like I never experienced before.

It was explosive.

After having Eva, could I ever go back to Marie? Did I still love her?

"We had better get dressed, Erik. Marie will start wondering where we have been."

The others had already finished breakfast when I walked in. Marie had tried her hand at it this time.

"Do you know where Eva is, Erik?" Herman asked.

"Yes, I saw her in the barn, feeding the horses. She should be in shortly."

"Quite a woman, that Eva," Abraham whispered to me as he passed by me in the doorway.

"Did Abraham ever tell you, Erik, how he met Eva?"

"No, he didn't, Herman, but I have a feeling I'm going to find out."

"Even with the Nazis all around, Abraham has been able to move in and about Vienna. He is not what you Germans would call, a *conspicuous* Jew. One evening at a local nightclub, he noticed a beautiful woman arguing with an SS officer who was trying to force himself on her. That woman turned out to be Eva. When they continued their argument outside, Abraham picked up a brick and struck the SS man in the head, knocking him out. He took Eva through some back streets and alleys to safety. She then vowed not to forget him.

Through the years, they stayed in touch. When Abraham found out that she owned this place in the country, he suggested to her an *appropriate* usage for it. It was only a matter of time for me to fit right into their plans to smuggle out of Germany and Austria anyone who wanted to leave for a price. By now, somebody must have told you that you are the first SS officer this place has ever had."

"So I've been told, Herman. So I've been told."

Abraham then walked back in.

"There is nothing like sitting in an outhouse, surrounded by nature. Don't you agree, Erik?"

Everyone smiled.

"Herman has told me that the hourly broadcasts about you have stopped. That is a good sign."

That comment got Marie's attention.

"Why is that *good*, Abraham?" she asked.

"The Gestapo must realize that they aren't going to find you. If so, then it's more to their advantage to keep your names out of the public eye. Perhaps then the public will forget you, or so the Gestapo hopes. Because then the public will perhaps also forget how such a *fine* intelligence agency could allow one of their own to be kidnapped with the perpetrators still free to do as they please."

Just as Abraham finished, Susanne began to cry.

Before Marie could comfort her, Eva appeared and put her arm around her.

"Little *Fraulein*, why are there tears in your eyes?"

"I'm afraid," she whimpered.

"You need not be afraid, little one. Your Papa and I will see to it that nothing bad happens to you and your sister." I knew that last comment wasn't going to go over very well with Marie. And it didn't.

"Eva, I hope you won't be offended by this, but I'm going to ask you to remember that I am their mother. I am perfectly capable to insure their safety."

"Marie, of course, that was very thoughtless of me! I did not mean to be offensive. I only tried to reassure the children. I'm sorry."

Marie only glared.

"I had better go back and tend to my horses. Marie, again, I apologize."

"The nerve of that woman for..."

"Marie! How could you be so rude to Eva. Don't you realize where we and the children would be without her?"

Everyone in the room was looking at Marie, waiting for her to do or say something. It didn't take her long.

"I'm sorry, Eva. You don't have to leave. It was very cruel for me to say those things to you. I don't know why I became so jealous."

"Come, children. Come, Marie. Why don't the three of you help me feed the horses? Would you like that, girls?"

Herman joined them. It left Abraham and myself alone for the first time since that fateful day when he had shot Dieter.

"Erik, there is something I want to show you."

"Yes, what is it?"

He pulled out a crumbled piece of paper from his inner boot.

"Read it," he said.

To the German Pigs: Sturmbannführer Byrnes and his family are in our possession. If you want to see these swine alive, you must pay two million marks, no later than Wednesday at noon. If a notice agreeing to these terms does not appear in the morning newspaper editions within the next 24 hours, all four of them will be shot.

"This is a copy of the note that was just delivered to Gestapo headquarters in Vienna, Erik. As you can see, the money we demand is much more than the Reich would pay for the return of Hitler, or anyone else for that matter."

I smiled.

"On the contrary, Abraham, I think you are selling me short, but it's over and done now so I won't make a big issue of it."

We both laughed.

"Erik, along with that letter was the family picture I had you give me some months ago. The Gestapo will never recognize the area. It will lead them to believe that we truly do have you captive."

"I have to admit, Abraham, that I am impressed by all that I have seen so far. Everything seems to have gone as planned."

"Yes, I must admit that I outdid myself this time. Neither the SS or the Gestapo have been anywhere near here in their search. And then, Erik, if they don't pay the ransom, we'll send them a picture of the deceased Byrnes family."

"Abraham, there is something I need to ask you."

"Of course, what is it?"

"Herman took more money from me, by force."

"He did what?"

"Yes, Abraham, he took my money. That was not part of the deal."

"That scum. I'll get your money back. He has been paid in full, and then some. I won't have my friend taken advantage of, especially when he is at his weakest."

That outburst satisfied me.

"So you will get it back? I have your word on it?"

"What, you don't trust me, Erik?"

"Of course, I do. It just... well, he works for you and I guess I was shocked when he demanded the money."

"I understand. Believe me. I will have your money back soon, and Herman will pay for his indiscretion."

"I don't want to cause a problem, Abraham, but if we don't get it back, what will we have to live on in South America? And how would I pay to get there in the first place? That money was for all of us, including you, Abraham."

"I know, Erik, and I appreciate it. You need not say any more. Like I said, I'll get back every mark for you."

I decided to leave it at that. I could tell he was starting to get annoyed with my constant questioning.

"How long will we be here, Abraham?"

"Not much longer. Things have gone so well that I think that very soon after we mail that picture we will be leaving for the next part of our journey to Switzerland."

"How will we cross the border? Isn't it heavily guarded? I'm sure there will be heightened security because of what has happened to me."

"We're not going to cross at any common place. No, my plan is to cross through the mountains, and then by boat. That way, we'll miss most of the patrols. Then, it is just a short way to the border, at a crossing which is not heavily traveled or guarded."

"But, Abraham... can the children stand such a journey?"

"The girls will have to be strong, but I think they can do it. I'll help you, of course."

22

On To Switzerland

A DULL routine dominated the next days. Eva and Abraham cautioned us not to go outside. There was a rumor in the village that search groups had entered the area. The boredom was starting to take its toll on the girls. They were tired of playing the same games all day long. All of the adults took turns in trying to keep them busy. Even Herman tried, but whatever relief was brought was only temporary.

I had heard nothing yet about Herman and the money, and although I knew it would be better for me not to say anything about it now, I was getting irritable and could not continue keeping quiet about it much longer.

As we sat down for lunch, Abraham walked in and made the announcement we were all waiting for.

"Erik, Marie... all of you. Tomorrow morning at dawn we'll move forward."

"You mean it is safe for us to go on?" Marie asked.

"Yes, Frau Byrnes, it is."

"On to Switzerland!"

"I'm glad to hear that, Abraham," Herman remarked. "I couldn't stand it much longer being held up in here. I prefer the ghetto rather than playing another game of cards."

We all laughed.

"The Nazis have not paid the ransom and they have been shipped the photo with the dead Byrnes family. They will be convinced you are all gone. This gives us the opportunity to leave. Tomorrow morning, a farm truck with a load of manure will arrive here. There is a large pocket built in the manure pile where we can hide. The next stop will be another farm near Lake Constance on the Swiss border for a night, and then we will make our move through the mountains. Don't worry, we will have a guide."

Abraham's tone of confidence lifted our spirits. Out of the corner of my eye, I noticed that Eva was smiling, too.

After Marie and I returned to our room to pack, she pulled me away from the children. "Well, Erik, I suppose you haven't gotten the money back yet, have you?"

"I told you already, Marie! Abraham promised me he would get it back, all of it. He's always kept his word to me and he will keep it again."

"But Erik, it's different this time. Before, if he didn't keep his word to you, it wouldn't have made a difference. You still were in charge. Now, this time, *he* is in charge. If they abandon us or even if they do take us where they promised, without all our money we are lost."

"I don't want to hear any more from you, Marie. Don't you trust your fellow Jew?"

"Erik, you've never said anything like that to me before. Why are you trying to hurt me now?"

"I'm not trying to hurt you. I just want you to leave me alone! Let Abraham handle this. Come on, let's get ready."

Again, as she always had in the past, Marie did exactly what I said. "I'll get started right away."

She was right about one thing, though. I should have gotten my money back by now. I decided to go upstairs to look for Abraham.

"Abraham, I..."

"Don't get excited, Erik. I know what you're going to say. I can tell by the look on your face."

Abraham reached into his back pocket and handed me a wad of money.

"Is this what you were looking for, my friend?"

I took the money from his hand and quickly counted it. It was all there.

"Thank you, Abraham. Thank you! What did you have to do to get it back for me?"

"Not that much. Not that much at all. I merely *reminded* Herman that he had already been paid in full and when he protested that he deserved more, I had to teach him a lesson in what you might call *memory conditioning*. He won't bother you any more."

This would be my last walk outside. I walked over to the barn, as I knew Eva would be there to release the horses. I had hope to *'talk'* to her alone before we left.

"Erik, come in here quickly." She motioned from inside the barn.

"What's the matter, Eva?"

"Quickly, come over here. Behind the hay pile! Please, Erik, you must help him."

Herman was laying in the corner exactly where Eva and I had made love. He was covered with blood, his face so puffed up, swollen and bruised, that I could barely recognize him. As we approached him, I could hear faint murmurs. He was still alive, but dying.

Eva knelt next to me.

Herman tried to speak, but all he could do was mumble. His lips and mouth were badly swollen and he was coughing up blood.

It seemed that he was trying to gather all his strength to tell us something. We leaned down to hear what he was trying to say.

Then, in a hardly audible voice and barely above a whisper, "Erik... you're in danger. You... all are... in danger."

He spat out more blood. I had seen men die before and I knew he had only minutes or even seconds left.

"What kind of danger, Herman? Tell me, please."

He gathered the last strength left in him. "Don't... trust him..." He was fading fast.

Herman reached for Eva's hand. She took his as he turned his head towards her. A small, forced smile crossed her face.

Then he was dead.

"Erik, what happened to him? Who did this?"

I was puzzled. I thought that she knew.

"It was Abraham."

"But why? Why would he do that?"

"Eva, listen. I told Abraham about Herman taking my money. He promised me he would get it back, which he did. He gave it all to me. Apparently, Herman must have resisted, so Abraham beat him."

"Oh my God, Erik, do you remember the young man in the car, the one who is in the shed near the road?"

"Yes, I do. What about him?"

"All I know is that Herman and he are close. When he finds out about this, there could be trouble."

I had forgotten all about him.

"Eva, I must let Abraham know that he could be in danger so that..."

"Thank you for your concern, Erik, but *that* danger has passed."

It was Abraham.

"I knew about Herman and the young man. So after I left you in the house, I paid him a visit. You can rest assured that he won't say anything one way or the other about Herman's unfortunate passing."

Eva lashed out at him.

"Did you have to go so far as to kill him, Abraham? Couldn't you have been satisfied with just beating him?"

"Eva, when a dog goes bad, some try to punish it, hoping that it will change its attitude. But most professionals agree that the only solution is to get rid of the animal. I agree with the professionals. But I want you to believe that I did not try to kill him. It just happened. I am sorry that I have taken your business partner away from you."

At first Eva said nothing. There was no expression on her face. Then a wicked smile crossed her face, and she looked directly at me. It took me a few seconds to understand why her emotions had changed so abruptly, but then it came to me.

I knew just what to say.

"Abraham, I feel responsible for the position we have put Eva in."

"Position, what position, Erik? I don't understand."

"It's simple. As you just said, now that Herman is dead, Eva's business enterprise will in all likelihood come to an end. If it wasn't for me, none of this would have happened. You would then not have *had* to kill Herman. I feel I must somehow make up for this."

Abraham sat down on a hay bale and put his face between his hands. He was in deep thought.

"Eva, perhaps Erik is right, but it is not his fault. I didn't think of you when I beat that dumb Jew to death. How can I make it up to you?"

"You both are right. My business is finished. I do have some money saved, though, and I can think of no better place to spend it than in South America with all of you..."

"How do you feel about Eva joining us, Erik?"

"I can't find anything wrong with it."

"*Ja*, Eva, you can come with us. I... we both owe this to you!"

The three of us decided it would be best not to mention what happened to Marie or the children. Rather, we would say that Herman had gone to the village and would not return before we left. When she found out that I had the money back, perhaps she would think that Abraham had removed him and the other man because of their indiscretion. I just hoped she would accept that Eva would be coming with us.

The day turned into night as Abraham stood guard. I sat down in the living room and turned on the radio. It was still set to the same station Herman had been listening to during the week. After some music, a news alert came on. I was impressed to hear them talk about the murder of myself and my entire family. The announcement did not say by whom. It seemed that the Gestapo had swallowed the bait, hook, line, and sinker. Yet, something just didn't seem right. No plan could be so perfect, or could it?

I hurried to tell the others about the announcement and we all shared our hopes for success.

I wondered what my father and sister were thinking this very moment and, for that matter, what Marie's parents were feeling. I hoped that Father would remember my words that he should not believe what he would hear. Should I try to get a message to him? No, that would be too risky. I would be putting not only the life of the six of us in danger, but Father's and Theresa's as well. No, I would have to wait and get them a message some other way and at some other time.

"Erik, Marie, it's time. Get up!"

Eva's voice woke me from my restless sleep.

"It will be light in less than an hour and we have to be ready to leave as soon as the truck arrives. I have some coffee and rolls for us to eat and provisions to take along. Wake your children and come upstairs as quickly as possible."

"This is it, Marie. Are you ready?"

"Yes, Erik, I've been ready for some time now. I want you to know something, Erik. Whatever happens, always remember that I love you and I wouldn't have given up my time with you for anything."

She put her arms around me and kissed me.

I should have felt ashamed, but I didn't.

It was still dark when the truck arrived but I could hear the birds announcing daybreak. At first, the children were afraid to climb onto the back of a truck full of manure, but when Abraham showed them the huge cavity which had been dug out and reinforced within the pile, they were more than eager to try this adventure.

The truck driver was a man whom I thought I had seen before. I think he was one of the men involved in our abduction.

Abraham pulled me aside.

"Erik, not one word about Herman. The driver is a good friend of his. I wouldn't want him to know what happened to Herman or the other guy."

"What did you tell him, Abraham?"

"I told him that they have gone ahead to make things ready for our arrival. He accepted that."

"What happens when we arrive and he asks about Herman?"

"If that should occur and if the driver gives us a problem, I will handle it, Erik. Don't I always deal with any problem that occurs?"

I nodded and helped Marie, Eva and the children into the truck. I then climbed inside along with Abraham. It was cramped.

Dawn broke, and we drove away from the farm house.

I had never been so nervous as I was now. It was dark in the pile, so Abraham switched on a flashlight.

"We will be on the road for some time, Erik. Unfortunately, there is nothing I can do about the smell."

We all laughed.

I couldn't help but watch Eva. There she was, in the middle of a pile of shit, but still beautiful as ever.

None of us spoke for almost an hour, including the children who somehow both managed to fall asleep. Through a slit in the covering, I could see light filtering in. When I moved my hand in that direction, Abraham's vise-like grip took hold of my arm.

"Don't, Erik. Don't take that risk. I know you're curious and anxious to see just where we are, but if you can see out, it's possible that whoever may be behind us could see in. It just isn't worth the risk."

Abraham was right as usual.

About half an hour later, the truck slowed down.

"Why are we stopping, Abraham?" Eva asked.

"I don't know, but I'm sure we'll find out soon enough. Just sit here quietly and whatever you do, don't say a word."

Fear began to grip us all as the truck came to a complete stop. Just then, I could hear another vehicle also stop. First one car door closed and then another. I could hear boot steps getting louder and louder as they approached our truck.

Suddenly, commands were barked to our driver.

"Get out. *Schnell*! *Schnell!*"

The truck door slammed shut.

"Don't you know that this truck is dropping shit all over the highway?"

The driver apologized in meek and humble tones.

"Where are your papers?" a second voice bellowed.

There was silence, dead silence. Marie placed her hand over Susanne's mouth and Eva did the same for Louisa.

"You are a long way from home. Where are you headed to?"

"I am going to visit my cousin. He lives in a little village just outside Innsbruck."

"And you are bringing him a load of shit? You must have great affection for your cousin!" The two men laughed.

"My cousin is a farmer. His cattle are very sick and don't produce enough manure for the crops, so I said I would bring him a load the next time I'd visit him."

Again, there was momentary silence.

"Lift open the canopy," one of the officers demanded. "Let's take a closer look at this shit."

The driver obeyed the command and lifted up the canopy. Although we were still hidden by the manure, trickles of light entered into our cavern. We were within inches of being discovered.

Silence again. The two of them were apparently looking at the pile.

"Come on, let's go," one of the men said. "I'm not searching through this mess."

"You're right," the other answered. "We've wasted enough time on this shit farmer."

I took a deep breath of relief as the sound of footsteps became softer and softer. We were safe.

"Mama, I can't breathe. Get your hand off my nose, please!"

Eva pushed Marie out of the way and smothered Susanne's mouth, but it was too late.

"What was that!" one of the voices hollered. "What's in that pile?"

Without hesitation, Abraham pushed himself out of the cavern, a Luger in his hand. He lifted the canopy. One shot rang out; then another; then two more. There lying on the ground were the two officers, local police. One appeared to be dead, blood oozing from his head. The other was only wounded in the shoulder.

"Who are you?"

Nobody answered him.

Marie and the girls remained in the cavern. Eva followed me out. I surveyed the surroundings. We were on a paved road in the countryside. Besides the police vehicle I could see no other cars but I could hear what sounded like motors not far away.

"Erik, you and Eva move the dead man into the brush off the road."

The wounded officer begged for his life.

"Please, don't shoot me. I won't tell anyone. You have my word. I have a wife and two small children. Please don't."

Eva and I watched as Abraham motioned to the man to head towards the brush where we had dumped his partner. He staggered, crying while at the same time saying his last prayers. Abraham pushed him into the brush and then shot him in the back of the head. He fell upon his dead partner. Eva and I covered the bodies with branches and leaves, while Abraham drove their car out of sight into the woods.

Re-entering the cavern in the truck, Abraham admonished us to hurry. "We have no time to lose. These men will be found soon and there will be a hunt. Maybe somebody has already spotted the truck. We must get moving. Hurry!"

The three of us got back into the truck. The children were hysterical.

"You must control those children," Eva snapped at Marie.

Marie said nothing.

"If you can't do it, I will. You almost got us killed and you certainly are responsible for the death of those officers."

Marie, typically, began to cry.

"Eva, enough, enough, it is over now and nothing can change what has happened."

I was glad Abraham said something. Although I felt sorry for Marie, I knew Eva was right. She had been careless with Susanne, and this carelessness almost cost us our lives.

"How much further is it?"

"Not much further, Erik, not much further."

We drove approximately another hour before the truck turned off onto what sounded and felt like a bumpy dirt road. It must be the driveway to the farm house.

"We've arrived," Abraham said.

As we stepped off the truck, we were met by an old man and an old woman. They said nothing, but motioned us not towards the house as I would have expected, but rather into the barn. They had cleared a place for us behind the hay pile.

"The Gestapo have been everywhere. You must be careful. You will stay in the barn tonight and leave in the morning."

The old man then left us and entered his home.

"When will our guides arrive?" Marie asked.

"You have already met him," laughed Abraham.

"You mean the old man?" I asked.

"Don't let his age or appearance fool you. He is strong as an ox and knows these mountains like the back of his hand. If anybody can get us out of here, it will be him."

The old man's wife brought us some cheese and meat to eat and water for the adults. She gave the children goat's milk.

"Eat, eat. You will need your strength when you cross the mountains with Josef. I used to make the hike with him for years, but my legs aren't that strong anymore."

She laid a large burlap bag in front of us, opened it, and took several weapons out of it.

"Herr Byrnes, this pistol is for you. Abraham, you take the rifle. And for each of the women I also brought a pistol. Take them. You may well need to use them."

We each picked up our guns. Marie hesitated, but at Eva's prodding she took the pistol in her hand.

"I've never used a gun before," she said.

The old woman laughed. "Hopefully you won't need it this time but in case you're caught, make sure you save enough bullets for yourself and your children. You don't want to get caught at any cost."

She turned away and slowly walked towards the house, laughing all the way back.

Abraham told us that we should all eat now and take care of our personal needs. "Then we must rest, for at dawn Josef will be ready to take us on our journey."

We did as he said. It had been a long day and we were hungry and tired. We ate quickly. Marie laid down by the sleeping children and was soon sound asleep. I picked a spot away from the others and lay in the soft hay. Just before I dozed off, Eva laid down near me. Before I could say anything, she placed her finger on my lips, kissed me and then curled up next to me.

"Get up! Get up! We leave in half an hour."

Josef woke us all from a deep sleep. It occurred to me that if we ever did get to safety in South America, I was going to import a huge load of hay and put it in my bedroom. I had truly grown fond of it.

Marie and Eva assisted the girls, while Abraham and I got the gear together. Josef had ready several backpacks full of provisions and camping equipment. There were ropes, hatchets, and knives, along with ammunition for the weapons.

When all was ready to go, Josef told us to begin. "Come, let us move on. We have a long way to go today before we can rest. Come. Come."

We followed him along a path which began behind the barn and continued into a woods at the foot of some prominent hills. Josef turned back to the farm house and waived farewell to his wife who watched us from the porch step. In the distance, I could see snow-covered mountains.

"Do we actually have to climb those mountains?"

"I certainly hope not, Erik. I doubt that any of us, except for Josef, is up to it."

Josef overheard us. "Don't worry, Abraham. The route I have chosen is difficult, but we can make it, even with the children. We will not have to climb over the top of any of the mountains you see in the distance. There are paths winding between them."

Marie held Susanne's hand and Eva took Louisa's. Although Marie had earlier tried to explain to the girls just what was happening, I don't believe they fully understood. Fortunately, they were young enough that in time they would forget Austria and everything that went with it. South America would be their new home. There, they could be Jews without fear of extermination or persecution from people like me.

I had heard that the countryside near the Austrian-Swiss border was beautiful. That was more than true. Words were unable to describe the beauty that surrounded us. I saw nature at its grandest. There was an abundance of magnificent trees, beautiful hills, valleys with small animals moving in all directions. The morning air was crisp and the temperature was perfect for the brisk walk and climb we had to undertake.

After an hour, I could tell that we were very slowly but steadily climbing higher and higher. When we reached a plateau, I looked back to where we began and could in the distance see Josef's farm house.

Another hour went by before Josef spoke. "We will rest here for about fifteen minutes. You should take advantage of this time. Every hour we travel will become more difficult than the last."

I sat down next to Marie and the girls. Louisa and Susanne seemed especially sullen. They were hardly saying a word and looked very, very tired.

"The girls miss their friends," Marie whispered to me.

"They will make new friends, better friends," I snapped back.

"I know, Erik. I know, but it's not the same. They don't understand why they are out here when all their friends are back home, playing in familiar surroundings."

I closed my eyes, ignoring the triviality Marie was referring to. Couldn't she see that I needed to get just a little sleep before we moved on again? After what seemed only seconds, I heard dogs barking in the far distance. Josef heard them too.

"Quiet, all of you. Be very, very still."

Quickly, I picked up my pistol, as did Eva. Abraham readied his rifle.

"Marie, take the children and hide in those bushes. Don't make a sound!"

Marie gathered the children and did as Abraham said. The rest of us joined Josef as we hid behind a large rock about ten meters off the path. The barking of the dogs got louder and louder. We could begin making out the sound of voices.

"It's a border patrol," Josef whispered to Abraham.

From behind the boulder I could see in the distance three, no four, men ascending the same path that we had taken just minutes before. They were regular Wehrmacht, a border patrol, just like Josef had said. Two German Shepherds on leashes were pulling their handlers forward.

"This is as good a place as any," Josef said to us. "You take out the leader, Abraham. I'll get the middle one and Erik and Eva, you're both responsible for the last two men. Shoot to kill upon my signal and fire more than once. Make sure your man is dead."

I never actually killed a man before. Yes, I was responsible for the death of thousands, no tens of thousands, but I had never had to actually pull the trigger.

By now, we could hear their voices clearly. They were joking about some women they had met in the village last week. Twigs broke beneath their boots as they ascended the path. Josef held us back with his left hand, gripping his weapon with the other hand. We waited patiently, a little farther, just a little farther.

"Now!"

Josef jumped up. In seconds, three shots rang out, knocking the first man to the ground and scattering the dogs. Seconds later, I heard Abraham's rifle crack two shots into the heart and chest of the second man. Eva had also felled her target. I hesitated. I could see the fourth man's eyes. He was frightened, just a boy, hardly twenty years old. He was so frightened that he dropped his rifle and raised his arms.

"Shoot, Erik, shoot!" Abraham scolded me.

As I began to take aim, Eva reached over and steadied my arm.

"You have no choice, Erik, no choice whatsoever. It's either him or all of us. Think of your children, Erik."

Just then, the young soldier turned and began to run. I didn't hesitate. I shot him twice in the back. He fell over dead.

The girls were screaming and Marie was crying.

"Erik, when is all of this going to stop? I can't stand any more killing."

Eva snapped back, "A fine wife you are, so prim and proper, with nothing to do but criticize your husband. You should be ashamed of yourself!"

Marie seemed startled and speechless.

"Erik is doing all of this for you and for your children. Don't you understand that? A war is going on and people are going to die. It is as simple as that!"

"Doing it for me? Doing it for our children? Don't kid yourself. He is as much interested in saving his own skin as he is interested in saving ours."

Eva's eyes were full of rage.

"Forgive me for saying this, Abraham, but Marie, you forget that if you and your girls weren't Jewish, we might not even be here. All those people who you are whining about might still be alive. Did you ever think of that?"

Marie's eyes were now equally filled with rage. She was no longer timid and meek.

"How dare you blame me and my innocent children for these murders. How dare you!"

She lunged at Eva. In an instant, they were on the ground. I just stood there watching, not knowing whom to help.

"Watch out, the cliff!" Josef yelled.

A shrill scream filled the air. It was Marie. She had fallen off the edge and landed five meters below. Abraham and I rushed down the side of the hill towards her.

"Marie, Marie, can you hear me?" I asked. "Are you alright?"

She was alive and conscious, but her left leg was seriously injured.

"I think my leg is broken, Erik."

"Mama, Mama!" the girls screamed as they ran down the side of the hill towards her.

"I'm alright, girls. Don't worry about me."

Josef bent down and grasped Marie's leg. Marie let loose a soft howl of pain.

Abraham went into the woods and came back with two sturdy branches which he cut in half with his axe. Josef, apparently familiar with this type of situation, quickly made a splint.

Abraham whispered to me, "This is as good as we can do for now."

"I don't know if I can make it, Erik."

"You have to, Mama," Susanne told her mother as she caressed Marie's hair.

"I'll help you, Marie," Eva told her. "I'm so sorry for what I did."

Josef motioned for me and Abraham to come by him. We considered whether or not we should return to the farm house, but we decided to press on.

"We have a long way to go. It is going to be very difficult for your wife. We have to make a stretcher and carry her. It's the only way. Heaven help us if we run into another patrol, and believe me, the patrols will be out as soon as these four are found to be missing."

I helped Abraham make the stretcher and we were on our way. Marie was in great pain but soon her moaning stopped as she fell in and out of a restless sleep. Abraham and I carried her and Eva helped the children, sometimes carrying one, then the other in her arms. She was terribly upset about what had happened, but was it really her fault, or had Marie overreacted?

I thought that under the circumstances we were making good time, but Josef was constantly looking at his watch, which convinced me that this wasn't good enough.

"We'll have trouble staying ahead of the patrols."

"We just won't rest as much," Abraham kiddingly told him.

Josef became very serious. "I know that each time I come out here there is a risk, but I always felt I could outsmart the Nazis. In this case, however, because of the stupidity of two women, it is possible that I will lose my life. I didn't bargain on this, Abraham. You did not pay me enough to take this chance!"

Abraham grabbed Josef by the arm and swung him around.

"Now, listen, old man! I hired you to lead us out of here and that is exactly what you are going to do. Now, shut up and keep walking."

Josef wisely said no more and continued forward, at a pace even faster than before, seemingly trying to punish us for our impudence.

We climbed higher, always looking behind us for the ever present Nazis. An hour went by before Josef signaled that we could rest.

I walked over to Marie. The girls were standing around her, caressing their mother.

After a few moments, Abraham took me outside the girls' earshot.

"Erik, Marie is not good. I felt her head. She has a fever and must be in much pain."

For the first time, I became alarmed.

"What are we going to do, Abraham?"

"Papa, papa, come here," Susanne called. "Mama wants you."

I ran to Marie.

"Erik, oh, Erik, the pain is so bad. My leg hurts so much. Please, is there anything you can do?"

I stood there, helpless.

"Soon, Marie, soon. We'll be safe soon and we can get you to a doctor. Don't give up. Please!"

I felt her head. Abraham was right. She was burning with fever. Giving her water helped momentarily, but soon she was crying and moaning all over again.

Josef's silence ended.

"Come on. We must keep going. We'll all be dead if the Nazis catch us."

Abraham and I picked up the stretcher and Eva took the girls by the hand. Josef told us we only had about another two hours to go before we would stop for the night. Tomorrow, we would be in Switzerland.

We reached the camp site Josef had chosen where we would rest until morning. My arms felt like they were going to fall off. Remarkably, Abraham showed little wear.

We didn't dare start a fire. It was likely that patrols were not far off. Eva fed the girls while I tried to get some food down Marie. Laying still seemed to help her a bit. The constant moving back and forth in the stretcher, even though we had been as careful as possible, had caused her great pain.

The children fell asleep quickly, each of the girls lying next to Eva. Children have short memories, or perhaps they don't hold a grudge. Abraham, Josef and I would take turns keeping watch. Josef took the first turn, Abraham would go next. I managed to fill a cup with cold water from a stream. I soaked a rag and placed it on Marie's burning forehead.

"Thank you, Erik. That feels so good."

Dear God, please keep her alive. She didn't deserve this. Don't let her die!

After Marie fell asleep, I laid down and dozed off within minutes, but it seemed like only seconds later that I felt Josef's hand over my mouth.

"Erik, Erik, keep still. Can you hear them?"

I rose quickly, still half asleep.

"Over there, look over there."

I gazed in the direction of his pointed finger. Down, far below in the valley, I could see lights, many lights, moving slowly, slowly up and towards us. They were quite a distance away.

Abraham had seen them too.

"Everyone up. We have to take cover. We'll get off the path and into the woods. Hopefully they will pass and we can continue down."

I thought to myself that this might be just the chance we needed. If the patrol passed us, we could wait and then go down the same way that they came up. It was unlikely there would be another patrol between the lake and here.

Distances can be deceptive, especially in hilly terrains such as these. The soldiers seemed to be farther away than they really were. Steadily and consistently they made their way up the path. Two kilometers away, then one, and soon they were almost upon us. I could now make out their uniforms. They were also regular Wehrmacht, but this time about twenty in number. I could hear their conversations. They were looking for the lost patrol. Little did they know that if they continued a way more, and if they searched off the beaten path, they would find their dead companions.

We stayed still, very still, our weapons poised and ready to fire. If we were forced to fire, however, even though we would kill some of them, they would because of their sheer number surely kill all of us. Perhaps they would spare the children? I really didn't know.

The first half of the patrol passed without incident, then a half dozen more until only the rear of the unit remained. It seemed like it took them hours but finally they passed as well. We were safe. Josef had us wait until all of the soldiers were out of sight.

"Abraham, Erik, come, let's move on. We can make it if we hurry."

Abraham and I picked up the stretcher. This time Marie didn't moan. Maybe she was actually getting better.

We proceeded quickly down the path, always looking over our shoulders. If we were noticed, it would be the end of us.

"Abraham, do you see that body of water in the distance?" Josef pointed his finger. "That is Lake Constance. Even in the busiest of times, there are seldom guards stationed here. I have two boats hidden in the cattails. We will use them to cross the lake."

My arms, which just a short time before had felt useless to me, suddenly had strength beyond belief. We all quickened our pace. The lake couldn't be more than two kilometers away.

"Slow down! We must still be careful. All it takes is for one of those soldiers to head back and see us. We must stay close to the edge of the path and move slowly, from tree to tree and from boulder to boulder."

Josef was right. We had to be careful. Now that we were so close, it was not the time to ruin everything.

"Papa, are we almost there?" Louisa asked.

"Yes, dear, we are almost in Switzerland. We will be free soon."

We reached the location where Josef had hidden the boats. "Get the boats out, and stay low," he said.

He had done a good job hiding them amongst the cattails.

"About an hour before daybreak, we will cross the lake," Josef said. I could see lights in the distance. Could we be this close?

"Josef, if we wait until then, don't we risk that this patrol will discover those bodies, radio their findings, and alert any border patrols? As long as the coast is clear now, why don't we make a try for it?"

This was the first time that Abraham had questioned Josef's directives.

"We'll be alright," Josef responded. "And besides, our contacts aren't scheduled to meet us until then. We have no other choice."

The girls spent time with their mother, obviously happy that she seemed to feel better. Abraham and Josef got some well deserved sleep, and I volunteered to keep the watch for the first hour.

Eva joined me.

"It's hard to believe, Erik, but I think we are going to make it."

I took her by her hand.

"Yes, Eva, just across this lake and then a little further. That's as far as we have to go before we will be free of the Nazi grip."

I knew that getting out of the Reich was only half the battle. We still had to find a way to get to South America.

Soon everyone was asleep, except for me. As I sat there watching, I had time to think about my future. If I ever did get out of this mess, I would have to start my life over, without any real money to speak of, with two children and a wife. A wife whom I now doubted my love for. I would be in a foreign country, not knowing the language or the people. If there were any Jews there, I could only hope they wouldn't find out about my past, and if there were any Germans, I hoped they wouldn't think less of me for running away from the Reich.

Soon, Josef relieved me and it was my turn to sleep, but I couldn't, unlike before. I think it was all the anxiety and apprehension building in me since I knew that by this time tomorrow, we would either be safe in Switzerland or captured. It was inevitable that one of the two would happen.

"Wake up, Erik. We must cross the lake now."

Everyone hurried, packing their things and putting them into the two boats. Even the children were excited and there was actually a smile on Marie's face.

"I think we are going to make it, Erik. I'm still having a hard time believing it, but it seems to be actually happening."

Eva, Abraham, Josef and I dragged the boats to the water's edge. Josef suggested that I cross with Eva and the girls, while Abraham would go with him and Marie. Abraham had placed Marie in a sitting position on the floor of the boat so that she would be as comfortable as possible. We pushed out from shore and were immediately engulfed by a heavy, fog-like mist, eerily rising from the lake like out of a novel by Shelley or Poe.

"The fog will make for good cover," Josef said.

"Hopefully it will last until we cross," added Abraham, rowing his boat. "Where will our contacts meet us, Josef?"

"Can you make out that small bay on the north-east corner?"

"Barely," Abraham answered.

"That bay is our meeting place. They should be there soon."

I was manning the oars in our boat. Except for a fishing boat to our right, I saw no other activity on the water. The surrounding shoreline appeared deserted, and quiet as death.

The journey across the lake would be longer than I initially thought, since our boats, although seaworthy, were not exactly made for speed, and the oars were more like make-shift planks of wood.

For a while all went well, but as we got past the halfway point, the wind suddenly began to pick up, blowing the fog away.

"I don't like this," I heard Josef complain.

I wondered if he also noticed how difficult it was to stay on course. The wind and the waves were gathering momentum. As hard as I tried, I couldn't keep the boat straight.

"Let me help," Eva insisted. "You take one oar and I'll take the other. It will be easier when both of us are paddling."

I gladly accepted her assistance.

I looked behind and I could see the difficulty Abraham was having, as strong as he was, in staying close to us. With every stroke we took, he seemed to be falling further behind.

As we got farther onto the lake, the wind picked up even more and now the waves were beginning to come over the boat's side. We still had a long way to go.

Storm clouds covered the darkening sky. Eva and I kept rowing harder and harder. Instead of moving straight ahead, our boat moved on an angle, not towards the safety of the distant shore, but rather towards the dangerous middle of the lake.

I looked back to where the fishing boat had been, but it was gone and nowhere to be seen.

"Erik! I can't keep the boat on course!"

I looked back. Even with Josef's help, their boat had completely turned sideways and was drifting out of control. "Papa, Papa. Do something!" cried Louisa.

I felt so helpless. Eva could see their danger as well as I.

"Erik, we must indeed do something. Their boat is going to capsize."

Abraham's boat was drifting farther and farther away. I stopped rowing. At least, that way we would drift with them.

Abraham was doing his best just to keep the boat headed into the wind in order to keep too much water from pouring over the front. Josef was trying to bail out the incoming water, but I could see that he was not keeping up with the deluge.

If only the wind would die down.

We were now far off our intended course.

"Erik, look!" Eva screamed.

I turned to where she was pointing and saw Abraham's boat about to take a huge wave of water. This would surely sink it.

"Abraham, look out!"

It was too late. The wave slammed over their boat, first knocking it backwards, then forwards, filling it with water from the rear as well as from the front. I could see Marie trying to pull herself up from the bottom. The top of the boat, which was at least one half meter above the water when we began, was now only slightly above the surface. Josef kept bailing while Abraham kept trying to keep the boat from capsizing. I knew they wouldn't make it.

"Eva, are there any life vests?"

"There aren't any, Erik. I looked already."

The girls were half submerged in water. I remembered that they had taken swimming lessons back home. I hoped that they would remember some of what they learned.

I looked back towards Marie and Abraham, their boat now barely afloat. Abraham yelled out to me. "Erik, we've got to get out of the boat before it pulls us down."

I watched with horror as he let himself slowly into the dark water, then placed Marie's arms around his neck.

"Hold on to me, Marie, and I'll take us to shore," I heard him tell her.

She did as she was told and the two of them slipped into the black water. Josef was the last to leave the boat before it disappeared from view. He seemed to be having great difficulty trying to stay above the surface.

"I'm coming to help you," I yelled to Abraham.

"No, Erik, don't!" Marie screamed back. "You and Eva help the girls. They can't make it alone."

I knew that our boat wouldn't stay afloat much longer so I told Eva to get the girls ready. The water was cold as I took Susanne and Eva took Louisa into the darkness.

"Don't be afraid," Eva said to them. "We'll all make it to safety."

Before our boat sank, I managed to kick out the seats. We would use them as floats.

In the darkness, I could barely make out the shoreline, but there was a flickering light, going on and off as if it was trying to signal us. Then there was a second light, and a third. The lights were moving towards us, along the water's edge.

I had always been a strong swimmer and Susanne's weight was not difficult for me to handle. Eva also seemed to be able to carry Louisa, and the four of us slowly moved closer to the lights.

I looked back towards Abraham and Marie. I could tell he was tiring trying to keep both of them from going under. I also looked for Josef, but he was gone.

"Eva, you and the girls hang on to the seats and try to kick your way to the shore. Do you think you can do this?"

"Yes, but where are you going?"

"Abraham can't make it alone with Marie. I have to try to help him."

After I made sure that the girls and Eva were alright, I swam away from them and towards Marie and Abraham.

"I'm coming, Marie. Don't give up."

Swimming as fast as I could in the darkness, I made it to where I had last seen them.

"Marie, Abraham! Where are you?"

Stopping in the water, I turned my head in all directions. The darkness and the waves lapping over my head made it almost impossible to see anything. I paddled around in a circle, looking in all directions.

"Erik, over here!"

It was Abraham. His voice told me he was not far away. I swam another ten meters or so towards the sound and then I saw him, straight ahead. He was hanging on to one of the oars, but it couldn't keep him totally above water. His face was pale and he was gasping for breath.

"Where's Marie, Abraham? Where is Marie?"

He didn't answer. I swam next to him and asked again.

"Where is she, man. Tell me!"

Gasping, between words, he answered, "I don't know, Erik. She was with me, hanging onto my neck. I thought we would make it, and then, without warning, she lost her grip. I turned around, but she was gone, gone."

"Where, Abraham, show me."

"About five meters that way. That's where I last saw her."

I swam to where he pointed and dived under the water, but it was useless. It was pitch dark underneath. I could see nothing. I tried over and over again, until I feared I would drown as well.

At the surface, I yelled, "Marie! Marie! Where are you?... Marie, Marie..."

Abraham then called out, "Erik, come on. We must get to shore. Marie's gone, Erik. We have to get to shore and out of here, quick."

I hesitated, looked around, but saw no Marie. Was this how it was going to end, the girls without a mother and me without my wife?

"Erik, come on, man. Remember your children!"

I swam towards Abraham, leaving Marie to her dark grave. With all the strength I had left, I grabbed my friend's shoulder and guided him towards the lights. We swam without saying a word. At shore, I could make out Eva and the girls. They had already made it to the shallows. There were others near them, presumably assisting them. Who were these men? Were they our contacts or were they just residents along the lake who noticed our distress? Or was it a border patrol?

"Can you make out who they are, Abraham?"

"I can't tell for sure but I think they are our contacts, you know, the lights we saw moving on the shore."

The winds had died down somewhat and we could now swim without too much difficulty. A short distance away, I could see two men swimming out to us. Soon we would be safe. I could just begin to hear their voices. They spoke German.

"Hang on, we will be to you in seconds. Don't give up!"

When they reached us, they asked, "Are there any others?"

"Yes," I said. "There are two others left behind, back there, a man and a woman."

"We will look for them. Here, take these vests. Can you two make it to shore while we look for the others?"

"Yes, please try to find them."

They swam towards where I had picked up Abraham. Maybe they would find Marie and Josef.

"Erik, until I'm sure who these men are, say as little as possible and let me do the talking."

210

I nodded as Abraham let loose of my shoulder.

Before I even reached the shore, I could hear Louisa call out.

"Papa, where is Mama?" I didn't know what to say to her.

"Where is she, Papa?" Susanne joined in.

I could feel the sand below me, and a tall man extended his hand to me.

"I am Ivan Kollmar. Which one of you is Abraham?" Then I knew these men were our contacts.

I went to the girls and took both of them in my arms. I looked at them, trying to see if they understood what happened. I couldn't tell if they did or not. The expression on each of their faces was one of confusion. I knew they understood that something was wrong but they were so young, far too young to understand the full meaning of death, far too young to comprehend that they would never see their mother again.

"Don't worry, little ones. Your Mama will join us later," Eva told them as she wrapped blankets around both girls.

I had to concentrate on us now. There would be time to mourn Marie at a later occasion.

Leaving the children with Eva, I walked over to Abraham who was talking to Ivan.

"Herr Byrnes, my deepest sympathies to you and your children," he said, pointing out towards the water. The two men who were trying to find Marie and Josef, were now swimming back to shore, only the two of them. Their search had been unsuccessful.

"Thank you," I answered. "Thank you for all your efforts."

"Abraham, I am sorry but we must leave right now. There is no time to lose. Soldiers will be upon us in no time."

I knew that he was right, but how could I leave Marie out there? Maybe she was still alive, grasping to a piece of the boat or to an oar, waiting to be saved.

"Abraham, you were with her. Tell me. Is there any chance that she could still be out there alive?"

He looked directly into my eyes and grasped my hand.

"Erik, I was with her. She was growing weak. Remember, her leg was broken. There is no way she could still be alive. She wouldn't have had the strength to make it. No, Erik, she is gone, gone to a better life."

"Was there anything she could have hung on to, to save her?"

"Nothing that I could see, nothing at all. Come, let's go. You now have your children to worry about. They depend on you. Marie wouldn't have wanted you to delay if that meant putting Louisa and Susanne in danger."

He was right. We must go on.

One of the men had brought a truck to the shore. It was a large truck, with a canvass cover. Instead of manure, this time the load was sacks of onions. We moved the sacks around and the five of us managed to get into the rear. Ivan looked nervous.

"Hurry, hurry, we must get going. The patrols will be here any minute. There is a good chance they saw our lights."

The truck sped off, and we left Marie and Josef alone for eternity. Eva could sense my sadness.

"Erik, I'll always be here for you and the girls. I mean that. Don't turn away from me now."

She was right. I needed her now. Since the girls were born, it was Marie who took care of them. I was always working and that's the way it should have been. Now that she was gone, I needed somebody to do what Marie did before, especially now that I had to devote all my time and attention just to keeping us alive. After all, the children were young enough. Hopefully, they'd adjust to Eva eventually.

"Thank you, Eva. I do want your help. Please do what you can to help the children."

A smile crossed her face. She bent over and kissed me on the cheek. Abraham could only smile as he watched on.

While the truck sped down the road, we and the onion sacks were being thrown in every direction. Ivan was in a great hurry.

"How much further to the border, Abraham?"

"I am not positive but it can't be far." He reached inside his jacket, then frantically started searching his pockets.

"My God, Erik, the papers. They are gone!"

"What do you mean, *gone*, Abraham?"

"Our identification papers to get us across the border, they must have fallen out of my pocket when the boat sank. How are we going to cross now?"

"Abraham, there is nothing we can do about it now. When we get to the border we just have to tell them that we lost the papers. What else can we do?" We would be there soon anyway.

"What was that?" Eva screamed. A loud bang had exploded. It sounded like the hand-held weapons that our infantry used against the Russian tanks. Then another loud explosion, now from ahead of the truck. The brakes screeched and we swerved to the right. A round must have landed in front of the truck, causing Ivan's evasive actions.

We were no longer on the road but rather in a field of some type. The children were crying as the heavy sacks of onions were falling all over and around us. Eva was doing her best to shelter the girls.

Now I could hear the rat-a-tat-tat of machine gun fire and the piercing sounds of bullets cutting through the walls of the truck and into the onions surrounding us.

The truck was still moving, swaying back and forth.

"How much further, Abraham?" I screamed.

"I don't know. I don't know!"

Eva, Abraham and myself huddled around the girls, trying to protect them from the bullets. Just another minute, just another minute. Please God, just give us a little more time.

Just then, we were tossed against the wall, as the truck tipped over on its side. A fire broke out in the front cab.

"We've got to get out, now, before the gas tank explodes!" Abraham yelled.

We struggled to get out. Less than one hundred meters behind us were our pursuers.

Abraham ran ahead to the front of the burning cab. "Ivan, Ivan, which way, which way do we go?" he yelled as he ran, but there was no response. I peered into the cab and saw Ivan through the flames, his body already semi-black. I could smell burning flesh, much like at Auschwitz.

"That way."

I looked in the direction Abraham was pointing, back to the road. About forty meters away there were several signposts, some in German and some in another language. There were men and vehicles parked there, just watching what was happening to us.

"That must be the border and those must be the Swiss. Come on, let's make a run for it. It's our only chance."

I picked up Susanne and Eva grabbed Louisa as we ran towards the Swiss. Abraham made up the rear, firing from his Luger.

Thirty more meters, the bullets whizzed over our heads, fifteen more meters, ten more...

"Keep going, keep going, don't stop!" Abraham yelled.

We were almost there. I could now make out the expressions on the faces of the Swiss. They were cheering us on. "Come on. Come on. You can do it. Keep coming."

Five meters to go... "Who pushed me?"

213

In that split second, as I flew through the air towards the border crossing, I landed face first on the hard, rock-strewn ground. A shell must have struck behind us. Fortunately, I didn't drag Susanne with me.

Blood was oozing from my upper shoulder as Eva stopped to pick up Susanne.

"Keep going. Get across," I hollered.

Just then, there was Abraham. "Hang on, Erik!" he yelled.

With all his magnificent strength, he grabbed me with both arms and carried me the short way to the border. The shooting had stopped. I looked up and could see why. The Swiss had their weapons raised and pointed them straight at the oncoming Nazis.

A loudspeaker bellowed out. "These people are now on Swiss soil. You will put down your weapons. These refugees are under the protection of the Swiss government. Cease, or we will shoot!"

23

Freedom?

WHILE the Swiss led us towards a small building, I turned to face the shouting Germans.

"Swine! Assholes! Someday, we will get you back in Germany and then you will die, you pigs. All of you will die, especially the three bitches."

"Pay no attention to those animals," our Swiss guard assured us in perfect German. "Every time somebody escapes across the border, it's the same thing. They swear and we all laugh."

"Does this happen often?" I asked.

"Frankly, I wish it happened more that it actually does. I would honestly say that of all the escape attempts I have either witnessed or heard of, less than twenty-five percent actually are successful. Another twenty or so seconds, and you would not have been here talking to me. You see, Herr..."

I didn't know what to say to him. Come to think of it, Abraham and I had never discussed what names we would use if we lost the papers.

"Schoflen, Erik Schoflen, and this is my family."

The guard smiled.

"Well yes, Herr Schoflen, as I was saying, you see, we are prohibited from crossing the border to assist anyone escaping here, but by the same token we will fire if theytry to tresspass onto Swiss soil. If the Germans had not put down their weapons when they did, those machine guns in the towers would have taken care of them. And, Herr Schoflen, they know that all too well. Believe me, they do."

"What will you do with us?" I asked.

"First of all, we will see to it that you and your family are given a place to wash and clean up and receive some food. Our commandant will then proceed with the standard questioning, just the basic questions, you know."

He could tell that I didn't know what he meant.

"Herr Schoflen, in the last few months, now that the Nazis will soon be eating their dead horses for dinner, the Swiss border has become quite, as you might put it, *open* for those who want to escape. You merely have to fill out some forms and produce identification so that you can get a visa and be on your way. Don't worry. Unless you are Heinrich Himmler or Herman Göring, you will have no problem."

He slapped me on the back and laughed. Little did he know how nervous his last words made me.

As we were led into a cafeteria-type room, I stole a glance at Abraham. The look on his face puzzled me. I saw no joy for escaping the Nazis nor worry that we might be discovered. No, I think it was more a look of guilt.

When Eva and the girls were out of earshot, I asked him about it. "Abraham, old friend, tell me, what is troubling you? You can be honest with me."

"Nothing, Erik, nothing. I'm just tired, that's all, just tired."

I looked intensely at him. "Don't lie to me, Abraham. I've known you too long. I know when something is troubling you, and believe me, something *is* troubling you right now. What is it?"

"If you must know, Erik, it's Marie. She is what's troubling me. I feel it is my fault that she is not here with you and her children. She was my responsibility and I let you and the girls down. I will never forgive myself for what I have done."

"You can't blame yourself," I soothed. "You did the best you could. With her broken leg, she was like a dead weight. With the waves and the wind and the darkness, what else could you have done?"

"I know, Erik, I know, but I still feel I let you down. I was thinking about this before. Do you know that I don't believe I have ever let you down before?"

"And I'm telling you this now, you still have not let me or my daughters down. I am holding no grudge against you. Without you, we would never have gotten as far as we have."

He smiled faintly. Either he didn't believe that I felt no malice towards him or, worse, he didn't care what I felt.

The Swiss meal was more than adequate. There was milk, bread, cheese, meats and some small fruits. We were all famished. Afterwards, the women serving the food were kind enough to bring some dolls for the girls. This brought back a smile to their faces. Eva was excellent with them.

"Papa, how long will we be here?" Susanne asked.

"And when will Mama come and see us, Papa?" said Louisa.

"We won't be here long, Susanne, just long enough for us to rest," Eva answered for me.

"But when will Mama be here?" Louisa insisted.

I looked at Eva, imploring her with my eyes to help me. I just couldn't tell the girls the truth, not just yet.

"Your Mama will join us later, children, when we get to our new home. But right now I want you girls to both play a game!"

"What kind of game?" they asked.

"I want you to pretend that I am your mother and that your new name is *Schoflen*. Whenever somebody asks you, you have to remember this. Won't that be fun, girls?"

Children are so trusting. Even so obvious a distortion seemed to quiet them, at least for now.

We practiced our new names over and over. It was about half an hour or so before we heard the outer door open. In walked a man in his fifties, thinly built and with reddish-brown hair. In perfect German he said, "Good day, my name is Otto Kentler. I am in charge of this outpost. There are some formalities I must go over with you, if you don't mind."

What could we say? "No, of course not, Herr Kentler, please sit down," Eva enticingly told him.

"Good, good, now let's begin. You are Erik Schoflen and this is your wife, your children and your..."

"My brother, he is my brother Abraham. My wife's name is Eva and these are our daughters, Susanne and Louisa."

"Very good, very good. Thank you. Thank you very much. May I ask you for some type of identification, Herr Schoflen."

"We have no identification on us, Herr Kentler."

"And why is that?"

"They were lost when we capsized in a storm on Lake Constance."

"I see," he acknowledged. "I see. This is going to make my job more difficult. You see these forms here?"

He showed us the paperwork he had to fill out.

"I'm required to indicate on these papers that I have personally seen some type of formal identification."

Eva took over. "Herr Kentler. Come now. A man as experienced as yourself must have come across a situation like this before. Not every escapee carries identification papers with them, do they?"

"Well... I don't recall not..."

"Really, just look at us. Two men, two children and one woman. Do we really look like anybody the Swiss government should fear or take a special interest in? We are just refugees, escaping the Nazi tyranny."

Kentler was obviously impressed by Eva, but then, any man would have been. For a second or two, I really believed he would accept her explanation and let us go without any identification papers.

217

"I'm very sorry, Frau Schoflen. I must have some type of documentation in order to let you all pass. The alternative is that you will have to wait here until my superiors arrive. They can of course make the decision to let you pass, papers or no papers. Unfortunately, I don't have that authority. With all the commotion that occurred when you arrived, it would be impossible to just forget about the whole thing."

"How long before your superiors will be able to see us?" I asked Kentler.

"They are scheduled to arrive tomorrow morning, at the latest. You see, this is not a heavily traveled border crossing and manpower here is still somewhat limited. But please, don't worry, you are the guests of the Swiss government and I will do everything in my power to make all of you, and especially the children, as comfortable as can be. You are free to walk about the grounds, but please, do not try to leave the perimeter. The guards have standing orders to shoot to kill and they make no exceptions."

With that, Kentler stood up, made a quick bow and left the room.

"Now, what do we do, Abraham?"

"I'm thinking, Erik. I'm thinking. By now, our next set of contacts must know that something went wrong."

"Erik, the girls are starting to get bored, do you mind if I take them for a walk?" Eva asked.

"Meet us back here in an hour. Perhaps by then Abraham and I will have come up with some idea."

"Come on, Erik," said Abraham. "Let's take a closer look at this place. Perhaps there is a way to get out of here."

"Abraham, even if we can get out of here, how do we get in touch with our contacts?"

"I know the town where we were to meet them. It is a small place, just down the road from here. If we could just get there."

Abraham and I took a stroll around the grounds. The border crossing itself and the few surrounding buildings had ten guards or so to cover the entire area. Much of the area was neither fenced nor guarded.

"Erik, I think that with a little planning we could get out of here unnoticed."

"Yes, but what then? Where could we hide, especially with the children?"

"If I could get to a phone, or even better, to that village, I know I could find our contacts. I am sure they are waiting for us there. We have to come up with a plan to get me into the village."

We walked further.

"I have it, Erik!"

"Well, what is it?"

"You will tell Kentler that the children need medicine for their asthma. You will tell him that you understand his reluctance in allowing you to leave and you will suggest that their uncle, that being me, leave with the children. You and Eva will stay behind. He won't suspect that a mother and father would allow their children to leave without returning. I will go with the children into the village, pick up some medicine, find our contacts, and return with a plan already set."

I thought about his idea. It sounded like it could work. Kentler seemed like a reasonable individual. Besides, we had to do something quick before the real interrogators arrived.

We ran into Kentler as he was about to enter one of the buildings.

"Herr Kentler. May I have a word with you?"

"Yes, Herr Schoflen. What can I do for you?"

"It's my daughters, Herr Kentler. They are both asthmatic."

"I am sorry to hear this. How can I be of service?"

"Would you be kind enough to allow their uncle here to walk with them to the village to get some medicine? Ours was lost. My wife feels so badly about this. I will stay here with her as a token of our good will."

Kentler said nothing, so Abraham weighed in. "Please, Herr Kentler. I am just a poor farmer, but I love my nieces very much. Please let me take them to the village to get the medicine. I could not bear it if something happened to them."

Kentler began to walk back and forth across the grounds, his hands crossed behind his back, his head lowered in deep thought. Another minute passed and then he said, "Very well. I have no objection, and besides, what harm can it cause? Herr Schoflen and his wife will stay here, so I guess that guarantees your return. Do you have any money for the medicine?"

Abraham hesitated, obviously not prepared for the question.

"Never mind, my friend." Kentler reached into his pocket and handed Abraham some currency. "Here, take this for the children. When you reach freedom, you can mail the money back to me."

Abraham smiled and gave Kentler a quick bow. He and I then left to look for Eva and the girls. We gathered around Eva.

"Now, listen to me. It's only about a fifteen-minute walk to the village. Once I'm there, I will surely be able to find our contacts. I will come up with something. I'll try to get some papers prepared. Don't worry. Everything will be alright."

Eva and I shook Abraham's hand. Then I walked up to the children. "I want both of you to go for a walk with Uncle Abraham. He is going to take you to the village to get you some candy."

The girls jumped up and down and danced around Abraham. They had such a look of joy on their little faces.

"Come on, Uncle Abraham. Let's go," Susanne said.

"Yes, little ones. It's time to go. Go give your Papa a kiss." I bent down as each girl reached up on her tiptoes, Susanne kissing me on the left cheek and Louisa on the right. "Bye, Papa. We will be back soon."

Eva and I watched as Abraham and the children walked down the dirt road. I gazed at them as they turned towards us, waving goodbye. Their silhouettes got smaller and smaller, and after a few minutes I could no longer make them out. They were gone.

"Well, what should we do now, Erik?" Eva said, taking hold of my hand. I didn't know how to answer her. It was a good question. What should we do now?

"Don't be shy, *Herr Schoflen*. After all, we are husband and wife, are we not?"

I thought about that. Now that Marie was gone, the girls would need a mother. They were young enough that, after time, Marie would only be a memory to them. Eva seemed fond of the girls and the girls seemed to have forgotten the fight Marie had with her.

"Eva, sit down on this bench. I want to talk to you."

She did as I asked.

"You told me that you would be there for me. Do you still feel that way?"

She did not hesitate. "Of course, my love. And what about you, Erik? How do you feel about me? Remember, if it wasn't for me, Marie would not have broken her leg and she likely would have made it off the lake. I blame myself for that, Erik. I will have to live with this guilt for the rest of my life. So I need to know, how do you feel about me?"

I put my arms around her and held her tight.

"Oh, Eva, I love you and I blame you for nothing. Nothing that has happened has been your fault. Can't you see that?"

Tears gathered in the corners of my eyes. "Eva, I will miss Marie for the rest of my life. She was a good and kind person who didn't deserve what happened to her. You need to know that I will never forget her. Can you bear that thought, Eva?"

"I can, Erik. I can, but you should know that if Marie came back today, I would not give you up. I would fight for you and still love you even if you would go back to her. I know that I can't take her place in your heart or in the hearts of your children, but I promise that I will make life better for the three of you if you give me that chance."

Marie had been gone less than a day and here I was seriously thinking of marrying Eva.

"I have not even given Marie the period of mourning that she deserves. And you, Eva, you don't really know me. You don't know what atrocities I have committed in the name of the great German Reich. You don't know how many thousands I have sent to their death, men, women and children."

"Erik, I don't care what you have done in the past. I only know that I love you and I love your children."

"There is something else you should know, Eva. People who get close to me seem to have a tendency to die. There was my best friend, Dieter Schmidt, who died trying to help me. Then there was my understudy, an officer by the name of Bach. He too died because of me. Then Horst Strasser, the SS investigator who also was killed because of me. If I am discovered, you will surely be caught as well. If that happens, they may execute you. Do you really want to risk that? Wouldn't you be better off trying to get out of here and as far away from me as possible?"

Eva didn't waste any time answering.

"No, Erik, I love you and I want you to marry me as soon as we can find a minister."

I looked into her eyes. I convinced myself that she fully understood the risks she was taking by becoming my wife. If she wanted me so badly, there was no reason why I should deny my desire to be with her. She would be a good wife and a mother to my children, a mother they desperately needed.

"Eva, I will marry you as soon as we can."

With a smile that covered her entire face, she got up from the bench and put her arms around me.

"Oh, Erik. I promise I will be a good wife to you and a good mother to your children. I will be strong and protect them as if they were my own."

As we were embracing, Kentler happened to walk by. Smiling, he nodded his typical short bow and continued on his way.

The hours passed on. Eva and I had walked the entire grounds at least twice and we had seen all the administration buildings as well.

"Don't you think they should have returned by now, Erik?" Eva asked.

"No, not yet. Abraham needs time to make contact and establish a plan. He probably is working right now on trying to get papers for us. They won't be back for some time. Don't worry. Abraham has been totally reliable in the past and there is no reason to believe that he won't get the job done now."

We spent the next hour seated by a small pond within the compound. Kentler noticed that we were not doing anything special, and he was kind enough to ask Eva and me to join him and a female member of the Swiss staff during a break. Although I dreaded getting into any type of conversation that might trigger a slip of the tongue, the idea of turning him down would have been the worse of two evils.

"It is very kind of you to ask us to join you, Herr Kentler."

"It is my pleasure, Frau Schoflen. Please sit down."

Eva and I took our seats between Kentler and his aide.

"Herr and Frau Schoflen, may I introduce Ida Schmidt, my assistant."

Then, what I feared began to happen.

"Herr Schoflen. Forgive me for being so inquisitive, but my curiosity gets the best of me."

I didn't want to offend him, so I told him it was alright for him to continue.

"I would much like to know, why did you and your family flee the Reich?"

I had been waiting for him to ask this question, or I should say I had been waiting for somebody to ask this question. I hoped that I had prepared myself properly.

"Herr Kentler, being Swiss, you have not had the *luxury* of living under a regime where the government is paternal and gracious enough to do the thinking for you and your family. In Austria, and throughout the German Reich, no one had to worry about such mundane things as *conscience* or *morality*. No, we had men such as Goebbels, Himmler and even the Führer himself to do that for us. They would decide what was right and what was wrong and what we could believe in and what would be too harmful for us to consider. Actually, these fine minds would even dictate who was fit to live and who should be put to death."

I could see I was making an impression. Kentler and his aide listened attentively to every word I was saying.

"Unfortunately for myself and my family, my wife and I did not agree with that philosophy. Like many other German-Austrians, at first we said and did nothing. It was about one year ago that Eva and myself decided that it was time for Austrian citizens like us to speak up and speak out against the tyranny and oppression that exists in our country. We had lived in the area for some time and knew most of the people, so our words did not cause us any harm from the local officials. Had we left it at that, we probably would not have gotten into the trouble that we did and probably would not be sitting here talking to you today."

Kentler's eyes were now riveted on mine.

"No, Herr Kentler, we went one step further." I grasped Eva's hand, indicating that we had been in this together. "We began to harbor Jews, Herr Kentler, Jews, the scourge of all Germany and of all good men the world over. We provided hiding places for them, the refugees of camps such as Mauthausen."

I could tell from his expression that he approved of what I told him we had done. I decided now was the time to tell him what I felt would be discovered soon, without my input.

"I have a confession to tell you, Herr Kentler. I have not been totally honest with you and I am not proud that I have deceived you."

He looked up.

"What do you mean, *not honest with me*, Herr Schoflen?"

"Abraham is not my brother, Herr Kentler. He is a Jew whom we had hidden and who escaped with us from Vienna. I am so sorry for not telling you this right away but I didn't know when I first met you, how you felt towards the Jews. It was only when I became convinced that you were a kind and good man that I felt I could tell you the truth."

Kentler began to laugh.

"Herr Schoflen, I also have a confession to make. I am not as naive as I might appear. In this position, I have seen many Jews trying to cross the border. Although most would not recognize your Abraham as a Jew, I suspected he was one right from the beginning. In fact, Herr Schoflen, I thought even the more of you and your wife because you saw fit to travel with this man and to trust your children with him. Erik, if I were wearing a hat right now, I would take it off to you."

Eva smiled at him with those beautiful blue eyes.

"Frau Schoflen, do you feel as strongly as your husband?" Ida asked.

"Why, yes, I do. It is strange. When the Nazis first entered Austria, back in 1938, my husband and I welcomed their presence and their protection. After all, most of us had German roots."

"May I ask you what made you change your mind?"

"As Erik said, Herr Kentler, it was primarily the persecution of Jews and other minorities that bothered us. No matter how much propaganda the Germans could put out, one could see that it was all lies. How could the Jews have been responsible for plunging Europe into this war? No, it was Hitler himself who caused all this suffering and misery, and after he had started it, he needed a scapegoat, and that scapegoat became the Jew."

"Quite well put, Frau Schoflen, quite well put," Kentler said. "But where will you go when you leave this place?"

I didn't want to tell him the truth. We might be hunted down later if I did. I had to come up with an answer.

"Uh, uh, well, you see, Herr Kentler, my wife and I decided that we no longer want to live here in Europe after all that has happened. We can't live with our own fellow Austrians who condoned such acts of barbarism. No, we must escape to a new world, a world where freedom reigns. We have decided to go to the United States."

"That is all very admirable, Herr Schoflen, but did you know that I have heard about anti-Semitism in America?"

"Yes, Herr Kentler. We have heard this too, but we have also heard that there are many Jews in America, and we need to find a place where Abraham will be welcome."

"Splendid, just splendid! Rest assured, Herr and Frau Schoflen, that I will do my best to make your exit from this place as quick and painless as possible. It is too bad that you don't have any identification papers. If you did, if you had anything at all, I could let you pass right now."

Kentler looked around to make sure there was nobody else besides his aide.

"You know, Erik, I am told that in that village where Abraham and your children are right now, it's not difficult to obtain, shall we say, new identification papers that could be useful to people like you."

"That's very interesting, Otto, very interesting. You wouldn't know exactly where to go for these papers, would you?"

"Well, what I've heard is just rumor, you understand, just rumor. In the village square is a shoemaker's shop. In the back of that shop, I'm told, is a printing press with some photographic and laminating equipment. I understand that this shoemaker does *excellent work* and he is quite reasonable. In fact, he even seems to trust people to pay him when they have reached the destination their *shoes* have taken them to."

"It is too bad that Eva and I did not accompany Abraham when he went down there."

"That would not have worked, Herr Schoflen," Kentler responded somewhat defensively.

"I meant no disrespect, Herr Kentler, none at all."

Then Ida had an idea!

"Otto, wouldn't it be possible for all of us to now go to the village?"

"I don't see how. I overstepped my bounds by even allowing Abraham to leave with the girls. My only excuse was that I have their parents."

"Yes, I suppose you are right," she sighed.

"Herr Kentler, what will Erik and I do, and the children and Abraham, when your supervisors arrive tomorrow? We have no papers. Will they turn us back over to the Germans?"

Kentler didn't answer.

"You know that if we are returned, we surely will all be shot, perhaps even the children."

"Shot, why would you be shot? Even the Germans are not that barbaric, to shoot refugees we return."

"Herr Kentler, Erik didn't tell you this, but I feel I must."

I looked at Eva with my mouth half open. Now what was she going to say?

"You should know that during our escape several German soldiers were killed. If we are forced to return, we will pay the same price, I'm sure."

Startled, Kentler got up and walked up and down the room. "This presents even a more serious problem. I'm sure you had every justification in doing what you did, but by tomorrow the Germans will put pressure on us, with every plausible demand to have you returned to them. If you were ordinary criminals, we would not hesitate to do so. I'm afraid my superiors might view you as such criminals."

He continued his pacing.

"We must do something today, before my superiors arrive. You must have credentials."

"Herr Kentler, couldn't you say that we, the parents, were worried and you agreed to accompany us to the village to look for the children?" Eva suggested.

Kentler looked up. "That is not a bad idea, Frau Schoflen, not bad at all."

This time I jumped in. "Of course, Otto, what a wonderful idea *you* have! Why didn't I think of that? Can we leave right away?"

"Yes, let's go now, but I'm not much inclined to walk the distance. I will go back to my office and strap on a firearm, for appearance sake, and so will Ida. We then will get ourselves a car. Come, there is no time to waste."

"Herr Kentler, my wife and I want to thank you with all our heart for what you are doing for us. We truly do mean this."

"I understand, Erik. It has bothered me for some time already that I have stood silent at this border passing, watching helpless refugees being returned back to the murderous Nazis, sometimes for no reason at all, except that they were Jews."

"Herr Kentler, you really don't have to go into this."

"No, I insist, Erik, I insist."

I thought it best to let him continue even though time was precious.

"You see, Herr Schoflen, for a long time we Swiss believed that the Germans would win this war. With that in mind, we were very concerned about offending the Nazis. Of course, we observed strict protocol and if the refugees managed to get to our soil and they had proper credentials, we protected their interest and did not return them. But if they did not, or if they were Jewish, then our agreement with the Germans mandated that they be returned, whatever the consequences to them. And believe me, we did return them, out of sheer fear. It is now time that I stand up for what I believe and do whatever is necessary and proper. Hopefully, Germany will soon be defeated and I will suffer no repercussions for my actions. It's something I should have done a long time ago. But I was afraid."

Eva put her arm around Kentler.

"We understand. Don't think badly of yourselves. You now are standing up for what you believe. None of us can change what we have done. The only thing that counts is what we will do now and in the future."

"Enough said. Meet me at the dirt road. Ida and I will be there shortly."

As Eva and I walked there, we couldn't help but smile.

"You know, Erik, he is such a sweet man. It is a shame that some day he might find out that he has helped *The Hangman of Vienna* escape from the clutches of justice."

"Don't say that, Eva. Do you have a better idea? If we don't get out of here by the morning, it might be all over for us. To me, that is more important than Kentler's pride, and who knows, maybe he never discovers who we really are."

Meanwhile, I tried as hard as I could to see if I could make out Abraham and the girls walking back this way. I strained my eyes, but I saw no one.

"You, know, Eva, I must admit that I am getting somewhat concerned. I would have thought that by now we should be seeing them coming up the road."

"I'm concerned, too, Erik. You don't suppose something has happened to them, do you?"

"I really don't know. I really don't."

Kentler and Ida arrived at the roadside just when we got there.

"Herr Schoflen, Frau Schoflen, please get in. You, Herr Schoflen, will drive the car and I will sit next to you. Frau Schoflen, you will sit in the back with Ida." And, smiling, but loud enough for the guards to hear, he added, "Remember, both of you are under guard, and if you try to escape, we will have to shoot."

"Of course, Herr Kentler. You need not worry about my wife and me. We only want to find our children."

The guards let us through and we began our way down the dirt road towards the village. I drove slowly, just as Kentler had directed. Still there was no sign of Abraham or the children.

"Erik, how does it feel to be on Swiss soil?"

"You don't know just how good, Otto, but to be quite frank, I won't feel safe until I am thousands of kilometers from the Reich."

"I understand. Let's see if we can find that shoemaker and get you started in that direction."

"Herr Kentler, there is one thing that bothers me."

Now what was Eva going to say?

"What is that, Frau Schoflen?"

"How will we explain that we now have these documents when we were unable to produce them when we first arrived?"

"That is my problem, Frau Schoflen."

Well, if Kentler was willing to take the chance, who were we to argue?

We continued slowly down the roadway. Where in the world were Abraham and the girls?

We entered the outskirts of the village. We passed one home, then another, then a petrol station. The roadway changed from a gravel road to a brick street. There was pedestrian and vehicular traffic. We were approaching the village square.

"The shoemaker is in that building, straight ahead," Kentler pointed out. "Remember, both of you are our prisoners so make sure that you behave that way." Ida laughed at that remark.

I managed to park the car directly next to the shoemaker's shop. I looked both up and down the street hoping that I would be able to see the children with Abraham.

"Do any of you see them?" I asked.

"No, I can't see them anywhere," Eva answered.

"We'll look for them later, Erik," Otto said. "Right now, let's waste no time in getting the proper paper work."

I didn't want to give up looking, but I knew that Otto was right. We didn't have a lot of time.

The three of us went inside while Ida remained in the car, as instructed by Kentler. She would watch for Abraham and the children.

As we entered the shop, a buzzer went off and soon a short, thin man in his late fifties appeared from behind a curtain.

"I recognize you. You are Otto Kentler, are you not?"

"Why, yes I am."

"What can I do for the Swiss government? Do you need your shoes fixed or perhaps you want some footwear for your two friends? I have some fine selections, all the way from Zürich."

"No, no thank you. That is not why we came."

The man stood there, saying nothing, waiting for Kentler to continue.

"I know of your reputation, so may I come straight to the point?"

"Please do. Tell me why you have *really* come to see me."

"Sir, I would like you to meet Erik and Eva Schoflen."

The shoemaker took my hand and then Eva's.

"You see, just earlier today, they managed to escape from Austria with their two children and a Jew they had been hiding. They need papers, papers that will allow them to cross over Europe and then to enter the United States."

"Uh, I see. They need papers, do they?"

The shoemaker stared first at me, then at Eva, then back at me. He looked at me for a long time.

"Herr Kentler, if they were just escapees from the Nazis, political refugees or the like, you and I both know that in light of how the war is proceeding, the Swiss government would allow them to pass within a reasonable period of time, papers or no papers. Is this not true?"

"True, you are right. Times have changed, but there is more. These people were forced to do things during their escape which, I'm afraid, would not be overlooked by my superiors. I'm afraid that by tomorrow morning, if they have no papers, they will all be turned back over to the Nazis as common criminals. That could mean death for all of them, including the children and the Jew."

"Oh, yes, the children and the Jew. Where are these children and this Jew? I'd like to meet them."

"We don't know," Eva answered. "They came into the village hours ago and did not return. We have come here to find them, and at the same time to try to persuade you to help us obtain papers for each of us."

"Yes," I added. "We are very concerned about them."

"Uh... Herr Schoflen? That's your name, isn't it?"

"Yes, that is my name, Erik Schoflen, and this is my wife Eva."

The shoemaker paced the floor, much like Kentler had.

"Well, will you help them?" Kentler asked. "I am risking my own neck by coming to see you and trusting you like I am, but I have stood silent too long watching the Nazis murder and kill and now I have a chance to set things straight. But we need your help."

The shoemaker stopped pacing and looked up at Kentler.

"Of course, for Herr Kentler, for Herr and Frau Schoflen, the children and the Jew, I will help. I will make sure everything is taken care of as it should be. Will you all follow me into the back room, quickly, please?"

We followed him behind the curtain into a back office.

"Please sit down, I will be right back with my equipment."

We sat down while the shoemaker went to another room, this one directly in the rear of where we were seated.

"I knew that he would help us, Erik. I knew he would," Kentler said with a look of success on his face.

We sat for several minutes waiting.

"Erik, I'm getting nervous," said Eva. "What could take him so long?"

"I don't like it either, Eva. Something is not right."

Kentler did not share our concern. "Patience, patience. Artists such as this one are a bit temperamental, you know. They cannot be hurried. They are perfectionists."

Just then the shoemaker returned, carrying a large case in one arm and some folders in the other.

"Now, I want you, Herr Schoflen, to move over against that far wall. Stand erect, about two feet from it."

I did as he said and moved over towards a white wall, obviously to effectuate a better background for a photograph.

"That's it. That's it. Very good," he said as I stood tall and erect, facing him.

"Now you, Herr Kentler, and you, Frau Schoflen, you move over near Herr Schoflen, but stay several feet away so that you don't get in the way of the camera angle."

Eva and Kentler did as they were told. Strange request, I thought. Why wouldn't he just have left them where they were? They obviously were not in the way.

"Now, just stand there, all of you, while I get out my camera."

The shoemaker bent over and unzipped the large case he was carrying, but when he stood upright, he held not a camera but a pistol.

"Kentler, Eva, look out, he has a gun!" I yelled.

"Stop, all of you, or I'll shoot. I promise," the shoemaker hollered as he waived the pistol back and forth in our general direction.

"What is the meaning of this?" Kentler asked in obvious indignation. "We trusted you to be a friend of those who escape the Nazis."

"Herr Kentler, you're a fool."

"How dare you call me a fool."

Eva and I just stood there. I glanced over the room, trying to see if there was any way the shoemaker could be distracted so I could overpower him.

"Sit down, Herr Kentler." The shoemaker pointed with his pistol to a chair. "You too, *Herr Schoflen and Frau Schoflen*, you too sit down."

Kentler looked at me, clearly confused.

"So you really don't know, Kentler, do you?"

"Know what?! I demand you tell me what you are talking about."

"That's a fair request, especially coming from somebody as gullible as you."

I caught the fear in Eva's eyes. The shoemaker must know who I was, and I suppose he thought Eva was Marie, my true wife.

"Kentler, do you know who this man is?"

"Why, of course, he is Erik Schoflen."

"No, Kentler, he is *not* Erik Schoflen."

Kentler became indignant again.

"Now, listen. To be quite honest with you, I don't really care if his name is Schoflen or Schmidt or whatever. That is not important. All I know is that he and his family need your help."

"Kentler, Kentler, I am amazed. I agree. I don't really care what he calls himself. You're right, that's not important. But what is important is the story I am about to tell you."

We all waited for what he had to say.

"You see, earlier today I had three customers walk into my shop, a man and two little girls. I knew right away that they were not from this area and that they certainly were not tourists who entered a shoemaker's shop by accident. I asked the man what he needed and at first he replied that he was looking for shoes for the little girls. They were beautiful twins, I might add. I told him that he was free to look around the shop if he wished to, and he did so for several minutes. It was obvious that he wanted something, something very different from what is on my shelves. You see, I am used to *shoppers* such as this man. They happen to come to my store many times a year, and at all different times of the day and night."

Sweat gathered on my forehead, both because of what the shoemaker was saying and because of the apprehensive looks Kentler was beginning to cast my way.

"At some point, the man walked up to me and told me a fantastic story about a man, his wife, their two children and a Jewish friend. I can assure you that he was very precise and very convincing. He introduced himself as Abraham.

He said that he was told to come to my shop in order to obtain the necessary papers for five persons to cross into Switzerland. Apparently, he met others in this village who knew of my reputation. The passes were for him, the two children and two others, a man and a woman, who were at your border station, Herr Kentler. Just before you arrived, I gave this man the papers he needed except, of course, for the photographs of the man and the woman, which I told Abraham I could take as soon as they came to see me. The three of them left by the back door, just minutes before you arrived."

Kentler could no longer keep silent.

"What's the point of all of this? Get to the point, man!"

The shoemaker told Kentler to keep quiet. He was not finished with his story.

"I have helped many people cross into Switzerland illegally. The Jew and the two girls really weren't anything special. I have helped many like them in the past. And when the three of you walked in and told me your story, I knew that Herr and Frau Schoflen, as you call yourselves, were the other two that Abraham had told me about.

At first I was just glad to take pictures of both of you and send you on your way. But then I stopped and took a long look at you, Erik. There was something about you. I had seen your face before, but where? Then I remembered! You were the kidnapped SS Sturmbannführer Erik Byrnes. Your picture was in a newspaper I had read. Everyone assumed you were dead, including myself until I saw you standing in my shop. When I left you moments ago, I went back by my workbench to look again at the newspaper photo. You definitely are this man. You, Kentler, obviously don't read the local papers, do you?"

"I don't have time for such..."

"Never mind. It doesn't make any difference now."

"Erik, is what he says true?"

"Herr Kentler, I am sorry for deceiving you but I had no choice. This man is correct. I am not Erik Schoflen. My name is Erik Byrnes. I am a Sturmbannführer in the SS and I have, along with Eva who is not my wife, attempted to escape from Austria to Switzerland."

Kentler was taken aback.

"Why the lies, Erik? I trusted you."

"Otto, your feelings towards the Reich, and especially towards the SS, were quite obvious. If I had told you who I really was, do you think you would have let me go?"

There was silence in the room. This was my last chance and I had better make it good.

"Does it really make any difference? So I am a member of the SS. Isn't the real issue here the fact that I, like anybody else you have helped in the past, am trying to escape from the Nazi tyranny? And what about Eva? What has she done? If you turn me back, she will certainly be executed, just like me."

Kentler was again in deep thought.

"Don't be a fool," the shoemaker shouted at him. "Kentler, this man is quite different from those I have helped in the past. He is a murderer. Have you not read about him for the last few years? He is known far and wide for his activities in Vienna. He is personally responsible for the deportation of thousands of Austrian Jews. He is a criminal and he must be brought to justice."

Kentler nodded. "Yes, you are right. He cannot be allowed to escape. I will take him back to the border station and contact my superiors. Since Switzerland is officially neutral, the only thing we can do with him is to contact the German authorities and inform them whom we have. I am sure they will come and get him."

"But what about me?" Eva said. "Herr Kentler, what will you do with me? I am not his wife. She died during our escape. Tell him, Erik. Tell him."

"She is right. She is not my wife. My wife is dead."

"You, Fraulein, present another question. What do I do with you? As I see it, your only crime was to help this man escape, and the only real question is whether or not for this crime you should also be returned to the Germans. If I have you sent back, I'm sure you will die, too. No, I feel that you should be let free." He nodded towards the shoemaker and added, "He can take your picture, and perhaps you can catch up with the Jew and the two girls. He will need somebody to take care of the girls."

The shoemaker nodded his head in agreement.

Kentler then drew his pistol and pointed it towards the outer room. "Herr Sch... Byrnes, you will come with me." I knew it was over. I marched in front of him and glanced back at Eva. Her eyes were moist and tears were flowing down her cheeks. We knew we would never see each other again.

I could only nod. My legs were weak and I felt faint as I walked through the door and towards Kentler's car. What I saw next made my stomach drop and my heart sink. There, next to the car was Ida along with Abraham and my two girls.

"Papa, Papa!" the girls shouted in unison, like they had always done in the past. "We were going to leave without you, but Uncle Abraham changed his mind. Now you come with us. Hurry, Papa. We have to leave now."

I looked at both of them and held out my arms to embrace them for the last time. They ran to me.

"My darling children. I cannot go with you just now. You will have to go with Uncle Abraham. I will meet up with you later. I promise."

As I released the girls, I looked up at Abraham. There were tears in his eyes.

"Don't worry about them, Erik. I promise I will take care of them."

He put his arms around the girls and looked them both in the eye. "Now, listen, young ladies. Your father has some business to take care of with Herr Kentler. He will join us when he is finished."

Susanne and Louisa looked at each other and then at me.

"Do you promise you will come back to us as soon as you are finished, Papa?" Susanne asked in a very grown-up fashion.

Choking back my own tears, "Yes, my angels, I will come to you as soon as my business with Herr Kentler is finished. Now I must go with him."

I asked Kentler if we could go now. It was obvious that he was very uncomfortable himself.

Kentler ordered me to drive. As the engine started and the car began to pull away, I turned back and looked out the rear window. There, I saw my beautiful girls, waving and calling to me. Tears flowed down my face, and I lifted my arm to wave back to them.

24

Back To Austria

AT the station, Kentler placed me under formal arrest. He escorted me to a small cell.

"I want you to know something, Erik. I don't know if I am doing the right thing or not. For what you have done in the past, you surely need to be punished, but what really bothers me is that I may never know if you escaped from the Nazis because you have reformed or because you had some selfish reason."

"If I told you, would you believe me, Herr Kentler, and even if you did, would it make any difference now?"

"Erik, I'm afraid it is too late. That shoemaker is undoubtedly bragging to all his friends by now, trying to make a jack-ass out of me, I'm sure. No, I can't help you anymore. By the morning, you will be returned to the German authorities."

"You're right, Otto. It won't make a difference but I still want you to hear what I have to say. Please, do it for me."

"Go ahead, Erik. Tell me."

"Herr Kentler... Otto, the reason I fled Germany was to save not only myself, but also my wife and children. You see, they are part Jewish and the SS were closing in on their true identity."

"Do you really expect me to believe that an SS Sturmbannführer has a Jewish wife and children?"

"Believe what you will, it is the truth. What good would it do me to lie now?"

Neither of us said anything. We just stared at each other.

"Otto, I know there is nothing you can do for me now, so I am not going to plead with you, but it does mean a great deal to me to at least know that you believe me, to at least know that one person will remember me as not being the man without any semblance at all of human decency."

I now broke down in tears.

"There was a time when people would have referred to me as *a good man*. I *was* a good man once! I cared for people. I loved my wife, my father, my sister, my country."

"But you hated the Jews, didn't you?"

"No, you're wrong. Damn it, you're wrong just like everybody else. I never *hated* them. Their elimination was only a *job* I had to do, much like the job you must now perform.

Admit it, Kentler. You really don't want to see me turned over to the SS, because deep down you know that you will be sending me to my death and perhaps I am not such an animal as some say I am. No, you are doing this because it is your *job*, and as a good civil servant you must do your duty. I too had to perform my duty. I did not hate the Jews just as you don't hate me."

He did not know what to say. He threw up his hands in disgust.

"Why did that shoemaker recognize you? Why couldn't he have forgotten about your picture in the paper? All this would have passed, and by now you would have been on your way."

Through the bars, I grasped Kentler's hand.

"Otto, I know you mean well and I know you're a good man. All I want you to tell me is that you believe that I am also a good man."

I couldn't sleep at all that night. A million thoughts crossed my mind. I would never see my wife, children, Eva, Abraham, or my sister and father again. Nor would I ever taste another day of freedom. How long it would take for the SS to execute me? Would I be put on trial or would they give me the opportunity to commit suicide, like they had done with others? If I had the choice, I would prefer to take my own life.

The morning came quicker than I would have preferred. It was about eight when I heard doors opening and the sounds of footsteps coming my way. I stood up, waiting to face the inevitable.

Kentler was accompanied by two Swiss officers and two SS. He said, "Erik Byrnes, by order of the Swiss government I am turning custody of you over to the representatives of the German Reich. You are being returned to them on suspicion of being party to the crime of murdering German border patrol officers. I am told that you will be taken back to Austria to answer to these charges."

I said nothing. What could I have said? The SS officers led me out of my cell and walked me to the outside compound. Waiting there was the familiar SS vehicle with two swastikas, one on each antenna. It was amusing. The car reminded me of the one Dieter used when I was driven around Berlin the day

I met Goebbels. This time, rather than being escorted as a welcomed guest of the Reich, I was being taken in disgrace as a traitor.

I didn't look back as the car crossed the same border gates through which we had entered. I wondered if the general public was aware of what had happened. Had my father and sister found out? Did anybody know that I was alive?

After an hour or so, the young officer next to me, a Hauptsturmführer by rank, finally spoke. "Herr Sturmbannführer, if you give me your word that you will not try to escape, I will take the handcuffs off. Do you promise?"

"Yes, Herr Hauptsturmführer, I do. I would rather enjoy the little time I have left in comfort. I appreciate your concern."

"Cigarette?" he asked.

He held one out for me, and even lit it. I could tell he was very interested in talking to me. I had to be careful, since I didn't know how much the Germans really knew. Perhaps, just perhaps they believed that I *had* been kidnapped and was forced to travel over the border?

"Herr Sturmbannführer, would you mind satisfying my curiosity?"

"Go right ahead. Ask what is on your mind."

"How is it that a man such as yourself, obviously very powerful and influential, a man favored by Eichmann, Goebbels, Heydrich, and the Führer himself, could have done such a very stupid, stupid thing? Do you know, Herr Byrnes, that in the SS Academy your name often came up as a role model for the recruits? I looked up to you and I was most interested in your career. When I heard that you had been kidnapped and then murdered with your family, I actually cried. I must know what you did and why."

Both officers waited very attentively for my answer. I knew then that it would do little good to lie to them or to ignore their questions. So I told them the truth, hoping that it would arouse some sympathy or understanding.

"Gentlemen, I was once idealistic just like you. Back in 1938, when I was first recruited into the SS, Germany could do no wrong in my eyes. I worshiped her policies and her beliefs, and as you know, I carried out these policies to their fullest. Countless thousands of innocent people died because of me. Yes, of course, for the most part they were *only Jews*, as you would say. I was told they deserved to be eliminated and I did as I was told."

"Please, what made you change your mind?"

"Herr Hauptsturmführer, I never said that I changed my mind."

"Then, if you didn't change your beliefs, what made you become a traitor?"

"Survival, pure and simple. You see, I found out that my wife and children were part Jewish and I feared that, because of the brilliant detective work of one now dead SS officer, they would eventually be discovered. That is why I did what I did. That is why I faked my own kidnapping and murder, and tried with my wife and children to cross the border to safety. It is not because of my *change of heart* towards the Jews. I did what I did to protect myself, my wife and my children."

The young officer smiled.

"Herr Byrnes, if you were so good at following orders, why did you not send your family to their death? Why are they less of a threat than the children exterminated at Auschwitz or Treblinka?"

"Because, Herr Hauptsturmführer, they were my family. And I loved them. How do you send someone you love away? Gentlemen, we could spend days debating this matter, but I have the feeling that I don't have this luxury available to me, do I?"

After another hour of driving, we stopped at a small café. I must say that I was treated very well. I was not handcuffed and I would guess that the few patrons who were there did not notice anything out of the ordinary.

We rested at a park that evening, each officer taking turns in watching me. The next day we continued our journey, and soon the countryside began to grow familiar. We were drawing near to Vienna.

"I can see familiar sites. Can you tell me where you will be taking me?"

I thought it could do no harm to ask and, besides, these men seemed to be quite decent to me.

"Our orders are to hand you over to the Commandant at Kovnas. We don't know what will happen to you after that."

At the ghetto stockade! They were actually going to lock me up there. This was something I did not bargain for. I suspected I would be taken to SS Headquarters in Vienna, but not there. Perspiration began to form on my forehead. Only few prisoners left there alive. It was used for torture in order to obtain information from uncooperative Jews. But what information did they need from me? Didn't they know everything already?

25

The Hangman Returns

IT was November 3, 1944, the day my escorts turned me over to an Untersturmführer, whom I vaguely remembered as having been under my former command. Before they departed, they bade me farewell and wished me good luck.

"You need not worry about this traitor!" the Untersturmführer told his superior officers. "He soon will find out what the consequences are of violating the Führer's trust!"

The stockade guards then grabbed me by my arms, dragged me down the corridor and threw me into the last cell.

It was a filthy two-by-four-meter area, with no windows, a wooden bed, no mattress or pillows or even a blanket. The only sanitation was a bucket for waste which had not been emptied.

But as I sat down, my fear seemed to have vanished. I should have been genuinely scared, but I was not. I suppose the greatest part of fear is the uncertainty of not knowing exactly what will happen. In my case, there was no doubt what would happen. I would be executed. It was only a question of when and how.

One might ask if I shouldn't be afraid of the method they would use to kill me, but I wasn't. Before I even left Vienna for Lake Constance, on the trip that would bring me either liberty or death, I had taken the precaution of bringing a cyanide capsule with me, which I hid in a compartment I made in my belt so that it would not be lost. Since the incident in the shoemaker's shop, I often clutched it for a sense of security, much like a small child would hold a stuffed animal. It was because of this small ampule that I felt the SS would never be able to make me suffer if that was what they chose to do. I decided to remove it from my belt and hold it in my hand. It was small enough that I could place it in my mouth if the guards arrived and still have the ability to speak if I were questioned.

As I lay there, I thought of Father and Theresa. If not by now, then soon, the Gestapo would visit them. Fortunately, they knew nothing of my plans and hopefully they would be left alone. Marie's parents, especially her mother, were in greater danger.

The holding area was quiet. The only sounds I heard were coming from the rats that made the prison their home.

My watch told me it was seven in the morning when I heard the outer door creaking to let in my interrogators.

"Good morning, Herr Byrnes. I am Hauptsturmführer Peter Naus. I have been sent here from Berlin to question you. Before we begin, is there anything I can get for you? Perhaps you would like a cigarette or coffee?"

I knew from experience that this officer was trying to get my confidence and trust. It was an obvious interrogation technique that I first saw the SS use years ago when a Jewish youth was fooled into betraying not only his Christian benefactors but other Jews as well. I decided to play his game.

"Thank you, a cigarette would be fine. You can ask what you wish."

He instructed those who accompanied him to leave the two of us alone.

"Erik, I won't pretend with you. We know that you planned your abduction and death and that you attempted to escape to Switzerland."

Clutching the cyanide ampule in my pocket, I took the offensive.

"If you feel that is the truth, why don't you just have me shot and get it over with? No, Herr Hauptsturmführer, either you are not certain of what you say or you have other questions you want me to answer."

He smiled, and said, "Just call me Peter, Erik," as he handed me the cigarette.

"You are quite right. There are some questions I need answered."

I stopped him right there.

"Forgive me for asking, but obviously I must begin to think selfishly."

"Of course, go ahead. Say what is on your mind."

"If I answer truthfully, what will I receive in return?"

"That's a very good point. What will you get in return? I can tell you this, and perhaps it will convince you to cooperate. If you don't answer me truthfully, I have been informed to tell you that your father and sister will be sent to either Dachau or Buchenwald. Your wife's parents will have the same fate. I can also promise you that you will endure, not by my hands but by others, a very painful interrogation. As you know very well, this will probably result in your telling what I wanted to know in the first place, so it's better to provide it without all these unpleasantries."

239

He got up and walked around the cell for a moment before sitting down again.

"Please don't put me in that position. I abhor violence but, as you know, there are others who thrive on it."

It now was time for me to do what I could to save my father and sister and Marie's parents. My life was, for all practical purposes, over.

"Herr Hauptsturmführer Naus, I realize that you will do as you please to me and my family whether I cooperate or not. After all, I was a Sturmbannführer and I had occasion to see how you work to get information. Therefore, I ask you to grant me several requests for my cooperation. After all, I did serve the Führer well for many years, as my record shows."

"It is true. You did serve the Reich well during your time. Alright, what are your requests, Erik?"

"First of all, my father and sister must be left alone. They had nothing whatsoever to do with my actions. Marie's parents must also not to be harmed."

"Agreed."

"Secondly, I want to be able to see my father and sister one last time, but not here in this God-forsaken ghetto. I want you to personally take me to Berlin to visit them at their home."

This time, he was not so quick to agree, but after some thought he consented.

"Finally, you will allow me to take my own life, as was permitted with Rommel."

"That, too, can be agreed upon."

"Do you have the authority to agree to my demands?"

"I do."

"You give me your word as a German officer?"

"You have my word."

I felt relieved. As I mentioned, the emotion of fear is primarily based upon not knowing what will happen. The unknown is what agitates us. In my case, the unknown did not now exist.

"Ask what you want."

I confirmed what he already suspected, namely how I planned my kidnapping and my escape to Switzerland. He asked who assisted me. He had little interest in Dieter's involvement, calling him a misguided individual. He was, however, most interested in Abraham. Apparently, he had known little about his role. I could detect anger when he heard how Abraham had killed Bach and then Dieter.

"I told you, Peter, that I would tell you the truth. This is what I am doing. I never told you that you would like what you would hear."

"This is true. Continue."

I told him about the young SS investigator whose investigation about the phone calls and Bach's and Dieter's death, was getting too close for comfort. Again, he was upset because this officer died trying to save my life.

"Herr Byrnes, it seems that many people who have contact with you meet with a tragic ending, trying to help you, mind you."

"Yes, that is true. You know, Peter, my wife said the very same thing to me some time ago."

"Oh, yes, your wife. Tell me exactly what you know about what happened to her and the children."

I told him how Marie had drowned and how Abraham and Eva escaped with the children. I didn't think it did any harm to tell him all about Abraham and the children. They were all now beyond the Nazis' reach.

"It is a pity about your wife. I have seen pictures of her in the newspapers. She was lovely and obviously a fine woman. Your children, too, looked like fine German youth."

"Yes, Peter, that's true. By the way, you say this even though you know that my children and my wife are part Jew?"

He smiled.

"I never said, Herr Byrnes, that I subscribed to the same philosophy that Eichmann and others adhere to."

"Your secret is safe with me, Peter. I no longer have any reason to cause anyone any more pain."

I spent the next hour or so answering all his questions until he finally concluded his interrogation.

"You have kept your word, Erik. I will see to it that you are allowed to change clothes, to wash up and have something to eat. We will leave for Berlin by train early tomorrow."

How different this was from the journey I took more than six years ago when I met Dieter. Now the train was almost completely filled with wounded soldiers. There was no joy or laughter. Now, there was only the constant fear of a bomber raid which could take out the train.

"What will you do after the war is over?"

241

"I'm not quite sure, Erik. I'm not quite sure. I am a realist. To me, there is no doubt that the war is lost. The talk of *secret weapons* is all garbage. We both know that there are no such weapons and even if there were, it's too late to make any difference. Do you know that I even had thoughts of taking you as my prisoner and turning the two of us over to the Allies?"

"What made you change your mind? From your standpoint, it sounds like a good idea!"

"I'm not really sure. Perhaps I don't want to be branded a traitor for the rest of time?"

I nodded. I understood what he was saying.

"How much time will I have with my father and sister?"

"No more than an hour, I'm afraid. I have orders to bring you to Gestapo Headquarters in Berlin immediately after your visit unless, of course, you decide to take your own life before then."

My self-confidence was now beginning to wane. Did I really have the courage to bite into that capsule? How could I get myself out of this situation? Who cares about my promise not to escape?

I gazed out the window. I could see the evidence of the Allied bombings. There wasn't a city that we passed through that didn't have a damaged depot or factory.

After a short while, Peter broke the silence. "Forgive me for asking, but I'm curious. What will you talk about when you see your father and sister for the last time?"

"I've been asking myself the same question for the last hour. I think that I will tell them how much I love them. I will tell them not to think too badly of me when I'm gone. They should try to find my children when the war is over. Hopefully, they will have the opportunity to have some type of a family again."

"Do you think often of your children?"

"I think of them every moment of the day. My only solace is that I trust that Abraham will take good care of them."

"It is very interesting, Herr Byrnes, how you became so close to a Jew, especially in this environment."

"Do you know, Peter, that besides Dieter I have never found a man whom I could trust more than Abraham? He never broke his word to me and it is because of this loyalty that I feel confident that my children are in good hands."

I managed to get a little sleep on the train and so did Peter. I thought several times about whether or not I should try to escape. There was no question that I could have overcome Peter on more than one occasion, but how would I get off the train? Where would I go?

"I have arranged to have a car waiting for us at the station, Erik, but don't worry, it will only be you and I going to see your father and sister. They know you'll be coming."

"What have they been told, Peter?"

"They have been informed that the reports of your death proved to be false, and that you would be in Berlin for only a short time to visit with them."

"It's probably better that way."

"Erik, I've been thinking. It might be better not to tell them everything. I gave you my word that nothing would happen to them and I intend to keep that, but if they start telling the world about what you did, or worse than that, that your wife and children have Jewish blood, other SS officers might not be so considerate, especially towards your wife's parents."

"That's a good point. I'll be careful what I say to them."

I gazed out the window at my beloved Berlin. The city had been devastated by the Allied bombings. I could not find a block that had not been struck. It seemed that every major governmental building and factory had seen some damage.

"So much for the Führer's *One Thousand Year Reich.*"

We both laughed.

"Peter, don't you ever worry about what the Allies might do to you after the war is over?"

"Of course I do. In fact, I carry a cyanide capsule with me wherever I go, probably very similar to the one which you must be carrying with you at this very moment."

I let out a laugh.

"If you worry about what might happen to you, maybe you should consider joining me in escaping from this Hell-hole."

"No, Erik, as I said before, that would not be very prudent. Besides, even though I am in the SS, I have never been even indirectly involved in killing any civilians, or in killing anybody at all, for that matter. Believe it or not, I have never even fired my weapon! I expect that when the Allies are done questioning me, they will conclude that I was nothing more than just an investigative officer and they will then hopefully let me go back to my beloved birthplace Hamburg. There I will be reunited with my parents."

"I certainly hope that you are right, for your sake."

"So do I, Erik. So do I."

243

The damage caused by the bombings diminished considerably as we drove out of the central city to its outskirts, where Father lived. Farther out there was no damage at all, and one wouldn't even know that there was a war going on.

When we pulled into the driveway, I could see Father and Theresa standing by the living room window, looking for my arrival.

"Erik, Erik. You're alright!" Theresa ran towards me and gave me a big hug. "I told you, Father. Didn't I?"she said.

"That you did, daughter. You absolutely did."

Father embraced me. "Come in, son. Come in and bring your friend with you."

Peter and I entered my boyhood home much like Dieter and I had many times in the past.

"We were so worried about you when we heard of the kidnapping, Erik. And when your death and that of Marie and the children was confirmed, I couldn't eat or sleep for days."

"Well, my dear sister, as you can see, the reports were false. I will tell you more, but before we continue, let me introduce you to Peter, a friend of mine who agreed to drive me here for a short visit."

By Father's look I could see that he knew I was not telling the truth.

Peter was kind enough to let me spend the little time I had left with my family alone.

"Erik, I think I will take a short walk. This will give you a chance to catch up with your father and sister. I know you have much to tell. I will be back shortly."

Theresa tried to coax Peter into having a piece of cake in the kitchen, but he politely refused. She seemed attracted to him. After he left, I asked them both to sit down. I decided that I would tell them everything. "There is so much to tell you, but I have so little time. Please let me finish all I have to say before you ask any questions." They both agreed.

"There was no kidnapping and there was no murder of me or my family. It was all staged by me, my plan in order to escape Nazi Germany, and it almost worked. I was arrested at the Swiss border. We had actually made it onto Swiss soil before I was discovered and returned to the German authorities. The children were allowed to proceed with a friend of mine. He will be in touch with you after the war is over. Marie didn't make it. She drowned when her boat capsized as we were crossing Lake Constance. I tried to save her, but she disappeared in the darkness."

Why was Theresa smiling?

"Erik, Marie is alive!"

I felt shock and disbelief.

"That's impossible! She is dead. She drowned in the lake!"

"No! Just today, Marie's parents called. Some farmers found her, half-dead, on the Austrian side of the lake. She insisted that, instead of calling the authorities, they call her parents. Her father went to get her. He brought her back to Berlin only hours ago. She is resting at their home right now."

"My God. Did she say anything? Anything at all?"

"Nothing that made much sense, except that she kept asking about the girls and you."

I got up and walked around the room, not knowing what to do and not knowing what to say. This changed everything!

"Father, does the Gestapo know what happened?"

"You would know the answer to that question better than I do, Erik. Would she be home with her parents if they knew?"

He was right. They didn't know.

"Father, the man who accompanied me here today is really not my friend, although he seems to be a fine man. He is an SS officer who is guarding me. Because I gave him a full confession, he allowed me this one last time to meet with the two of you before they execute me."

Now it was Father's and Theresa's turn to be shocked.

"What are you talking about? Execute you? They can't mean you. You are a Sturmbannführer in the SS!" Theresa shouted.

"It doesn't matter, Theresa. To the Reich, I am only an embarrassment. Perhaps they will be kind enough to allow me to take my own life. At least I will ask them to let me."

"Oh, Erik. How did it all come to this?" Theresa cried as she embraced me. "I won't let anybody hurt you. I just won't!"

Father, too, came up to me and took me in his arms.

"Erik, we have to do something. We can't just sit still and let them kill you."

"I knew the chance I was taking, Father. What's important now is that I see Marie one last time."

I looked at the grandfather clock. Peter had been gone only about ten minutes, but I was sure he would return soon.

"Father, is your car still parked in the garage?"

"Yes. The keys are in the ignition."

"Good. Here is what I want you both to do. I am going to their home to see Marie. Call them and tell them I am coming, but if Peter gets back when you are on the phone, make sure he doesn't hear what you are saying. When he

245

comes back, Father, I want you to tell him... I want you to convince him that I *will* be back in one hour. He won't believe you at first. Perhaps he won't believe you at all, but just tell him that I *do* keep my word. If he asks where I went, don't tell him. You have to lie to him."

"But where should we tell him you went?" Theresa asked.

"Tell him you don't know. Tell him anything... Tell him I went to church to see a priest for my last confession. Yes, that's it! Tell him I went to a church. I don't care what you tell him, just convince him I will be back."

I embraced them. I hoped it wouldn't be the last time.

When I entered the driveway, the shades were all drawn and there were no lights or signs of life at the home of Marie's parents. I drove into their empty garage.

"Hurry, Erik," Johan said. "Get in before someone sees you."

I closed the door behind me.

"Where is Marie?"

"She's upstairs, with her mother."

"Did you call a doctor?"

"Yes, he just got here. He is with her now. We had to find one that we could trust."

"How do you know you can trust him?"

"There is no doubt he can be trusted, Erik. He is a Jew, just like your wife."

I ran upstairs to Marie's old room where I was met by Brunhilda.

"Erik, she is very weak. Sometimes she knows who she is talking to and at other times she does not. The doctor just arrived."

At Marie's bedside was a shabbily dressed man, likely in his forties, but looking more like sixty. He was one of those Jews whom the SS were always on the search for, Jews whom we missed the first time and who evaded all subsequent round-ups. He must have known who I was, because when he turned around and saw me, he quickly lowered his head and turned away from me, much like the Jews in the ghetto did when I was in their presence.

"Don't be afraid of me," I told him. "The SS want me more than they even want you."

By his slight smile, I knew that he understood what I was saying.

"Herr Byrnes, your wife is very weak. Her leg is mended, but she is suffering now from the effects of exposure. The greatest danger right now is that she contracts pneumonia, especially in her weakened situation."

246

Marie coughed, her eyes still closed. I moved closer towards the bed. There she lay, the Marie I once so loved, the mother of my children. If only she would wake up so I could tell her that I still loved her and that the girls were safe. I knew that the news would help her recover.

"Doctor, I don't have much time. There is an SS officer waiting for me at my father's home. If I don't return soon, there will be Gestapo all over the area. I must speak to Marie. Can you please wake her?"

The physician looked at Marie's parents, trying to see if they approved. They both nodded in agreement, and he began to wake her up.

"Susanne... Louisa... are you here? Mommy is looking for you..." As she muttered incoherently, she began to stir and to move her head. Her eyes opened and she looked straight at me.

"Erik... Erik... Is that you?"

"Yes, Marie. I am here."

I sat on the edge of the bed.

"Where are the girls?"

"They are safe, Marie. They are with Abraham. They will be with you soon."

"Can they come to see me now? I want to see them now, Erik."

"Soon, Marie, soon. As soon as you are better, they will be here."

My assurance seemed to give her strength. The doctor and her parents seemed to be pleased.

"Marie, I want you to drink this," the doctor told her.

"Drink Marie. It will make you feel better," I insisted.

With my help, we put her in a sitting position which enabled her to drink the broth that her mother had prepared. After just a few sips, she seemed to do a little better.

I asked her parents and the doctor to please leave the room since I had very little time. I told Brunhilda that my father would call her and explain everything. They left without saying a word.

"Marie, I want you to know that Abraham and I tried to find you. We couldn't. The men who would guide us into Switzerland also looked for you. I'm sorry, so very, very sorry."

She pressed her fingers to my lips.

"Erik, I know you tried. I could hear you calling, but you couldn't hear me. The wind blew me away from Abraham. He tried but he could not find me either."

"But Marie, you are not a great swimmer and that broken leg didn't help. How did you manage it?"

"I was lucky to latch onto a large log, and I managed to hold onto it until I drifted to shore. The men who found me were very kind. But what about you, Erik? Why did you come back to Berlin?"

"I've been caught, Marie. I was discovered at the border by a Swiss national who knew who I was. The SS interrogated me and they know everything, except they don't know that you are alive, or where the children are. I am here under the guard of an SS officer who is waiting for me at Father's home. I will have to go with him, Marie. There is no escape."

"Erik, there must be something you can do. Run. Get out of here. Take your father's car and escape."

"Escape where, Marie? There is no place to hide. Besides, I gave him my word that if he gave me this last time to be with my parents, I would go with him and not resist. He is a good man and I wouldn't want him to get into trouble because he trusted in me."

She started to cry.

"Oh Erik,I love you so! There must be some way out of this. Don't think about your word to an SS man, but think about your family. You must escape. You must!"

I knew she was right, but where could I go now?

"Marie, the authorities don't know that you are alive. Stay hidden. The war will soon be over and then you will be safe. Stay indoors. Let Father find the girls, and be strong for them when they return."

"But, Erik, what is going to happen to you?"

"I don't know for sure, but whatever happens to me, Marie, just know that I love you and the girls very much. Tell them that I love both of them very much."

I took her into my arms and kissed her one last time. Sobbing, she returned my embrace.

"Erik, remember, I have always loved you. If there is any way you can escape, promise me you will. I will always wait for you. There will never be another for me. I swear it."

I had to go now. I thanked the doctor and said farewell to Marie's parents. Would I ever see her again?

I sped back to Father's home and pulled into the driveway. As I entered the living room, there stood Theresa, covered with blood, clutching the same knife she used so often to cut meat. On the floor lay Peter, blood flowing from several wounds in his back. Father stood by, as if in a daze.

"My God, Theresa, what have you done?"

"I couldn't let him take you, Erik. I just couldn't. I tried to talk him out of it. I even offered myself to him, but he refused. While he was talking to Father, I went into the kitchen and got the knife. When he turned his back, I stabbed him over and over and over again, until he fell dead to the ground. I had to stand up for you, Erik. I've always stood up for you!"

"You have to leave, Erik. Leave right now. You kept your word. You had no idea what Theresa would do."

"Father is right, Erik. Go, go right now. Don't call us until it is absolutely safe."

"Erik, take the officer's car and leave it by the train station."

"But Father, what will you say when they come looking for him?"

"This evening I will bury the body in the dirt floor in the garage. Nobody will find it there. Go, my son, go. We will see you again. At least I know that this way you have a chance. When Marie is better, we will let her know, and I promise you, the children will be re-united with her."

I had no choice. I had to give it a try. If I stayed here or turned myself in, I would not be the only one who would die, so would Father and Theresa. I checked to see that I still had my money and turned towards the two of them. "I love you both and I will return!"

I headed towards the Anhalt Station. There I would leave the car in the middle of the packed parking lot where it would raise little suspicion. I still had time before the search for Peter and myself would begin.

Then I had an idea. Kovnas! I would go and hide in the ghetto! The SS would not think of looking for me there and Abraham had shown me all the entrances and hiding places.

I boarded the train for Vienna without incident. Nobody even checked my papers, and why should they be concerned? There were few, if any, Jews left in Berlin, and the war was obviously lost.

I arrived in Vienna the next morning. I didn't take a cab but rather payed a farmer to drive me to the ghetto. My biggest concern was to keep the SS from recognizing me. If they got a close look, I was sure they would know who I was.

I snuck in unseen, just where Abraham had told me to.

I felt alone as I walked through those dark and dirty streets. The only inhabitants now left were those still in hiding and those *lucky* enough to be left with the task of whatever maintenance duties were still to be performed.

Although it had only been a short while, Kovnas was not as I remembered it. When I made my frequent visits here, the area was full of people. I could hold my head up high for I always kept my word to *my Jews*. As long as they did as I said and worked according to the quota I set, I fed them as promised and caused them no unnecessary suffering. There must have been a mass deportation in just the last few days.

I found the building where Abraham and the other Judenrat members would meet with me. It was now vacant and closed, but I was able to push a board to the side and get in. There, in the center of the room, was the same large table that I used when I conferred with the Jewish elders. There was my chair and also Abraham's, at the head of the other council members' chairs. Here, I was the King, the *King of the Jews!*

After a few minutes, this momentary illusion of grandeur faded for I realized that now I sat here alone. My wife was in Berlin, and my children were who knows where, with my father and sister in danger of being arrested for Peter's death. Dieter was dead and Abraham was no longer here to guide and protect me.

As I looked out the cracked window, I saw dust blowing in the empty streets. How ridiculous was my plan! How long could I stay here without any food or water? If I didn't starve to death, I would surely die of thirst.

For the next hour or so, I just sat there, torn between thoughts of sympathy for myself and thoughts of how much suffering I had caused others.

Suddenly, I heard activity in the streets, an SS patrol. Were they looking for me? It couldn't be. They had just come out of what appeared to be a vacant building, but they were not alone. They were dragging a man and a woman. They shoved them into the street and while the two were kneeling and pleading for their lives, they shot them.

Now they were moving this way! I had to hide. I found some old boxes and clothes piled up in the corner. I had to hurry, the SS were almost here.

"Let's go in here, Otto. I think I smell a Jew."

I was shaking as I heard them enter the room and then stop not far from me.

"Somebody's been in here since yesterday, Ernst. You see that the board has been pried open. Here, Jew... here, Jew... come on out, Jew..."

They laughed as they opened the cabinets and doors looking for someone, anyone.

They stopped about five meters from where I was hiding. There was silence in the room.

"What do we have over here?" one of them laughed, pointing to the pile I was in. "Let's see if anyone is hiding here."

I heard footsteps moving close to me.

Suddenly, a bayonet was trust into the pile where I was hiding, entering barely a meter from me.

"Nothing there. How about over there?" He stabbed again, to my other side.

"Ernst, you're not very good, are you? Let me try."

Ernst handed the rifle to Otto. I had to come out because the next thrust would likely be right where I was crouching.

"*Warte, bitte!* Wait! I'm coming out."

I came out of hiding with my hands held high.

"Well, what do you know? We found one, another rat hiding in a corner."

The SS stood there with their rifles pointing at me.

"Wait, I'm not sure this one is a Jew."

"You're right, Ernst. He certainly does not look like one."

"Who are you and what are you doing here?"

If I told them who I was, I would be back in the same position I was before. I had to think quickly.

"I said, who are you and what are you doing here? I won't ask you again!"

Otto lifted his rifle and pointed it directly at my forehead.

I blurted out the first thing I could think of. "My name is Otto Kentler."

"Papers! Papers! Give me your papers."

"My papers have been taken from me. I was on the Aryan side of the ghetto when I was kidnapped and brought here. Go ahead and search me. See for yourself."

This time, I was fortunate that I had no papers.

"Why would anybody kidnap you?" they asked.

"I was carrying money, a lot of money. The Jews, they were Jews. They didn't want to rob me on the other side, so they brought me here and took my money and my papers."

"You know, Otto, I think he is telling the truth. Let's take him to headquarters and file a report."

"You're right. He's obviously not a Jew and he doesn't match the description of any common criminals in the area. Come on. You come with us. You'll get something to eat and perhaps you can give us a description of those Jewish swine who robbed you."

They lowered their rifles and walked me outside to the street. These men were obviously new recruits, because they didn't recognize me. If I went with them to the SS Headquarters, I'm sure there would be somebody there who would know who I was. In fact, the last time I was there, there was a picture of me on the wall! Depending on what they knew up to now, I was either a fallen hero or a traitor. In either event, I would be discovered.

"You really don't have to go through all that trouble just for me. If you could just get me to a phone, I could call my family and they could come and get me."

"Nonsense," Ernst said. "We are going that way anyhow and it is not safe to walk in this area. There are still a few Jews left here, you know."

We continued walking towards the gate that separated the Aryan side from the Jewish ghetto. I hoped to God nobody recognized me.

On seeing us approach, the guard on duty joked, "How was the hunt today, Ernst?"

"We got about a half dozen, mostly hiding in the abandoned buildings."

"Who's this one, Otto? He's no Jew."

"We know that. Why do you think he is still alive? He was robbed. We're just bringing him out safely so he can file a report and then contact somebody to take him home."

Thanking my *protectors,* I tried not to make eye contact with the guard. I had almost made it past his post when he called out to me. "Wait a second. Come back here. I want to talk to you."

My blood chilled as I stopped at his command. Again I tried not to look at him. "Herr soldier, are you speaking to me?"

"Yes, come here for a second. You look familiar."

I knew I couldn't avoid him any longer so I approached. He asked me my name and I gave him the same name I gave the SS troops. "I could swear I have seen you before, but where, I can't place it."

I played along with him, but denied that I had ever seen him before. My memory was better than his. I did recognize him as a young recruit who arrived under my command just shortly before I left.

After some more discussion, the guard and the SS men told me to forget about the report and be on my way. They pointed out a location where I could make a phone call. I thanked them and started walking down the street. I had fooled them again!

Just then, a voice called out. "Herr Sturmbannführer Byrnes, Erik Byrnes!"

The moment I turned towards him, I knew that I had just made the most fatal mistake of my life.

The guard tricked me!

I began to run down the roadway with all of them in pursuit.

"Halten! Halten!"

I didn't stop as I ran by merchants, past people waiting for the trolley and through groups of school children playing in a yard.

"I said halt!" one of them hollered. "If you don't stop, I will shoot."

This time I yelled out. "No, you won't. Your superiors certainly would reprimand you for not taking me alive."

I looked behind me and saw that although they were younger than I, they were tiring and I was able to pull away even farther. But where would I go? Where could I hide?

I ran, unseen, into a department store. I had lost them momentarily, but soon the whole area would be covered by SS and Gestapo. There was only one place I could hide. I had to get back to my ghetto, but how?

I would hide in the store's restroom until after it closed and make my way back at night. After all, I did know where the secret crossing was.

After a few hours, all the shoppers and employees had left the store. I managed to find some food and blankets and to evade the cleaning personnel. I needed to get some rest. Huddled behind a store counter, I fell asleep.

The chiming of a grandfather clock, not far away, woke me. It was midnight. Now was the time for me to make my way back to the ghetto. I found a suitcase and a change of clothes, with glasses, a hat and an overcoat. Perhaps this disguise would work.

I made it down two flights of stairs to the first floor. In the distance, a light was indicating an exit. As I walked down the corridor, I noted there was a section devoted to uniforms for children. They were Nazi uniforms, size extra small, some SS and some Wehrmacht. They were made for the children of the Reich, the Hitler Youth, who wanted to be just like their beloved Himmler, Göring, Goebbels and all of them. There, amongst the figurines, stood a statue of Hitler, presumably addressing his loyal followers. I stopped. I knew I shouldn't, but I could not resist.

It had all come down to this. Germany and all its protectorates were on the brink of ruin, yet this store still had these wares for sale, to gullible patriots who still believed in the impossible.

I mounted the podium, right next to *The Führer*. I gently removed the shirt from the manikin and put it on. I then moved *him* aside and took *his* position addressing the crowd.

"Faithful members of the Reich. I am here addressing you on an issue I raised in 1933 when I became Chancellor. At that time, I warned you that there was an epidemic in our great land, a disease which grows like a cancer. It spreads over and into every fabric of our society. I told you then that if it is not stopped, it will create ruin and chaos."

I paused just like the Führer did in order to gain control over the crowd.

"This cancer is the Jew! He is the disease that I promised you back in 1933 I would put a stop to and, as God is my witness, I did put a stop to it. Look around you. There are no more Jews!"

I said it again, but this time much louder.

"There are no Jews!!"

The store lights turned on. In front of me stood armed policemen.

"Get off the podium. Get down right now."

"How dare you speak this way to your Führer!" I countered.

As the police officers stood there, I heard them talking back and forth to each other.

"He must be the one the Gestapo are looking for, some type of SS officer. Be careful not to harm him. They want him alive."

The fools! Don't they know I have escaped death more than once? Do they really expect that they can stop me...??

Epilogue

I WAS told that they never found Erik. Just seconds before they were going to drag him off the podium, an Allied bomb hit the store. After the war was over, the German government declared him *missing in action*. They never investigated or bothered to explain what happened at Lake Constance, or the deaths of Dieter, Bach and all the others. SS officer Peter still lies buried underneath Erik's father's garage floor. I stayed hidden in my parents' home until the Allies liberated Berlin. Nothing ever happened to my parents.

The Allies were too busy trying to reconstruct Germany and keeping the Russians from gaining control, to worry about what happened to just another Nazi.

In June of 1945, Abraham knocked on my door, and with him were Susanne and Louisa. He never left Switzerland, but remained there until the end of the war. He now lives in Berlin and visits often. Eva, so he thought, was on her way to South America to start over again.

Erik's father and sister see the children often. Erik's father seems to have adjusted well, but Theresa took Germany's defeat very badly. She still believes Erik is alive.

Each night, I think about Erik. I think about the good and the evil of this man whom I once loved... no, whom I still love! I know he can't come back to me *yet*. In fact, I don't know for sure if he is even still alive, but I believe he is. If he is, he will come back to us some day.

What helps me believe that he is still alive is the poem I received in the mail, just the other day. There was no return address. I learned that it was a poem written by a German minister, Martin Niemoller, who also survived the war.

"They came for the Communists, and I
didn't object- For I wasn't
a Communist.

They came for the Socialists, and I
didn't object- For I wasn't
a Socialist.

They came for the labor leaders, and I
didn't object- For I wasn't
a labor leader.

They came for the Jews, and I
didn't object- For I wasn't
a Jew.

Then they came for me-
And there was no one left to object."

Marie Byrnes
December 4, 1945.

* * *